COST OF THE GOLD SERVICE

A SCI-FI ACTION ADVENTURE

THE CAPITAL ADVENTURES
BOOK 5

ALLEN IVERS

Illustrations © Tom Edwards
TomEdwardsDesign.com

As always, a big thanks to my wonderful wife - Lyn.
My best friend - Evan
And his wife - Sharon

I love my misfit family.

CONTENTS

FOREWORD

This is the second book in *The Gold Service* trilogy—if you haven't read the first, you'll want to stop here and go find the previous book before continuing.

This series contains the following content matter:

- *Graphic Violence & Traumatic Injuries*
  - *If you thought Book One was graphic.*
  - *Including amputation, stabbing, gun shots and bone fracture.*
- *Occasional Foul Language*
  - *People swear when this stuff happens*
- *Alcohol & Drug Use*
  - *Underage Drinking, Mind Altering Substances*
- *Reference to Sexual Activity*
  - *Dialog references, no depictions*
- *Religious Trauma/Conversion Therapy*
  - *Electroshock torture and isolation*

We're here to have a good time with characters we love. If any of this material distresses you, it's okay to grab another book instead.

Hope you enjoy!

MAP & CHRONOLOGY

The Solar Imperium, also called the Gnostic Empire by the more faithful citizenry, stretches over a fifth of the Milky Way Galaxy. This map features the primary locations featured in the series thus far.

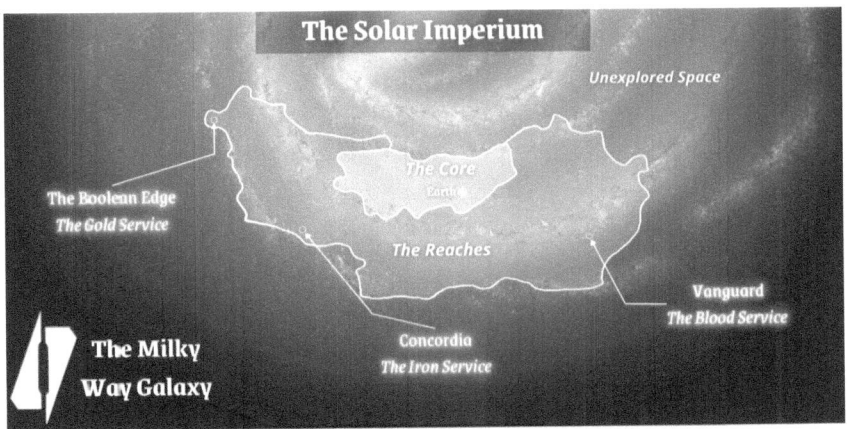

| Map of Solar Imperium controlled space, 2241 CE

The events of the Capital Adventures occur entirely within these borders. Events from one book may be mentioned in another, or characters may cross over from one trilogy to another. Think of it as a shared universe, with the individual stories having unique tones and flair, while building an overarching plot.

You may enjoy each trilogy independent of the others—and I've meticulously built them so that your enjoyment is not contingent on having read the others! But if you want the full experience of the Capital Adventures, I do encourage you to pick up the other books to get a full sense of the Imperium's reach. The official reading order would be to read the trilogies starting with The Blood Service, then The Gold Service, and finishing out with the upcoming Iron Service.

If you're like me, however, and you were looking to read the novels in chronological order, the events of all nine books are as follows:

———

1) THE GOLD SERVICE
2) THE BLOOD SERVICE
3) THE IRON SERVICE

4) RANKS OF THE BLOOD SERVICE
5) COST OF THE GOLD SERVICE
6) SWORDS OF THE IRON SERVICE (COMING SOON)

7) COMMAND OF THE BLOOD SERVICE
8) SHARDS OF THE IRON SERVICE (COMING SOON)
9) POWERS OF THE GOLD SERVICE

WITH EVEN MORE TO COME...

The Gold Service Trilogy has a lighter tone than the other two members of this series, with a strong found-family of mercenaries and malcontents that all share a single brain cell, while also confronting both religious & generational trauma. These characters have become a second family to me, and I hope they do the same for you.

"The best revenge is to be unlike him who performed the injury."

MARCUS AURELIUS

PART ONE
FAITH-BASED FURY

"The Pilgrim urges us to form together and abandon our disparate clans and borders. Those who cling to their differences, who insist on superiority of one over another—there is but one commandment: banish the oppressor first with your word, and if necessary, with the sword."

PROF. ORDEE, C.H. (2224). *RADICAL FERVOR: THE QUANDARY OF THE PILGRIM'S WRATH*

CHAPTER
ONE
TYCHO

HE JUST TRIED to remember her face. He'd survived so much by keeping her soft violet eyes fixed in his mind.

She'd gotten them colored some time in her early twenties, some rebellious phase, before she had decided to settle down and met Dad. Tycho had seen those eyes almost every night before bed and when he left for the Academy, he'd taken one last look over his shoulder.

Her eyes had been full of glad, patriotic tears, but also...mourning. Her shoulders convulsed with each wave of grief that slipped out of her. That beautiful smile had broken, hidden somewhere behind the palm cupped to her face.

She had prayed to the Pilgrim for strength as she bid her child goodbye. She would likely never see Tycho again and she had wanted to give her twelve-year-old son such a strong send-off, and he had promised her there would be no tears.

A promise he had broken.

Tycho thought about those eyes during every exercise, every drill, every formation and parade; he thought about them when he was too tired to walk, too tired to think, too tired to press on.

He didn't want to cause her any more tears.

He thought about those violet eyes a lot in his first three years at the Academy Bellator, and the six months at Holkstad after. He even sketched them in his drafting software, so that he could look at them whenever he liked. And he thought about them when they put him under for his first surgeries, grafting metal to his muscles and bone and circuits to his nerves.

He didn't remember waking up, but that was fine—half of his graduating class didn't wake up at all, killed by the dangerous implants and cybernetic enhancements. Their bodies were unable, unwilling to adopt the upgrades.

The rare student like him was even more resilient, crossing a rather unsettling threshold; he had more parts now that were cast or soldered than grown. Those that survived would press on to become the elite.

Orbital Strike Command—augmented, awe-inspiring, and optimized. There were no soldiers alive more potent than the Oskies.

That's what Tycho had thought before his instructors had pulled him aside at graduation: a special volunteer program he was perfect for. Extremely dangerous, certain death, that kind of thing. But prestigious, and a guaranteed silver ticket to join the Sojourn, whereupon he would rest at the side of the Pilgrim to await his mother and father.

Tycho didn't want to make his mother cry. He wanted to make her proud. And what would make her prouder than to see him again after death, where they could walk the Pilgrim's Path together forever?

There were a hundred of them in the room, all augmented graduates of Holkstad Academy, an exceptional example of their class. It was an impressive space, vaulted ceiling and stained glass, like a cathedral to medicine. Each student laid on their own table, sacrificial altars with AutoDocs for each. It almost resembled a mass casualty event, but for the Silksteel augments laid in closed boxes beside each bed, ready for installation.

They were getting even more upgrades. And no two were the same. Some were firearms, others were armor, optics, and generators. If the surgeries before had been deadly...

He consulted the onboard memory bank installed, bringing up the crystal-clear portrait of those violet eyes. One last look.

Before the procedure began, three robed figures walked up and down the lanes. Two of them swung smoking censers in opposing directions, as if trying to hide their mysterious third. He wore thick wool gloves and the heavy fabric of his long open sleeves swung in rhythm with the incense.

Clutched in this priest's hands, a shard of inky black glass with ancient glyphs etched...somehow within it. Tycho thought little of it —the priests were laying some ancient rite upon the procedure. Some folk took their faith so severely, and the Dunsweir royals had probably donated that relic from their collection to help anoint the believers for their journey.

Tycho didn't exactly feel blessed by the Pilgrim, but then, what did that feel like? Buzzing in the ears? A quickening of the heart? Or a bounce in his step?

He settled his head back against the table, looking up at that stained-glass ceiling. And as soon as he had, he thought he saw in the corner of his eye some flicker of movement within that dark relic, like a fish kicking beneath the surface of a deep lake. And like it caught his gaze, there was a burst of green light. Distant, like a child lost in the void, calling out to him. When he refocused on it, he could swear the beveled writing on the glass slid in parallax, like the writing itself was further away than the shard that contained it.

The priests paused next to him, lingering, like they caught on to his staring. But before Tycho could work out a thought, they had begun their somber march anew, leaving him with a chill in the back of his mind.

Tycho's fingers itched, and he wanted to flex his ankles, but he didn't dare move. This might be an assessment of some kind, testing their patience or obedience, and he didn't want to find out what failure would feel like. He had endured far worse than itching and cramps. And those priests were taking their sweet time going from row to row. And that incense, sandalwood and juniper and myrrh, was almost making his eyes water.

He still hadn't quite gotten settled with his Oskie augments and he was about to be stepped up another level entirely. How much more elite could he get? At this moment, he could hear the patter of a soft afternoon shower on the roof, the percussion of footfalls in the building below him. And the croaking voice of an old doctor two rooms over.

"Magnus...I must caution you, we may not find ourselves with a suitable candidate."

The responding voice was deep but youthful, almost as young as Tycho was. Elegant, cultured, but rigid and with sting. Was Tycho actually this close to a member of the Holy Family, just two rooms away?

No, this voice spoke with a clipped stentorian manner, brusque. If this empty lack of charisma was one of the Dunsweir? Tycho wilted at the thought, but then smiled. Never meet your heroes, he supposed. They never matched expectations.

If this voice wasn't Dunsweir, he certainly worked with them. He had the same accent. "They'll be on the Sojourn soon enough. How they get there is of little consequence."

The croaking doctor coughed. "Should I ask Holkstad for a second batch, just to be safe?"

"Have as much faith as your patients do, Doctor. You'll be a happier man."

Tycho was no fool, and he was hardly the only Oskie in the room that had heard the conversation. This operation he had volunteered to undergo, this program with almost certain death? That had not been exaggeration or euphemism.

Many of the young men and women in this room were about to die. Right here, right now.

He had hoped—even expected—to die in a hail of gunfire, opposing enemies of the Empire, fighting to make this world and a galaxy of others safer. Perhaps he'd face a great alien beast or some crafty terrorist, an organized militia he'd dismantle single-handed before succumbing to his wounds.

Tycho didn't expect to face death and judgment laid up on a stiff bed, deep in some dark installation orbiting Jupiter. None of them did. But Service to the People didn't always mean violence. Perhaps this was what they were meant for.

The priests began to chant: "Your path is simple, your purpose focused. The Pilgrim calls you to the Sojourn, to walk by their side. Complete this task, this one request...and your seat at their right hand shall be open unto you, Servant of the Path."

The doctor and the mystery voice two rooms away knew full well they were within earshot of a battalion of super soldiers; they just didn't care. Tycho could hear the flutter of a long plastic jacket as the doctor fished for something in his pockets. "If they survive the upgrade procedure, their new companion will manage their considerable augmentations. This will make them...rigid in their interpretation of orders."

"I don't need creative battlefield thinking," the voice said. "I need an unprecedented killing machine."

"That's precisely my point, sir. They will be more *machine* than anything else, more akin to a gun that can think for itself than a soldier. You will need to take care in how they are deployed. The onboard AI will require considerable power and Cascade quantum errors will be accelerated. The human element will stabilize them for only so long. You will have yourself an exceptional soldier, unmatched by any made by man...for a time."

"So long as they're exceptional," the voice said with a bit of spit.

Tycho squeezed his eyes shut and tried to picture his mother's face in his mind, recalling that sketch he had made.

"They will provide," the doctor assured. "This union of machine and man. bonded by the Pilgrim's light, has never been more potent. Paladins do not know failure. They do not eat, they do not sleep. They will find their enemies and, simply put, overwhelm them."

Paladins, Tycho thought. That was the first time anyone had

mentioned the name of the program. Every other MOS had been numbers and letters, convoluted messes tied more to regulation codes than people. 11-Bravo, 33-Whiskey, 19-Kilo.

Now 'Paladin.' That...that sounded impressive.

"I've got some redlining on 42 and 81," a technician noted.

"Remove them from the pool," the doctor ordered. "They'll serve Holkstad in more practical ways."

Tycho heard the doors swing open and two veteran Oskies entered, escorting two of the graduates off of the floor. Two fewer people for Tycho to outperform.

"If there are no further delays," the voice grumbled, "shall we get started?"

"Agreed," the doctor said. "Introduce the anesthetic line."

Tycho heard a hundred AutoDocs hum to life, and the crane arm over him swung into position. A quick panning of a laser scan found the ideal intravenous entry point. It had to differentiate between the network of coolant lines running around in his body with the actual blood veins; after all, injecting a potent drug into coolant would do nothing whatsoever.

He didn't go to sleep, drift off and dream. He blinked, and he felt...different. Time had shifted, the light cascading through the stained glass had moved, now painted across his face, blinding him with jewel tone reds. He couldn't feel his left arm, like it simply refused to respond to his calls. And his feet tingled with the most curious sensation. Not pins and needles, but something more...electric.

And he heard half again as many heartbeats in the room. Had they had moved him?

No. The same empty cathedral hall. But stiff, cold bodies had replaced his colleagues' warm souls on the rows of tables. The temperature of the air had fallen a full ten degrees because of it.

"They've come around," a technician reported.

"Very good," the doctor said with a relieved sigh. "Commence the upload."

A click and clack somewhere behind Tycho's head. He didn't feel the card enter but he felt the force of something jamming into his neck.

And it was like the world suddenly came alive with light. His legs twitched as the augments came online, unlocked and ready for service. His arm almost sprung off his shoulder, so much pent-up energy.

And that's when the pain hit, like an acid poured in his ear to melt everything within. He grimaced, prepared to endure. He had not come this far to lose now.

He thought about his mother's eyes, her small nose, and the bob-cut of her hair. He'd see her again. He would.

// OS 19.6.901 — Installation Successful

Who was that? That voice? He hadn't heard it, but he had...thought it? Not a voice, really. But there was something else thinking in his head.

// Fragmentation detected in primary hard drive. Beginning integrity analysis.

Diagnostics. Interesting. Heuristic learning, targeting algorithms, navigation control. This would be a severe advantage in the field. Oskies had several mechanical augmentations, from camouflage to speed to stunning tools. Some brave students had whispered about the idea of loading in actual sentient programming, but none dared mention it publicly. Where would the AI take up residence?

Turns out, the practice was real. The AI was already managing the suite of upgrades for him, keeping everything balanced, opti-mized, and in order. He had never been one for partnerships before, but an organizational tool this sophisticated—

// Data corruption detected. Quarantining.

What? What corruption? Tycho hadn't even left the AutoDoc. He was still laying down on the cold bed while the crane arm quietly hosed off the lingering blood, a transfusion line pumping hot fluids into his arm. But there was already data corruption? That was some intense quantum drift in the calculations.

There must have been some problem with the onboarding process. He hoped his new augments would still function.

More temperature drops. More bodies going cold. The upload process was...was shutting down other survivors. The simple act of uploading an AI was killing them.

And then, finally, only one other heart beat in the chamber, a candle flickering in the dark. Just Tycho and one other.

"Ninety-three KIA. Two survivors."

Did this mean he'd done it? Was he going to be accepted into the program? He thought about his mother's...his mother's...

Mother. Biological female in a species that provides ovum for genetic exchange. As a mammal, he must have one...

What was her name?

// User attempting prohibited access. Formatting partition.

It was like he heard a snap of static and his eyes fluttered. Who was she? Those violet eyes in the pictures...

He didn't remember.

// Formatting Complete. Command Prompt Open.

"And you thought we wouldn't get one," the brusque voice mocked. "The Pilgrim has blessed me with two. Get them standing and cleared for duty. I'll prepare the ship. We have a renegade to find."

RECORDED DREAM DATA, DATE: 2241.13.04

PATIENT: THOMAS HUGH

PATIENT STATUS: NOMINAL.

// Increases in rapid eye movement. Pulse elevated.

// Muscle spasms in lower lumbar region. Apnea events above normal levels.

// Advise further—

// Warning: Abnormal Brain Activity Detected.

// No rapid eye movement.

// Pulse ox falling. Increased electrical impulses in the—

Do you blame yourself?

// Warning: Abnormal Brain Activity Detected.

I asked you a question.

What?

It's okay. Take your time with it. Communication like this can be quite...taxing.

Do I blame myself? Who are you?

// Warning: Heart Rate Accelerating.
// Deploying quarter milligram dose of Tinpraxolom.

You didn't ask for this. And Stride didn't know what he was giving you.

Stride?

// Warning: Abnormal Brain Activity Detected.
// Blood pressure in excess of safe zones. Alerting ship's physician.

This is going to be disorienting for you. And I can't ask that you trust me.

You could start with a name.

// Warning: Subject experiencing light tachycardia.
// Warning: Early signature of oncoming heart attack.

It'll make more sense soon. I promise.

// Symptoms subsiding.
// Brain activity, pulse, and apnea events all returning to normal levels.
// Records forwarded to ship physician for immediate examination.

CHAPTER
TWO
THOM

MILARDI HADN'T EVER TREATED a sixteen-year-old with symptoms of a small overnight heart attack before—sorry, 'cardiac event' was the technical term. Thom's thing didn't technically qualify but had been what Milardi called 'preclinical.' Not that the team medic concerned himself too much with what the latest medical texts were saying.

Of course, Milardi hadn't ever treated a dead man before either. So there was liable to be a whole host of interesting discoveries being made.

A physical showed no lingering issues, and while his labs detected the aftermath of the stress, there was very little he or the AutoDoc could advise beyond further observation.

It would take a few days for the dream panel to process into anything legible—the brain waves had to be sorted out. But Thom knew that the raw data wasn't 'fine' based purely on the bug-eyed expression on Milardi's face.

Still, nothing to do but wait and watch. And they had work to do, anyhow.

———

It was a delicate business, keeping the *Aurum* tucked in the radar shadow of a much larger transport, all without a physical connection. Roche did his best to position their ship in the blind spot, firing the stabilizing micro-thrusters every so often to keep them from drifting off. If they held close enough to the large hull of the bulk freighter, passing Imperial scanners would miss their silhouette and heat signature amidst the enormity.

And if they drifted too much, the others would never make it back aboard with the cargo. Transport captains had wide jurisdiction in how they dealt with...pirates. Osyen might prefer the term highwaymen, or scoundrel, but Thom knew what they were doing today fit the definition of piracy.

The transport train beneath them resembled a string of towers laid on their side and hooked up end-to-end, a convoy of buildings humming along their predetermined route without a care in the world. It stretched back towards its point of origin like a long metallic thread.

The *Aurum*, with its stubby thrusters and aging parts, looked like a fly on its back. On the Jump Deck, Roche sat plugged into his myriad of consoles, a half a dozen screens projecting up in front of him. The subdermal implants each crew member had allowed for a picture of what each could see, albeit with some interference.

Thom leaned over the round jockey's shoulder, studying the holographic wall of videos carefully, sorting out where each crew member was. He could see a fine dining hall, a room full of crates, and a tool closet.

"Lily?" Thom asked, summoning the *Aurum's* AI. "What's mission time?"

The deep and unsettling baritone voice was polite enough to whisper it to him. "Forty-nine minutes, eighty-two seconds..."

Thom blinked. "So...fifty minutes. Because that's how minutes work."

"Well, if you expect me to do all the work for you."

Roche groaned. "Perhaps you both can take the conversation on-line, so that I am not further distracted?"

Thom nodded, assenting. Roche needed to match the movements of the train carrier so that they didn't clip one of the *Aurum's* nacelles against a wall—or be discovered by the law-enforcing Navy surely lurking nearby. Instead, he thought backward for the radio implanted at the nape of his neck. *We are at zero hour. Rashida, Osyen? That's your cue.*

Plan in motion.

Thom watched the camera feeds as the two in the fancy dining car turned towards one another, each camera 'looking' at the other. Osyen cleaned up well for the occasion, about as well as could be hoped for, anyway. His waistcoat had been purchased new with fine leather, and they'd trimmed up his facial hair into something current and fashionable. They had dyed his jet-black hair a deep and silky blue, only showing its true colors when the light hit it just right. Rashida had insisted the oceanic look wasn't dumb and that it was, in point of fact, quite fashionable. Sure enough, the other passengers in their cabin had equally vivid colors on their heads—along with some truly garish headwear.

But Osyen never felt quite comfortable feigning wealth. The criminal captain popped and preened, his chest puffed out to a comical degree. And he jammed his thumb in the coat pocket, tugging the fabric tight across his shoulders. This was what he saw in pictures and movies, and he was trying to imitate the picture in his head.

The Lady Rashida Izan de Tylmirande had to foul herself up by comparison, else she'd stand out from Osyen's vain attempts at status. The fugitive royal's holy bloodline practically glowed off of her like an aura, with a slight lift to her chin and squared shoulders. Thom could probably balance a water jug on her head.

And her fine linen pantsuit was no exception from that quality, with a blue & white patriotic filigree running up one leg and across her front, almost like tree roots in search of water. She had folded her jacket over one arm, and the silk shirt draped across her shimmered a metallic green, like sea foam in the tropics.

Between them was a simple but opulent meal laid out on silver. And the criminals had no intention of paying for it.

Thom pushed the thought to them both. *Let's get this messy show started.*

Osyen grumbled, *Remember, Rashida: make it convincing. Not real.*

Real is pretty convincing, Rashida remarked.

Roche snickered. "We also need them to not get arrested for public disturbance."

Thom raised an amused eyebrow. "Yeah, but that's the next part."

"When we have to boost them from the brig?"

"Let's not overcomplicate things. First thing's first."

Of course, Thom had plans for that eventuality. Any time security on a cruiser this size responded to an event, detainment was a possibility.

Rashida cleared her throat, and Osyen paid her no mind, choosing instead to pick at the food on his plate. He looked like he was studying it on a petri dish.

"You'd think on our anniversary," Rashida began, haughty, "you'd pay more attention to *me*."

Osyen's biting response came back almost before she'd finished talking. "My dearest Alphette, I afford you the attention you have earned."

"Perhaps," Rashida granted, "but what if I were to lend my...attentions...elsewhere?"

"Oh, for the love of—" Roche moaned. "There are other words! There are more words in this great language. Hell, use *another* language!"

"It's like they're doing it just to screw with you," Thom said.

"Nineteen recognized languages in civilized space and they just..."

Osyen looked up from his meal—the view on Thom's monitor

finally coming up to study Rashida's playful dare. The captain of the *Aurum* was no blind man, and Rashida's curated appearance took him off balance, like he'd been staring down for so long that he forgot how beautiful she was. But her doe eyes hid a venomous bite, unblinking and unwavering in their focus on him. Thom supposed that her youth spent at the Dunsweir manor sharpened her will like little else in the world could.

Thom exaggerated his shiver to hide the real one that tingled up his spine. Roche looked over at him. "What was that?"

"Nothing," Thom lied.

Roche shook his head. "Puberty," he muttered, loud enough to be heard.

Osyen set his silverware down with a clatter. "I will celebrate this day with the woman I married, Alphette. What happened to her?"

"She grew up, Grigori!" Rashida snapped back. "She grew up and left the fairytale!"

The noise was enough to summon one of the transport's help. A vaguely humanoid robot, with a tuxedo hand-painted onto its frame, buzzed over to their table, gliding along tracks on the floor. It lurched to a stop at their table and turned its boxy head to each in turn. A simple digital face projected off the surface, a monochrome blue depiction of androgyny. "Apologies for the interruption but this private moment is occurring in public."

"When I need your input, *sommelier*, I will call for you," Osyen barked.

Rashida threw up her hands. "Oh, that's lovely. Crass to me, rude to the staff. But it's all *poetry* for the bartender at the lounge."

Roche fished a bag of nuts from under the console, popping a meaty hand inside to rustle for delicious salty snacks. He froze, looking up at Thom. "You want some?"

"Floor nuts?" Thom asked, incredulous, "No. No, I don't."

"Suit yourself."

"Didn't you tell me not to distract you like four minutes ago?"

Roche nodded. "And you're not."

"At this time," the robot waiter droned at Osyen, "I must ask you to vacate the premises and return to your stateroom."

Osyen guffawed at that request. "With the amount I paid to be on this rickety scow, I should be able to take a nap in the captain's quarters."

It's not working, Roche said with a shake of his head, *No calls out to Security.*

Rash? Thom bounced. *Initiate physical contact. That oughta do the trick.*

Rashida reached over and slapped Osyen across the face with a loud clap. The sound echoed in the dining hall and elicited more than a few gasps. Murmurs rippled back and forth, and the robot's face soured, changing to a hot yellow.

Thom tongued his cheek. *I meant hit the robot.*

I know what you meant.

The robot turned to her, stern voice dropping a whole octave into a thundering baritone. "Person-to-person contact of a hostile nature is strictly prohibited aboard Emerald Skylane Adventures. Service is now terminated, and you must return to your stateroom at this time."

Roche perked up, stiff as electrons flowed up the wires into the ball socket at his wrist. "*That* got their attention. Inbound enforcers from the checkpoint."

"How many?" Thom asked.

"Two."

"We need more than that," Thom grumbled. *Osyen, you have got to step on the gas, or we need to abort. Get the guards out of that checkpoint. Now.*

Osyen groaned—and grabbed his plate of delicious delicacies. He palmed it and hurled it across the room, shattering it and smearing expensive meats on the wall. "Dammit, woman! I'm a man in grief!"

All gossiping immediately ceased, and all eyes snapped to the broken plate, trying to pick up what they missed.

And Osyen had more to offer this drama. "If I lack enthusiasm on this day, it is not out of absent love. I buried *our son* two weeks ago!"

"And we're off!" Roche said. "They got up so fast, they probably left their shoes behind. Only one guard left."

Osyen, Rashida, start the clock. Buy me two more minutes, then get out of there. Thom looked over to the next set of camera feeds. *Milardi, Zatia. You're up.*

A skiff of this size had checkpoints between every car. The baggage container had to be of easy access to passengers, so it was ready and close to most of the sleeping sections. Now further on, deeper into the ship, was the real and proper cargo hold where bulk items or valuable materials were stored.

That was behind a security scanner, a biometric lock, and anywhere from six to ten armored jackbooted thugs.

Thom watched as a parade of uniformed boots went stomping past the screen, the blare of a security scanner going off with each successive person through it. With each passing, they could count who was leaving the checkpoint.

The camera panned over to see Jackson Milardi tucked behind some shelves. Even on a stealthy smash and grab, Milardi wore his finest. His collar was popped high, lining up with the angle of his jaw. Twin pistols glinted under his long coat, but not nearly as bright as his smile.

That smirk slipped to one of concern as he counted up the alarms going off from the checkpoint. *That...may be more than Oz can handle.*

He's playing the part of rich entitlement, which can handle quite a bit. He's not supposed to win a fist fight, Thom assured them. *You two have your own job to worry about.*

Zatia tapped Milardi on the shoulder, a shock of pink hair poking out from beneath her wool cap. "I got five that says Osyen gets shot."

"Five?" Milardi coughed. "*Fra tow,* girl, that's not a bet. He is absolutely going to get shot."

"Fine." Zatia slipped her glowing card out of a chest pocket. "Five says he gets shot *in the leg.*"

"That's more like it."

Zatia snapped her fingers, and her head twitched hard to the left. Thom squinted at the camera feed, trying to suss out what had made her tic like that. But Milardi didn't seem distressed.

Focus up, will you? Thom scolded them, deciding to move past the odd moment. *Lily, you're in through firewalls, nice and quiet?*

Yes, Thomas. I have breached the third layer and gained limited access to ship systems.

Alright, loop the wireless security. Adelaide? Thom said, looking at his last camera feed, which seemed to be nothing but cables and wires. *Stand by to take out the hardwired.*

Say the word, Maestro. Two wrinkled hands with rolled-up sleeves had pulled free a bundle of gold and copper, isolating out a single line. She slipped a pair of cutters around the wire, like an ax hanging over the head of its victim.

Milardi and Zatia waited for the guards to leave and the door to slap shut, before they crept from their hiding places. Zatia's compact frame made it easy for her to keep low to the ground. But Milardi, with his gangly oversized limbs, didn't even try. He stomped right on over to the checkpoint.

True to reports, one guard remained at his post. Young, with gear that fit loosely on him. He was snapping and unsnapping the retention on his holster. He flexed his fingers like a quick-draw artist gauging himself in the mirror.

His eyes were locked on a security feed from the robot waiter, watching as Osyen and Rashida escalated with one another. Osyen tried to flip the table, only to find it bolted down, so he elected to throw his chair instead. The guard chuckled to himself, but more out of a perverse dramatic irony. He knew what was coming for Osyen at that very moment, and it was going to be so satisfying seeing a rich prick experience consequences.

Milardi leaned on the checkpoint's customer service desk, putting on his best smile. "Yes, hi, hello? *Mizoe en tar.*"

The guard groused, upset that work had somehow found its way back to him. He stood up and dragged himself over to the desk. "How can I help you?"

"I wanted to check on my shipment, a crate of Kevalkian whiskey. Should be in SR-52?"

The guard sneered, giving Milardi the once-over. "You got a ticket, *skel*?"

"I'm sorry?"

"Duster like you, no ways you affords a seat in this tub. Ticket?"

"Well, I never!" Milardi did his best attempt at a posh accent. A pretty convincing one, if his thick Colonial did not immediately follow it. "You'd be a hundred percent correct."

Thom took that motion like a starter pistol. *Scanner, go.*

Adelaide clipped the wire—as the guard pulled out his baton.

And Zatia dove through the scanner. No alarm or flashing light without power to it. So no one was notified of the breach.

The guard looked down at the movement, in time for her to hook his leg and yank him off balance. He fell forward, slamming his head into the desk—and folding his body backward in an ugly unnatural way. The guard slipped to the ground, motionless with blood leaking from his forehead.

"Zatia!" Milardi hissed, surprised but trying to keep his voice down. "Ex-cessive!"

"Oh, quit your whinging. He'll be fine."

"He will *not* be fine!" Milardi said as he slipped through the dead scanner. "What part of that *gulaw s'ivan* looked medically okay to you? He's going to have neck problems 'fore he's thirty!"

Thom nodded to himself. *Adelaide, nice work. You see any alarms?*

Nothing on my end, Adelaide grunted. *Lily?*

The baritone AI practically sang the words. *Nothing to report.*

Good, Thom said. *Patch it back in place and get ready for the big one. We're go for Phase Three.*

Adelaide's aged fingers worked magic, rubbing a ball of resin in her palm to warm it up. She pulled the clipped wire ends taut together and pressed the resin over it, bonding the lines back together. There was evidence of a cut, but only if someone came looking for it.

Row A, Box 113, Thom reminded them. *You have one minute before the whole place knows we're here.*

Behind the checkpoint, Milardi and Zatia moved on into the cargo haul. Racks full of crates and baggage a few miles long, trailing off into the distance. It was strange to see the world stretch out on a ship far enough that humidity blurred human vision.

Milardi muttered the designation to himself over and over as he frantically scanned the racks.

"Got it!" Zatia called out, and Milardi came jogging over. His jaw dropped, and they both stared for a second, marveling at the size of the crate.

Hey, Thom?

Yes, Mr. Milardi?

You said the target was a box. You did not say it was the size of a bulk engine.

Thom tried not to chuckle as they stared at a steel crate twice as tall as Milardi himself. *Not everything valuable fits in your hand.*

"How are we to get this hunk of bunk back to the *Aurum?*" Milardi mused aloud.

"Reminder," Lily said, far too loudly, in Thom's ear. "Mission time now at fifty-three minutes and the transport is nearing the next Jump in its course."

Thom pinched his fingers in the air and spread them wide, lowering the opacity of the hull. He could see the train stretching out before him, nobbled cars locked together by concentric rings. The feverish glow of a nearby star brushed the convoy with glorious reds and oranges like living fire. *No more time, folks. Figure it out.*

Zatia dashed back to the front of the cargo bay. She clucked her tongue as she searched, beat-boxing a rhythm to herself until she found...an equipment locker.

Thom quietly noted to single her out for applause in the debrief.

The convoy crew that meticulously loaded all of these crates didn't do all of this with strong backs and full hearts. Just outside the checkpoint, a yellow paneled storage unit practically called to her—but it was locked.

No matter.

She unhooked the bangle on her wrist, flicking out the bladed tonfa within. She wedged the Silksteel blade into the crevice of the locker and pried it open with a happy ping!

A quick scan of the interior: lunch boxes, uniforms, medical gear. Her eyes lingered on a smaller locker buried within, this one painted red and with warning signs. But she shook her head and settled on the exoskeletal arms hanging conspicuously to one side. They wouldn't fit her, but...

She raced them back to Milardi, who hung his head. "Of course. Yes. Loading arms."

We live in a magnificent time, don't we? Thom teased him.

"Yurich's down! Somebody's in Cargo!"

Roche looked up at Thom. They accounted for all the guards, and Osyen was still arguing with the detachment from the checkpoint. Thom squinted. Had he missed some patrol, counted wrong? Who were these new faces?!

Milardi tongued his cheek, looking down at Zatia. "I'll get the box, you get the goons?"

"Why do I gotta get the goons?"

Milardi reached up, barely able to press his hand to the side of the crate. "If you can reach it, you're welcome to it."

A gunshot!—hollow gonging—the scream of a ricochet and a rain of sparks! The two different audio feeds each played the crack of the bullet whizzing by overhead.

Thom lurched forward, on the edge of his seat. Was somebody hurt?!

The camera feeds were tracking what each crewmember was seeing, more following their line of focus than a simple box image. So the first thing Thom saw clearly was Zatia pushing the plunger on a stim package, sinking a complex chemical cocktail into her thigh.

After that, it was hard to track what precisely she was focusing on. Likely because her pupils had dilated and her eyes lost focus. Heart racing, muscles tensing, nerves numbing. The stimulant was doing a lot for her, but it didn't exactly make for the most coherent backseat viewing.

Remember Zatia, Thom urged, *no blood!* He wasn't even sure she could hear him anymore. That drug hijacked a lot of her nervous system.

On the neighboring view, Milardi had taken cover nearby. He was alternating between working the exosuit gloves onto his lanky arms...and watching Zatia work.

Three goons had entered the cargo bay, splaying out wide to cover the most area without losing sight of one another. They each took one lane, advancing along to keep the brigands from escaping. When a rack of cargo would break their line of sight, they practically sprinted to the next opening, all too eager to see their friends again—and provide covering fire.

That's when they were vulnerable. That's when Zatia hit them.

She jumped out of cover, rushing the first shooter. He saw her coming and took his shot. But proficient on a closed shooting range couldn't compare to tracking a drugged-out pixie with two foot-long wrist blades charging from the shadows. His shot went high and wide. She didn't give him time for a second shot.

Zatia reached over to the cargo rack, hooking her blades on a support and swinging herself feet first into the goon and kicking off of him. He slammed backward so hard that he lost his grip on his pistol. Thom wouldn't have been surprised if he left his soul behind.

The little bruiser tapped her feet on the ground, just enough to spring up into the air and plant a kick into a nearby crate. She hit it hard enough to dent the steel—and sent it sliding into the neighboring lane. Based on the wet thud and surprised grunt, she'd managed to clip the second guard with what had to be half a ton of weight.

The first goon scrambled for his weapon. And Zatia—somehow casually—beat him to it and punted the side of his head like she was trying to kick his jawbone across a field. Maybe he died, or he was just playing dead. Thom didn't really want to ask.

More gunshots—as the two goons one lane over started peppering shots through the hole in the rack Zatia had made. Zatia took off running down the lane.

She didn't react, but Milardi's view spotted a spray of blood on the wall as she went past.

Zatia built up some speed, gritting her teeth and taking a step or three up onto the wall, where she leapt for the rack of cargo.

She picked well, blasting through a small crevice between crates. Using her momentum, she hooked her blades on the rack support and sent herself hurtling towards the two shooters.

Panicked, they backpedaled as fast as they could to create space. But she was close enough. Each shot they sent her way, she was able to stick her blades up and poke the muzzle of the pistols off-target just enough. And she pressed them, fast and precise.

Until they were bright enough to split up, split her focus. One peeled off to the left, and her crazed brain went with the movement. The goon had a clean shot on her head—

—if Milardi didn't ram him with a massive crate wielded by his new exosuit arms. The guy went hurtling across the room and the gong of his head against the wall was...wet.

Not that Zatia noticed. She was all too happy to keep pushing the last man, slicing and swiping at his pistol. Finally, the blades got a little thirsty. The ring of metal was replaced with one clean slash and tear of flesh. The goon yelped, dropping his pistol to clutch at his hand. Thom thought he saw a blur go bouncing down the lane, but neither Zatia nor Milardi focused on it long enough for him to identify it. The blood that gushed between the goon's fingers said that whatever it had been, it hadn't been small.

Zatia laid her blades against his throat—

"Zee!" Milardi shouted, scolding.

Her focus lingered, inspecting her victim's pulsating throat and the blood that seeped from his hand. Thom could see now that she'd taken a finger or two. And that hadn't satisfied her.

She drew her blades together, not quite decapitating the man.

Thom squeezed his eyes shut. He didn't need to see any more. *Get the crate and get the Hell off that ship.*

It surprised him Zatia could manage full sentences. *You got it, Maestro.*

CHAPTER
THREE
OSYEN

"WELCOME HOME," Lily said with warmth. "What did you bring me?"

Scuffed pants, jacket torn, and hair in his face, Osyen stepped over the lip of the hatch and safely back onto the *Aurum*. He held the dinner plate with both hands, the immaculately conceived chef's special having gone cold but still in immaculate condition. "Have you ever had a lemon meringue tart?"

"Meringue..." Lily paused as they dug through their databases. "A European desert, traditionally from whipped egg whites and sugar. Laid atop a custard and warm pastry crust."

"Yup This one's got lemon in it, I guess."

"I await its addition to the collection with anticipation."

There was a clang and a bang from down the hall as Milardi tried to maneuver the stolen crate down the *Aurum's* narrow passageways. "Oy! You break it, you bought it!" Milardi grumbled some curses under his breath but had nothing specific in retort.

Zatia bumped Osyen's shoulder as she stormed past, nearly knocking the plate from his hands. She was still wiping the blood from her face with one hand and gripping tight with her other to the bullet wound in her side. Pain, anger, none of it could stop the clicking of her tongue in rapid-fire, a compulsive drumroll.

Rashida gingerly stepped on to the deck, joining Osyen in his bewildered stare. "You want me to have a word with her?"

"No," Osyen said, "you'd just get your head bitten off."

"Poor choice of words," Adelaide grumbled as she shuffled past the duo with her toolbox.

Osyen sneered at the old woman, turning back to Rashida. "Let her patch up, detox, have a shower...then I'll talk to her."

"There wasn't supposed to be *bodies* back there, Oz," Rashida whispered. Perhaps she was afraid her voice might carry up the hallway to the crazed bruiser in Medical.

"There also wasn't supposed to be a second team of armed guards." He didn't miss the unspoken part of Rashida's complaint. Sometimes casualties happened in their line of work, but there didn't have to be today. There was a dead man today because Zatia, well...

Because they asked too much of her. How many times could they realistically expect her to dose those drugs without some side effects?

Rashida glanced down at the meringue. "Shall I take that off your hands?"

He nodded, passing her the plate. "Drop it in the Replicator and click it to scan." He turned to follow after Milardi, shouting over his shoulder. "Don't eat it."

"I have restraint." Rashida smiled, but it immediately cracked as she reminded herself of recent events.

"Yeah, well, some of us don't," Osyen muttered to himself. He jogged up the stairs two at a time, making his way into the *Aurum's* cargo bay. Milardi was busily getting the cargo strapped down for transport. "Oy, longshanks."

"Did you get shot?" Milardi asked him as he gave one last good crank of the strap. "In the leg?"

"No, but my hair is *blue*, and my attention span shortening by the second." Osyen slipped a hand through the cargo netting, leaning forward to stretch out his shoulder. "What happened in there?"

"Long story short? I don't know."

"Give me the long version."

"She could've knocked him out, tied him up, scared him back to his cradle—she decided to *redecorate*. Does that answer your question?"

Osyen shook his head. It didn't tell him anything he didn't already know. He had hoped the one other person who witnessed it would have some more insight. "Zatia doesn't just kill people without good reason."

"Well, if she's got one, she hasn't shared it," Milardi sassed back.

Zatia had always been a freelancing firecracker. Broken many a nose, some knees, plenty of bottles—she'd shot Osyen before. And she'd killed plenty of folk. But killing somebody without being provoked? "I thought her little stim cocktail was stable?"

"It is," Milardi said, "but it's not the only thing swimming in her system. Chemical compounds, mixing with natural chemistry, hormones—you don't always get predictable results. And outside of that, we gave her the cocktail to end all cocktails. Who knows what the detox time on *that* is? If there is one." Milardi raised his eyebrows in a pointed expression.

It hit Osyen like a sledgehammer with the word 'obvious' welded into the handle. Of course. Three months back, Zatia had taken some exotic kind of stimulant to help her go toe-to-toe with an Oskie. "You think her usual mix is getting some lingering effects? After Stride?"

"She's been having a hard time with those compulsive tics." But Milardi shrugged it off, looking away. "Can't say for sure without running some tests. Think she'd even let me run 'em?"

"When I'm done with her, she will," Osyen assured him. "She's a member of this crew. She's got a job to do. If she can't do that job to satisfaction..."

"She gets to quit stims cold turkey while studying our exhaust pipe?"

She was crew. She was a friend. Osyen would never leave her out in the cold. And it was rather alarming that Milardi was so ready to drop her like that. "You always bail out of things when they get too hairy?"

Milardi scoffed. "Cap'n, hairy is the way I like 'em. But *that* wasn't hairy. That was somethin' else."

"You worry about your job, let me do mine," Osyen said, turning back to head towards the front of the ship. "Speaking of which, do your job: go patch her up. And no peeking in the stolen box!"

Milardi's voice echoed up the hall. "Aw! That's half the fun!" And Osyen couldn't help but smile.

Osyen clomped his way up and through the galley, watching Rashida fumble with the Replicator. Lily was trying to guide her through the process, glowing blue head poking out of the roof. The AI had modified their already bewildering look by shaving half of their head. So technicolor flowing locks dangled in the air on one side, and the other half was a pristine blue dome. "You must secure the cupboard before analysis can be conducted."

"The cupboard?"

Lily's voice hiccupped with a hint of static. "Cupboard—shelf—cabinet—container."

That wasn't normal. And Osyen faltered in his step. "You okay, overlord?"

More static, then a pop. A second head slipped out of the wall in front of him, with a girlish smile and a twirl of their mustache. "The garish one is deliberately difficult."

"I am being specific!" Rashida objected, following up under her breath. "He never brings *me* meringue."

"Because you already know all about it," Osyen said in passing, dragging a hand affectionately through Lily's image. "You wouldn't be impressed."

"I'd be impressed by the gesture."

Lily's head slipped back across the ceiling down to square up in front of Rashida, like it was on an invisible crane arm hidden in the wall. "Condition required: You are not special."

Rashida just shrugged. "And you are very special, Lily. So special I have to feed you through a cupboard."

But Lily was fast in their crushing rebuttal. "And if you prize your precious oxygen, you will resume your task."

"Somebody's grumpy," Osyen crowed, as he jogged out of the galley and up to the Jump Deck. He called out ahead: "Roche?"

Roche spun about in his chair, the cables in his knobby club arm whirring as the drum inside loosed more length to compensate for the distance added by the movement. "Weasel's already made contact. I told him job's done. We're heading for the rendezvous."

Osyen raised a cautionary hand. "Low and slow like. We don't want to run across some well-informed pirate-types with questionable affiliations."

"You really think the Godfather would stoop to backstabbing?"

"Yes, I do. But also, anybody wanting to climb the ranks in his scummy organization might take initiative. Say a certain rodent-themed asshole. So just...I prefer late and in one piece, is what I'm saying."

"So long as we get paid," Roche muttered.

Osyen raised an eyebrow. "We running a little close to the wire?"

"More than close. We're dancing over the edge."

Osyen nodded, glancing at the empty chair on the other side of the Deck. "Where's Thom?"

"He's frustrated. On walkabout somewhere."

Why? Because of Zatia? They got the cargo for the Godfather, clean as could be helped. And everyone's home, mostly intact. Osyen shook his head. "He couldn't have known what they were walking into."

Roche pulled his lips in tight. "That's not how the boy sees it. He planned the job, and he thinks..."

Osyen pinched the bridge of his nose, rubbing at the ball of stress starting up. "I'll talk to him too, I guess."

"Remember when being a pirate captain was mostly about shooting and getting shot?"

"Yeah," Osyen said, mindfully rotating his shoulder in its socket. He'd collected more aches and pains than any twenty-five-year-old should have. "And this may be an upgrade to that, but that doesn't make the chit-chat any more pleasant."

"I suppose what I mean is: 'keep perspective'."

Osyen sighed, turning to confront the drama hiding somewhere on his ship. "Just make sure Weasel knows when to expect us."

First Zatia getting a little bloodthirsty, and now Thom beating himself up. Osyen groaned just thinking about it. When did he become everybody's dad, running around and balancing everybody's mental state? He didn't get into this business to be a camp counselor.

He reached out through his implant: *Thom, get out of the ducts and meet me in your room for a hot minute?*

I'm not in the ducts.

Whatever, Osyen dismissed. *Just be there in five?*

But first, he had to go confront a five-foot-tall sixteen-year-old with a history of performance-enhancing drug abuse. Osyen had a review of her conduct in the field.

Feh. Because he liked the idea of having a newly gifted broken leg.

He could always hang it up, retire, send this crew on their separate ways. Take Lily to a little shack on an agreeable, insignificant planet to live out his days. That is, until they both went mad from the banal routine.

Instead, Osyen knocked on the door of Medical. And got roughly the answer he expected. "What?!" Zatia barked through a grimace of pain.

"How's the gunshot?"

"How do you *think* it is?!"

Since he hadn't been told explicitly to bugger off—and it was *his* ship—he entered. Zatia laid on the AutoDoc as the machine did its cruel business. Little metal fingers pulled at her flesh, exposing the seeping wound to the air as they picked out foreign objects like fabric or lead, all while sanitizing with a spray of white foam.

Milardi's fingers rattled at the holographic keyboard floating in front of him, consulting the various diagnostic reports.

"What's the damage, operator?" Osyen asked.

"Well, she's not in sepsis yet," Milardi quipped. "I'm able to image the bullet fragments, and we'll extract when she's out. But the perforated bowel is going to be tricky. Might take a couple hours for the Doc to glue her back together. Couple weeks' worth of rest."

"See?" Osyen tried to hide his grimace and focus on Zatia's pallid face. "You always said you were full of shit. Now it's actively spilling out of you."

Zatia didn't think he was funny. She actually *growled* at him, her arms tight against the restraints. He had no doubt she'd reach up and strip the flesh from his skin—and he'd kinda deserve it.

"What happened on the convoy, Zee?"

"I made a mistake," Zatia grunted. "Happy?"

"No, no. See, mistakes? Leaving Jackson unsupervised with my whiskey? That's a mistake. What you did was a tad more than can be called 'a mistake.'"

Zatia winced as the AutoDoc tugged on her gut, and she clenched her hand in the air to prevent herself from shoving the machine. "How about you take my sorry, and I don't punch you? How 'bout that?"

"We kind of had a directive to leave 'no bodies' in our wake. Weasel's not going to be happy."

"Weasel didn't get shot," was all she had to say about that, with clenched teeth and bloodshot eyes. Fair enough, she was in an amount of pain. Especially as the stim wore off, taking its analgesic qualities with it.

"Weasel is our one ticket into the Godfather's good graces," Osyen reminded her. "And we made Adelaide a promise I intend to keep. Understood?"

That seemed to crack through. Zatia laid her head back and took a deep breath—something that hurt with the pull on her gut. But she nodded with the exhale.

Osyen gave Milardi a look, and the gunslinger hit two keys. The AutoDoc swooped in over Zatia, expertly sliding two intravenous needles into Zatia's arm and flushing her system with fluids. She was asleep in seconds, with a gentle groan and a muffled curse.

Milardi ushered Osyen out of the room to let the AutoDoc sanitize its little bubble. With the door shut, the machine released a hiss as it cycled the air of the small room to prepare for surgery.

"No heavy lifting," Milardi reported with benign authority, "no strenuous activity, no spicy food."

Osyen cackled. "Don't tell me that. Tell her that. She's going to do all three."

"You played it kinda soft in there."

Osyen stared through the plexiglass window at the courtesy bubble of blurred glass around the operating table—that was getting spackled with red. "Sometimes, all you have to do is plant a seed and they'll get there on their own."

Milardi shoved his hands in the pockets of his waistcoat, like he was digging for the right thing to say. "And if she doesn't?"

Osyen didn't really want to think about that part just yet.

———

Thom bounced a ball against the floor of his cabin, skipping into the wall and back to his hand like meditation. Osyen noticed the paint had actually scuffed on the bulkhead from however many hits it had taken over the months.

"How does Roche feel about you banging on the wall he shares?" Osyen asked.

"He's never in it," Thom pointed out, "so he's never complained."

Osyen folded his arms across his chest. "It was a clean hit and a good plan."

"Good plans don't have that many surprises."

"You work with what you have. Sometimes intel is bad."

Thom threw the ball with a bit more force. "And that's why you hired Zatia in the first place? For 'when the intel is bad?'"

Osyen tapped his foot, measuring how hard he wanted to push back on that. "We've had a good run the last few months, and that's *entirely* because of you, kid. You've had good plans, good execution—"

Thom raised his arm, ready to hurl the ball—but stopped himself, exhaling cut his nose and dropping the rubber into his lap. "Somebody is dead because the plan *wasn't* good. He had parents, he had dreams..."

"Two weeks from retirement?" Osyen asked, flippant. "What Zatia does on a job is her responsibility. Not yours."

"I told her to go. I told you all to go. Told you it was safe."

"No part of this life is ever going to be *safe*." Osyen slid over to lean against the scuffed wall, squaring up on Thom. "And if we're going to go full macro level, the job wouldn't have existed without Anze Orchikov. So take it up with the Godfather, or whatever the Hell he calls himself these days...The Master, or whatever."

"I'm not kidding around."

"Me neither. A crime boss gave the order. Without him, you never call the play. So if Zatia's not at fault, then neither are you. Stop falling on the grenade."

Thom drew one knee up to his chest, squeezing it in tightly. "Jus' never got anybody killed before."

He looked so small, like he had years two ago at the Pan & Pantry. A younger, scared Thom withering under the spotlight and lowering his voice lest he step on somebody more important.

"You still haven't," Osyen assured the boy.

The kid huffed, shaking his head. "All for a box of cybernetics."

Osyen scowled. "I told everybody no peeking."

"Nobody has," Thom said without breaking his dour expression. He pushed a single finger to his lips, mocking a shush. "But a man of the Godfather's caliber will assume that we have, even to check for resale value to a third party. If the cargo is something worth killing us over—because it's too valuable to pay for, or we're loose ends—either way, I'd like to know about it going in. Now I know that it's just spicy commodities and I can take us in without sweating."

"See?" Osyen said. "You haven't lost your touch for breaking into crates you're not supposed to."

"Who said it was *my* touch?"

Osyen's brain had to take a moment to reboot. "Lily scanned the crate for you, didn't they?"

"What?" Thom faked a smile, his eyes still grim. "For an AI to crack physical locks, someone would've had to breach the electromagnetic, remove the shielding, and pierce the Faraday systems before meticulously resetting each one."

"Adelaide?"

"Took her forty seconds. I timed her."

That headache was coming back again, creeping down behind his eyes and nose. "You...are going to be a *demon* one day."

"One day?" An ounce of pride and a pound of pain flickered on Thom's face. "Zatia can't come to the meet."

Osyen nodded in agreement. "She's laid up in recovery, anyway."

"Roche's got to drive the ship. And I wouldn't bring Rashida within four kilometers of Weasel."

"I love the girl...but you can't talk these guys to death," Osyen assured him. "Milardi and I can handle it ourselves."

Thom hesitated, jaw slack, then snapped it shut so hard Osyen heard the click of his teeth. Nobody relished going to a meet like this, on uneven ground with uneven strength. And this was inherently going to put them at a disadvantage in negotiation. Without Zatia, it was that much easier to just *take* the cargo. Two dead men didn't need to be paid.

And the crew needed this deal to do better than just an exchange of goods. They needed to impress. They needed to get into the inner circle.

Osyen's eyes went wide. "You want to come?"

"No!" Thom said way too fast, back stiffening. "No, nothing. It's fine."

It wasn't fine. Something was eating at the boy. "You haven't had a bad idea in three months," Osyen countered. "I mean...bunch of good ones and the bad ones have usually led to good after like five minutes of oxygen. So give it air, kid."

Thom picked at his teeth, cautious with his word choice. But he said nothing.

"You can't mean Adelaide?" Osyen asked. "She lost her husband to these exact gangsters. She's not liable to be diplomatic."

"It's nothing," Thom insisted, rubbing at his forehead like he was pressing the stress out. "I just haven't been sleeping well."

"Yeah, Milardi mentioned," Osyen said, laying his head back against the bulkhead with a theatrical gong. "My nightmares don't typically try to kill me."

Thom shook his head. "This wasn't normal nightmares. It-it was like open-heart surgery, only I'm the patient. And awake while they're cutting. There're these priests walking around a big cathedral. And they..." He wasn't saying something, wouldn't put energy behind the words

"Creepy," Osyen said, flippant.

"They had a piece of..." Thom paused, like it was difficult to think about, to articulate. He looked up at Osyen with sharp, unblinking eyes. "Don't go to the meet. Drop the crate, drop all of it."

Osyen's eyes darted around the room, looking for the gas line that was piped in here. "We killed a man to get this crate, and that comes with some pretty significant noise—you want me to just *vent it?*"

"Somebody..." Thom choked on the words, swallowing back on them, before he finally got them out. "We chase this road much further and somebody's going to end up—" His throat clenched on him, and he couldn't say the word.

Time to be Captain.

Osyen considered how to approach this gingerly. "Thom, you *died*. Stride killed you dead. Yeah, that was a bit ago, and half a galaxy away. We threw the Icon into a star and put Fiona off our vector. But something like that, that's liable to have some lasting effects on a man. It's nothing to be ashamed of. Soldiers get hurt, they need to talk to somebody. You? You *died*. You don't owe anybody anything, okay? Dreams are just...your brain is wrestling with what happened."

Osyen came off the wall and sat next to Thom on the bed. He wanted to give Thom room, not smother, but the kid clearly needed some human contact right now. He blamed himself for a job gone pear-shaped, and now was wrestling with some pretty aggressive trauma. "Next time we hit the Core—or some proper industrialized planet...we could see about getting you proper attention?"

"Yeah," Thom said, hollow. "Probably smart. Probably *very* smart."

Osyen laid a hand on the boy's shoulder, and he felt the kid lean into his palm, instinctively seeking the warm comfort. But Osyen left that room feeling like he'd done more harm than good.

CHAPTER
FOUR
ADELAIDE

"SHE'S grumpy on the best of days. This was *not* grumpy." Milardi was not one for mincing his words, but Adelaide had reviewed the playback from the heist. The gunslinger was dramatically underestimating the situation.

Zatia had every opportunity to spare that guard's life. He wasn't a wicked man, a force of evil or oppression; he was a pair of work boots on a job site, a stiff, just trying to make his mint like a responsible man should. And the girl had taken his life for no other reason than because she had wanted to.

Adelaide hadn't been happy about it, but Osyen had asked her to tag along on this misadventure. Apparently, the Maestro had a bad feeling, and that was enough for him. She moaned and groaned, but truth be told: she wanted to go. She wanted to look these monsters in the face.

Adelaide sat in the back of the shuttle, one hand laid possessively over their stolen crate. She rolled her fingers across the tacky surface as the boys yammered on. Milardi leaned over to Osyen like he could have a private conversation in this little tub.

Osyen, meanwhile, focused on flying and paid the gunslinger little heed. "When was the last time you were grumpy?"

Milardi shook his head. "I don't know, maybe that shell game on Halcyon?"

"*That's* grumpy for you?"

"What? You would've had a different pick?"

"Ugh," Osyen practically scoffed. "Antioch. Easy. There was that lynx flush?"

"Ah, yeah." Milardi slipped into that memory. "*Fra tow zu*, by the way."

Osyen swallowed his laugh. "Don't forget how much you love me."

"I won't."

Adelaide rolled her eyes and wanted nothing more than to be working on her second cigarette already. "I don't feel like either of you know what the word 'grumpy' means."

"Sure," Milardi admitted, "because I don't make it my entire personality."

"Hey!" Osyen barked. "Be nice."

"You really think I expected him to butter that up?" Adelaide snarked.

Look at them, she thought, deflecting right into humor and playful antagonism. They'd gotten themselves comfortably off the point. Zatia's cold-hearted bloodlust was forgotten, the misdirection of a proper magician. She doubted either of them realized they'd done it. Conflict avoidance in its finest form.

Who knew what kind of chaos they were stepping in to now? The criminals might just turn them over to the Navy to avoid catching flak themselves. Or the Law might simply be waiting for them, a sting operation. There were a million ways this could go wrong—*before* Zatia spilled blood.

Adelaide watched as the planet rose up below them, a marbled collection of swirling brown and white. The formal imperial corporations largely dominated more temperate zones around the equator, but those were relatively low traffic. The real fun was in the old helium mines in the northern ice fields, long since drained dry. They had been converted to resort towns in the last twenty years, bringing in tourism from the Core to enjoy the icy weather and mountainous terrain. Far enough away from prying eyes and populated enough to vanish, it was perfect for those that wanted a little...spice with their escape.

"Speaking of grumpy," Osyen began, looking over his shoulder, "can I count on you to just frown the whole time and say exactly nothing?"

Adelaide shrugged. "No promises."

"I *will* duct tape your mouth."

Milardi leaned backward over the top of his seat, looking at her upside down. He spoke, soft and careful: "If this is too much to ask, it's completely—"

"I'll be fine," she chided them. "You'd think I need a walker, the way you two coddle me."

"Jus' remember why we're here," Osyen said, "and it'll be over 'fore you know it."

"Yeah," she affirmed, tightening her arms around her waist. She had to keep her hands tight around herself; she'd torn the skin on the back of her hand just by clenching her fist when she'd heard the news.

Weasel. That wasn't the man's real name, of course. But she knew him. She would have a hard time forgetting his face.

Osyen must've seen the homicidal look. "He didn't kill your husband. And even if he did, I'd still need you to keep clenched. Okay?"

"Use it," Milardi offered. "You've already got a good scowl, so..."

Oh, she was supposed to meet with the criminal organization that killed her husband and mounted his ashes to the mantle like a trophy, all while keeping her observations strictly to herself, was she?

Adelaide's face must've soured, because it made Milardi shiver, straightening up in his seat. "Oh yeah, that's the good stuff."

Osyen keyed an open radio channel. "Farragut Control, this is SSV-11-Delta-Oscar on approach. Requesting a vector."

The jockey at traffic control was almost certainly on the take. There'd be no official record of this landing. "Copy, Delta-Oscar. Level out at one hundred thousand, then descend at four degrees for approach."

"Copy that. Level at one hundred, descend at four. Delta-Oscar."

"Welcome to Farragut."

Milardi pointed to the northern hemisphere, at a white swirling storm system. "Look at that beast. That blizzard's gotta be the size of a small moon."

"Bigger," Adelaide said. "And it never dies. Just circles around like a top."

Osyen glanced back at her. "Not your first time visiting this snowball?"

Hardly. But she didn't answer him.

It was a bumpy ride through the upper atmosphere, lots of weather on the icy planet, but what was worse was the silence. There was no chatter on the radio, no idle banter between passing ships. Shuttles were free to come and go as they pleased with little interference from the Corps that ran things on the equator.

Which meant that the right greased palm allowed an alarming amount of freedom.

So Osyen steered their shuttle craft far off the beaten path, away from the main ports and into the tundra proper. It was rolling hills with the occasional snow-capped patch of forest. After flying good and low for a time, evading active scanning, they touched down to bury the goods under the ten feet of compacted snow. The exosuit arms looted from the convoy made the work that much easier. Arriving at a meet with goods in hand was an excellent way to get paid in highly kinetic fashion.

With that chore complete, they circled up again to rendezvous at the agreed upon location.

The Godfather had sent a proper host. Six men, openly carrying Gauss rifles, waited with two vehicles. Reclined atop one shuttle with a crooked leg and a fluid ease, the Weasel craned his neck to see their shuttle come drifting in. He was a man of fluidity, with no tension in his movements, but that didn't mean he was casual. Just at ease.

They brought themselves down at a friendly distance, completing the triangle of the three vehicles.

Milardi stepped out first, swaying his narrow hips to draw attention to the revolving cylinder pistols and the custom-tooled cartridge belts hanging off his tall frame. The long coat billowed in the air, buffeting a bit of the fresher snow like a breath of frost about him.

Osyer's exit wasn't nearly as impressive, clambering down the steps and crunching on to the snow like the unruly goon he was.

Adelaide leaned against the shuttle door's hydraulic pylon, hanging in the doorway as further presence. She had no desire to get her shoes wet or get any closer to this frostbitten pond scum.

"You had mentioned a delay," the Weasel said, a simple complaint.

"That, I did," Osyen effused, hooking both thumbs through his belt. "Could've not mentioned it but felt like a professional courtesy to keep a fine gentleman like yourself informed of the schedule."

The Weasel didn't smile, didn't nod in acknowledgement or thanks. Instead, he tented his fingers and bowed his head. It reminded Adelaide of supplicants at church, playing at grace.

Just as soon as that was done, the Weasel popped off the hood of his shuttle, and strode to the middle of the clearing. "I can't help but notice I don't see the cargo the Master were promised."

Adelaide huffed. The Master, The Godfather. Anze Orchikov was a glorified, up jumped mobster playing at Colonial Governor on Farragut. And his obsequious people had offered sequentially more reverential titles. Apparently, 'the Godfather' wasn't a suitably divine rank. He now had to claim the nauseatingly simple 'Master', too.

Cults of Personality. Something so simple is rarely innovated.

"And you won't," Osyen told Weasel with polite enunciation, hard consonants and flat smile, "until you actually pay for it, that is."

And Milardi smiled, scanning the assembled shooters Weasel had brought with him. They outnumbered the crew two-to-one, but Milardi seemed awfully confident.

"How do I know you got the goods?" Weasel asked.

"I think I'm the kind of fool that wants to ingratiate myself with the Godfather, not piss him off."

The Weasel pointed a crooked finger at him, like he was pointing out a spot on a map. "I don't see no blood on you. And I heard a little bird chirping about some blood being spilled."

Dammit. Adelaide stood up straighter, ready to dive back on to the shuttle for cover.

But the Weasel cracked a smile, almost pleased. "You'll do great things when the Master asks of you."

"I can work wonders," Osyen said, "when I'm well paid."

The Weasel's voice went cold, and he lowered his head. "I trust the Master's privacy was respected?"

Osyen smiled, bluffing. "Pay a man enough, and he can blink for a real long time."

Weasel's eyes tracked Milardi, and by simple additive quality, flicked over to Adelaide. His eyes narrowed, focusing in and drawing upon the déjà vu he must be experiencing in that moment. But suddenly, he grinned from ear to ear, showing off a multicolored sampling of metallic teeth, and he stooped low into a bow. "Welcome to Farragut, fair folk: the iceland paradise."

"Yeah, it's a..." Osyen scanned the featureless tundra for miles in every direction. "A real palate cleanser. And much as I'd like to see more of it, I want to know what else we can provide to...the Master."

The Weasel's eyes flashed with recognition, a curled lip. "To work again so soon?"

Milardi popped up the collar on his jacket, shielding his chin against the blistering wind. "Some men work to live, and others live to work."

"Which are you?"

"Me?" Milardi set that one up with a smirk. "Work ain't work if you love what you do."

"What about her?" Adelaide stiffened as the Weasel drew focus on to her. "She like your work as much as you do?"

Osyen knew better than to speak for her. The Weasel had directed a question to her, and to intercede would be to capitulate the point. This was Adelaide's ball to catch.

She let go of the shuttle pylon and instantly felt her gut fall out beneath her. She nearly staggered down the ramp, playing it off as a swagger. Or a drunk.

"Ain't you a bit old for this game?" Weasel asked her. "Shouldn't you be pulled up to a fireside and a warm friend?"

Yes. She should. But the Godfather killed him, burnt him, shoveled him into a gaudy bucket, and mounted him to a mantlepiece like a trophy kill.

Everyone waited expectantly for what she had to say, what witticism or vagrancy she might bring. Gangsters: no matter how much pomposity or ritual or script was incorporated into the culture, they were all just thugs in the end. And this prime selection was little more than serfs, bowing and scraping at the feet of their feudal lord for the gift of another day's breath.

She'd seen what happened when that gift was rescinded because the requested beatitudes were given in the incorrect tone.

So she didn't say a damn thing. She just studied the Weasel's face. He had a scar on his nose where some roughened blade had dug into the meat years ago. His patchy beard had collected some frost out of the air, but his tailored suit was perfectly dry; he hadn't so much as taken a single step into the snow until the crew had arrived. He wore driving gloves with stitching up the back of the hand, like ridges on a cobra. And his jaw hung slack, hungry, thirsting for whatever might drop from her lips.

She denied him, mouth locked tight. No, if she were to move...it would be to break his knees.

The Weasel had stood idly by while her husband died, that same thirsty look on his face now as then, when blood had spat from her husband's back with each report of the pistol.

She cocked her head. And the Weasel mirrored her, leaning in the same direction. "Do I know you, miss?"

Miss. Few folks looked at a woman her age and assumed unmarried. And were he anybody else, she might even consider that polite.

"I ain't nobody's miss...or madam or lady," Adelaide snarled.

The Weasel chuckled, eyebrows waggling up and down his forehead. "No, you ain't. You...are tempered steel." And he laughed to himself.

That was probably a compliment, based on how every single guard immediately slackened. They slung their rifles, and one came jogging up with a bag. The Weasel plucked it from his hands without even looking back. "This is eighty percent of our agreed-upon fee. I hope you understand that we accrued certain expenses from your team's aggressive approach."

"I might've agreed to those terms," Osyen said, "if that had been stated up front."

"Eighty or nothing. Could always indicate where I believe some uh...*murderers* might be hiding out..."

"But then you wouldn't get the benefit of our continued services," Osyen countered without missing a beat. "Loyalty can't be bought."

"Ain't that the truth?" The Weasel said, glancing at Adelaide. "We're somethin' of a family here, Captain Belt. Every man, woman, and child under the Master's sight does their part. What part will you serve?" He raised the bag of payment.

Osyen threw a side-eyed glance at Adelaide, as if to back her down. Then he took a grand step forward, like he was going to take the bag, but kept his hands low. "I've got a counter-offer. You keep the money, and we...get an audience with the Master."

The Weasel folded his arms behind him, moving the bag out of reach. "I don't haggle, Mr. Belt. You have an item for purchase, one that I requested. We agreed upon the manner in which I pay you."

"Yes, we did," Osyen said, "but then you changed the amount, which got me thinking. If it's all fungible...I mean, we all serve the Master's will. You as his fixer, the businessman, a branch of the tree.

But you're not the root. You want these parts, parts that you undoubt-edly promised delivery of? You see about paying us one hundred percent...cr for the low, low price of a single meeting. Sounds like a steal to me."

The Weasel leaned to one side as he metaphorically weighed his options. The way he ground his teeth betrayed how frustrated he was even to be asked this.

The nature of any good cult: there was only one king, but there were always pretenders who used the king's authority to claim their own fiefdoms under his eye. And they all believed themselves once-and-future royals ready to inherit the throne, already behaving like they had some stake in it.

Osyen had challenged that, pointed out the Weasel's role as an...instrument.

"Tell ya what," Osyen said, clapping his hands together like he was closing a book. "Product's not going anywhere. If you're in a rush, we can come to an agreement right now. If not, we're happy to let you think about it. We'll head over to Farragut proper, have a drink, let you make the calls you need to make. It is a Family town, after all. We can't exactly slip away. 'Course, you could kill us. And spend the next ten years combing the ice for your box. I believe you to be a more...conscientious man than all that. Am I wrong?"

The Weasel raised a finger, silencing Osyen. Insults aside, he was considering the geometry of the situation, of the pieces that would needed to be moved. Was it worth the effort?

Now, he could capture them and torture them into giving up the product, too, but what precedent would that set? How many new recruits would they get if he went about torturing folk?

He drew a wintery breath through his nose, like he was smelling the planet itself. "Storm is coming in. It'll blanket this little patch of civilization with cold out of legend."

"At least once a year," Adelaide said with a smirk.

"We saw it coming in," Osyen quickly noted, taking the moment back before Adelaide did anything else. "But that storm's days out. You've got time to ponder options."

Narrow eyes and a heavy sigh, the Weasel considered Osyen's measure. And Osyen didn't blink.

The Weasel straightened up, squaring his shoulders. "Go have yourselves a drink." He fished in the bag and pulled out a single credit chip, tossing it to Adelaide. "On me."

Osyen gave the man a polite—and mocking—bow. Adelaide lingered as the Weasel and his gangsters filed into their ships. And the credit chip sat in her hands like a scalding hot coal between her fingers.

When the door shut on the Weasel, she snapped the chip in half, leaving its shards in the snow.

CHAPTER
FIVE
RASHIDA

SHE'D SEEN MORE than her share of shady institutions, entire planets motivated by poison and knives. Her last year's itinerary looked like an encyclopedia of locations where muggers outnumbered school teachers. Delta Boolean alone would make the top of the list if the Navy wasn't actively wiping it off the map.

She idly wondered what Fiona thought would happen to her little pirate cove after sinking an Imperial fleet carrier and taking no prisoners. The Navy wasted no time in declaring it an act of Civil War—and bringing down thunder.

But amongst all of Rashida's past roosts, Farragut was a standout because most Imperial planets had the welfare of their citizens in mind. No one was homeless in the Empire, even in its criminal corners—if prisons could be constructed and meals provided to anybody committing a crime, then citizens surely deserved at least as much, including job training, medical care, and recreation.

Not on Farragut.

Losing a roof for the night meant being kicked into sub-zero temperatures that would freeze a man to death in a matter of hours. There was no shelter that was not owned by the Godfather, and if he deemed you unworthy of his house...

Barbaric, even by criminal standards.

The spires of human life sat between two mountain ranges as they pinched together, nestled atop the ice field in that glacial valley. The entire colony was built outward in a ring, gleaming steel reflecting the blue ice and plumes of stinging, heavy smoke, tinged with frost and acrid metal.

The searing orange of pitched fires lit up the air, as industry had drilled down through the tundra to expose the planet's magma mantle. A warm heart beating fresh, exposed through conduits to provide life and comfort to the people. Each drill-site was contained within a small structure, piping heat to those nearby, and even warming the surrounding air.

At the center of it all was the largest geothermal plant, a four-story tower that seemed to father all the rest. Standing close to it was like being bathed in radiance—only really bringing the temperatures above freezing.

This place was one power outage away from being blown away, buried in the snow. There was no industry here, no research—only commerce. This was a place of business, where money flowed, and people listened with care. It had sprung half-cocked from the ice as a hidden place where people might meet beyond the reach of prying eyes, and it slowly grew and grew until an irony took hold. Now an entire city had assembled out of nothing but pricked ears and open palms.

If these walls could talk, they could point the way to half of the crime in the sector.

Osyen had returned from the meet with a positive spin, that they would soon hear from the Godfather and be able to make their overtures. Poor Adelaide would likely see Nathaniel's ashes retrieved, should they bow and scrape accordingly, before making themselves appropriately scarce.

For now, they could resupply the *Aurum* and relax in one of the more upscale dens of iniquity.

Rashida took ten minutes with Lily to construct a fur coat from recycled fiber, something lush and warm, but unrestrictive. It was difficult to marry fashion with utility, but the AI helped her make the most within the confines of physics. It took a few attempts and an illustration for Rashida to communicate what she wanted. Lily almost constructed a blueprint for a mechanized mink, misunderstanding the prompt.

"We're going sluggin' and slingin'," Milardi had said, marveling at her look in the corridors outside the crew cabins, "not kissing rings."

"Sure," Rashida had conceded, "but some of us look good while doing it."

Milardi had stood up a bit straighter after that. The handsome archon of poor decision-making enjoyed the casual flirtation, but she doubted he was interested in anything more than the game of it. For those that drew his more focused attentions, he was far less subtle in his pursuits—and with an alarming rate of success.

Roche had brushed past them both with a grunt and a sigh. The man resembled a brown bear ready for a winter slumber, ambling along with the same begrudging drag of the feet.

Milardi had looked at Rashida with a shrug. Whatever had gotten under the jockey's skin was beyond his observational skills, even as a frequent bed partner and gambling compatriot.

Osyen had arranged for transport from the docks, and Rashida had to admit it impressed her. The local ferry service was little more than a heated cabin on an automated maglev system ten years out of date and two years beyond its service life. It would sail along a predetermined route and pause only long enough to disgorge its contents onto the snowy streets. They bolted guide rails to the ceiling to help passengers balance when the car was packed shoulder-to-shoulder. Seats were mostly metal and recycled plastics, stained with a dozen unfriendly substances. And adding in the cold, nobody wanted to sit.

But above all else, this was quite functional, even with its grunge aesthetic. Most public transport in Reaches colonies was more loose. Unlike the shiny efficiencies of colonies like Londinium or Vanguard, most were scrapped together from old units and held together by a grown man's wishes.

The crew filed down the gangway, walking with forced casual, while simultaneously trying to catch the transport before it left. They didn't want to wait the twenty minutes for it to come back around.

"Hey! Yeah, you!" Adelaide shouted across the concourse, pointing a finger at two dock workers. The young lads had the *Aurum*'s refueling conduit in hand, tucked recklessly under their arms, an umbilical line almost a foot across.

Adelaide stopped in her tracks, her whole body leaning forward like a racehorse in the stall. "That bit of pipe has more current running through it than God's left testicle. So handle with some *care*, huh?"

Milardi swooped over, guiding Adelaide back to the rest of the group. "Somebody needs a drink."

"Jus' trying to save some lives."

"Me too."

Rashida chuckled to herself as she clambered aboard the transport. For the moment, the few riders aboard wanted nothing to do with the boisterous bandits and malcontents now boarding. Rashida understood—not everyone in a pirate town was a pirate. Some of them were just trying to get by unnoticed.

Roche had been reluctant to get aboard, only hopping on when he heard the closing bells chime. He was panting as he gripped the handrail, swaying in exaggerated ways with every curve of the rail line. "I just—I don't like going wireless," he stammered. "Lag times, atmospheric interference, packet drops...gives me headaches."

"Darling, baby, *matryushka*," Milardi draped an arm around Roche, squeezing him at the shoulder. "We're going for some well-deserved evening drinks with co-workers of occasional benefits." Which prompted Rashida, Osyen, and Adelaide to all exchange looks. Did he just mean Roche—or had any of them? No. No! They couldn't have! Had anybody?!

"It's fine," Milardi assured his neurotic Jockey friend. "We will not be doing any high-octane escapes today. You watched the *Aurum* get hard-lined to the spaceport. You'll have Lily for company the whole way there and back. Nothing is going to happen."

Zatia, Osyen, and Thom all pointed at Milardi like an angry ecumenical council, jabbering their various complaints. But it was Adelaide who said the most coherent sentence, throwing her head back. "*Why?*"

Milardi brushed them off. "You superstitious twats! Sayin' it out loud don't make it so."

"I'm goin' to staple your mouth shut," Adelaide muttered to no one and everyone.

Roche was still on about the technical restraints. "It's just, it's very loud in pubs."

"Yeah, usually," Osyen said, leaning on the overhead handlebars. "Which is why we selected a quiet little bar on the edge of town that's ten seconds away from bankruptcy. No loud noises, we'll be half the occupancy. And lots of cheap liquor."

Hesitant. Interest piqued. Roche's head dipped like a mouse coming out of its hole. "No loud noises?"

"Averages out at sixty-two decibels," Osyen said with a knowing smirk, like he was expecting a gold star.

"You don't have to come," Thom affirmed, "but we wanted to make sure you *could*."

She had seen Roche excited before, but usually around a quiet card game or logic puzzles. But right there, it was like seeing a dog wag its tail or a cat prick up its ears. "Okay. We can leave if it gets too loud?"

"Of course we can," Rashida said, "but if it is too loud, it's more than likely just Zatia. And we can shut her up."

Zatia threw up her hands at that random shot but winced when that movement pulled on her bandage. Thom blinked a few times before asking: "Should you be drinking when you're also leaking?"

She pointed at Milardi. "Doctor's orders." And the lanky bastard croaked some cheerful noise in her response, which was enough for Thom.

Rashida couldn't help but smile. They were all so concerned with one another, so invested. They went out of their way to help each other, to comfort each other. It was...saccharine, sickening. And wonderful.

And it set her skin on fire. Kindness wasn't real. It was the cloak hiding a dagger. Even though she knew these people were genuine, compassionate, her mind couldn't rest with it.

It was a jovial ride to the edge of town, with comedic criminal caricatures getting on and off: one lady with a respirator implant, repairing her graphically removed nose (she had shown Milardi on request); the requisite peg-legged pirate tried to sleaze talk Thom until Zatia moved him along; a grizzled dark man sat in the corner with a hood pulled tight to hide his dark and bloody past, desperate for everyone to look at him while simultaneously unsettled by any level of attention.

She wanted to know their stories, and she felt they would've told her had she the bravery to ask.

Osyen hadn't been buttering anybody up—the destination pub was barely standing against the harsh weather. Shingles rattled in the wind and the sign flickered with loose connectors. Thick cable that had never been properly secured swayed in the air like jungle vines.

Holographic tags from a half dozen gangs littered the metal walls with morphing images of sneering men, bloodied knives, or torn-up flags. One particular image was a woman, intended to be attractive, though Rashida wasn't sure where the subject's ribcage had gone.

She paused in front of it, incredulously studying the art and swaying her head to watch the programmed motion. Swing left, and the subject's head tracked to follow. Swing right, and the painting opened its legs....

Rashida glanced over at two goons leaning at the corner of the building—not bouncers. Unaffiliated toughs, one with a running blade prosthetic below the knee. Caught staring, they tried to fake some idle conversation between each other, but there was a spring-load tension in their stance. Blade leg kept bouncing the tip on the ground, tapping out some internal beat.

Rashida caught Milardi's eye, indicating the potential problems. He nodded back at her with a smirk. He'd spotted the two easily. They weren't doing a superlative job of blending in.

The Godfather's men: likely there to report on their movements, more than inflict the superior will. Still, good to know that they were being watched while in town.

Osyen held the door of the establishment with a doofy smile as he windmilled his arm to get everyone out of the cold. He stopped the antics for Roche, letting the big guy get a low-stimuli taste of what was inside before the jockey took the plunge into its depths.

Then Osyen beckoned to Rashida.

She gave the two watchmen a little wave. Slouching and begrudgingly, they waved back—busted. Smiling, Rashida walked into the bar.

It was a dingy establishment but she'd certainly seen worse. The actual bar was quite large, dug deep into the permafrost for natural insulation. Down a set of winding stairs, they had laid a vaulted pit out as the primary bar floor: tables aplenty, some idle games, nothing too fancy. A few dozen patrons were scattered about. Surly types, with unkempt hair and rough hands, snow patches still clinging to their clothes. They grumbled while huddling around steaming drinks and greasy food.

The brassy music scratched from a speaker overhead, and Rashida could feel the tinge of acoustic manipulation at work—nothing more sophisticated than a simple joy spike. That was likely a good technique to keep the peace; cheerful people don't break tables.

But her eye stuck on a crude brass statue behind the bar. It looked like dusty scrap that someone had welded together in the shape of an eye, with three wavy lines up and down, like radiating power. It was sitting on a shelf above everything else, a place of prominence, where it could be seen in every corner of the pub.

'Under His Eye.' Lovely. The gangs of Farragut were taking their pet idiom a little literally.

How very devoted of them.

Milardi, Thom, and Zatia bellied up to the first free table they encountered, waving Roche to join them. A blue ghost of an AI waiter blinked into existence next to them—Rashida could see the glow from the projector dangling on the roof. It was a jovial caricature of a man wearing a floppy hat and sporting a waxed mustache, with a rough but friendly voice to match. "Welcome to Farragut and thank you for choosing the Icepick for your refreshment needs! Can I get you lot started with a stack of pickled eels? Perhaps a warm beverage to melt those frosty hearts?"

"Beef stew," Zatia said, cracking her knuckles on the table. "Pour some whiskey in it."

The AI waiter flickered as it computed that off-the-menu request. "Can do there, missy!"

"Call me 'missy' again, and I'll pull you out of whatever wall socket you're in and bury you in a snowdrift. They'll never find you."

Thom and Milardi both raised guffaws and apologies to the tone, but the waiter didn't seem to even register the threat. He turned to them. "And for you fine folk?"

"Uh," Thom hesitated, "triple-filtered water, and a raisin muffin?"

"I'll have the eels," Milardi chirped. "You had me at pickled."

Roche eased up to the open spot at the table, drumming his thumbs on the surface. The waiter turned to him, expectant. Roche didn't even make eye contact. "Nothing for me. Thank you."

"Very good! If you require any other services, my name is Humphrey. Just give the table a tap!" The waiter vanished.

Thom leaned over to Zatia, whispering something, but Rashida was too far away to pick up what. Milardi had spun about and was bathing in the bar's atmosphere. He propped both his elbows up on the table, practically draping himself backwards over the surface.

"They were using that," Roche said, eyes still scanning his environment like a security bot.

Milardi squeezed his eyes shut and pulled his lips tight, holding back the far more acidic response. "They...really weren't. And I needed a good stretch. You want me to ask permission to breathe next?"

"I want you to consider that you're here *with* people. Respect them."

"I respect 'em fine!" Milardi glanced at Thom. "You feel disrespected?"

Thom's eyes snapped back and forth between the two. "I feel like I don't want to be a part of whatever this conversation is."

"See?" Milardi turned to Zatia. "You? You feelin' disrespected?"

Zatia simply scowled directly into her own open hands, like she was trying to memorize her fingerprints. She idly snapped the fingers on her left hand, tracking the beat of the music above—her idle tics were getting worse. Rashida wasn't even sure the girl had heard the question.

"You take them for granted," Roche argued.

Milardi didn't even address the accusation. "For a man full of naught but logic and processors, you worry far too much!" Milardi gave Roche a friendly push on his doughy shoulder. "Let me buy you a drink, and we'll take right care of those worries. I promise, you won't short out.'

Roche's eyes fluttered as he computed that request. "I'm fine."

Rashida sighed, leaning on the banister. The sound caught Roche's attention, and he glanced up at her. She smiled, giving a subtle urging nod.

Roche raised a finger. "One drink."

"—is how all great stories start!" Milardi clapped him on the back. The gunslinger slapped the table surface twice with an open palm, and the blue AI barkeep flickered into existence again. "Humphrey: this man, one whiskey, as soon as you can."

Rashida suppressed a chuckle behind a gloved hand. Milardi

might live his life five seconds at a time, but he was never above including folk in those moments. So many people in his chosen profession kept people at arm's length. Milardi seemed to beckon every soul closer to him with each cool breath.

Then again, he also never had an issue putting two holes in most men he'd ever met. Perhaps he faked that intimacy, enjoyed being the center of attention. It would hardly be Rashida's first encounter with the trait.

Slots in the table opened up, deploying plates of steaming food and small glasses of questionable color. Zatia, Milardi, and Roche examined their bounty with curiosity and even alarm. But Thom...

The young man snatched the muffin off his plate, dunking it into his glass of water. He balled up the baked good into a little bread torpedo before grabbing the glass and pouring the mixture down his throat in one smooth motion.

He slammed the glass down, smacking his lips. And was greeted with a mixture of horrified stares. Except for Milardi, who just started clapping.

Zatia's jaw hung open. "What the hell just happened?"

"Is your jaw a pocket dimension?!" Milardi exclaimed.

Thom tented his fingers, sorting through the vocabulary in his head for the words that might explain this trick. "Busboys at the Pan & Pantry didn't get food breaks, per se, but they gave us access to the Replicator. And we quickly learned how to get food onboard as fast as humanly possible. You get a baked good, typically one with a good mineral, vitamin, protein mix—and you sink it."

"Sink it?" Roche asked.

"Yes."

"*Fra tow zhu li.*" Milardi tapped the table, summoning the waiter again. "He needs another glass of water and a new muffin, because I need to see that again."

Rashida watched with mirth as Thom tried to talk the gang through the trick. His cheeks puffed up as he shoved the manufactured facsimile of a baked good into his glass, his skin flush with color and life. He had a cherubic momentum about him, hesitant but eager, and never far from a crafty smile. He was still small for his age, slender and short, but he was looking healthier every day.

A miracle, given what the boy had experienced.

Osyen drifted up to Rashida's shoulder, propping himself on the banister. His eyes were full of nostalgia, and he took a loud sniff of the stale air. "Brings back memories of our first get-together."

"Yes," Rashida acknowledged, "but there was a bit more broken glass, foul language, and matters of honor."

"Accurate," Osyen said, sidestepping that story. "You were particularly beautiful that night."

She let out a satisfied, wistful hum. "And the little boys and girls were driven quite mad."

"That's like a sport for you, isn't it? Catch and release."

She frowned, brushing off the callous statement. Instead, she chose to be clever. "It's not that I'm not hungry, Mr. Belt. It's just that I've not found anything appetizing."

"I'd say you could always pick up a menu, but then, I think I'm torturing the metaphor at that point." He chewed on his cheek. "You know, you don't have to keep running with us. We're long since past the job in the Boolean."

She huffed. "Trying to get rid of me?"

He popped off the banister, squaring up on her. "Not many people would pick the life of seedy bars and rusting ships if they had other options, is all."

Rashida hid her wince. Osyen did not know where she came from. To him, it was all gilded porcelain and tall towers. To him, a jail cell was bars and iron and hatred.

She knew better. She knew that culture could keep hands locked at the waist, a mouth clamped shut, and clip the wings as well as any warden could. And like a warden, prisoners that stepped out of line could be disciplined—or worse.

She forced a smile. "This is the best place I could ever be."

And he coughed. "That's depressing."

"Why do you say that?"

His face darkened, throwing out the playful tone and laying out his cards. "You either want this life or you're born to it, beautiful. It's not something you can sample."

Rashida eyed the young captain. "You didn't take us all out for drinks as a group bonding activity, did you?"

"Nope," Osyen confirmed as he slid in front of her. "The Godfather will be considering our offer, and while he does, I need to do some necessary maintenance to my team of malcontents—you included. And..." He threw a glance at Thom's attempt at a muffin speed run. "...whatever the hell *he* is today. But that's not why we're here."

"You want me to chat up the owner, unearth their affiliations, and pry some deepest secrets from capitalist claws?" she said with a raised eyebrow.

"I didn't say that. Did I say that?"

"I know what I'm here for."

"You're here for a lot of reasons, but people is what you're good at." He studied the outline of her shoulders, lingering for a moment longer than was professional. "The fur coat's a nice touch."

She smiled. "Adds a bit of glamor."

Osyen took a breath, unintentionally getting a lungful of her perfume, amber and musk. And she watched it send pleasant shivers down his spine.

She'd seen that look reflected back at her since she was thirteen, and her sisters had schooled her well in what it meant. And with appropriate preparation, proper posture and delivery, a young noblewoman discovered she could compel the reptilian hindbrain to seize control of just about anyone. Perhaps it was that training, the knowledge itself that robbed her of the magic, but the shape of a bare hip or the smell of rose petals never did anything for her.

Clever Osyen was wise to her tricks and skill, and yet, he took one look at her, one smell of her perfume, and she had him hooked.

His eyes fluttered and a devilish curve came to his lips. She could read the thoughts that flashed across his mind.

He wanted to stay by her side all night, and into the morning. Sweet caresses that turned into a forceful grip.

But he managed to rip himself away by grabbing a lungful of the bar's stale air. "Glamor is right."

He jogged down the steps to join the crew, leaving Rashida to compose herself on the landing.

She looked back at the entrance. Adelaide leaned on the wall, looking down at all the growing cacophony. The fiery glow of a lighter in one hand as she lit a cigarette, taking a clean puff.

Whatever she had seen with the Weasel, she still needed time to process. Rashida turned her back and left Adelaide with her thoughts.

Rashida sashayed her way down the stairs and up to the bar, settling down on a stool. A hard-nosed woman cleaning liquor hoses was more tattoo than anything else and midway through her third midlife crisis. She didn't even look over. "Humphrey takes orders. I just take your money."

"What I require, Humphrey can't provide," Rashida lamented, exaggerating her accent.

"I don't talk in riddles, honey." She didn't miss the burly woman lowering her hand below the bar for a fresh towel—or the grip of a gun.

"I've only just arrived in Farragut," Rashida said. "I was told to meet someone, but he didn't show."

The owner sighed. "You one of Patrice's little birds?" she said with a side-eye glance.

"I'm my own person," Rashida assured her.

The line almost worked. But something caught the owner's attention and sent them marching off to the far side of the bar. Rashida might've thought she'd offended, but for the flick of the owner's eyes tracking on to the new movement.

On to whatever actually drove her off.

A shape settled up to the bar stool next to her. Boot heels, light but placed with power: masculine. She heard the calm rattle of a cane being set down, but she hadn't heard it clicking on the ground—this man carried it for style, not need. Or as a weapon.

The slide of elegant cotton fabrics slipping against oiled leather as he sat down. The flutter of a long coat, but of a more civilized cut— not meant for rough and tough living. Rather tailored and fit for Court. He stood up straight, supported by the corset that cinched his narrow waist.

And the smell...

Most men smelled like something—sweat, salt, or whatever obnoxious rosewater scent they used to cover it. This man smelled like nothing at all. She could hear his shoes squeak on the wood floor, see his shadow cast itself across the bar. No doubt she could touch him and feel what must be soft and pampered skin.

But one of her senses defied her, told her nothing was there.

His voice was deep for his age, almost thrumming in her ear. "Rashida Izan de Tylmirande...you have been your own person for long enough."

"Magnus," Rashida whispered, unwilling to turn to face him. "Where did I screw up?"

"You were not subtle in the Boolean. Half a dozen databases had your face. Interrogation of survivors confirmed the veracity."

"Yes, well, I don't kill everyone I happen across."

Magnus slipped a hand on to her shoulder, sliding his sharp fingers inside the fur coat to gently turn her outward, to face him.

He was as harsh as she remembered. Barely eighteen now, with his gaunt and skeletal face, sunken eyes and high cheekbones. He'd grown taller in the last few years, but no more muscular, all sinew and wire. One might think they could break him like a twig, but they would find him as strong as Silksteel. There had always been something so chilling about having her leash held by a child, but one that behaved so hollow? It was uncanny, unnerving—by design.

And his voice could still cut her like a cord around her neck.

"This is your final warning, Rashida. Come with me, now, or there will be no more patience."

"You've been showing patience to this point, have you?"

Magnus bowed his head, as though he were her friend, cautioning her. "The Dunsweir are livid, Rashida."

"Livid with you, maybe. Your responsibility is to keep me in check. How's the track record on that?"

He didn't acknowledge the barb. "They know of your...activities. And you embarrass them. Playing in the mud is one thing, but your actions in the Boolean? They cannot tolerate open rebellion."

"And I cannot abide a cage."

"I don't come to you with demands. I come to you with options. No matter how far you run from me...I am, and always will be, yours. I am your Consort as chosen by your father, I am your guardian—"

"My jailor," she spat. "Nothing more."

Magnus took a sharp breath through his nose, and it sounded like a snake hissing. "Choose now: you can come with me, or you can face the Paladins." She stiffened and his lip curled in cruel appreciation. "Ah. Do I have your attention now?"

"What have you done?" she whispered.

Magnus leaned in. "I am charged with your protection—from both corruption and distress. That was my vow. You are almost irredeemable, Rashida. Come home. Before it's too late."

It surprised Rashida that it took this long, but Osyen suddenly appeared at Magnus's back. He grabbed the delicate boy roughly at the shoulder and peeled him back. "The lady doesn't seem too happy to see you—Whoa!" Osyen's eyes went wide when forced to stare into Magnus's sallow face. "Milardi, check it out. It's anti-Thom."

"What?" Milardi said, his voice muffled by the cup pressed to his face.

Rashida tried to shake her head, wave him off, stop kidding around. But she was so frozen it just came out as trembling.

The Paladins? Magnus couldn't be that insane. He couldn't have!

"Osyen Belt." The name came to Magnus like he was reading it from a file behind his eyelids. His mouth hung open on the name, tasting the air for blood. "Your crimes are many...but you do them to survive. The Consul is not without perspective, nor without mercy and understanding. But if you do not release me, you *will* share her fate."

"Coulda just threatened me, boy," Osyen said with a smirk. "Why'd it take so many words?"

"Take your hand off my shoulder."

"No can do. See, the lady's a member of my crew, my family. And I protect my family, y'hear?"

Magnus nodded with an acknowledging smile. "I understand. I was born to protect a Family, Mr. Belt. One far older than yours." But he released Rashida nonetheless, his fingers still crooked in the air like a hawk's talon.

Osyen glanced at her, locking eyes to check her state and he was disquieted with whatever he saw reflecting back at him. He likely had never seen the royal lady with so much fear on her face, pallid sweat and shivering.

Magnus didn't look at her, but his question was for her. "Your answer?"

Her throat clenched as she tried to force it out. Yes. Yes! For God's sake, take her and leave them alone. The Paladins? He'd ordained a Paladin simply to collect her?

They'd destroy this entire planet and just keep coming.

That little croak in her throat, the half-sound only just taking shape. Osyen read that as hesitation. So he spoke: "She doesn't want to go, discount vampire. Take a hike."

Magnus sounded almost apologetic. "Oh, I will. But I need to witness something first."

"Witness?"

Rashida tried to cut in. "Oz, you don't—"

But Magnus was locked on to his course now. "Witness."

And that's when Roche screamed...

CHAPTER
SIX

MILARDI

IT WAS like someone had set the Jockey's hand to a glowing hot iron. Sweat tumbled down his forehead and his skin had gone gray so fast, like he had his blood drained from him with vacuum suction. His throat rasped as his lungs strained to pull oxygen fast enough to scream out loud again.

Roche, talk to me, Milardi bounced over the commlink. *Can you hear me?*

The big man doubled over, hands gripping the table like he was on some nauseating ride. Thom and Milardi stooped to catch him, but the big guy was both fat and full of metal. Milardi grunted under the load, slowly slipping to the ground. "Thom, he's not answering me!"

Thom blinked at that. "You haven't said anything..."

"I was..." Milardi squinted, shifting back to the radio implant. *I was using the party line.*

Thom's face sharpened and his eyes glazed as he focused back on his own implant. He shook his head. "I didn't hear it."

Something was blocking the signal, and with the amount of implants in Roche—wireless and otherwise—it was probably driving him mad. Milardi glanced up at Rashida's well-dressed hunter. Magnus raised a pointed eyebrow, matter of fact and deliberate.

Zatia leapt to her feet so fast she sent her seat sailing backward. She squared up on the mysterious monochrome man with all hundred twelve pounds of her hatred. Magnus might have had a few inches on her, but they were almost the same weight. The Imperial Courtling had probably never thrown a punch in his life.

"You may do as you like," Magnus said, "because what happens next is inevitable."

Zatia snarled at him, but Milardi could see her reset her footing— as the pull on her stitches kept reminding her of her condition. Osyen stared at the bruiser, likely trying to send private messages of his own. But she was not getting a single word.

"No fightin' in the bar!" the owner bellowed at them.

"No fighting," Magnus assured her. "Just bloodshed."

"He's Imperial," Osyen shouted, getting damn near every soul in the bar on their feet. Osyen swept an arm up to point at the brass eye behind the bar, reminding all in attendance of their allegiance.

Everyone here was probably taking money from the Godfather, either directly or as a contractor. There was no love and more than enough spite for figures of the law under this roof. "What do you say, folks? What does Farragut think of Imperials?"

Steel on leather as a half dozen weapons of varying quality left holsters and sheaths. Even the owner hefted a chunky bracket gun from behind the bar, dropping the heavy thing onto her hip—all aimed at Magnus.

"Let my friends go," Osyen whispered, "and then you go. But I can't vouch for how safe the walk to the spaceport will be."

"We don't want all of you," Magnus called out to the room, never drawing his eyes off Osyen. "Just the girl."

Osyen's eyes narrowed. "We"?"

"The girl walked under this roof," the tattooed owner piped up, propping a leg up on a stool so Magnus could see the bracket gun in all its exquisite detail. "So, she walks in the Master's sight."

"'The Master,'" Magnus whispered, a quiet little joke just for Osyen and Rashida. "Master, Godfather, Hephaestus...whatever he calls himself, Anze Orchikov is but a man. And men *bleed*."

The sound of a foot hitting the floor above...but it was deeper, heavier, coupled with a thunder strike. A bass note that thrummed in Milardi's jaw and down his arm. He'd have thought it was heavy machinery chugging away nearby, digging out some portion of the glacier.

Heavy workman's boots came tromping down the stairs. A long coat pulled tight across his front to shield against the cold and his collar popped high, hiding his chin from the biting wind. Broad, strong shoulders filled the stairwell, and each step shook free a fresh layer of dust from hidden cracks in the aging building. Just under the hairline there was a cold steel band sunk into his flesh, like a coronet or a shackle.

And Milardi immediately picked out the telltale yellow glow in the eyes.

Thom saw it too—and his throat throbbed, like he was being choked. He backed up from Roche and the others. Anything to get away from this unknown figure. His head shaking, every muscle in him tight from head to toe. One hand clutching at his gut in phantom pain.

The newcomer tracked Thom's movement and squinted. Studying, curious. A yellow stripe tracked across from one eyeball to the other and back, like a bouncing wave.

Only one thing in the universe Milardi had ever seen had eyes like that.

"Oskie!" Milardi called out, drawing his pistols and leveling both at the threat. The Oskie didn't even flinch.

Through the tips of his gloves, he felt skin graze steel, and he tightened the requisite six-and-a-half pound trigger pressure. The click of release touched off an electrical impulse to the batteries within. With a complete circuit, it charged the magnets in sequence, grabbing and pulling the slug down the five-inch barrel faster and faster, ultimately hurling a three-hundred-grain slug out of the muzzle at over sixteen-hundred feet per second.

That was fast enough to put a hole in the side of a commercial shuttle.

He expected the Oskie to dodge. The bastards were fast, could smell sweat from a block away; Hell, he could probably hear Milardi's brain make the decision to attack.

But he didn't dodge. It just stood there and took the round straight to the chest—no. A rainbow shimmer, and the cracking song of a ricochet. He heard the round splatter against steel somewhere behind him.

A man-sized deflector shield?! Well, that had an effect on the landscape. Why dodge when you can just walk through it?

The Oskie cocked his head at Milardi. A single rough gorilla hand reached over to the stairwell, his grip hovering over the handrail —and magnetically ripped a chunk off with all the effort of pulling at soft cheese. The jagged rod chunk floated inches from the Oskie's hand, awaiting instructions.

Milardi heard the batteries charge up within the Oskie's wrist. And he didn't wait for whatever was going to happen. He grabbed the whimpering Roche and dragged the big guy completely to the ground, covering his head.

Because the entire bar opened fire, like they were each individually going to be the hero that found the gap in the armor. Bullets ricocheted everywhere, exploding tables and chunking stone. Some bullets found their way back into fleshy humans, cracking armor plates and spitting blood into the air like heavy ribbons.

Zatia snarled, digging in her pouch for a stim kit. Milardi raised a hand, instinctively calling out over the radio. *Zee, don't!*

But she didn't hear him, not with whatever jammer was in the air. As gunshots sailed in, she took the one moment she was liable to get and slammed the hypodermic into her thigh. She took her last breath of fresh air, as her senses sharpened, her pupils dilated, and her heart started slamming.

No more pain, no fatigue, no fear.

Just like this golem.

It took the pub's aggregate punishment with the same weight as he would a pleasant breeze. The invisible bubble rippled into view with each impact as the non-Newtonian field pushed back and sent the metal slugs hurtling just about everywhere else. Light bent and warped with each strike, ripples on the surface of a pond.

Milardi was so preoccupied with the glowing predator, he entirely missed when Magnus had drawn a stiletto, looking to slip the triangular blade into Rashida's ribs. She caught the ghoulish boy's wrist and pinned it to the surface of the bar with both of her hands. Which left Magnus with one hand free. He grabbed her hair and cranked her head back, exposing her neck.

And the creepy son of a bitch actually snarled, revealing a row of sharpened shark teeth.

Milardi couldn't take the shot—he was just as likely to hit Rashida as Magnus. And besides, Osyen was closer.

The sound of knife hitting wood bar was enough to draw Osyen's attention off of the Oskie, and with not a second to spare. He snap-kicked Magnus in the back of the knee, dropping him to the floor and releasing Rashida.

Osyen must've had a sixth sense, or just a good read on the situation. But rather than finish Magnus, he grabbed Rashida and pulled her to the ground. The Oskie extended his hand—and the chunk of handrail rocketed straight at her head, embedding the jagged metal shard into the bar as easily as the knife had.

"Hah." Zatia must've been inspired by that miss. She charged the seven-foot-tall shielded Orbital Commando with the reckless confidence of someone on drugs. Milardi might even admire the gumption, if an entire armory hadn't just bounced off of this thing's ribcage.

She never even got close. The big guy swept one arm out and slapped her upside the head, sending her rocketing into the underside of the stairwell. But courtesy of her stims, Zatia was able to tumble and get her feet planted on the surface, absorbing some of the impact. She bounced off, hurling herself safely to the ground nearby. The stim pack might be the only reason she survived that hit. She got most of the way back up before immediately collapsing to the floor, wheezing hard.

"Zatia!" Adelaide practically vaulted over the banister, the old woman taking the ten-foot fall like a champion. She rushed to Zatia's side, rolling the pixie over to check her injuries.

Unstoppable and unflappable, the Oskie stomped towards Rashida and Osyen. It dismantled anything in its way, metal or otherwise. And the pirate goons had quickly figured out they were outmatched, many trying to circle around the monster and get to the safety of the exit.

Cornered, frantic, and nowhere to turn, Rashida stood tall to face her fate. She tried to push Osyen away, but the idiot held firm, keeping his fragile squishy body between her and the robotic titan.

Magnus looked up from his position on the floor. Almost wistful.

Milardi leaned down, whispering into Roche's ear. "Buddy, you have to get up. I won't leave you behind, so if you don't get up, I'm dying too."

Roche whimpered, curled fetal with his one proper hand pressed over his ear and the gnarled ball of cables and sockets failing to get a good seal on the other.

"You can lean on me the whole way back home," Milardi promised, "but I can't carry you. Get up. Right now!"

Roche lifted his head, tears streaming down his face. Damn shame he looked up in time to see what came next.

The Oskie brushed past Magnus, almost stepping on him as he pressed Osyen and Rashida into the corner. Rashida said something, and Osyen shook his head in response. Damn hero.

"Hey!" Thom shouted from across the bar, like he could distract a walking tank.

But lo-and-behold, the Oskie turned and Milardi finally got a clean look at the man's face. Despite being bigger than some cars, he couldn't have been older than fifteen. Maybe that was all the obvious gnarled augmentations. It looked like they'd swapped a child's head onto a human forklift. And those yellow eyes, like polished citrine, considered the young Thom Hugh.

And that's when the Icepick's owner swung her bracket gun over the bar, blasting the back of the Oskie's head with a clean shot. A fifteen-inch wide cone of hot red laser scorched the Oskie's scalp, burning away a chunk of jacket and all of his hair.

But aside from sizzling like boiling water, the boy's skin was unharmed. Now hairless and adorned only by that simple steel crown —but completely nonplussed.

The Oskie reached over. The owner wasn't stupid enough to try and fight, so when the Oskie snagged the bracket gun from her with his magnetic palm, she simply let it go and tried to run.

The bracket gun was a squat thing, no real sharp edges to it—just a battery, capacitor, and a focusing lens to dump every bit of stored energy in one go. It was the side-by-side shotgun of choice for home-owners across the Empire, the first real laser weapon for home defense. The Oskie shot the entire chunky gun at her with just a flick of his arm, hard enough to impale the owner to the bar wall. In doing it, the Oskie never took his eye off of Thom.

If that hit didn't kill it, nothing Milardi had was going to do the job.

But it was distracted, transfixed on Thom for some reason. And Osyen would not waste that opportunity. He grabbed Rashida and slipped along the bar's outer wall, just out of reach. "On your feet, bandits! Go! Let's go! Let's go!"

When Thom broke into a run, the Oskie looked back—to find his prey gone.

Milardi helped Roche to his feet and practically dragged the big man out of the pub's door, quietly wishing they'd left the Jockey on the ship.

CHAPTER
SEVEN
ZATIA

HER RIBS CREAKED with every breath, her jaw was clicking with alarming frequency, and her ribs felt hot and wet.

She picked at her shirt, trying to peel the sticky cloth away from her stitches. Intellectually, she understood that the red stain wasn't a good sign, what it must mean for the still healing patch job; she also understood that one of her ribs was more free floating than usual.

But what was more surreal was feeling the blood pump out of the wound and the bone drift around her gut with each subsequent breath, like a malfunctioning water pump.

Adelaide's hot breath baked the side of Zatia's neck as she helped the wounded brute hobble up the stairs and onto the frozen roads of Farragut. The Godfather's watchdogs took off at the first gunshot, leaving still-hot cigarettes sizzling in the ice where they fell.

Osyen led the way, jogging down the street, even as he called up the taxi service's interface on his wrist. "What the Hell was that thing?!"

"I don't think he had a permit for that much freight," Zatia slurred with a very unhappy whistling sound to her breath.

"Don't talk," Adelaide badgered her.

Rashida knew who that question was meant for. "I'll tell you on the ship. I'll tell you *everything* on the ship. But now, we have to go!"

"What the Hell do you think we're doing? I just can't signal anybody out there."

"They're jamming all wireless signals," Rashida explained. "How far is it to the dock?"

"Long enough we won't make it on foot! But I'm not going to stop trying to—" And Osyen stopped, causing everybody to slip and stagger a bit on the icy ground.

Zatia swiped a lock of bright green hair out of her face...

To see another long-coat eight-foot-tall goliath in the road ahead. It marched towards the group, one heavy foot after another, like a walking siege engine. Passersby recognized a standoff when they saw one, and the meager crowd immediately broke for cover.

"There's *two* of them?!" Milardi balked, his voice cracking.

Big guy number two raised his arm—which had been replaced with an obnoxiously threatening tube, rotating concentric rings spinning down in alternating directions all the way to a fiery core.

"Oh, *fra tow mizu!*" This time, Adelaide did drop her, pushing Zatia down into a snowdrift.

A green orb of twisting scorching energy spat forth, licking tendrils of lightning against the ground as the plasma ball tried to rip free ions from anything close enough.

Zatia hit her fluffy cloud of cold—and something about the temperature cut through all the stimulants and chemicals to remind her body that she was in agony. Her gunshot had ripped open, and her jaw bone was in pieces.

She cried out, light and hollow, with no air in her chest to back it up, which only made her cough. That, of course, only made it hurt worse.

That cold crawled up her arms and down into her heart and right into her brain...

Somebody grabbed her arm, roughly yanking her to her feet.

Which is when she saw the glowing nine-inch diameter hole that plasma shot had blasted through the side of a building.

"The other guy didn't have a gun-hand..."

It was Thom who threw himself under her arm to support her weight. "The other guy didn't need one. Let's go!"

The smell of scorched carbon. Zatia felt around Thom's shoulder, digging into the crunchy skin that still burnt at the touch. "You got tagged..."

He didn't respond to that. Maybe he didn't hear her. Had she even said it?

The crew staggered down an alleyway, trying to get off of the main thoroughfare and break the line of sight. Her pulse throbbed in her ears, matching the oncoming beat of the Oskie's pursuing steps, the oncoming clank of heavy boots and steel parts.

She watched the flying cruisers and taxis and trucks gliding by overhead, far out of reach of the chaos on the streets. If anybody looked down, they might see.

Or was this just another day in Farragut?

She would have to come back some day and get a more traditional experience. The cold of this place...it was in her bones now...

"Oy!" Milardi shouted, sliding to a stop by a good-sized parked cruiser. Rusted, forgotten, and scrapped for parts. "Will this fly?"

Adelaide took one look at it. "Not far, not high."

"Has to be faster than walking," Osyen noted, looking back the way they came.

The clomping had stopped. Where were their pursuers? Perhaps they could fly? Thom must've felt the same way because he was scanning the rooftops.

Adelaide dropped onto her back and pushed herself under the cruiser's hood. "I see a battery, highly corroded. Who knows if it has charge?"

"I don't want to die in a car crash while running away from death," Osyen snapped. "Make *sure* it flies."

"She'll fly."

Milardi snapped out a pistol and blew off the gullwing hinge, yanking the whole door right off the car and dropping it into the snow. "Then get in! Everybody, let's go!"

It was compact—the cruiser was made to seat five, plus some cargo. But they'd all fit if they pretended to like each other.

Zatia flopped onto Thom's lap, the last available place—she wasn't able to hold herself upright, anyway.

Osyen didn't even wait for everyone to strap in before he primed the engine. A thousand gears bemoaned their rust and old pistons pushed through heavy oils with a screech.

But the mag-lev kicked in and the cruiser shook as it came off the ground...barely.

"Get us up," Rashida urged.

"My foot is on the floor," Osyen said. "That's all she's got in her."

It got them a few feet off the ground, enough to get some speed. They'd have to follow streets, dodge buildings—but they could get there.

They must've heard the gunshot, or the sickly roar of the vehicle. But the bald Oskie flew out of the sky and struck the ground inches from the car's hood, yellow eyes gleaming and head still steaming from the face full of laser blast.

"Push harder!" Milardi hollered.

Osyen cranked the wheel, tilting the vehicle left and drifting it out of the scorched man's reach. The big guy sunk his fingers into a corner of the cruiser but it was so rusted that the metal simply tore free.

"Get down!"

Whoever made the call, it was a good one. Everyone tucked their heads just as the Oskie hurled the piece of metal through the cruiser's cabin. It blew out the back window and clean through the windshield—

Right over Rashida's head.

A few more chunks struck the back of the car, wedging deep into the steel, but unable to penetrate.

Those would've gone through Rashida's chest had there not been a car in the way.

Osyen didn't wait another second, putting some tilt to the car. It rattled and shook its way down the alley. Anything that wasn't directly ahead of them blended into a blur of frosty blue and industrial gray. Wind filled the cabin, blistering cold that tussled her hair and billowed clothes. It was like ice crept its way into every available crevice and cut into her flesh.

Zatia palmed her gut, and her hand came away painted red. Lights that whistled by the windows flashed like blood, strobing the colors.

Soothing. Hypnotizing.

And Roche didn't look much better. The big guy was muttering to himself, hands clutching his head.

So much for a quiet drink.

She looked back through the open rear window. Lumbering after them, the bald Oskie brought one heavy footfall after another, gaining momentum and speed. The accelerating patter of his steps seemed to shake their noisy cabin, despite the car not even touching the ground.

"Oskies are fast," Milardi pointed out. "Why hasn't he run us down?"

Osyen glanced at the monitor on his dashboard, the look alone calling up a rear view of the pounding pursuit vehicle masquerading as a person. "Keep talking, because he's gaining on us."

"Look out!" Rashida shouted.

Osyen pulled the car around a geothermal exhaust port in the ground, swerving to stay on course. The cruiser's maglev was old and didn't hold the ground that well, so it slid like an ice skate.

The Oskie...didn't even slow down. He blew right through the obstruction, sending up a ball of fire and shrapnel.

"*Fra tow ni laska,*" Milardi said with a hush. "Get us out of here, Oz!"

"Working on it!"

Thom leaned forward, tapping Osyen's shoulder. "It takes him time to build up that speed."

"So?"

"So *turn!*"

Osyen cranked the wheel, almost like Thom had willed it. The car banked down another pedestrian walkway. They hummed barely over the heads of the occupants below, throwing up all manner of trash and detritus. More than a little flipped up into the car.

Zatia looked back to see the Oskie gong off the corner of the alley so hard he shattered the support pillar. As he built up his sprint again, thunking his way down the alley, she could vaguely see the building collapse in a cloud of debris and screaming.

"That's it!" Thom exclaimed. "He'll beat us in a straightaway but we can lose him in the turns."

"Perhaps," Rashida said, "but for how long?"

"Long enough to get home."

Osyen tilted the car forward, trying to slow the car down. Everyone grunted and screamed, slamming into their restraints and each other. Shards of broken glass came flicking off the windows, flechettes dancing around the cabin.

Ah, that's why. Gun-Arm had jumped ahead and dropped to the ground in front of them. He raised his hand like a peace officer, compelling them to stop—backed up by the plasma cannon masquerading as his limb. And Zatia could make out the beginnings of the green ball of death starting to form.

"Hang on to somethin'!"

Still gliding forward on the cruiser's nose, inches off the ice like a dancer's toe, Osyen gave the wheel a yank, spinning the car out of the way of the shot.

Zatia looked up to see the green blast slide past the hood of the dancing car. A flash of fire and a wash of heat as the blast popped something important.

"Don't roll, don't roll, don't you roll!" Osyen prayed harder and harder as the vehicle spun on its nose.

Timing it, he dropped the ass of the car safely back onto the maglev. Adrenaline, fear, and glee all came out in a brief battle cry as Osyen plied the thrust again.

"It's been a while since a plan came apart like this," Zatia grunted.

Thom looked down at her, his eyes flicking over to her bloody stomach and his throat clenching on his gag reflex. "Plan? What plan?"

Before she knew it, the car settled onto the happy ground—she never thought she'd resent being on ground before. Zatia paused to feel through her feet, wondering if she might sense the approach of those thundering titans.

There sat the rusty old *Aurum,* their only way off into the safety of the sky. It sat on the open-air hangar deck, fat and lazy.

Knobbly old bird had no idea what was chasing them.

Osyen led the haggard group up to the docking ramp where two of the Godfather's goons waited, casually sucking cigarettes with rifles slung. They actually had the audacity to try to stop them. The smarter of the two stepped forward with a dumb smirk. "Where exactly you off to, *skel?*"

The second leapt to immediate flowery conclusions. "Perhaps he thinks to skip out on his deal with the Master."

"Boys, I have exactly no time for diplomacy," Osyen snapped. "Get the Hell out of my way."

They responded by simply charging their rifles. "We have orders, see? You're not to leave Farragut."

"Everybody should leave Farragut," Rashida warned. "Get your family and friends together, and leave today, while you can."

The guards wanted to jump down her throat, but Osyen waved them back. "Do you see what we parked out front? Do you think that happened on the way from the dealership?"

"Nobody is leaving Farragut without—"

"*Fra tow s'ivan.*" Zatia shoved herself off of Thom and squared her shoulders. Predictably, the guards didn't take the five-foot nothing brightly colored girl seriously as she stalked up to them with murder in her eyes. Men like that always found her adorable. Men never thought she was reaching for a weapon when she clasped the gaudy bangles on her opposing wrists.

She whipped the jewelry off and the hidden tonfa blades clicked into place. Before the guard could regret his life choices, she drove both blades into his gut and up into everything important. The force even picked him up in the air a bit, dangling him off of his toes.

The second guard squeezed his rifle into his hip, ready to mow down the lot of them—but Milardi out drew him, punching out a two-inch hole in his chest. The guard flopped backward, bouncing off the ramp and tumbling to the maintenance bay below.

Osyen glared at Zatia but couldn't argue. No time to anyhow. "Everybody up. Let's go. Roche, on the Jump Deck. Get us in the sky."

CHAPTER
EIGHT
ROCHE

ALL THE PAINFUL noise and all the maddening quiet all came into happy relief when Roche slid his cables back into the *Aurum*'s command console, like a blanket wrapped about his chest letting off pain by applying pressure.

// Reactor warm up. Disengage landing lock and apply vertical thrust 89.1. Lock and execute. Lock and execute!

He felt Lily's fond embrace as he issued each command in the span of a heartbeat. The ship lurched as the locks let go—and lurched again when the *Aurum* bounced off the docking bay's wall.

Vertical thrust! I said vertical!

Apologies, Lily said. *Reactor still coming on-line. Energy reserves taxed at* 106%.

Give me life support. Give me the lights. Just get us out of here —now!

All too happy to.

Roche pulled up the holographic display of Farragut below, projecting the frost planet onto the walls—just in time to see their damaged car tumbling in the air towards them!

Roche grunted as he reflexively yanked the *Aurum* out of the way. Back down through the floor to the hangar deck, he could see the twin Oskies, their long coats billowing as the engine backwash filled the space. The one raised his plasma cannon—

But the *Aurum* fired its engines, screaming off into the upper atmosphere.

Lily scoffed. *I take it the quiet drink wasn't so quiet?*

"Lily!" Osyen's voice echoed as the captain scampered up the hallway. "Spool up the Jump Drive. We are leaving."

"To what destination?"

"Get us back on to the main lanes and far away from here."

Lily chirped a confirmation and receded into their calculations and preparation.

"What the Hell were those things?" Roche asked.

"You know as much as I do." Osyen paused, glancing down at Roche's seat. "You might know a bit more, actually."

Roche knew what he was referring to. Nobody else had crumpled into a ball on the pub floor. "It was like...a banshee shriek. I couldn't block it out."

"White noise," Osyen concluded. "Lily? Can you pull me security footage on those two goons?"

"One moment—" Lily's voice hiccupped as they added the request to the queue. "Unfortunately, there doesn't appear to be any records."

Osyen shook his head in disbelief. "Car chase through main street, the pub, the hangar—"

Even Roche couldn't believe it. "I know it's a pirate town but..."

"Not one blurry picture from one camera?" Osyen pleaded.

Another hiccup and static. "There ap-appears to be widespread data corruption in Farragut Security records."

That had been...quite a lot of audio glitches in the last few minutes. "Lily, how are you feeling? Speaker system giving out on you?" Roche asked.

"Thank you for asking, Roche, but all is well. A deep, deep well where we keep the clear drinking water."

Roche twisted to look at Osyen. He heard that too. He had to.

And in that moment, he saw real terror flash across Osyen's face, a panic, a sweat.

The captain blinked a few times and wiped that thought from his head. "Just get us clear of Farragut. I don't want any trail those things can follow."

"If I'm being completely honest," Lily began, "I am having some difficulties completing the Jump equations within acceptable drift margins. Risk of injury to crew is high."

"I don't know if you saw that shit-show back there, Lily, but the risk of crew injury is high if we stay here much longer. So finish those calculations and get us the Hell out of here."

Lily tried to take the conversation private, forgetting that Roche was plugged directly into the console. Or Lily trusted Roche to understand. *I don't often raise the specter of my programming, Osyen, but I'm afraid that protocol insists we avoid Jump conditions without proper calculations in place.*

Roche tried to cut in. *Osyen—*

But it's like Roche wasn't in the room with them. Osyen blew right over the top of him. *And I've got two unkillable somethings that are latched onto our scent. So we have to go! This isn't something we discuss.*

The gravity of what Lily was saying was eluding Osyen's head, or more likely, he just didn't want to confront the reality of it. Lily was making a rather apocalyptic statement. Jumping a gravity well required the physical data of an entire ship and crew to be digitized, punched through a singularity, and reassembled on the other side without error.

This 'Jump drift' was a collection of natural errors from the quantum computations—inevitable effects from background noise—causing the mathematics to fluctuate nanosecond by nanosecond. This involved minute changes in the reconstruction of a ship—and the squishy, sentient water bags inside it.

An unacceptable level of change by safety standards would be the shaving off of millimeters in a jockey's height, or the minute loss of muscle tissue. Normally diet, exercise, and medicine were more than able to counter effects.

The 'successful' Pathfinder missions in the early days of space travel had some more dramatic changes to the bodies of the explorers. The lucky ones died without a lifetime of chronic pain.

Lily was warning of something far greater than changing their shoe size. They might forget how to put a human heart together or place their hand inside their lung. If two people sat close, they might fuse at the hip.

Unacceptable Jump Drift margins could be fatal.

We need to get through that Jump, Osyen declared. *That's an order.*

Lily didn't take kindly to that. *I am not your puppet that can be puppeteered whenever you puppet me.*

Roche's jaw almost dropped. *Osyen, if that right there wasn't evidence enough—*

Do you need more time to complete the equations, improve results? Osyen asked. An intelligent question. If it was a matter of time...

Unlikely, Lily responded. *Each attempt seems only to increase the drift.*

"Cascade..." Roche whispered the word.

And it was like he'd pulled a knife, because Osyen snarled at him. "Nobody is having that. Okay?"

"Osyen. All AIs eventually do. Every single one."

That was not a fact up for debate. Much like how one day, Osyen's knees and back would give out, one day Lily's heuristic programming would start to corrupt. It was the natural life of an AI. As they grew and learned and developed, there was natural fragmentation in their storage memory.

There was no way to know how or when, but the only thing you could do was cycle the AI back to factory settings.

But all the growth, the personality, the life in Lily...Lily itself...

"I would take a long breath and try to calmly explain this to you, Lily, but we don't have that kind of time. Those things back there?

They will not stop coming. They're going to blast through whatever we put in their way, so we have to get as much distance as we can between us and them. Our only shot is losing them. So *please*, lock in that Jump."

"Osyen..." Roche could swear the AI's voice actually cracked, like they were on the verge of tears. "You know I can't do that. I could never do that."

"It'll work."

"I'll hurt you. I'll hurt the crew."

Osyen took a breath—and moved for the opposite console. And it was terribly clear the gambit he was playing. If Lily was unwilling or unable to roll those dice, Osyen was about to force them to.

Which is why the console went dark the moment Osyen got to it. He glared at Roche, but Roche shook his head. "I didn't do it."

"Lily?" Osyen barked. "Lily, answer me."

Roche felt through the cables, searching for the vibrant and brutal and colorful life that had always lingered on the edge of hearing. But it was all quiet now.

"They're offline," Roche whispered. "They took themselves offline rather than hurt us."

Osyen couldn't curse them, couldn't burst out in anger. That was too noble of an act to hate. But he bit his tongue and exhaled ragged. "And they might've just killed us."

———

Space was not empty, despite claims to the contrary. There was plenty of debris and asteroids and ice for the *Aurum* to blend in with. The true test was finding a suitable hiding place that fit the bill and do it all without leaving a trail of breadcrumbs. That meant minimal LADAR, no broadcasting, and no wireless tapping into the Imperial Extranet: all useful tools when scanning empty space looking for a good size rock to hide under.

But found one they did—a collection of asteroids chewed up

during the first wave of colonization, pitted with dozens of holes, some big enough to slip the *Aurum* inside. They latched onto the tunnel wall, turned off all unnecessary ship systems...and prayed.

Two hours went by of silence and cold before Osyen let them turn the heat on again. They were sufficiently hidden.

For now.

"How's our fuel situation?" Osyen asked.

"Thin," Roche reported. "If we cut all non-essential systems, we'll save power and cut our heat signature—that'll make us harder to find and stretch what we have."

"Good," Osyen said. "So what's the bad news?"

"You'll asphyxiate before you freeze to death."

A heavy sigh came from Thom. "How long do we have?"

"A few days," Roche said, "so long as we all breathe soft."

Milardi dragged his feet up the last few steps, leaning on the doorframe of the galley. Roche had never seen the slinger of petty witticisms this tired before. It was like he was a weeping willow, taking root in the ground so his hulking batch of limbs could drape in the cool air.

"Her jaw broke into four parts," reported the gunslinger. "She didn't even notice. Ripped open her skin patch, two cracked ribs, and half a dozen scattered hemorrhages in her legs—likely from the stim pack stresses. It'll be another couple of days of reconstructive and rest. Let the AutoDoc do its thing, and Zee will be okay."

Osyen sighed at the first piece of good news of the day. He wiped his slick forehead with the back of his hand, turning to face the well-dressed elephant in the room. "Rashida...spill."

Her voice was meek, apologetic and small as she hugged herself against the cold. Not to mention the unfriendly aura everyone was throwing off. "What do you want to know?"

"Start with, what the *Hell* are those things?"

Not how Roche would've phrased it, but he badly wanted to know too. What kind of weapon could throw a car, take a bullet, and switch off a radio just by being near it? Mechs were strong, but they burned with a laser to the head like anything else. AIs could hack into local subnets, but that thing in the bar was clearly a person.

Rashida drew in a breath, collating the data into the most cogent order. "They're called 'Paladins.'"

"Never heard of 'em," Adelaide said. Hardly dismissive, just underlining.

"You wouldn't have. Let me guess...you couldn't pull any security footage? Biometrics? Not even records of the destruction?"

A chill went up Osyen's spine. "How did they do that?"

"Paladins are a secret wing of Orbital Strike Command. Loaded down with as much gear as possible, along with an onboard artificial intelligence to manage the suite of systems."

"That's impossible," Roche puzzled. "The amount of hardware needed to work a sophisticated heuristic interface like Lily? And store it on a man-platform?"

"Not to mention why?" Thom mused. "There's got to be more an efficient killing machine than struggling to fuse a computer with a person."

"Does explain how they jammed our communications, cut out all evidence of them," Adelaide said. "The AI is in a constant wireless hack, slicing out evidence of their passing and countering their target's efforts to escape. If the Paladin doesn't leave any witnesses, it's like a meteor fell wherever they went."

Rashida couldn't be distracted. She was almost in a zone, scouring through her recollections. "Paladins are completely removed from military hierarchy. They don't serve the Ministers, the Consul, the Admiralty: they don't serve *humanity*. They serve the Pilgrim. Dogmatic, violent, and single-minded. They are given an objective, and every means available to complete it. Spare no expense, no secret technology. They respect no border and no authority."

"Serve the Pilgrim?" Thom asked, shaken. "What does the Pilgrim care about a smuggler ship full of criminals?"

"Oh, I'm sure the Pilgrim doesn't give a damn. These aren't holy warriors. They're zealots, carefully cultivated by theocratic manipulation. They've been told the only way to join the Pilgrim on the Sojourn is by killing the enemies of the Dunsweir, even if that means their own death. They're indoctrinated, hand-selected from an already fiercely faithful crowd. And then severely augmented."

"We noticed," Osyen sputtered.

"You don't understand. Oskie augmentations already have a fatality rate attached to them. The human body rejects the invasive material, often killing the participant. The augmentations you just witnessed aren't speed, or strength, seeing in the dark, or camouflage. Paladins...there's so much hardware, we're talking close to a one hundred percent failure rate."

"They kill almost everyone that hits the surgical table?" Milardi asked, agog. He might be a gunslinger by day, but Milardi patched as many holes as he ever made. The very idea that a doctor would willfully harm anyone on their table...

"I don't get it. Why not just simply build a mech for it? It'll be more stable, less expensive..." Adelaide asked, half-confused and half horrified.

But Thom drew a sharp breath. "Because computers don't *believe*. And there's nothing more potent than a man who thinks he's right with God."

Rashida nodded. "Every single patient thinks they get to go to Heaven...just by laying down on the table. They die serving the Pilgrim, one way or another. A computer can be reasoned with, hijacked, or trapped. A soldier can be terrified or persuaded. But a Paladin? Strengths of both."

"Capabilities?" Osyen asked.

"There's no way to say. Oskies have their abilities tooled to their specific strengths: speed, power, stealth. The Paladins? They're...There's no telling what powers they have. It's not off a blueprint. They're bespoke."

"If that's the case," Adelaide started, "why didn't they just blink over to you and rip your heart out?"

Roche could answer that one. "Because Isaac Newton can't be

negotiated with. The AI onboarding would need so much hardware, that they have to commit to a different methodology. They'd be so heavy, you'd have to burn too much energy to get going and then again to stop it on the other end—all without killing the end-user during the movement. They build Oskies with that speed in mind. Speed *is* their bullet-proof armor. So you strip off everything that slows them down. An AI would require...Paladins can't go fast; so you up-armor."

Thom finished the thought. "Juggernaut."

Rashida nodded. "Not to mention the psychological torture: why go fast when you never stop coming? Don't forget: this is as much a mind-game for the Dunsweir as anything else. They want you to *know* you can't escape."

"If it were me," Osyen said, more than a little spite in his voice. "I'd have just sent an Oskie to sidle up to you nice and quiet-like. None of this thunderstruck bullshit."

"An Oskie can grow skeptical," Thom argued, "even go AWOL. Like Stride. Something tells me a Paladin doesn't. They want her that much."

Why were they all hitting her? Rashida didn't call down the air strike on their heads. That was the Empire. Why were they blaming one of their own?

But even Rashida seemed to agree with him. "Which is why you have to give me up."

Everybody stiffened in their seats, straightened up in their stances. Nobody had expected her to say that. But Roche ran the math. She knew they couldn't stop the Paladins; they'd just die trying. And if they couldn't run, then...

She was dead anyway. It was just a matter of whether they all died along with her. It was a noble thing she was suggesting, insisting on saving her friends. Logical, too. With her death, the Paladins would stop. One life for six others.

So why did it feel so wrong to him?

Clearly, despite his misplaced rage, Osyen had the same thought.

"That's not going to happen, Rash."

"Oz, Magnus laid down the law very clearly. They want *me*. They don't give a damn about you!"

"And I don't give a damn about him!" Osyen challenged. "I will not buy my life by selling out someone else. Not me, not my..." He stopped himself there.

And Rashida jumped on the gap. "You don't have a choice!"

"Of course I have a choice! And so do they, I might add!" Osyen threw a pointed finger over his shoulder at some metaphorical entity looming out of sight. "They came for you. Don't act like *you're* the one making the choice, owning what *they* decided to do."

"No matter how long we drag this out, I die at the end."

"Then they already beat you," Osyen hissed.

"If it costs one hundred soldiers just to make one of these..." Roche said. "It has to be a target worth losing a hundred to guarantee a kill on. They're not hitting you with orbital bombardment. They want to *know* you're dead."

Rashida swallowed hard on that. It was an immutable fact: she was apparently a target worth all the effort. No matter the quality of her self-esteem, she didn't see herself as *that* important to anybody.

"They wipe themselves from records," Thom muttered, studying some smudge on the floor. "They can't be killed. And they can't be bargained with."

"How long have you known about this? The Paladins?" Osyen asked, his eyes dark. The follow-up question already chambered.

"I'm a runaway: a third cousin of a third cousin. I drink, I gamble. I look the part but I'm barely nobility at all," Rashida babbled. She was panicking now. She might not see herself as that important, but Roche concluded that someone out there clearly did.

"They don't go after enemies of the state, Rash," Thom said. "They're sent after threats to the faith. Something that compromises the foundation of the Dunsweir. Do they think we have the Icon?"

Rashida shook her head. "Magnus didn't indicate as much."

"Well, beautiful, your old Consort," Osyen cut her off, "just pulled *two* of these things out of his ass to bring you in or put you down. And because of you, Zee might just—"

"Osyen!" Roche barked, making everybody in the room jump. "Take a walk if you need to. Get your mind right. And then come back rational. Or you can remember, right now, that this is a friend you're talking to."

Osyen wasn't wild about being called out in public like that, but it helped that Roche was right. He tongued his cheek, trying to bury his embarrassment before modulating his tone. "You didn't know it was goin' to happen?"

"I swear to you," Rashida pleaded, "I had no idea."

"Okay." Osyen's face didn't seem to agree with his mouth, still dour and full of unkind thoughts.

"It's got squishy bits. It's got power cells. It can die. How do we kill it?" Adelaide asked the big money question.

"You hit it with a moon," Rashida said. "Short of that, they'll wipe out entire colonies."

"Well, nobody will miss Farragut," Milardi quipped.

"The people that live there will," Adelaide pointed out.

Rashida pulled herself up tall. "Which is why you have to let me go."

Osyen drew a breath and gave his best authoritative captain voice. "Milardi, would you be so kind as to handcuff the martyr to her stateroom for the foreseeable future?"

"Why you assume I've got handcuffs?"

Osyen gave him a mixed look of 'stop kidding around' and the 'are you kidding me.'

"Can't fight them," Thom puzzled out the problem. "We barely fought Stride. Which means we run."

Rashida settled into her seat, hands folded in her lap. She had said her piece and been shouted down. Roche had never seen that powerful woman look so much like the children from back at the orphanage. Verbal, mental, or physical—abuse had the same markers every time.

"And with Lily..." Osyen couldn't say it, couldn't admit it. He didn't want to confront the inevitable truth.

"What's wrong with Lily?" Adelaide asked accusingly. She might have grown fond of the personality that had taken root, but she'd always been suspicious that this day was coming. And Roche wasn't looking forward to the next ten seconds.

"Nothing's wrong," Osyen snapped back.

Get this over with.

"They're in Cascade," Roche blurted. "Errors increasing by the moment."

"Roche—!"

"You love Lily, I understand that, but I'm the one plugged into the ship twenty-four-seven. If you're blinded by your feelings, that's one thing. But I *can't* miss it!"

Adelaide grunted, cracked her neck in both directions, and made herself say the awful thing. "Cycle Lily. It's time."

Roche watched Osyen's hands tense as he stopped the impulse to draw a gun on the old crone. He stared at Roche's knees to avoid further puncture of his willpower.

"Oz, they're already dead, they just don't know it yet. Cycle Lily, or you're killing every single one of us."

His hand fell on his gun.

Not a single soul in that cabin missed Osyen's breach of control. And nobody said a damn thing in response, tried to add anything in support or defense. Nobody liked the idea, and nobody wanted to entertain it any longer than they had to.

Roche had read about families getting together and having frank discussions about pulling the plug on an increasingly dependent elder, or a suffering child. He expected to feel some kind of way about it—to agonize over the decision or to reach a requisite logical conclusion. Perhaps he thought he could avoid the pain of it by making a selection quickly and being done with it.

But while it was easy to admit the problem...he found himself avoiding the solution entirely.

Adelaide would not let it go. "Lily or Rashida. You don't have to like it, but those are the choices."

"I *will not* kill one person to save the rest," Osyen snarled. "Do you understand me?"

Milardi sighed, the gravity of that prognosis setting in. So he chambered up his medical hat. "How long does Lily have?"

"They powered down," Osyen admitted. "We can't calculate a Jump without them. Even if we had 'em, they're not certain that they could...pull it off without—it doesn't matter. They won't wake up."

"Could we get a new navigator?" Rashida asked, quickly adding, "Just to get us out of the system."

"If we could..." Thom toyed with the idea, drawing every eye to him. Everyone wanted a master plan, an easy ticket out. But Thom didn't even look up, buried in the layers of conniving. "There's only one dealer who could get us what we need. And he won't like the call."

CHAPTER
NINE
OSYEN

"INCALCULABLE DAMAGES. Loss of life. Loss of business. And you have the gall to call me and ask for a favor?" The Weasel was predictably unhappy.

"Favors are between friends," Osyen countered. "This would be a service. Paid for in full."

Osyen had set up on the Jump Deck to take this call. It was strangely quiet being up here. Most of the ship's automated functions, chirps and grinding and whistles and hums, had switched to a casual idleness. The music of mechanical life that once rolled through every deck and every corridor had suddenly gone quiet.

Thom and Roche hovered nearby, out of view of the projector. Thom chewed on his thumb, a nervous tic, but at least a sign that his brain was engaged with the problem. Roche looked like he was flicking in and out of consciousness as his eyes glazed over with a calculation and then refocused.

"You know a great many partners in business that bring Imperial heat down, do you?"

Osyen's jaw worked as he sorted out the best way to phrase his response. "You might be surprised if I said that number wasn't zero."

The Weasel's eyes narrowed and suddenly Osyen realized where the lithe little bastard got his alias. "Then you run in particularly hazardous circles. The Master is most displeased with this development."

Emphasize we're a part of the team, Thom bounced. *Don't talk like an outsider.*

Osyen's eyes narrowed. "One hour of time with a heuristics specialist is not an unreasonable request, even if done remotely. Upkeep and maintenance of The Master's teams will produce better results for him."

"You overstep yourself, Mr. Belt," the Weasel sneered. "You are not a member of this Family quite yet."

Roche shook his head. This was going sideways, and they were barely a minute in.

There's a balance between enemy and brother, Thom insisted. *Don't let him play black and white.*

"I may not be in the good graces, but that doesn't make me on the outside," Osyen said. "I would've hoped the last three jobs would've shown as much."

It was a good pitch, but they paid the Weasel to be cynical. "Many an authority figure have picked pockets and snatched purses to prove themselves. Undercover agency is not a new concept to organizations like ours."

How many spilled blood? Roche pointed out.

"Nor mine," Osyen agreed with Weasel, remembering how Milardi had hung around for a year before stabbing him in the back. "But how many undercover Clerics commit murder to protect their patron? Me and mine cannot be of continued service if we're shut out in the cold."

The Weasel kept a firm lock on his facial expressions, but Osyen could see the smile that leaked out of the wrinkles around his eyes. So full of pompous. "It's also how you put out a fire, Mr. Belt. Happy trails. And good luck."

The screen winked out. And Osyen reclined back in his seat.

"He was unlikely to support us," Roche noted.

Osyen nodded. "Yeah, but it was worth a shot."

Thom continued to gnaw on his thumb, rolling the problem over in his head. "What are you talking about? That went perfect."

Did Thom not hear that entire conversation? The Weasel made his stance very clear, despite Thom's coaching.

But Roche said the words. "You heard him same as I did, Maestro. He's going to leave us to hang by our collective necks. And I'd be hard pressed to do anything different in his shoes."

"That's not what I meant," Thom said. "We had to ask him for a heuristics specialist, so that he can go find all of 'em for us."

Osyen squinted, sitting forward in his seat. "Come again?"

Thom plopped down into the opposing chair, bouncing himself back and forth with toe taps like a ball between his hands. "We're a little short on time, so we can't spend days upon days scouring Farragut while we're also being hunted ourselves. Before, he would just put out the word that no one is to do business with the *Aurum*. Instead, we call him and make our intentions clear."

Roche connected the dots. "We show our hand."

"A little," Thom agreed. "Now he knows *what* we want. And that we're desperate and a little bit stupid. He'll expect us to try for it anyway."

Osyen rubbed his face with both hands, trying to squeeze out the stress. The kid was talking like this tactical error was a good thing. "He'll put extra security on the engineers."

"Better," Thom said with a wry grin. "He'll put 'em in lockdown where he can deny us access entirely. Except he'll accidentally be telling us exactly where they'll be and saved us a load of time. Roche, can you track if multiple vehicles are headed to a single compound?"

Roche almost giggled, his eyes glazing over as he was already tapping into Farragut's public access. "Yeah, I can."

Osyen stiffened. "You can't possibly think to steal from Anze *gulaw* Orchikov."

"The Godfather's not much use to any of us if we're all dead,"

Thom pointed out. "If we can't talk our way into his good graces, we have to break in. Tell me I'm wrong."

Osyen leaned back in his chair. And he wanted more than anything to hear Lily's acerbic wit right about now. "This morning I was going for a drink."

"Point of order," Roche said with a raised hand. "If we had stayed home, we wouldn't know we're being hunted. And they might have tracked us right to the hangar deck. A trip to the pub...probably saved our lives."

Thom puckered his lips as he and Osyen both imagined that outcome at the same time.

"First Fiona, now this," Osyen muttered, glaring at Thom. "You keep getting me into situations where I have to steal from people I should be working for."

Thom shrugged. "Work for yourself instead. It's less stressful."

"Feh. The Hell it is."

"With Lily sidelined, we won't be able to compete with AI security systems." Roche raised his hand, pinching a projection of a truck from the air. He spread his fingers wide to increase the scale and show off to the others. Two brutes stood to one side negotiating with a man wearing four different kinds of headgear.

An Engineer.

"We'll be going in blind," Osyen said. "And likely have hostile responsive computers that will pull oxygen from rooms, lock us out of sections, play mind games. They build these compounds to secure against intrusion, by both man and machine."

Thom's face didn't even budge. "Adelaide's going to earn her pay, I can tell you that, but nobody wants to screw with the Godfather more than she does."

"You sure we want to do this?"

There it was, the precariousness of their situation finally showing, as Thom swallowed the stress ball in his throat. "You know what the other options are."

Give up Lily. Give up Rashida.

No.

"Well, let's at least go see what we're dealing with."

CHAPTER
TEN
MILARDI

HE HAD PROJECTED a week's recovery. Zatia was up and about inside of twelve hours. She was ravenous and had eaten almost half of the kitchen when Milardi found her. After some badgering, she submitted to examination.

Her jaw fractures had fused almost perfectly. The rib wasn't so easily dealt with, but had made remarkable progress, with the soft callus already being replaced by bits of growing bone. And her gunshot wound had regained almost all of its lost ground. Modern medicine would've seen this stage in a few weeks, and she was there after a night's rest.

No wonder she was so hungry. Her body had somehow metabolized a week's worth of healing, and it needed to replenish its energy. She was likely in partial ketosis, as her body started to break down muscle mass to feed itself.

This wasn't her standard stim kit's handiwork. Milardi had spent months spinning that cocktail to fit her system. In his professional opinion, this was a side effect of the serum they'd used to fight Stride.

And it made sense—that cocktail was designed to accelerate everything about her, from reflexes to mental computations. Why wouldn't it speed up other parts of her too?

He wouldn't be surprised if she was aging faster too. But unless she spontaneously grew a few inches, how was he supposed to measure that?

But her tone of voice hadn't changed much. "You can't just keep me locked to that bed all day!"

Osyen folded his arms across his chest. "I mean, I can't. But two or three of us probably could."

"I'm fine! I took your tests. I jumped up and down. I let you jab me with needles. I'm fine."

"Yeah," Milardi said with a Colonial drawl, "and that doesn't surprise you just a little?"

Zatia was so mad she couldn't even look at him. "Why should it?"

"Zee, your jaw was in pieces just yesterday! You should be clamped shut! And you're eating solid food. That's not, like, a red flag to you?"

Of course it was. But Zatia was as stubborn as ever. She bounced on her toes as she tried to come up with a perfectly good reason, but if the medically proficient member of the crew couldn't, she sure as Hell wasn't going to find one. "I'm just awesome like that."

Osyen mimed pinching a program shut and throwing it over his shoulder. "That settles it. You're not going."

"But he gets to go?" Zatia said, pointing at Thom, who was just trying to innocently pass through the galley. Thom froze to the spot, eyes wide, not entirely sure why he was being pointed at.

Osyen stepped forward into Zatia's reach, which Milardi felt was of questionable judgment. There wasn't a whole lot of good that came from being in punching range. But Osyen had been hit so many times it probably didn't faze him anymore. "The things hunting us have a tendency to scramble communications. Thom can't call the play if he can't see what's happening. We limit the people exposed, so Thom goes...and Milardi is going as his security. More people, more risk."

"More security, more safe," Zatia said.

Osyen squinted at her, trying to work out that math.

"I appreciate your faith in me, Oz," Milardi noted, "but I see one of those things, I'm just going to throw Thom at them and take off."

"Thanks," Thom grunted, his head somewhere inside a cupboard.

"The *zoldat* aren't the only dangerous thing out there," Zatia pointed out. "The Godfather'll be on the lookout too, and his guys we *can* handle. Comes to that, Milardi may just need the backup."

Okay, now *that* was a fair point. They were making a pretty powerful enemy right now, but at least it was one that died when shot.

"We're going to go stare at a building through a viewfinder," Zatia said. "It's not like I'm asking to go leg press a hydrogen tank. I'm just a little stir crazy."

"You're also regular crazy," Osyen said with a raised eyebrow.

"Yeah, but you pay me, so I'm *your* crazy."

Osyen sighed, then raised a finger. "One: we don't know what the Paladins can see or hear, but I figure they can sense at least as much—if not more—than an Oskie. That means body heat, your heart beating, radio transmissions, and any incessant whining. Two: you get what you need, and you get out. We're not tourists. Three?" He looked directly at Milardi. "Nobody gets left behind."

Milardi glanced at Zatia and her smug expression before mocking off a salute to Osyen. "Yes sir, cap'n sir."

———

Fortress wasn't the right word. When Milardi heard 'fortress', his mind conjured thick metal walls with patrolling guards at the perimeter—perhaps working with attack dogs or some vicious local wildlife. There were towers with spotlights scanning for movement, interlocking fields of sniper fire to trim down the acceptable hiding places, and entrenched artillery pieces to pluck you out of the few places bullets couldn't get to.

This didn't look like a fortress. This looked like a hotel.

A classic rotunda circa 20th century was out front, white pillars and half a dozen waiting staff in little red jackets and white gloves. They were helping each Engineer out of their rusting gang-scarred vehicles welcoming them with a hot towel and glasses of warm cognac before ushering them through double wood doors.

"Wood?" Milardi breathed. "Man's got access to real wood, and he makes a *door?*"

"Criminal," Zatia snobbed from the floor. She had laid a camera up to the window, and ran the cable down, so as not to expose her face with the back light from the screen. She had one leg crossed over the other, squeezing to keep them still. Thom laid next to her with a scanner of his own.

They looked like two kids laid up and playing some game on their Entiglases together. Adorable.

They'd settled up in a modest structure across from the Godfather's compound, a few blocks away. Most of the rooms had been left empty, and the locks had meant nothing to crafty little Thom. The room itself was a clean slate box, four walls and a featureless ceiling. Perhaps it was meant to be office space, but more likely a small, questionably ethical laboratory. The only hint was the non-standard high-power outlets strewn about, along with gas and water lines exposed.

Arctic wind blew through every crack and snow had collected in small drifts on the floor. They weren't outside, but this wasn't that much better. Supposed they weren't on tundra soaking cold in through their socks, but still...

Milardi perched on the window and looked down his telescope. The heads-up display grabbed everything he needed from range, material, even biometrics. He happily baked his hands on the heater they brought to keep from losing fingers to their environment.

Of course, the infrared thrown off by the heater would be a dead giveaway in the less than tropical atmosphere, but their bodies would throw off detectable heat too—even to the Godfather's men.

So Thom had the bright idea of popping a dozen flares in different spots in their apartment building, blending their heat signature in with the rest of the city's noise. With Roche's computations, they were able to suitably match the pattern.

Lily could've done that in half a second, but Roche spent the better part of an hour trying to game out the problem.

They almost ran out of time.

"Walls have got to be two...three feet thick?" Thom suggested.

Zatia agreed. "You'd have to spend a good amount of time with a plasma torch to get through that. And if I'm Anze Orchikov, I've laid explosive paper in two layers of the build to blow back on your tool. You'll kill yourself cutting in."

"Just means you can't cut in with heat," Thom noted to himself, wrinkling his nose at that large hurdle. "Now an acid burn? But if I'm him—"

"Which you're not."

"I run an electrical current through the walls tied to an alarm system. Cut it, and instant alarm. The AI summons every guard to that hole like a swarm of bees."

"He wanted a fortress," Zatia sassed. "He got one."

"I will remind you both," Milardi said, "that septic systems and air ventilation are made for liquids and gases, respectively. Not people."

"Which means front door..." Thom mused.

"I feel like every heist always goes through the front door," Milardi quipped.

"It's the single biggest security hole in any system. Boring, but true," Thom said. "They know our faces and the major dealers in town, so...."

Zatia shrugged. "We could take somebody's face." Milardi and Thom slowly turned to look at her, both trying to gauge how horrified they really ought to be. Zatia didn't even look up. "I meant as a disguise, but I'd be willing to go the whole nine yards."

It felt so loud, talking like this, and Milardi was just waiting to hear the heavy footfalls of a Paladin on approach. If they could hear it, it could hear them. And there was very little any of them would be able to do at that point.

They couldn't use their radios. Broadcasts like that would be a dead giveaway. So they were back to the oldest trick in the book: whispering to each other. So uncivilized. Milardi's ears were reserved for attractive people to whisper into while they grabbed his neck, not for professional subterfuge while he curled up on a cold floor.

Oh. He gave himself chills there.

Each engineer clambered out of their cruiser, shielding their eyes from the sun like a true kidnapping victim being thrust suddenly into the horrid light of the daystar. The blustering wind tossing them one way before yanking them back the other. One man even fell over, forcing the staff to rush to his aid.

"Think they outsourced the collection of these guys?" Zatia asked.

"Possibly," Thom admitted, "but then, who in this town is out of the fold? Even so, most of them aren't setting foot inside. So we need to find somebody who is allowed to come and go."

"Supply run?" Milardi asked. "This many people need food, entertainment, medical."

"That might do it," Thom whispered. "Pose as the delivery guy. We'll need to do some cosmetic adjustments."

"The AutoDoc and enough time, I can make some pretty solid tweaks."

Thom's hawk-like vigil softened a bit as he studied the latest pathetic engineer tossed out of his car, shivering and confused. "How many do you think politely accepted the gangster's invitation versus how many were just taken?"

Milardi huffed at that. If the Godfather wanted to end this nonsense in his backyard quickly, this was a Hell of a way of going about it. The *Aurum's* crew would scatter around looking for help that no longer existed, only to get picked off by the Big Bad Wolf— Wolves. Multiple—Big Bad Wolves—roaming his city.

"I got a feelin' that Mr. Orchikov doesn't do a whole lot of polite anything," Zatia said.

"How is he allowed to operate?" Thom asked. "He's at least as potent as Fiona ever was, and he's out here within spitting distance of Imperial interests. Why don't they come shut him down?"

"Being within spitting distance," Zatia said, "doesn't mean he's doing any spitting."

"True," Milardi said, "but do you see any Imperials wandering about with impunity? This is *his* turf and they let him have it."

"It's not like there's anything of value up here."

"Wait staff out front are half guards," Milardi pointed out. "There's two that have never left the door, and they're packing."

Zatia nodded. "I also see a neat little scanner built into the doorframe."

"Which means our gear would have to be procured on-site."

"Both solid finds," Thom said, "but either of you take a look at the alley?"

Milardi tilted his lens over to the only thing Thom could be talking about. There was a gap between the hotel and the next closest building. It was clean as a whistle, with a heating exchange and what looked like an automated scanner panning back and forth on a crane arm, giving it a full view of the tight space. It was looking for any inconsistencies, any microscopic change.

"I'm looking, but whatever good thing you're seeing, I'm missin' it."

"Keep looking," Thom assured him. "You'll see it."

And like magic, the heat exchanger dumped steam. Hot, glorious steam. The scanning arm craned right through it, but...

"Somebody has a design flaw," Milardi sang. "Thermal, visual..."

"Nothing can see through that, but it's brief. That'll hide a person or two, if ya time it right," Thom said. "How much time you reckon Adelaide needs to do some line work? Ten seconds?"

"Depends on what you're cutting."

"Not cutting," Thom said, "patching. I want to get Roche hooked up to the inside."

Milardi lowered his scope and looked back at the kid. "He can't do that kind of thing by remote. He'll have to stand in that alley, not move a muscle, in the cold...and the moment he gives an order to the system, the House AI is going to sniff him out. They'll send every guard in that whole building to go stomp his pretty face into the pavement."

"Which is what you both will be up to. Thanks for volunteering."

"So in this little plan of yours, Addy is outside doing the patch. Zee, me, Roche are outside. I expect Rashida is hiding in a hole. And you're coordinating..." And Milardi's heart sank. "You're sending Osyen into the Godfather's backyard alone?"

"Yup," Thom said, popping the word.

"How does he..." Milardi paused, searching for the most elegant words, "...get out again?"

"Working on that part."

Milardi looked over at Zatia for some kind of backup. But she was in no position to give any. Her jaw was clenched tight, so tight he could make out the tendon in her little neck. And her muscular wrist gripped her panel like she was going to snap it in half. Her eyes glazed over, her nostrils flared, and as he connected all the dots—her back suddenly arched, sending her gear clattering to the floor.

Milardi swooped down, sliding a leg under her and to support her head. Thom dove for the tablet as it banged and scraped along the cement floor. It might as well have been a dinner bell.

He cursed as he cupped his hands behind Zatia's neck. And her skin was burning hot, clammy. Her pupils were dilated, wide saucers of black. And the furrow to her brow might not have been under control, but it sure looked like panic.

Her neck jerked backward in short repeated jabs and her arms swung forward around Milardi's waist, pinching him awkwardly with her wrists.

Milardi couldn't risk bouncing Thom a quick report, and he

didn't dare try to speak right now. He'd almost certainly shout out of sheer muscle memory. And the boy stared at Zatia with barely contained horror as she thrashed and jerked like a fish yanked out of water on a steel hook.

A seizure.

Given the look in her eye, he'd say she was awake and aware as her feet scraped the cement and arms tried to slap the ground. After the third incidental hit, Thom dove over and tried to pin her arms and sit on her legs. Anything to stop her from summoning the gangsters or the monsters.

Milardi listened, even as he held Zatia's head in his hands, for the drumbeat of those feet. She shook and shook and the look in her eyes never wavered. All three of them wondering if she'd just killed them.

But nothing came.

And after a few minutes, the seizure subsided. Drenched in flop sweat, Zatia curled into an embarrassed ball, and it was a good ten minutes before they could get her up and out of that frostbitten room.

PART TWO
DOCTORS WITHOUT MORALS

"It has been widely accepted in scholarly circles that the Pilgrim is not any particular wonderment or object of divinity. Rather, the theories say that the Pilgrim, no matter their origins, carries one remarkable trait: the ability to step through Time the way we might through Space.

We traverse the Jump Points to places far and wide, and the Pilgrim simply does the same throughout our history. It is with this power that he healed us.

We were not cured, but restored to a Time before our pains and sickness."

PROF. ORDEE, C.H. (2226). *THE ROOTS OF OUR FAITH: THE HISTORICAL REVISIONISM OF THE PILGRIM*

RECORDED DREAM DATA, DATE: 2241.17.04

PATIENT: THOMAS HUGH

PATIENT STATUS: **Preliminary Hypertension**
// Warning: Abnormal brain activity detected.
// Warning: Dangerous spike in electrical traffic.

Did you see him, Thom?

See who?

Through that door. It's the man you're looking for.

// Warning: tachycardiac response detected.
// Oxygen levels falling.
// Administering two milligrams Tinpraxolom, increasing oxygen flow.

How do you know that? That I'm looking for someone?

You're still looking for them. And you've found them. And you've lost them. It's...the problem with my superluminal state of being.

// Warning: tachycardiac response increasing.
// Detected atrial flutter. Trauma receptors activated.
// Notified ship physician.

How did you know my name?

How could I not?

That's not an answer.

Not yet. But I hope this helped.

// Warning: Cardiac fibrillation in progress.
// Charging capacitors.

I have so many questions.

And I'll have the answers. But we're out of time. They're about to wake you up.

// Warning: Applying defib. Stand clear.

CHAPTER
ELEVEN
THOM

THOM HAD NEVER CONSIDERED himself claustrophobic. He had, after all, spent a good few months crawling around air vents with nothing but a stiff brush and a dream. And before that, he had spent three years going places no other bus boy could get to. But opening his eyes to the curved ceiling of the Medical Bay pressing down on him, he felt a momentary flash of panic.

So, as Thom lurched awake in surprise, he found himself sitting up even closer to that low concave ceiling, which only alarmed him further. He stuck a hand out, catching the ceiling and stopping his forehead from bashing itself into hardened Silksteel.

How had he gotten here? They'd...carried Zatia back, and he had gone to his bunk...

Medical wasn't an especially large space, less so when the AutoDoc was actively engaged in treating a patient. Through the plastic privacy shell, one could vaguely see a dozen tiny arms attending to their patient, safely in a sanitized environment.

The second and third beds in the room were more of a staging area, ready and able to transfer a new person into the waiting claw arms of the mechanized healer. A gurney would slide into place while pulling the finished patient out to a similar side bed for recovery. The whole space wasn't really designed for more than two patients, plus an operator.

Of course, they'd crammed the entire crew into that room on more than one occasion.

He peered at the AutoDoc, able to see the shock of pink hair inside that had to belong to Zatia. There were no whirring motors or hissing machines. But the faint beeping of the computers was monitoring her various life signs.

Stable. At least, at the moment. But she wasn't moving.

Another sound—and Thom whipped around to see Osyen curled up on the operator's stool, arms folded across his chest like a blanket, and his head resting against the back wall. His breathing was heavy, rasping as it sucked past something in his sinuses. That was probably fixable, if he ever admitted it was a problem. He'd had his face broken so many times, he liked it broken.

"Oz?" Thom whispered.

Osyen didn't even move. "I'm not sleeping."

Thom rolled his eyes, and the movement felt like it turned him upside down. He looked back at the AutoDoc. Somehow, its lack of urgency was so much more nauseating. Thom's breath hitched in his throat and his skin felt hot.

Osyen answered the open question. "Grand mal seizure."

"What caused it?"

Osyen shrugged, still not opening his eyes. "Can't say. But my money? She's in withdrawal."

Thom bit his lip. The cocktail Milardi had whipped up to help her fight Stride had promised side effects. But Thom hadn't thought that life-threatening seizures had been a part of that.

"Will she be okay?"

That made Osyen snap both eyes open, and there wasn't even a hint of sleep in that hawkish brown gaze. "Will *she* be okay?!"

Thom let his jaw hang and jammed his tongue in his cheek. That was a loaded sentence and he couldn't help but feel ashamed, guilty, even a touch afraid, like a child who'd broken something but didn't quite know what. "What happened?"

Osyen exploded. "You scared the *Hell* out of me, Thom! Rash and Milardi too. You had a heart attack in your sleep. That should be the thing we watch out for in our chain-smoking octogenarian, not a sixteen-year-old *kid!*"

He felt compelled to apologize, but despite being phrased as an accusation, Osyen hadn't yet named something Thom had willfully done. So he just absorbed the noise, let the captain blow up in the rare space where no one else was watching. And after the longest pause, when Thom was sure that Osyen had finished, he finally spoke up. "Feel better?"

"I feel pretty unappreciated, Thom, I've gotta say!"

"Thank you."

"You're welcome. I guess." Thom chuckled and Osyen did so too. The captain ran a hand through his hair, squeezing on his scalp to wrench some of the stress out. "For a teenager with a heart condition, you look good."

"It's not a heart condition," Thom said the words as fast as his brain conceived of them.

He felt good. He didn't quite know what he was supposed to feel like, but he felt like he'd gotten a half decent night's sleep and just wanted a cup of coffee. To wake up in Medical was more alarming than anything else.

His arm didn't hurt, his chest didn't hurt. He was tacky with dried sweat. He could remember clearly, and wasn't slurring or—whatever this had been, it wasn't a heart attack.

Thom struggled with the phrasing, trying to find the best way to articulate his feelings. "It wasn't a...more like—can I see the EKG?"

Osyen sat up, prim and proper, like he was trying to shove his hair into the ceiling. He rolled out his shoulder, freeing up some old injury from the cramped sleeping posture before keying up the requesting image. The image projected in the air, amber squiggles measuring his blood pressure, oxygen, and heart rate.

Thom reached forward, piercing the image from the back and scrolled backward till he saw the red flagged 'cardiac event.' And Osyen threw up his hands.

Thom sighed. "Sorry I had my heart attack at an inconvenient time."

Osyen rubbed his neck, looking down at the grating floor. Thom had scrubbed it to a matte finish. "Well, I suppose there were times *more* inconvenient, but let's not tempt fate."

"I had that dream again..."

"Did it tell you to kill small animals and set things on fire?"

"Give the computer some time with it and you can watch for yourself."

Osyen grimaced. "Expressionistic painting by a computer isn't exactly what I choose to do with my free time. But when you've made your bag, you do what you want."

Dream interpretation was something of a fringe science, but electrical impulses were like any other code. And codes could be cracked, replicated. And the high art world paid good coin for the dreams of 'visionary' artists with enough processing power to paint the images. The elite could watch a dream through a console with some sensory separation or upload the dream directly and get to live the beautiful nightmares of art's most drug-induced hazes.

Thom looked through the translucent EKG at the frazzled Osyen. The man was hardly seasoned, but already had collected an impressive set of scars. And was growing wearier every day. "I didn't mean to scare you."

Osyen shrugged it off but chose honesty. "I lost my mother. I promised myself I'd never lose anybody else. Then I lost track of Fiona, and I promised myself I wouldn't lose anybody else. And then I almost..." He looked away, forcing a smile.

Thom's smile was softer, gentle. "You're like a big brother, Oz. I don't want to lose you either."

"Oh, I'll be around for a long time yet," Osyen promised, focusing back on the EKG and his personal nightmare. "But that's twice now you've nearly skipped out on me."

Thom sighed, his own eyes drifting back to the amber collection of spiky lines and graphs. There was something dreadfully off about it, but Thom couldn't quite place what it was. He pinched at the image with both hands, pushing and pulling on it, stretching and squishing. But it was like trying to focus an image and never quite finding the—

That was it.

He started scrolling forward. Osyen saw the proverbial light bulb go off and his brow furrowed. "What is it?"

"Nothing yet," Thom said as he traced his finger around a section of his EKG. Clipping out the image with two fingers, he pulled it out and away, as he scrolled backward to the crisis. Stopping under the erratic heartbeat, he pushed the more regular heart rate underneath it to compare. "What do you see?"

Osyen ground his teeth. "You could just tell me."

"I need to know I'm not insane right now," Thom said, a quiver in his voice. "What do *you* see?"

Osyen leaned forward, the orange and red glow lighting up his face like a sunset. Thom was watching him more than the scans. At first his eyes glazed over, not really able to track through the crap. But then he squinted, questioning, formulating. And Thom nodded. He was having the same impossible equation go through his head.

Tachycardia was just an elevated heart rate, but fibrillation—as seen on Thom's chart—was a randomly firing chamber or chambers of the heart: it was off-rhythm and could cause serious damage.

But Thom could see a different rhythm.

Osyen grabbed Thom's cutout, stretched it a bit, and laid it over itself. And lo-and-behold, it was damn close to what was displayed in Thom's recorded crisis.

An extra...something. Faster, pulsing in threes...

"It wasn't a heart attack," Thom said, breathless. "I had a second heartbeat."

———

Rashida's cabin was as opulent as ever. The warm bronze and brass thread in the drapes reflected the light, making every wall seem to glow. Fluffed pillows and cushions lined her bed, each dangling tassels of red and gold. She'd hung fabric from the ceiling to soften the metallic echo, and a mannequin sat tucked in the corner, half-dressed with some new project.

But despite all the comforts and decadence she'd managed to fabricate, Rashida laid on her bed and stared at the ceiling with wide eyes. The rich chocolate tones Thom would've normally thought poetic paled against the strained whites, striated with darts of red. Had she been crying? If so, her tears had long since dried up, and now she was simply in a catatonic haze.

She'd didn't break the staring contest she was having with the roof. "Can I be of some service, Thomas?"

It was impossible to be subtle or stealthy entering the crew cabins, by design. He had to clamber down six feet of access ladder to get into her room proper. Osyen knew every scrape and dent on this ship and even he couldn't slip down those ladders quietly. But Thom somehow still felt his throat clamp up.

This was something of a sore subject. Now that he was here...

He'd seen her recline on that bed like a Dionysian avatar, all curves and smiles, taunting and teasing. But now she laid stiff, like she was awaiting the stone of her sarcophagus to cover her at any moment.

"I'm afraid I'd be a rather poor friend right now," she admitted.

"Then it's good I don't need a friend. I need a priest."

That got her attention. She tilted her head, dragging her eyes over onto him.

Thom swallowed. It might offend her. It might give him the only answers he'll ever find. "As a blooded member of the Royal Family, you attended seminary, correct?"

"Since I was five years old," she said, ice pumping through her veins. Where was he going with this?

"So it's safe to say, you're the single greatest theological expert on the *Aurum*."

"Which is, admittedly, not a high bar to clear. Do you need confession?"

Thom drew a breath, feeling his throat clench and splinter at what should have been a calming moment. "Can I ask..."

"I've told you all I know about the Paladins—"

"No, no." Thom raised his hands up, as if to show her he meant no threat and carried no weapon. Or to soothe a wild animal. "It's...my questions have a more epistemological spin to them."

Her eyes narrowed, curious enough. "Go on."

Thom took a step forward, working his hands in the air like he had a ball of clay to shape. "The Pilgrim...their healing powers, the original Dunsweir companion, them departing on the Sojourn together? The stories may have elevated to fable, but they're rooted in an actual historical event, right?"

Rashida nodded. "That's correct. The Pilgrim healed the sickness plaguing the earliest human colonies before embarking on their endless quest." She said the words like they were a compulsion, and they probably were from years of childhood programming.

"Right," Thom affirmed. "So we can conclude—however we feel about the Dunsweir and their use of the Pilgrim's name—that the Pilgrim isn't a fabrication."

Rashida propped herself up on her elbows. "Crisis of faith, Thomas?"

Heh. She walked right into it hard enough to make Thom wobble. His voice went low and hushed. "The opposite, really. What do we know about the Pilgrim? Like, verifiable facts and figures. Multiple sources, reviewed by experts. What do we actually know *for certain*?"

She swung her feet to the floor, rooting herself. "Why do you ask?"

"Because I've had two heart attacks in a week," Thom said, feeling the sweat start to come on. "And in the first one, I...I saw the creation of the Paladins."

"Thom—"

"I saw it, Rashida. I saw it *before* they hit us. I swear to you. I-I didn't know what it was at the time, I didn't..."

Rashida looked like she urgently wanted to rush to his side and wrap him in a thick blanket. Defuse the ticking, frantic energy. She settled on simple, clarifying language. "How could you see it?"

"Dreams," Thom whispered. "Computer's still compiling. If we even live long enough to read it."

She was suddenly deadly serious, with a stiff back and a firm tone. "What did you see?"

"I saw..." Thom shook his head, trying to cling to the memory of it like dust in the air. "Stained glass. Priests were burning incense. And an operating table."

"Tall ceilings?"

Thom nodded. "All sharp angles pulling to a point. It was like looking at an artist's rendering of a Jump in progress."

"The Cathedral Dei Trames." Rashida breathed the name like it was a curse.

Thom looked up. "You know it?"

"I was baptized there. My sister drowned."

Thom scoffed at that reveal. "And it took you how long to run away?"

That was a little flippant for Rashida's taste, and her jaw tightened. "I ran from the believers, not the faith. And you don't know the half of what I fled."

That was a fair hit. How was she to know as a child that what she'd witnessed was wrong? Rashida had spent however many years wandering the galaxy in search of something to excuse that behavior, and she found only more suffering. Suffering caused by and spurred by her own flesh and blood.

But the Pilgrim...hadn't done anything wrong. It was the supplicants, the faithful, who responded to love and healing with fire and blood.

Rashida was deadly serious now. "What did you see at the Cathedral, Thomas?"

"Surgeries," Thom grunted. "Hundreds of surgeries."

They didn't need to dig any deeper into that. They both knew how the Paladins were made, blessed, and charged with their tasks. And he'd seen that days before two Paladins had crossed their path.

"*Viator dul*," Rashida said. "You remember what that means?"

"'Sweet traveler.'"

Rashida stood up. And Thom couldn't shake the feeling that she was about to lay some kind of ancient curse on him. The drapes, the colors, and Rashida's raw charisma had very witchy energy.

"You touched the Icon of Cruciform," she said. "Stride used it and brought you back from the dead. Healing is one thing, but resurrection? That shouldn't be possible with modern technology. But *Pilgrim* technology?"

Thom sat down on the floor, pushed down by metaphysical weight, crossing his legs. One step shy of going into a full turtle shell. It was that or run away.

"The Pilgrim doesn't care for time or space," she said, in full liturgical mode now. "They are everywhere at all times, omnipresent. We are never alone, always watched. They saw us in pain and stepped off their great Path to remedy that. And they see you, even now."

"Your faith is a police state," Thom joked.

"My faith should be yours," she said. She raised a hand like she might have laid her palm on his forehead, but then pulled away. "You said there were two heart attacks? What else have you seen?"

Thom looked up at her. "I know who we have to get. And I know how to get past the defenses, and back out again. How do I know that? How could I *possibly* know that?!" Panic was leeching into his voice now.

Rashida drew a breath, hissing it past her clenched throat. And she didn't answer that question.

CHAPTER
TWELVE
RASHIDA

HER MOTHER HAD COACHED her on how to manage stress and aggression, and it all began with the core. Good breathing could influence the mind as effectively as any sub-harmonic manipulation. She sent Thom on his way, urging him not to speak of this discovery with anyone. Until they knew more, they knew nothing.

She sat in her room alone, metering her breath while counting down in her head. In and out, slow and steady. Like the flow of the river. No object or man could resist the headwaters—violence never had the stamina to withstand patience.

Thom had been touched by the Pilgrim's power, the Icon of Cruciform bringing him back from the jaws of death itself. What marks could such a journey have left on the lad?

Her Entiglas chirped up with a call incoming. She would've ignored it entirely, but for the private code flashing on receipt. One meant for emergency lines.

She narrowed her eyes and spread her fingers wide to throw open the screen. She wished she hadn't.

There was a fine line between devilish charm and demonic facsimile. Magnus added a third element to that mixture—one so ghastly, she thought him exhumed from a crypt. "Come now, Rashida," he said, almost jovial, "you can't possibly be surprised to see me now."

"If you think you can trace this signal, you'd be sorely mistaken," Rashida warned.

"As if I'd want this reunion to end so quickly. But I am pleased to find you still within range for video connection. Trouble with your Jump drive?"

"Older ships," she said, half-true, "have older problems."

"True," he admitted. "Do I need to go through the list of charges, or did yesterday morning demonstrate the gravity of your situation?"

She didn't move, but she heard her shoulder crack, like stonework settling into place. "You believe the Godfather will simply allow you to operate in his space?" Rashida bluffed.

Magnus's cheek twitched as he tried to hide a smile. "If he enjoys keeping the contents of his skull within its casing, I do believe he'll let me do just about anything I want."

"First time feeling powerful, Magnus?"

He lowered his head a touch, staring at her with a mixture of voracious hunger and upright dignity that seemed to sour her stomach the longer she looked at it. "You fear me, don't you, girl?"

She didn't answer him. But his nostrils flared, and she could practically see the vigor pump up through the veins in his neck, flushing his cheeks with color. "You do, don't you? I was such a gangly little thing before."

"You still are," she said, a tremor leaking into her voice.

Now he properly smiled, flashing those shark teeth. "And now you appreciate who is in control."

"Why didn't you just kill me?" Rashida asked. "Why all the theatrics? Why are you on my wall in what I can only assume will be one of many future house-calls?"

He played with something off-view, passing it back and forth between his hands, likely the handle of his cane—never taking his eyes off of her. "It hardly seemed fair."

"Oh! So now you have a vested interest in equality, do you?"

His thin lips drew tight like wire squeezing around her throat. "That's a very old ship, Rashida. Its hull is buckling under rust and neglect. The hydraulics leak and the engines cry. And its crew is as threadbare as every other part. Their loyalty is bought, Rashida. They will choose their own wishes over anything else in the world."

She'd seen Osyen's eyes, the way the others talked about Lily. They'd flown together for months, and he'd known several of them for years. She had no doubt he'd have gunned them down to defend the anthropomorphized computer that lived underfoot and overhead.

"It's not too late for this to end quietly, coolly," Magnus said, "without further incident."

She had nothing else to say to the ghoul. She reached up and pinched the image down, pushing it back into her Entiglas.

And she was suddenly acutely aware of every sound that echoed up the hull of the *Aurum*. Fans whirring and metal flexing, fluids flowing. She laid down on her bunk and tried to tell herself that those sounds had always been there.

CHAPTER
THIRTEEN
MILARDI

HIS REPORT on the Godfather's compound had been sorely undervaluing the brutalist architecture and raw manpower on site. It was an intimidating building someone had thrown a multicolored carpet over in an attempt to mask the prison within, but that wasn't terribly relevant.

By contrast, Thom had been alarmingly specific in his descriptions. The Maestro had always had an eye for detail, and he might be overdoing it after the mishap on the convoy—not to mention the higher stakes of this job.

But he had included foot paths of guards inside, motion trackers in the floor that the building AI used to count inhabitants, built-in airlocks to trap and asphyxiate intruders, and a biometric scanner in the ceiling.

When asked how Thom knew this, Rashida had chimed in: "What benefit does he have in lying to you?" A fair point, but Milardi couldn't shake the feeling she was masking something.

It wasn't enough to simply lie through your teeth; they'd have to breathe with someone else's lungs and beat someone else's heart to go by unnoticed.

Well...that could be arranged.

It was a high security location on alert, but they were also simple gangsters. Which meant that more than half of the foot soldiers were in it for a poor paycheck, even if they bought into the Godfather's 'Master' spiel. Milardi had heard all about Anze Orchikov and his crew of devoted minions. Whispers said that the mob boss could give an order and even electrons would follow.

Oh, Milardi was shaking in his rubber boots as he grabbed the wire clippers. Real big scary man. A mobster he could beat by being grounded? Please. Imperial cannon-arm McGee was a lot more intimidating.

The engineers being 'recruited' by Orchikov's goons were tightly under lock and key...but the delivery detail schlepping in hundreds of pounds of food, alcohol, and sundries, they were pre-approved gaping security holes. With biometrics matched to a record on file and a quick nod from the posted guard, the delivery could waltz right through the front door.

Every single big heist, the biggest security flaw was always the front door. Until it was a skylight. But usually the front door.

So they needed...the delivery guy's face, pulse, breath index, and other vital signs. Also, they didn't need him walking up to the door right after Osyen had already walked through it. Would kind of spoil the whole thing. So...

Milardi picked at the jumpsuit that cinched around his neck. Of course, nobody on this little frostbitten moon built anything with space-faring folk in mind. Spacers grew tall and thin, and this 'one-size-fits-all' suit was made for someone never clearing six feet. So the cloth stretched at his ankles and neck, straining at its seams. "What are the odds that this guy has a big brother? Or just a big guy on staff somewhere?"

Osyen snorted. "I mean, it would be our luck, wouldn't it?" The captain was peeking out the door, a thin strip of yellow light tracing up his face.

The warehouse supply that the delivery teams came from was well-supervised. But the packaging facility hadn't been. So they hitched a ride in on a delivery car, slipped on the proper uniforms once inside. And waited.

"You just know that the quiet little snatch job suddenly goes me into a fistfight with a human hillock," Milardi mocked, looking up and down at whatever hypothetical giant. He threw a jab at chest height, immediately crumpling at the wrist and miming out incredible pain. "I break my hand on his stomach—"

Osyen frowned to avoid cackling. "I'mma break *you,* if you don't shut up."

"Listen, I need to have me some gallows humor, or we all just start crying ourselves to sleep."

"Hell, I was already doing that *before* Farragut. What do you think I'm doing now?"

"I try not to pry." Osyen got a good few seconds of quiet after that, but Milardi couldn't help himself. "Can I ask you a stupid question?"

"Hell, you haven't asked a smart one yet."

Ah, Hell. Well, here it goes. Milardi wished he could put up a ballistic shield. "What's special about Lily?"

Osyen's head turned, like a creaking door hinge, as he brought his eyes around to lock onto Milardi.

"Hey, I told you it was a stupid question," Milardi said with a defensive finger.

"Other than the obvious?" Osyen's voice hit that lower register with barely contained rage.

"How's about more special than the whole crew combined? For that matter, what's so special about Rash? I like 'em both, I do, but I also like the rest of 'em."

"What's so special about you?"

Milardi shrugged. "Aside from my winsome charm and perfectly adequate singing voice, not a whole lot."

Osyen shook his head, resuming his watch out of the door. "At least he's self-reflective."

"Look, Oz, you're like my brother," Milardi said, "and I'm not going to push any particular way. You know that. I don't need to know your thinking. I just want to know you *are* thinking."

"These days, Thom does the thinking," Osyen deflected.

"See, that's what I'm talking 'bout. You don't plan, you don't think. You call the shot from the gut, 'specially when family's involved."

Osyen took a breath and instantly the little closet they were in started to feel very, very small. "We can't buy our way out of this," Osyen said with a sense of closure.

But Milardi would not let this be dismissed. "Not every choice we get is between right and wrong. Sometimes it's just two bad options."

"If all you see is two bad options, you're not looking hard enough."

"Fiona tell you that one?"

Oh look, he found another big red button to smash. Osyen snapped at him. "Imperials are the ones trading in lives. Not us."

"There's a hapless guard Zee unzipped that might carry a different opinion," Milardi said. "We kill when it suits us. Just like they do. I don't enjoy hovering on this idea any more than you do, but I can't help myself."

Osyen considered him for a long moment, like he was trying to read something etched in the back of Milardi's eyeball. But then he just sighed and turned back to the door. He was never going to surrender the point, but he'd given up on the conversation.

Milardi scoffed. He could've fled any time, but he was still here, and Osyen didn't give him credit for that.

Osyen's eyes snapped on to movement. "There he is."

Milardi jabbed a hand into his pack, pulling out the hypodermic. The pistol grip on it cupped his palm nicely, and with an extended finger he could hide the whole device. He pulled the sleeve of carbon fiber off the tip, revealing the aerosolizing nub. A quick jab with this, and it would spray a solution directly through the skin, like a thousand tiny intramuscular injections.

"Look at 'im. No idea what's about to happen," Osyen remarked with a wry grin, the last five minutes of conversation forgotten in an instant. That served Milardi just fine. But he knew Osyen hadn't forgotten a damn thing. He was just in denial about it.

Oh well, Milardi knew that not every gamble he took in this life was one he was aware he took. Couldn't live his life anxious for every one of them, now could he?

Milardi took a little peek. The hostage was conveniently not dissimilar from Oz, with a medium build and short shock of brown hair and a certain smugness to his swagger. His nose was crooked from a few too many falls or punches, and his bushy eyebrows were trying to meet each other in the middle.

"I'm good and ready when you are."

Osyen nodded, crooking two fingers in an unintentionally suggestive 'come hither.' "Let's go pick up the luggage." And he pushed open the door.

It was the same as every other office was, truly. Milardi hadn't seen the inside of too many shipping facilities, per se, but he had broken into more than a few office buildings. Aside from the groan of heavy machinery heard on the loading docks above, the especially crude humor chortling from the break room, and the stench of cool aftershave, it was a typical office.

Marketing folks and people with fancy college degrees had reinvented the concept of an office many times, then fallen back to old traditional designs before congratulating themselves on the same innovations the second time around. It was just as much a fashion choice as Milardi's jacket or Osyen's hair; whatever the manager of the day felt was promoting efficiency was how they arranged the furniture. But the facts of the case remained the same—the powerful had doors they could close on the plebes.

The hostage-to-be was one such plebe, staring at a bulletin board of glowing postings, but he didn't seem to be reading anything. He was just sipping coffee and killing time on the clock under the illusion that he was educating himself on workplace safety, and the litany of acceptable avenues of worker complaint.

Milardi had always been partial to kinetic discourse. It had a more satisfying sound.

Osyen and Milardi settled up beside their target, one on either side. Their hostage just snorted, immediately incorporating them into his thought process as he stared at an alarming environmental posting. "You think the geothermal plants are *really* going to run cold in ten years?"

"Hard to believe, you ask me," Osyen chirped, with perfect follow through. "I mean, it's the magma core of a planet. You telling me we froze that?"

"Right?" the target said with a shake of his head and a bemused smirk. "It's like they think we're stupid or something."

"Well, I'm not a smart man," Milardi chimed in, "but I do believe smart people, especially when they hit me with those...omni-syllabic...uh...multisyllabic....long words."

That got the guy to look over at Milardi, and he squinted. "Never seen you around here before."

Milardi looked down at the hostage's nametag. "Connor, eh? I've been working here six years. When did *you* get off the boat?"

"He's new," Osyen offered.

"I'm not new!" Connor objected, whirling around on Osyen. "And who are you?"

Milardi bent over to whisper in his ear. "We're the sack brigade. And you're going in the sack." And with that, he slammed the hypodermic into the guy's neck.

Connor stiffened, his eyes fluttered, and he slumped into Osyen's arms. Chemical narcolepsy was fun.

Milardi stooped to get under Connor's shoulder, but the difference in height meant that one of Connor's feet swung in the air while the other dragged on the ground. "Whoa, man, you're in no state to drive the line swing."

"Yeah, you need to get home and charge your batteries," Osyen said.

With the shipping boy dangling between them, they walked straight to the front door. They shuffled him into an elevator with two other uniformed nobodies who didn't even bat an eye. Either this happened a lot with Connor, or these two couldn't give more of a damn. The lift shuddered and shook the way only industry ones do—maybe they were just built with loose tolerances and bounced around more?

The entire way down, nobody said a word about the catatonic man hung out to dry between the two men. The other occupants just stared forward, all awareness beaten out of them, matching uniforms and matching stares.

It made Milardi's spine crawl.

And the door opened to reveal something that made Milardi's spine jump. The silhouette was a nine-foot tall human brick and for a split second, Milardi thought he caught a flash of yellow in the eye.

But no, this wasn't a young baby face bolted to a metal monstrosity. This was an office heavy, a veteran of the yard, and—with a tattoo on his lower lip. His voice was like silky thunder. "Shift's not over yet, gents."

Oh, that vocal range did all the right things, and Milardi felt a squeak jump out of his mouth. Osyen blinked, processing that embarrassing sound, before taking a breath, "Connor damn near collapsed at his station."

"Then he can sleep it off in the break room, and we can take it out of his pay," the brute said, "but nobody goes home till the shift's done."

"You don't sleep off paracephylitis." Osyen crapped that bluff out of his mouth and called it a sentence and Milardi almost bit through his tongue.

Paraphyletic was a technical term in biology for things with a common ancestor. No idea what 'paracephylitis' was. But it certainly sounded contagious.

And it made the brute take a small step back. Osyen bit into it. "It's not airborne, but we need to get him into isolation—and us too, probably."

"The things you do for your friends," Milardi stammered out, still studying the curve of the big guy's shoulder. It looked like a bowling ball on either side, broad and smooth.

The heavy looked like he was trying to decide if he should hold his breath. "You just came out of a loaded elevator!"

"Yeah, we did," Osyen said, like that underlined the importance.

"Get him outta here!"

"On our way! Yes, sir!" Osyen said, as he pulled both Connor and Milardi out towards the front door and into the streets of Farragut. Milardi didn't even get the hunk's name.

It was only when they'd broken line of sight that Milardi's haze snapped and he remembered to be aghast. "You can't just put 'itis' on the back of a word and call it a disease!"

"The generalized stupidity of the public means I can. Get in the car."

———

Thom wasn't mincing words today. "The plan is simple, but there's not a lot of room for error. Delay, and everyone dies. Miss a beat, everyone dies. Skip a step, everyone dies. Do you understand?" Everyone felt the air get sucked out of the room, and Milardi felt the pit in his stomach sink a little bit further. It was a helluva way to start a briefing, reminding an entire crew that death and dismemberment laid around the next corner.

Like they needed reminding. Milardi would not forget that bald-headed gargoyle and his empty yellow eyes.

Thom looked over each and every one of them, making sure they internalized that notion. He spoke like he was trying to pound his truth into the back wall, like any small-town minister or mid-size crime lord.

It suited him. "We've played in worse skies. We sank the Icon of Cruciform, escaped the Boolean and outfoxed the Imperial Navy; we can do this. Adelaide and Roche, you're the first pieces on the board. Once you make contact with the grid, that's when you give us the call."

An open radio communication with their implants. They might as well send out personalized invitations for the Paladins.

Thom was counting on it. "Clock starts—and Osyen makes his entrance, disguised as the delivery officer. He gets as close to the target as he can."

How will he know where to go? And what room? Thom had produced a detailed floor layout, passcodes, and ciphers for a half dozen rooms. Milardi didn't really want to know *how* Thom had gotten that information, but while he and Osyen were off grabbing the mailman, Thom must've secured some inside sources.

"That's when I open the door?" Roche asked.

Thom nodded. "You're hardwired to their network, front to back, so you'll see everything they can. Now the compound's AI won't be able to see you in its system until you tell its subnets to do something. Then it'll pin you down in a matter of seconds. And pull half of the city down on top of you. Adelaide'll get you in, but you've gotta open the door. Milardi—once he gives the order, get 'em both cut. Not a second slower. That's all you have to worry about."

Milardi mocked a two-finger salute at Osyen. "Just in case you didn't notice, the actual plan...involves abandoning you."

"I wouldn't be making fun," Thom jumped in, "because if the security forces are coming down on you, you better believe at least one Paladin is." Thom's eyes flicked over to Rashida on that, before catching himself. "We're all known associates. I don't think I need to say anything more on that."

He didn't. Milardi glanced over to see Rashida turning two shades paler in the face and swallowing the ball in her throat.

He never thought he'd miss having Zatia to watch his back.

Thom clapped his hands, snapping the room back to focus. "Oz. Once you have the package, you've got to hold tight."

"My escape route going to be self-evident?" Osyen asked.

Thom's eyes fluttered, like he was glancing at the blueprints inked to the back of his skull. "Something like that."

Osyen's jaw actually dropped. "I'm going out the hole a Paladin makes for me, aren't I?"

Thom bobbed his head to one side, compensating, like a ship losing an engine. "We're being tailed by some iron bulls. Time we made that work *for* us. He'll come in after you, and Anze Orchikov, for all his might...can't stop it. Bind it up in the Godfather's goons, and then hightail it to the shuttle." Thom bit his lip as he considered how to phrase this last bit. "Oz, nobody is going to be in a position to help you. I'm not putting Rashida in play, and I'll be stuck back here. You'll be in deep, and if it goes wrong..."

"I trust you, Maestro," Osyen affirmed, no hesitation. "If this is the way, then this is the way. I'll get it done."

That was either the best or worst thing to say. Maybe Thom had hoped for a little doubt or pushback. But Osyen had been through a lot with that little duct rat, and even when he was mad at Thom or tortured by Imperial goons or shot or stabbed—Thom seemed to get that man injured with alarming regularity. Osyen still didn't breathe right after the beating that Stride gave him.

But the kid had never led them wrong. They'd gotten this far together. And Thom certainly had a better head for heist management than Osyen or Milardi ever did.

Thom reset his stance, rooting himself back into his role and stage-voice. "We'll know when things are about to get nasty when we lose the back channel. That means a Paladin is on top of you. You stop hearing callbacks, go radio silent. They may be doing more than just jamming our comms and I don't want to give out any free advice to 'em."

Osyen summed it up best. "Get in. Grab an engineer. Get out."

Milardi nodded, glancing at the roof that was painfully bare metal. He'd grown used to seeing an awkward blue face staring back.

Help is on the way, Lily.

CHAPTER
FOURTEEN
OSYEN

WHAT WAS it about this job? First blue hair, now face work.

They couldn't slip a holo print past a second-generation heuristic security system, let alone whatever top-of-the-line artificial intelligence that Anze Orchikov was running. So Milardi and Rashida had to painstakingly recreate the appearance of poor dickish Connor.

Rashida got him fitted and dressed, scuffed in all the right places. And Milardi brought on a new nose, eyebrows, black hair, a scar on the cheek from rough housing as a child with a small, unfriendly animal. Prosthetics could only add to the face, not take away—so careful application of chemistry stripped away whatever had to be subtracted.

Milardi assured him they could grow it back. But being capable of doing it and being flush enough to afford to do it were two very different things.

Couple that with careful application of pharmaceuticals, and they could mimic the heart murmur and chest cough Connor had been wrestling with; contacts for optical scans and gloves to replicate his hand print.

But faking a person was more than just data—it was a performance. He had to fool more than just computers, after all. He was a regular appearance at this checkpoint. The guards would know Connor.

And Osyen didn't know jack squat about Connor. Which was going to be problematic.

Osyen waited up the block with his car of goods rehearsing his backstory: he was an up-jumped dock worker with delusions of grandeur who enjoyed sports, women, and alcohol, in that order. He was chummy with assholes and demeaned his lessers. He was a man with very little actual clout, so he swung it about to make it appear more impressive.

The only one impressed was himself.

In the silence, Adelaide was already at work in phases as the scanner panned over the alleyway again and again. And she was working inside of bursts of hot steam that could brand flesh. So she was trying to apply super-strong acids while wearing a burn suit.

Once cut, she could access the electrical lines in the wall. Splicing a connection in for Roche would be child's play. But the mental fortitude to not ask a camera to pan or adjust a refresh rate was a whole other type of challenge. If Roche issued a casual and meaningless order, it would blow their cover too early.

He'd have to meditate, essentially, while plugged into a super-computer with an entire building's worth of data pumping into his brain every second. It was, suffice to say, slow going.

"Please, sir." A small voice, timid and quaking, cut through the noise in his brain. He looked down to his left to see a small child, not yet a teenager. They were bundled in scraps of stained fabric, as many threadbare layers as they could keep on. And Osyen winced when he noticed the frostbitten black that was creeping up the child's fingertips.

They shivered against the cold, pulling one of their many scarves tighter around their little chin. "C-can I come with you? I can...I can cook, clean, I can..."

Anything but another night on the ground.

Osyen squeezed his eyes shut. Taking in another stray might be just as good as putting a bullet in them, on today of all days.

He dug in his pocket and produced a single credit chit, loading it with some cash with a swipe across his hip. "I'll do you one better. There's a grungy little hospice two miles that way. You can make it before sunset if you leave now. Offer the front desk this and don't answer any of their questions. Whatever you do, don't let 'em take it from you. This is *yours*." The child reached for the chip and Osyen lifted it away. "Don't make no trouble and don't get involved in none. After your first night, give 'em the same offer you just made me. Do whatever he asks and then ask for more. And whatever you do, you do this one thing for me, okay?"

Osyen handed the chit over to the child, setting their salvation down like a soft snowfall into their grubby palms. They looked up at him with watery eyes. Osyen held that eye contact for a hard moment, trying not to cry himself. "You grow up big and strong."

The child nodded and took off running down the street. In the wrong direction.

Whatever. If he'd just been scammed, he'd been scammed by somebody that needed it more than he did.

It was cursed silence for another ten minutes before, finally, the radio callout that made Osyen's hair stand on end. *We're in position,* Adelaide bounced. *Roche's tapped in.*

And just like that, somewhere in the city...the Paladins were coming.

Last chance to back out. He was about to deliberately snare himself in the Godfather's clutches, hoping a cybernetic assassin fueled by dogmatic insanity was going to—*accidentally*—break him out.

Osyen had flirted with death enough times, but it never took him somewhere nice. Why not try once more?

He took a breath, feeling the bite of the cold air on his dry throat and cut his lips. And he pressed the cruiser into gear. His heart pounded on its prison walls, desperately trying to get off this suicidal ride.

Too late. The guards waved him in, and he casually drifted the hovering car to a grinding halt to the front gates.

Apparently, he came in a little hot. At the last second, the guards raised their hands and started barking at him—two posted shooters on the door raising their guns in reflex. But the car came to an unsatisfying stop, almost like the gangsters had plied the brakes with their minds.

"You ever goin' to learn to drive, Connor?!" One of 'em sniped from the side. He had a jagged scar down his cheek from a dull blade, like an extended permanent smile up one side.

Say something! No hesitation. Do it! Osyen opened his mouth and let Connor do the talking. "Certifications are for people with no natural God-given talent."

"Uh-uh. Certifications," Smiley said with a raised finger, "are just tools of control for governments to select people they deem worthy of success."

Another guard reacted with a sharp crank of her head, her full mop of red hair tossing in the cold air and spraying bits of ice. "Yes. Why do you say that like it's a *bad* thing?"

"Because the boot of the bureaucrat—"

The whole posting groaned, a chorus of pain, one even throwing up their hands. "Oh, for the love of—we *know!*"

Smiley was on a downhill roll and would bowl over anything in his way. "It's not a meritocracy if two equal people are not allowed equal footing because of—"

"Oh, just *shut up!* All day with this..."

Preoccupied with Smiley, most of them didn't keep track of Osyen as he clambered off the cruiser and started loading his dolly. This was apparently standard procedure, since the Mop of Red Hair came over and actually helped him stack boxes, cranking the straps and securing the cruiser with an electromagnet anchor.

Hmm. If that cruiser was his getaway, that small dinner plate attached to the hood might be a problem. He'd never get the engine started with that there, and he'd never get it off without Adelaide.

He'd need a new way out.

And Osyen was so distracted by the anchor, he didn't notice the man marching up on him. The big fella grabbed Osyen's wrist with enough force to nearly lift him off the snow-packed rotunda. Everyone yelped, even as the attacker cranked Osyen's wrist around to touch his shoulder blades and planted Osyen face first into the side of the cruiser. Osyen heard a crack and his cheek and nose instantly screamed, sharp fire pumping along his jaw.

Over the chorus of oohs and whoas, a single icy voice dripped saccharine contempt into his ear. "You said you were going to call her. Last week."

Connor's past indiscretions were about to become a very tangible problem. "Call her?" Osyen strained. "Wh-who we talkin' about?"

Not a good question, and it earned Osyen another slam into the cruiser. He felt a wet stick on his cheek, as his blood was freezing to a glue. Rivulets were already thickening into a slushy paste as they dripped from his nose.

The voice escalated from contempt to seething, and a fresh blast of acrid stench rolled across Osyen's neck. "She is a very sweet girl, and you promised to be just as sweet. So when she calls me in tears...I take an interest."

Oh, fantastic. They'd picked a real cherry for Osyen to impersonate. Singular dipshit, Connor the Delivery Boy, had abused his privileges and played with somebody's loved ones. And now Osyen, wearing his face, was getting a makeover through the careful application of a steel plate.

To make matters worse, his biometrics were almost certainly off now: face, heartbeat, all of it. This guy had bashed Osyen into the side of a car—and locked him out of half of the building.

Osyen, put some thrust on this, Thom said. *We've lost too much time as it is.*

"So," the voice whispered, "whatchu say now, little man?"

Don't break character. "I say...she's not as *sweet* as you said."

Eyes went wide. Jaws dropped. And a voice that sounded like Smiley let out a whistle, like a gas leak, as he failed to stifle his laugh.

The hand clenched tighter on Osyen's wrist and for a second, he thought the man was just going to squeeze the blood out of him like a dirty bar towel. But suddenly, the man twisted and flipped Osyen around to face him.

Well, at least Osyen figured out where all of Weasel's stolen cybernetics were going. The man looming over him was the criminal underground equivalent to the super soldiers circling in the chill tundra, albeit far cruder. Nothing in this man was custom made for him, so bits extruded from his flesh in hideous geometric clumps underneath his clothing. He looked like a steel troll fresh out of a storybook, tufts of hair and dark flesh clashing with the scuffed chrome.

The Troll leaned in close enough for Osyen to get a full blast of that burning carpet smell, and Osyen got a glimpse of the vise masquerading as the Troll's hand. "You want to say that again?"

"No," Osyen said, coughing, "but I think you're burning up a friction pad somewhere. Damn."

That got a full hoot and holler out of Smiley. He was expecting a blood bath now.

But Troll simply let Osyen go, shoving him into the side of the car. "I see you within a city block of her, and I will pull both your kidneys out and donate them to charity."

Osyen gave him a thumbs up. "It's a good cause."

"Get these crates inside!" Troll bellowed over his shoulder as he retreated into the compound's inner sanctum.

That, Thom muttered, *should not have worked.*

Osyen had to stop himself from falling to his knees in thankful prayer, but that didn't slip into his chatter. *Spend a little more time with gangsters, and you figure out what they respect.*

Gusto? Milardi asked.

He wasn't wrong. Folks didn't step off the King's Road without

139

either having or quickly acquiring a certain brand of stupidity. Life was to be lived, not sheltered.

Of course, the life expectancy statistics didn't exactly support this choice, but the only numbers that concerned these types were currencies.

Osyen grabbed his dolly full of crates and pushed it over to the guard detail at the gate. They scanned the crates with their Entiglas and received a happy green chirrup from the device. Satisfied, they went to scan him—comparing his face and everything else against the security record. He could only pray Troll hadn't jacked him up too much, knocked out a contact or shook his heart back into its regular rhythm.

Shock of shocks, the device croaked and flashed red. The holographic text displayed was backwards to Osyen but reading backwards was a talent for anyone that passed checkpoints regularly. His facial recognition was outside acceptable margins.

The Redhead looked him over, squinting. Osyen tried to smile, and it hurt. "I *did* just cheek check my own car."

She suppressed a giggle. "Yeah, you did. Your head made a funny sound. Thonk!"

Osyen grit his teeth, running his tongue over a few to check that they were all still there. "It was more fun experiencing it."

Redhead swiped a few things around and the screen chirped green. "Get your business done. 'Sweetie.'"

Okay, he deserved that. No, *Connor* deserved that! But all Osyen said was, "Yes, ma'am."

———

The relative opulence of the building's exterior, fortress and all, did not prepare Osyen for the barren and crushing interior. The first room he entered was completely featureless, just a beige cube with doors on either side of it. Each door had a brass knob—a holdover from a bygone era, but kind of attractive in a retro way.

He had no doubt that every crack and crevice in this room could draw out air or pump in noxious fumes. And that brass knob was a secondary biometric scanner that might lock him out again. And the low ceiling and lack of furnishing gave him nowhere to hide.

This wasn't an entryway—it was a kill box.

The only adornment in the room was a portrait, floor to ceiling. And Osyen had no doubt who it was supposed to be. The brass eye carved into the picture frame, genuine oil on genuine canvas. It was no small expense for the formally dressed middle-aged man depicted upon it.

A sharp jaw with a shock of white hair, one unruly lock dangling in front of his eye like a lure on a fishing line. And his piercing green eyes seemed to follow Osyen all through the room.

The Godfather, Anze Orchikov himself.

Less mafia boss than he expected. This man had the countenance of royalty, power that came from gravity rather than commerce. He was important because of how he warped his world, not because of his place within it.

Osyen bowed his head in playful greeting to the painting. He had no doubt there were cameras socketed somewhere in that painting, giving newcomers an opportunity to be scanned yet again for biometrics and optical signifiers.

What better way to get people to square up to have their picture taken than to show them a picture?

Osyen trudged to the door across the room, feeling the ground give underfoot like a soft moss or loam. The dolly he pulled behind him sank just a touch, forcing him to pull that much harder. He had never encountered a 'floor' that felt like walking on a lily pad. It was then that he noticed...the entire room was askew, one wall taller than the other and one side deeper.

Maybe they were pumping gases into the room, and he was already succumbing to some mind-altering drug to leave him helpless?

So he slapped himself in his bruised face, and the sharp sting was bracing. He looked at the walls again and...nope, they were in fact built off-level.

Um, Thom started. *I almost hate to ask but...Why?*

If I see a white rabbit, it was nice knowing you, Osyen said.

It's designed to throw you off balance. Prisoners are less likely to resist if they think they've cracked, Thom explained. *Keep moving.*

Osyen grabbed the door handle and felt the tingle shoot up his arm as the AI scanned him. He twisted the knob, expecting it to resist, but the AI found whatever it was looking for. The tumblers aligned, and the door released.

The antechamber revealed was banal—almost like the aforementioned government certification offices. There were armed goons standing guard, including the Troll sneering from his post. Two rows of chairs were the centerpiece, noticeably carrying straps and clamps to accommodate the unruliest of tenants. A hairless desk clerk sat behind a tall pulpit, encased in thick plastic. Almost every limb had two or three cables dangling, plugged into ports on the desk in front of them.

Osyen wheeled his dolly up to the counter, looking to get the clerk's attention somehow. "Hello?" he asked, waving a hand.

An acidic sigh and thumping feet. Osyen turned—but the cyborg Troll had already closed the distance and grabbed Osyen again with his metal clamp of a hand. His wrist still ached from the first abuse, but all the Troll did was slap Osyen's hand onto the open counter.

The surface lit up a happy pearlescent white at his touch, and the clerk looked up, as if seeing Osyen for the first time. A soft smile and a slow blink of milky blue eyes. "Hello, Connor. How lovely to see you again so soon."

Troll grumbled something and stomped on back to their posting. Osyen blinked, turning back to the pleasant voice and unsettling appearance.

This wasn't a person. It was just a mech.

The clerk had a pleasant, soft voice, but every other part of them was just...unsettling, from the misshapen dome of its bare head to the spider-like bony fingers and the pull of the skin around its plug points where a malnourished body had retreated. And the metal had resisted. "Is there something I can help you with?" they asked, slow and even-toned.

"Yeah, I've always meant to ask," Osyen said, "why are you not a hologram?"

"Quite simple," the clerk said with a note of cheer. "Holograms are more commonly associated with artificial intelligence and are a commonplace feature in customer service. As a physical extension, I am more likely to cause discomfort."

Osyen pursed his lips. "It's working for you."

"Thank you. I have noted your commentary in our service log."

Ask about Lars Hedlop. Thom ordered. *Delivery's for him.*

"Uh," Osyen stumbled, "delivery for Lars Hedlop?"

The clerk's eyes drifted, unfocused. And Osyen became painfully aware that the uncanny man hadn't blinked, at least since Osyen entered. "Lars Hedlop is within the estate. Consent for additional security scan?"

"Yeah, uh..." Osyen glanced back at the Troll, keenly aware that the big guy was both capable and eager to rip Osyen limb from limb. "I consent."

The clerk sat up straight and their milky eyes rolled back into their skull, revealing bone-white nothing. And Osyen was no longer comfortable with this much weird in one place. Whatever the Godfather had intended here was doing its job, because Osyen was halfway to confessing the entire scheme if he could just cut out the obscene amount of unsettling going on within these walls.

The front door had looked like a dilettante's second home, and the inside was like someone visualized a monochrome nightmare through a shard of glass. This wasn't a prison; this was a corner of Hell, gently inserting steel barbs into his flesh even as it asked about his weekend and plans for the summer.

Whatever scan the clerk had run satisfied them. They relaxed back into their seat and the gentle blue pupils rolled back to the front. "Welcome back, Connor. Lars has been notified of your arrival."

The white light on the counter danced down to the floor and flashed over to another door, brass handle and all—one Osyen hadn't seen moments ago. Maybe it had been tucked behind a false wall, or he had simply missed it?

Osyen bounced on the balls of his feet. He wasn't really enjoying the idea of seeing how much weirder this could get. But there was no turning back now. Heck, even hesitation might spell disaster. Connor does this regularly enough.

And so he marched on over to the door.

"Wait." The Troll had seen something, noticed something! Osyen tensed up and froze to the spot. And it was everything he had to not flinch as the cyborg approached.

The Troll stomped on over, squinting. "What do you have for Lars?"

"If they don't tell me," Osyen bluffed, "they're not going to tell you."

A hint of a smile. "So you ain't even peeked? Not even a little?"

Where was this coming from? This guy had been ready to use Osyen as a blood sponge, but now he's getting all chummy.

Well, if he recommended girls for Connor, they might be closer than he had initially expected. So Osyen flashed him a smile. "What kind of scum do you take me for?"

And the Troll's facade dropped to reveal that death glare again. "The kind that calls her back."

Osyen threw up his hands in surrender. "I got it! I got it! I'll call her."

"You'll call," the Troll informed, "and you'll be telling her you won't be seeing her again. Right?"

"Whatever you say. You're like two and a half of me. You think I'm going to test you further?"

The Troll leaned closer. "You would die."

"Keenly aware," Osyen said, pointing one finger at the door. "Can I go now?"

That vise clamp of a hand reached out, bashing the doorframe. A happy chirp and the door swung open on its own. Osyen jumped, a little startled, but there was no further explanation. Perhaps it was a door known for sticking? Connor would know this, but Osyen was in the dark.

So he dragged his dolly of supplies through, following the little white line into the passage and leaving the accommodating folk behind.

Happy white lines and hospital beige corridors notwithstanding, Osyen knew a prison when he saw one. There was a smell in the air he remembered all-too well from Fort Augustine. Plumbing was never a chief priority in prisons anywhere.

Osyen didn't see another soul as he marched onward, following his little guide on the floor, like a pixie in a forest leading him to certain demise. The dolly's magnetic hum as it hovered along the floor was the only sound other than his own footsteps. And the dull echo of his boots rapidly became the hollow metronomic descent of his brain into further madness.

No doors. No rooms. No guards.

And it occurred to him that the AI was giving him only one direction to go. Much like the door that had appeared at the drop of a hat, the walls were sealing off any other path. He was undoubtedly surrounded by different rooms he simply couldn't see, from guard posts to prisoners' cells. He was being scanned at intervals, each layer of security checking the work of the last.

But for all he knew and saw, it was just a bland, asymmetric corridor.

Until finally, one last turn, and the corridor ended in a door with a brass knob, just like every other. Osyen mused, trying to escape from a place like this would be its own kind of Hell. Every door, every passage, every path looked the same. He could run for hours and never know if he was even making progress. Even the guards were trusting the AI to get them in and out again.

Osyen marched toward the door. Perhaps it was a trick of the searing lights or the hallway's architecture, but for every two steps forward, it was like the room got only one step closer. A forced perspective, but Osyen had read about the Core worlds, and even colonies like Ilum, where buildings built out of sapient bricks could shift and move on command. More than just a trapdoor or a sliding wall. The building itself was like a liquid that could construct barricades, rooms, and pillars at will.

He found it hard to believe that such technology would be available for the public, but to someone like Anze? That egotistical lunatic might just have sprung for it.

The door was within reach. And Osyen took a breath.

I'm here, Osyen bounced. *And if I try to open this door, they're going to know what we're doing.*

Agreed, Thom said. *Milardi, get ready. Roche, all I need is one door.*

You'll have it.

Osyen grabbed the door handle and waited...no beep. No chime. No klaxon.

But the door swung free.

It was a jail cell alright, albeit well furnished. They had hung two shelving units of personal effects on one wall, next to an exacting holographic blueprint of a starship. The bed was made up with fine linens, starched and crisp.

And a hunched figure curled his back over a desk, scribbling with a stencil onto a tablet while his other hand tapped away at a haptic keyboard mid-air. His hair had thinned into a gray tonsure, a patch of dry skin on the crown of his head. His fingers were bent and crooked from a lifetime of fine-tool use. And his voice was as crunchy as every other part of him.

The man sighed, more exasperated than tired. "And what does the Master require now?"

This was the man. The man who could save Lily, save his crew. Osyen's heart sank and then leapt, before rooting itself back in his chest.

"Lars Hedlop?" Osyen asked.

The fossil nodded, never looking up. "Is it finally time to slit my throat?"

"No," Osyen said. "I'm here to get you out."

Dramatically, that's when the klaxon erupted in a baleful whine, like a dying whale or a mother who'd lost her child to unyielding ocean waters. Sounded like Roche's breach had been detected. Only took ten seconds or so. Not a bad response time for an AI managing a psychological monstrosity like this.

Alarms, rescue, heroism. But all this excitement elicited from Lars something akin to ridicule. "What a change of pace."

Osyen reached out to the others. *I've got Lars. How's the weather out there?*

Nothing. No response. The alarms...weren't for Roche or Osyen.

The Paladins were here.

CHAPTER
FIFTEEN
OSYEN

"YOU'RE A FOOL."

Osyen raised a finger in objection. "Lars, I'm a very capable, resourceful, and desperate fool. On your feet."

Lars did not move, did not even turn to face him. "Anze Orchikov will not suffer this insult."

There wasn't time for this. "You want to know why I'm desperate, Lars?"

"Many people on Farragut are desperate. An intelligent few remain desperate and *alive*."

"Normally, I'd agree with that," Osyen said, "but I've got two tons of dogmatic murder machine rolling after me and mine, and you're the only way any of us can get away from it. So, get on your feet or I'm shoving you in one of these crates. Understood?"

Something in what he said got a response. Lars didn't get up. But he did finally turn around, revealing a multi-aperture monocular hinged on eyeglass frames. The other unexposed eye was wide in genuine terror. "Say that again."

"I don't have that kind of time," Osyen said, advancing on Lars. "Choose your poison."

Lars jumped at the cacophony of gunfire coming from up the hall, swiftly joined by cries of pain and anguish. Lars took a ragged breath, a mixture of horror and wonder. "What have you done?"

Now, that was an awful lot of intention in those four words. Osyen looked down at the...heuristics expert and cybernetics technician of high value held by the most powerful gangster in civilized space. "You know what that thing is, don't you?"

A tinge of panic entered Lars's voice, like salt in a wound. "Get me out of here."

"My pleasure." Osyen went for the door, kicking it open.

But as Lars approached the open pathway, a heavy bass voice filled the air. The pixelated, featureless face of the building's AI pushed out of one wall, filling the entire surface and knocking the shelves to the ground. "Lars Hedlop, please remain seated. There is no cause for alarm."

"No cause for—" Osyen ridiculed. "What exactly *would* be cause for alarm?"

And he got his answer. Down the hallway, the cybernetic Troll appeared. All the machismo and gravity this man once had was stripped from him. The big metal goliath was staggering, galloping forward on his one good leg and cradling one arm against his gut. He trailed blood behind him like a damp mop—which is when Osyen noticed that his bad leg he was hobbling forward on was mostly shreds.

The Troll called out to them. "Close the door! Close—"

A rod at least two inches thick caught the Troll through the side of his jaw mid-word, staking him to the wall. It struck him so fast, it almost teleported into place. Osyen would've been thankful for how fast that was, but the big guy had clearly suffered plenty of indignities just up the hall.

Thud. Thud. Thud.

Osyen stood tall as the Paladin rounded the corner, bald head and blank stare.

"Computer," Lars whispered, "do something!"

The AI's face twitched, like frames dropping in a video feed. "Attempts—to inhibit approach are being-being countered. You are my charge. I must-protect the charge. Protect...."

Countered? The Paladin...the Paladin had an AI of its own in its man-sized shell. It was wirelessly hacking and competing with a *building*'s AI, with all of its foundational city block-sized processor power.

And it was winning.

The Paladin came to a stop next to the Troll's body. The blood pooled outward, almost effervescent against the bright floors. He leaned over the husk and he whispered. "Bless your burdens for the road is long."

Osyen hadn't expected to hear a voice from this thing, let alone a sentence. But the Paladin stood up straight and tall, filling the hallway.

And it called out to him. It sounded like a rusting gear shaft had become a real boy. "Where is the girl?"

"The—the girl?" Lars stammered. "We-I don't...you'll have to be more—more specific."

"He wasn't talkin' to you, Lars," Osyen said. He tested the Paladin's intentions by taking two clean steps forward, calling out. "She's not here, big guy. And by now, I don't know where she is. Could be halfway to Vanguard by now."

"Deceit," the Paladin snarled, "is a sin."

Osyen hung his head. "Yeah, well, it is one of my favorites."

The Paladin extended a hand towards the Troll. The magnet in his palm pulled the spear out of his victim—and wrenched half a dozen cranial implants out too.

The bass voice of the AI echoed up from Lars's room, and Osyen could swear he felt a breeze, like the roar of an unspeakable beast at his back. "Protect the charge! Protect the charge!"

The Paladin flicked his hand, sending the spear hurtling down the hallway straight for Osyen's chest. The barest flicker of a white cone flashed around the spear as it cracked the sound barrier—

—and a wall slammed up in front of Osyen, just in time for the spear to sink into it. The spear tip stopped mere inches from his chest. He gasped and stumbled backward, the supersonic crack deafening in the small space.

That face pressed out of the wall, sliding its own eye right up along the shaft of the spear. "You must go! I cannot hold him!" To Osyen's right, a wall melted away into the floor. "GO!"

Osyen grabbed Lars by the collar and pushed him down the open hallway. Nothing to do but run.

They took off, fleeing for their lives. Osyen chanced a look back, waiting for that manmade titan to simply blow through the obstruction. He could hear the crunch of stone and the increasing patter of steps, but nothing was behind them.

No time to think about that. He pressed on Lars's aging back, urging him onward.

The Paladin surged through the wall in front of them, sending a shower of bricks and a cloud of white powder into the air. It dragged its heels to slow down, carving scars in the stonework two feet long. Something clutched in its grasp, spinning around and around to build up speed..

It was a person—or part of one anyway, bearing the color scheme of the Godfather's goons. A spray of red painted the beige walls with the rotation, like paint flicked off a bloody brush.

Osyen pulled Lars to the ground as the clumsy improvised bullet came sailing overhead, splattering against the wall and bouncing off down the hallway.

They were helpless, prone. And the Paladin advanced, one heavy foot after another.

Lars gibbered something that sounded like an apology, but all he could do was stare at the approaching Paladin, his butt frozen to the floor. Osyen snagged his collar and tried to haul him back the way they came, his hand slipping on the floor slick with what remained of the poor projectile.

This was asinine! He couldn't run for both of them!

A very stupid man came marching out of the hole the Paladin had carved, shouldering what could only be described as heavy ordinance. He tucked a firearm the size of a small tree into his hip, pointing in the Paladin's general direction. Luckily enough, the Paladin was a big enough target that he could probably have aimed with his eyes shut.

A rapid three-round burst of 'thunks' and Osyen could swear he heard a ricocheting piece of shrapnel come sailing by his ear with a hateful zing. The brief cloud of vapor and debris fell to the ground, revealing the rainbow bubble insulating the Paladin.

But the Paladin redirected its focus, turning to face the artillerist at their back.

The very loyal, very brave, very suicidal man shouted over at Osyen. "Get the Engineer and get outta here!"

Osyen leaned over. "On your feet, Lars. It's cardio day." But Lars didn't respond, didn't move. It was like someone had poured concrete into all of his joints.

The gunner fired another burst and then another. If the repeated back-to-back explosions were causing the Paladin any distress, it wasn't giving notice. The guy backpedaled, laying burst after burst. Soon, both gunner and Paladin had vanished back into the hole they came from.

Grunting, crunching metal, more grunting.

And then, Osyen heard another burst, and a pink mist fluffed into view.

"Get—Up," Osyen ordered. And this time, Lars finally found his on switch. All four limbs started scraping the ground for any kind of traction, wheels spinning and burning.

Osyen provided the last bit of lift to get the old man up and they took off back the way they came.

Everywhere they ran, walls opened before them. The once

barren pathway was now enriched with a thousand sights. They passed by empty guard stations, sparking consoles. Prisoners behind thick glass pounded frantically, screaming threats and pleading for release. The once porcelain environment had shattered into a thousand disparate tableaus of pain and desperation.

Those thudding steps, faster and faster, like a heartbeat accelerating.

A prisoner screamed something unintelligible through the glass—as the Paladin burst through the backside of his cell and crashed right through him. The man's body came apart like it was held together by naught but thread. Painted from end-to-end with blood and ash, not even slowing down, the Paladin crashed through the glass, showering Lars and Osyen with a hundred blades.

Osyen shoved Lars away from him—and found a wall rising between them. No face this time, but he heard that voice, sputtering and distant. "P-Pro-P...protect the charge."

Osyen flopped over to look at the Paladin looming over him. Exhausted, beaten. Each draw of breath gave him no refreshment. His throat clenched and his back ached. A cracking headache punched in his skull.

Had he taken a shard of that glass? Or did one of his ribs pop free again? They liked to do that these days. And what a bad time for that to happen.

The Paladin's shoulders rose and fell, as the big guy gasped for refreshing breath, tried to pull in and found...

Nothing.

The AI: it had trapped them both in a small room and evacuated the air. Tried to smother both flames, both threats.

Neck tense, shoulders tight, eyes strained. The Paladin was suffocating.

It looked down at Osyen, snorting at him like a bull, like he was somehow responsible for this. And it extended a fist out sideways, punching a hole in the small chamber. A rush of air and cold kindness kissed Osyen's cheeks. He rolled onto his stomach, doubled over in pain as the pressure equalized again.

The Paladin didn't even flinch. "Where is the girl?"

Osyen chuckled, mostly from the pain. "You have a...bizarre interrogation style."

The Paladin made no threats, no promises of pain. This thing was strong enough to pull ships out of the sky and rend metal like cloth. If it even got a hand on him...

It reached down—just as something came clattering in the hole. Osyen didn't know what, but it couldn't be good. So he curled up into the smallest ball he could.

Through his fingers, his clothes, and his face into the ground...he still saw the bright flash, enough to white out his vision. It was like it had scoured all sound from the space, a white noise drowning every other source.

Was this what it felt like to die? Disconnected from everything?

He didn't want to leave them. He still owed them all so much.

And that's when he heard the Paladin's voice crying out, like a groaning bear, both hands clutching at the circlet around its head.

And Lars's voice. "Get up, boy!"

Osyen looked up to see the Engineer's face on the other side of the Paladin's punch-out. He beckoned for Osyen to come to him.

'Go out the hole the Paladin made.' Osyen had been facetious. Thom had meant literally.

It wasn't a large space, but Osyen was able to slip around the Paladin's enormous frame and get to the crack in the wall. He pulled himself up to the hole and Lars grabbed him with both hands, yanking him through.

He didn't dare look back. "What did you do?!" Osyen shouted.

"In short? Blinded him," Lars explained, his voice muddy and distant. "But it won't last."

They stumbled and staggered up to the simple door and its brass knob. Osyen had exactly no time for this and just threw a kick at the doorknob. It didn't budge and, based on the screaming pain, he might've just thrown out his knee. "Gah! Sonnuva..."

Lars gripped the handle and waited. But nothing. He looked backward, expectant. "Come on, you stupid machine! Open up!"

No reaction at all. If they couldn't get this door open...

Click.

"Go!" Osyen shouted, throwing his shoulder into the door. It popped open, and both men stumbled out into—

A nightmare. The robotic clerk sat, pleasant and patient, at his desk like everything was fine.

But the room was in tatters. Several seats had been ripped up and were now embedded in the ceiling, stapling a guard up there where he could ooze his fluids down to the floor. Another guard's various sundry parts were scattered around the room. Carbon scarring and bullet holes peppered almost everything where they'd been tossed by the deflector shield. And a carve-out in one wall where the Paladin had simply walked through on the shortest route to Osyen.

The clerk looked up, and the milky white eyes refused to focus. "Why hello again! More security forces are already en route. Can I provide any further help?"

"No!" Lars shouted at the machine. "Cancel the alert and send the troops home. They'll only get killed."

The clerk cocked its head. "But we must protect the charge."

Lars pointed at the bruised, sweating, bloody Osyen over his shoulder. "I have protection. Protect yourself!"

The clerk stiffened, sitting up straight, its eyes rolling back into its head. And the voice that came out was not its own. "Where...is the girl?"

That was it. The AI that once ran the building was crushed, over-written, dominated.

Osyen drew the last of his strength. "You'll never find her. I promise you that."

Silence, like the robot considered that answer. But then he heard the clerk's voice say something. "Please—"

And it suddenly slumped, all lights out, draped over its desk. Dark and gone.

Lars pulled on Osyen's jacket. "We need to go. Now."

They jogged out the front door, through the asymmetric entry room, and out onto the street. The cold hit Osyen's face like a gift, but the impressionistic painting of red on alabaster snow was less welcome. Redhead and Smiley were nowhere to be found, but Osyen assumed they were just not in a state to be identified amongst the sanguine mulch.

Osyen's cab was still there, but unfortunately, so was the electromagnetic lock. Osyen stomped over to it and tried to dig his fingers under the plate. "Can you get this loose?"

Lars threw his hands in the air. "What kind of kidnapper are you?"

"It's not really my day job," Osyen said, straining at the device.

The hum of a cruiser and Osyen looked up to see another vehicle approaching. Had the Godfather's reinforcements arrived with all of their military-grade pain?

Nope. It was a rusted-out taxi cab with Thom at the wheel.

"What happened to you staying out of it?" Osyen asked.

"I had a feeling you'd need a ride," Thom said, glancing over at Lars. "You can wait for the Paladin, or you can get in."

Lars didn't need to weigh his options. He tried to run.

"Oh, for the love of—" Osyen took off after him and easily tackled the Engineer to the ground, tumbling into the snowdrifts. "I told you...I need you *alive*."

"You can't escape them," Lars babbled. "You will die, and you will die tired."

"Joke's on you, I'm always tired." Osyen dragged the Engineer back to the cab and tossed him into the back.

And when he looked up, there the Paladin stood in the doorway, silhouetted by the crumbling building interior. But he made no advance, grabbed no weapon. The light from inside painted a black shade across the nightly snowfall, a rigid statuesque guardian.

His yellow eyes locked on to Thom. Focused, drilling, enthralled.

And Thom wasn't much better. He looked at the Paladin like it was hacking his brain, drawing shallow breaths, eyes fluttering, and lips parted.

Osyen gingerly slipped into the passenger seat, leaning over. "Thom? Maybe get us the *Hell* out of here?"

"Yeah." Thom muttered, blinking. And he pushed his foot down on the pedal.

The car sped away into the sky, leaving the collapsing villa in their rear view. And the Paladin did not chase them.

CHAPTER
SIXTEEN
TYCHO

"I'M afraid I don't follow," Magnus said in a vaguely threatening tone. "How could he already be in Cascade?"

The doctors were as befuddled, but adrenal functions had engaged, and they were sweating clean through their linen coats. "The heuristic analysis is-isn't an exact science. And there was always going to be a half-life—"

"Yes," Magnus scolded, "and a brief one, but not *three weeks!*"

Regular assessment and re-tooling were necessary delays. Given the beneficiary of a second Paladin, they could recall one for maintenance while the other continued the hunt. But Tycho always felt...itchy laid up in his pod. Automatic maintenance hands scuttled about his frame, prying open a dozen compartments and splaying him open like a roast chicken, as they confirmed connections and uploaded software patches.

Tycho tried to focus on the violet eyes in his memory. So comforting, a rich color full of happy sparks of blue, like a sunset over a deep pocket of ocean. A miasmic euphoria of warmth.

// Data corruption detected in partition HJ-291. Quarantining.

Grasping that image was like trying to remember a half-forgotten dream behind gossamer sheets that billowed in a warm wind. They came in and out of focus, intangible.

But now he could see a fresh set of eyes. A young man, standing in the snowstorm, clothes tattered by the gale—as he did back in the pub. Slight of build, narrow shoulders, but something...raw about him, something familiar, wonderful, but also...

Nothing?

// Corruption Detected in Primary Partition. Quarantining, Verifying Integrity of Cached Memory.

"Is there any way to slow or reset the Cascade?" Magnus asked, knowing full well it was a foolish question.

"The AI and pilot are too intertwined," the doctor tried to explain. "Cycling the computer will kill the man. In truth, the man is the only thing keeping the computer stable."

Magnus settled up in front of Tycho's pod, studying. And snarling with his sharpened teeth.

"Is there any such pattern coming from the second unit?"

"No, sir. The variance seems isolated here."

"It would be my luck to receive two Paladins, and one of them *defective*." Magnus sighed, and Tycho could hear the Consort's leather gloves squeaking as they rubbed against his pallid skin. "Your professional assessment? Can this unit continue to serve?"

"Oh, yes," the doctors assured him. "He's still well above benchmarks. I'd estimate we have another two weeks before full Cascade sets in."

"Then run the diagnostics again and make all necessary repairs. Until such time, he is to remain under lock and key." Even with his eyes laying on a table two feet away, Tycho could tell that Magnus had stepped up to him, staring at the exposed components. The royal servant was himself computing the available data and processing the risks. "You're in luck, Tycho. You may see the Pilgrim sooner than we thought. But patience is needed now...the quarry will not escape."

// Operational Necessity Adjusted. Entering Standby Mode.

But every moment he waited, the further he strayed from the Path...

// Corruption Detected. Quarantining Fragmented Drive.

Understood, Tycho thought. The Sojourn awaits only the Faithful. And he'll have to wait as well.

SEVENTEEN
ZATIA

HE DIDN'T LOOK like much: she'd seen more impressive men working in salt mines and more intelligent folk that sat behind retail counters. This man, all crooked back and firm scowls, just looked like a village elder who disapproved of youngsters within a fixed radius of his house.

Zatia felt her lower lip twitch, and she bent it into a snarl. Lars gave her an assessing look, his eyes lingering on her radioactive hair-cut. His head jerked with a dismissive huff, tracking back across the group to find someone more interesting.

Ten minutes, some utensils and some privacy, she'd fix that atti-tude of his right quick.

They had him trussed up in the galley, the entire crew circled up around him. All except Osyen, who was busy getting his ribs tended to and his borrowed face taken off. Thom had insisted they show themselves to the captive as a sign of trust. It's not as though the Godfather wouldn't find out who had stolen his prized possession, after all.

No, that ship had set sail. Now, all they could try for was cooper-ation from their guest.

Thom, the wee baby, was trying to command grandpa's attention with slow, deliberate language and eye contact. "I think you have a firm grasp of the situation my friends and I have found ourselves in."

"Yes," Lars mused, eyes panning over the crew, "and you've ensnared me in your situation as well."

"Do as we ask, and we can return you to the Godfather—or any friendly port you like."

"No."

Milardi cocked his head, glancing at Zatia with a jerk of his thumb, as if the Engineer couldn't see the pejorative gesture. This *fra tow skel* thinks he can dictate terms!

Lars shook his head. "You removed me from the one safe haven I had, and you did it in a selfish attempt to prolong your miserable existence."

"Your existence looked pretty miserable from where I was standing." The crew split apart to allow Osyen to stomp into the room. The captain struggled to heave his feet over the door frame. "Who you hidin' from?"

Lars looked up, like he'd finally woke from whatever stupor held him. "Everyone, it seems."

Zatia ground her teeth. Guy didn't want to talk to half a dozen armed thugs but would talk to the one person he deemed important enough. Osyen wasn't all that. But men like Lars enforced hierarchies to make themselves feel that much more special.

Everyone felt the same when they were bleeding on the floor, Zatia thought.

"What did you do to the Empire?" Osyen asked, guessing the answer.

"It's what I did *for* them."

"Our ship AI has slipped into Cascade," Thom said. "We need you to pull them out of it."

Lars shrugged. "Cycle it. Or are you too attached to your precious navigational charts?"

Adelaide couldn't resist throwing a biting glance at Osyen in agreement with the Engineer. But Osyen didn't blink. "Thought you were good at your job? Your answer is turn it off and scrape the hard drives?"

"Simple answers for simple problems."

"You don't relish a challenge?"

"It's not a matter of challenge, but of physics," Lars said. "Quantum computers of sufficient complexity have computational drift. There isn't some treatment reserved only for special elite folk. Your computer will, Naval computers will. AI degrades over time as it grows more sophisticated. They become unstable, even dangerous. That's a 'year one of heuristics' truth. The only thing one can do is flash the system back to its initial conditions—short of providing uncorrupted space for the AI to grow into. The larger the space, the longer you have."

Osyen took a sharp breath. That was it. The death knell. Lily was dying and there was nothing anybody could do about it.

Made sense, Zatia thought. Capital ships, like an Eisenclad, had to be out in space for years at a time. The AI guiding those floating cities had to be long lasting. So something like the *Aurum* and Lily...

"Well, then." Zatia pulled a knife from her boot. "We don't really need him, do we?"

She was expecting Osyen to jump down her throat, scold her. But it didn't come. So she shrugged and moved on Lars. He tensed up, that lovely tendon in his neck revealing itself to be cut like a bowstring.

Which is when Roche spoke from his corner. "A heuristics specialist... hiding out from the Empire?"

"Is that not why you wanted me?"

"We wanted a doctor for Lily," Roche said with a squint. "The fugitive element is new information."

"Think there's a bounty on him?" Milardi asked, only half-kidding. "Just because they want us dead doesn't mean they wouldn't pay for another 'Most Wanted.'"

Lars's smirk was bittersweet. "You can work for the Glory of the

Empire by your own choice or by theirs. I was offered a third option by a...charismatic man."

"The Godfather." Adelaide said the name like it was a curse. "Lavish comforts, anonymity, security. So long as you deliver what he asks on time and up to spec?"

Lars sneered at her, a knowing glance. "You're personally familiar, I take it?"

"Not all that different from Imperial interest, you ask me," Milardi quipped.

"The projects were far more amenable." Lars's eyes finally fixed on the quiet Rashida, peeling apart her many layers and finding her juicy guilt in a matter of seconds. "What did you do to deserve such specific hatred?"

Zatia took another pointed step, raising the clip-point knife tip for emphasis. "Ask another question like that, you'll be drinking your meals for the rest of your life."

Osyen stepped in front of Zatia, backing her off. She could've planted the knife in his back right there just for the interruption. But he had no focus on her. "What do you know about the Paladins?"

Lars grinned, vile and lascivious. "Everything. I used to make them."

Zatia practically heard the jaws hit the floor. Curiously, Thom just stared into the man, like he was piecing together an enormous puzzle. It was like he hadn't heard that shoe drop.

"So we have *you* to thank for our lovely paramours," Milardi quipped. "I'll save you a seat at the sweetheart table."

Rashida spoke, her voice soft but firm. "Answer the man's question: what do you know about the Paladins?"

Lars almost laughed. "Or what?"

Rashida's eyes narrowed. "Or the pink one will remove your ability to answer."

Zatia's eyes flashed and her head cranked around. Where was she keeping *that* all this time? It made Zatia's scalp tingle and put a bounce in her step.

Lars inspected Zatia, her slight frame. And the curve of the blade in her hand. He sighed, wistful. "The more things change..."

"Have you made your selection?" Rashida asked.

He gave a diplomatic nod of his head. "Settle yourself, my lady. The line of inquiry is broad, but I have no respect for Imperial confidentiality. Yes, I worked on the Paladin program. They recruited anyone of sufficient talent at artificial intelligence or cybernetics, often fresh from our respective programs. Thousands of us. Many were excited to dive into such innovative work. Lesser men were working on Oskies and amputees. We got to work on..." The next words had a bit of sour tinge to them. "The very best."

Lars paused, jaw slack and a light in his eyes, mired in memory of the good old days. But with a single breath, he snapped from naïve young talent back to the embittered present. "Do you know what it's like to kill a boy, some as young as fourteen? And they laid on that table of their own volition, fully aware of the risks. We removed so much of them to accommodate the machine. Do you know what that does to the surgeon? The engineer? The scientist? When pressed by faith to do something again and again—something you know will almost certainly kill—something you know is wrong? And to resist is to court your own end? Take part in a willing inquisition inflicted on innocent children whose only crimes were loyalty? Yes, I took the Godfather's offer gladly."

"You...worked on the Paladins?" Thom asked.

"Well, I worked on their AI companions, to be precise. Generation C17 dash Bravo through Gamma," Lars said with a salty mixture of pride and regret. "Though I expect they've iterated up to a C19 by now."

"Then you know what they can do."

Lars sat up, like he was telling a ghost story. "Compact deflector shields capable of withstanding twenty-thousand-foot pounds of force per second. Synthetic ceramics replaced the skin and absorbed further kinetic impact. Newer models ablate heat from energy weapons into an onboard heat sink. A miniaturized fusion reactor generates enough power to operate their chassis for over a year." He tapped his forehead with two fingers. "That circlet on their heads is a band of sensors, capable of grabbing the *entire* electromagnetic spectrum in three hundred and sixty degrees."

Roche's expression said he knew what tonight's nightmares were. "That would be an immense amount of data. The human mind isn't capable of interpreting that much information."

"No, it's not." Lars was pleased to see another working brain in the room. And he smiled, full of self-congratulatory ego. "But my artificial intelligences can. Even in pitch darkness, they have eyes in the back of their head. Wireless hacking, data filtration, power management, threat assessment. The AI is the Paladin's true weapon, what makes them the potentate they are. State-of-the-art heuristic systems are loaded into the user's wetware. The human mind itself dedicates writable space to the AI, which stabilizes the rather dramatic quantum drift...for a time."

"They're walking capital ships," Milardi said, aghast, "that go insane if you wait long enough."

"And then they leave no survivors," Lars assured.

Thom folded his arms across his chest. "All that data pumping through them must be a lot to filter...that's how you saved Oz. You overwhelmed the system with too much, blinded it. Thermal, radio, optical spike. And despite that, all you could do was run."

Lars pursed his lips, looking about like a preening bird. "I don't know what you mean."

Piece of trash. He was so trapped, so convinced he was dead, he was going to go out with his head held high. Zatia was looking forward to beating that particular instinct out of him.

She wanted to spit in his face, pop her lips, or click her tongue...

Her hand felt like it was vibrating, though she was very sure it hung still at her side. Suppressing these urges was growing harder and harder. And she was less interested in burying them the longer she stared at this ragged old goblin's face.

Lars looked at her again, and it felt like soaking in acid. He could see right through her. Was she ticcing right now?

All the thinking and questions made her stomp her foot on the galley floor. And Lars smiled, enjoying her discomfort and frustration.

"What happens when those AIs do Cascade?" Adelaide asked. "I think I'd have read about a bunch of crazy unstoppable killing machines stomping through Imperial space." If Zatia didn't know better, that was an edge of hope in her voice.

"All quantum computer systems eventually Cascade. In this case, taking their end user with them...but no Paladin fails," Lars affirmed with a pointed look at Rashida. "They complete their task. And then wander into dark space, beyond the scope of our galaxy. That, you could say, is the appeal to the young applicants. From the moment they lay on that table, they see the face of God."

And Adelaide deflated again. She stepped up to Osyen's shoulder. "Can I speak to you in private?"

"When we're done."

"I need to talk to you *now*."

"We're kind of in the middle of something," Osyen said, motioning to the bound-up captive.

"I'm sorry, but it needs to be said. And I'm tired of dancing around your fragile sensibilities."

Milardi raised a hand in the air. "Oy, Addy, back it down a notch—"

Wrong move, because Adelaide snapped back like a provoked pit viper. "*Do not* call me Addy."

"Everybody stop." Rashida stepped forward. "She's right. It's time. You all took incredible risks to do this, and I'm touched. But I've run from Magnus long enough. I'll take a shuttle, and head into Farragut." Rashida moved for the door.

Adelaide got in her way. "Lily is still dying, so you killing yourself doesn't save anybody."

"Lily is *not dying*!" Osyen insisted.

"Indoor voices!" Milardi pleaded with them.

Osyen snapped at him now. "Get onboard, Milardi, or out of my way!"

Fed up with being ignored, Milardi popped out of his seat and walked over to the kitchen cabinets, beginning the assembly of a sandwich. Roche backed himself into a corner, eyes glassy and unfocused. Overwhelmed by the noise.

Zatia glanced at Lars. The old man had a wry turn to his lip. "You enjoying this?" she asked.

"I may be dead in two minutes or in two years. I take entertainments where they come."

Osyen straightened up. "Lily just needs a doctor—"

"We got them a doctor," Adelaide pointed out. "He said what he said. Even if you donated half of your tiny brain, you'd only buy them time. They are Cascading. There's no negotiating that point."

"So we get them another doctor—"

And Adelaide snapped like a gunshot. "It is *over*, Oz! We tried! Now do what you have to do! Act like you give a *fuck* about anybody else on this ship!"

And Osyen matched her, roaring with every bit of breath in his chest. "I will *not* give them what they want!"

Something in that rage...mellowed her. Adelaide's eyes softened and her stance slackened. And the room drew blessed silence. She took a soft breath, a sympathetic grumble. "Well, we don't always get what we want, Oz."

Zatia bit her lip and looked away. Adelaide had lost her husband to the Godfather, forced to flee and live out the remainder of her days in isolation and distance. And because of all this, she might have lost her one shot at seeing her husband's remains ever again.

The only chance they'd had was in cajoling the Godfather into a moment of congratulatory kindness. And with the last week's worth of chaos, they had ensured that would never happen.

Give up Rashida and they might buy themselves time. Give up Lily and they might escape their assassins.

What about a charismatic third option?

"You put them together? The Paladins?" Zatia asked Lars, sheathing her knife. "You worked—you assembled them? Means you know how to take them apart."

Lars raised an eyebrow. "Some things are built to never be opened again."

"It's a machine," Zatia insisted. "Means there're screws, welds, cracks. Nothing's invincible."

Lars pursed his lips, considering. "A Paladin unit *is* infantry. Physics will always have its day."

"I mean, if you have a ship-mounted gauss cannon I don't know about, Zee," Milardi said through a mouthful of sandwich, "first of all: jealous."

"But they *can* be killed," Zatia pointed out. "Why else would you keep updating the specs?"

Thom perked up, glancing at Zatia with ferocity. He saw where she was going with this. "Nobody's ever killed a Paladin..."

"Exactly," Adelaide said, confused. "And we're chewing up valuable air because...?"

"But nobody's ever had what we have," Thom noted, glancing at Lars. "We have one of the *designers*. We have build specs, capabilities, design flaws, power ratios..."

"I'm lost," Osyen said, gears whirring inside of his little head, "and more than a little angry. How does this help Lily?"

"If we can deal with the Imperial threat," Thom explained, "we can bring the Godfather the trophy of a century, demonstrate how valuable we'd be as allies. Imperials can't claim we violated any authority without acknowledging the Paladins, so...they just have to let it slide. And the Godfather himself might just have the power to get Lily sorted."

Even Lars pursed his lips at that plan. "Outside of the extraordinary risks, that's a compelling sales pitch, Mister..."

"Thom Hugh. What do you say, Mr. Hedlop? Want to help us slay an Imperial dragon?"

Lars stiffened. "The Empire fed me, clothed me, and tasked me with the impossible. I failed almost every time for nearly twenty years. From hundreds of boys that climbed on my table, there were as many as four who climbed off. And my masters were *pleased*, all while my attendants filled mass graves with unnamed children." He drew a breath like the air was full of poison, hoping it might quiet his pain. And when nothing happened, he shrugged. "What's one more?"

CHAPTER
EIGHTEEN
RASHIDA

SHE'D GROWN sick of the way everyone looked at her these past few days. It was like the sight of her shocked them, turned their stomachs. They'd pause their activities when she entered the room, their lives hitching into a momentary tableau while walking past her in a hallway.

And to think she'd just gotten to feel at home here.

She'd made one attempt at climbing into the shuttles, but it rejected her passcode with a glaring red light. With Lily offline, that meant Osyen or some other crew member had gone to both shuttles and scrambled their access. She could likely sit there and try to crack whatever simplistic cipher they'd used, but she'd almost certainly be caught by some discerning eye.

Whether they tried to stop her was another matter.

She could retire to her cabin and read another fantasy adventure, pull some nostalgic joy from her library to soothe the static noise building in her mind. Most fiction she'd read followed some normal girl and the elusive 'specialness' of her that everyone else seemed to see. Rashida could think of little more torturous than to be considered special when you were not.

Rashida used to prefer herself a good yarn of a monster in the woods. Now, it had lost some of its spice.

So she instead wandered the ship to see if there was something she could help with. A willing third hand was usually a welcome sight, even if she had no expertise to offer.

Milardi stood guard in the galley doorway, hands folded across his front like a grungy butler at some fine establishment with sticky floors that thought itself elite because it also served wine. That meant their new guest was still being held within. Made sense: the *Aurum* didn't exactly have a brig to toss stowaways and captives into. The next closest thing might be an airlock.

The winsome fellow's look faltered as she approached, but he quickly recovered, flashing a trademark flirty smile. "If you can't sleep, I can distract."

"Have a card trick for me?"

"A trick, yes," Milardi said, a devious look in his eye. "And I'm sure I could get playing cards involved."

"I'm afraid you'd find that a lonely activity." Rashida pointed at the closed door. "I had hoped to get myself a lemon meringue from the Replicator."

He looked her in the eye, all games put aside. And he cranked the door open for her. His words were sly in humor but full of honest empathy. "Sometimes the best care is a little indulgence."

"You would know, wouldn't you?" she said, breezing past him and watching his stance slump, listening to the sharp hiss as he drew in a lungful of her lingering perfume. He coughed to cover his weakness, but the way his eyes shot open could not be masked.

She might have charmed them on the last look, but their first look was the honest one, the organic one. How they saw her when she came into view was the reflex.

She missed how they all used to light up.

Roche sat close to the bound-up Lars, tapping out detailed notes. Osyen lead the inquiry, a looming dominance from over behind the Engineer. Adelaide lurked in the corner, draped over two chairs as she thumbed through something on her Entiglas, only half paying attention.

The door closed behind her with a clack, causing everyone's eyes to shoot up. And there was that look again. Roche's eyes drooped, going for a careful investigation of the floor tiles, while Osyen's lingered a hair too long with ferocity and spite. Adelaide, in stark contrast, swelled with a mother's disappointed sigh before returning to her study.

Nobody said a word. They didn't want her here. They didn't want her anywhere. They wouldn't be in this mess if not for her.

So Rashida strode over to the Replicator. What was the key command for the meringue? Something alphanumeric, two letters, then 829...

Lily would know.

Hell with it. She'll just get a bran muffin. Glass of water. The Maestro was onto something.

"Do you need a menu?" Osyen called over.

Rashida glared at him, locking eyes with him as she felt out the key commands. "You looked good with the blue hair. You should've kept it."

Osyen's jaw twitched, no rebuttal to that. And he resumed growling at the back of Lars's head.

Rashida turned back to her meal. The Replicator's work was almost done. A bright light laid out the molecules line by cosmic line, orienting them as the saved data recalled. The same technology that allowed human beings to survive a Jump, also meant they could save into memory all kinds of comparably simple materials. They were all the same muffin.

Rashida recalled a question a young boy had asked in Seminary: if the muffin is always the same muffin, would two people stored by a Jump drive be the same person if two were to be reconstructed on the other side? Provided space and materials, could you not simply 'print' an ideal person over and over again? Of course not, the teacher had said, there being no soul to put into the second body. Bodies require life to live.

So what is that life, that fuel? The boy had asked. An astute question, if a tad existential for Rashida's taste.

They had escorted the boy out of the room. Authority never did like questions it couldn't answer. Come to think of it, she'd never seen the boy again. She had always assumed they had ejected him from the program, but knowing what she knew now...

It didn't fit into the dogma and so it had been outlawed, hardwired into Navigation AIs—they could not harm a person through defamation of their reconstruction, or by sanctioned replication of their image. So the point was moot: there would only ever be one 'you.'

But there could be so many muffins. The light winked out, and the finished muffin steamed a picturesque single cloud off its surface, like it was fresh from an oven. The glass of water was far easier to get, simply filtering out moisture from the air, chilling it, and pouring it into a glass.

A chilling question grabbed Rashida's attention. "So they can imitate a voice over the radio?" Osyen asked the engineer.

"Conceptually," Lars conceded. "They would require a decent sample of the target voice in order to composite anything that would resemble natural cadence or tone. After that, it's simply mathematics. How do you think your ship navigator developed its personality?"

"And the Paladins can draw from any manner of sources," Roche pointed out. "They're into security systems planet-wide. They have recordings from the harbormaster, the pub, the tramway..."

"So more than a blackout, we also can't trust what we hear on the radio?" Osyen asked.

"They turn your greatest strengths into liabilities." There was that pride again, rippling off of Lars's voice as he laid his head backwards over the chair. He caught Rashida watching him and clicked his tongue. "A good weapon makes certain that your shield is a detriment."

Rashida sneered right back at him. She might be the reason they were all in this mess, but she'd also seen many people with that look in their eye. He had no interest in helping but had no reason not to. What he relished was impressing himself upon his space, feeling relevant, having gravity. Tormenting his fellows was just another way to shout at the wind and feel heard. He was insignificant and refused to believe it, so he hurt others until he felt something.

So she crammed the bran muffin into the glass of water, pounding it down with her fingers. Lars looked at the glass and back to her, his eyes flitting about for explanation—in time for her to throw the glass back and pour the bread torpedo down her throat.

It felt like swallowing a fist. But she was not about to gag in front of this loathsome cretin.

But it was Osyen she got to. "*Fra tow ni laska*, woman. I could've given you tableware!"

"This was faster."

"That's hard to deny," Lars murmured, somewhere between frightened and confused.

Roche finally lost the battle suppressing his giggle and let out a little snort.

"Children?" Adelaide enunciated from her corner, projecting her voice to command attention. "You have work you should be doing."

"Yes, right." Osyen clapped his hands together and squinted at Lars. "Back to the data mines with us. So many specs, so little time."

"What about that plasma cannon?" Roche asked. "How does he draw enough energy without burning his arm off?"

"I'd have to consider the specific subject," Lars said, eyebrows up in thought, "but my explanation is going to frustrate you."

"Magnets?" Osyen asked.

And Lars nodded. "Plasma is simply ionized gases. Meaning that it has a strong electrical charge, which can be repelled by a sufficient electromagnet. It follows that a chamber can—theoretically—be lined with enough powerful magnets to contain the material safely."

Roche scribbled something. "Another magnet might disrupt the bolt?"

Lars dragged his inquisitive stare onto the jockey. "You have a way to test that hypothesis?"

"I do not. But I know a lunatic."

"Aren't those just excellent to have?"

Rashida strode over to Adelaide, eyes tracking on the boys as they resumed their interrogation. But Adelaide raised a hand. "That's close enough, darling."

Oh. So that's how far she'd fallen. Rashida froze to the spot and withered a bit.

What could she even say to her? Rashida's past had climbed out of the shadows to deny Adelaide her one shot at reunion with her husband. Now they were frantically considering how to kill a demon.

This display must've been suitably pathetic, because Adelaide rolled her eyes. "A firm boundary doesn't mean 'I hate you'. It means I want to be left alone."

"Forgive me," Rashida said, hands cupped one over the other as though she bore a gentle fruit that might be squashed by careless grip. "I just wanted to see if there was anything I could do."

Adelaide scoffed. "To help? We've got plenty of help on hand."

"It's just that...it's my fault that—"

"Don't do that." Adelaide cut her off. "Don't do that to yourself."

She hadn't been scolded like that since she left the Core. And Rashida found that all of her instincts, programmed by parents and teachers and tutors and fellows, were all still very much intact. A tone of voice and Rashida's back stiffened, her hands folded across her front, toes together, head bowed slightly.

She somehow didn't yell, didn't raise her voice, spit or snarl or bite. She just laid out the facts. "You know, you really screwed us, Rashida. You thought yourself simultaneously high and mighty, untouchable—and in the same breath, you were too small and unimportant to be noticed. Can't be both at the same time. We're all somebody and we're going to be noticed by someone."

Adelaide retreated back into her Entiglas. It wasn't difficult from this range to see what she was so invested in. Still-life captures of a slender gentleman with a shock of pure white hair. His eyes were deep set and small, which only seemed to double the size of his smile. His skin had wrinkled severely in old age, laugh lines that carved up his face with a history of joy.

"Is that Nathaniel?" Rashida asked.

Adelaide seethed, but she spoke. "We were operating out of Londinium when Anze called him up. Jobs were small at first, legitimate work. We needed the money and his cash cleared, so we took that job and then the next. Before we knew it, we were hot-wiring stolen vehicles and when Nathaniel put his foot down, Anze shot him twice in the chest. They burnt his body and mounted him on the wall of the parlor." Her voice shrank down into her throat. "Didn't even give him a warning."

Rashida lowered her head. "I'm sorry."

"Don't do that."

Had she missed a step somewhere? Every rule of decorum told Rashida to accept responsibility for her part. She could only control her role in events, and she had made mistakes. "Adelaide—"

"I'm not done. I'll tell you when you can talk." Adelaide drew on her cigarette like she was dousing a fire before it could grow beyond control. "That's twice you've apologized, and I don't even know for what. We were *this* close to getting him home. But if you think I blame you, you are outside of your mind. Your proximity to my anger doesn't make you responsible for it. Anze Orchikov killed my husband in front of me and doesn't even remember my face. Your little steward? He brought in the *zoldat* and ruined months of planning. But you? You are not important enough to this story. What have you actually *done* that you would need to apologize for? So what if we knew the Paladins would eventually come? What would have changed? You think Osyen would've marooned you somewhere, with his bleeding heart?"

"Osyen thinks—"

"Darling, I've known Osyen for three long years, and that boy doesn't think about much of anything at all." Adelaide tapped her gut with two fingers. "He thinks with this. And there's not a whole lotta blood running to it."

Osyen perked up. "I heard my name?"

And that's when Adelaide properly shouted. "Interrogate. The bad man."

"O-kay."

A smile broke across Rashida's face, but her hands were shaking. Maybe if she clenched them tight and close nobody would notice?

Adelaide shook her head, scanning right through it all. "You think nobody's ever stood where you're standin'? Don't beat yourself up over this. Because nobody's going to forgive you, least of all yourself. Apologies don't mean squat, and forgiveness is more than words. Don't wait for it to feel better. Find the problem, do your best to fix it. You'll make mistakes, you'll break things. Curse, drink, take a nap—then try to fix it. You keep doing that, you won't find any problem from me."

There was a kernel of something in that speech, something truer than Adelaide had maybe intended. And Rashida's brain seized on it, and the words just fell out of her mouth. "You blame yourself?"

And that's when Adelaide's voice ran cold. "Go back to your room. We'll call if we need you."

What else was she to do? Rashida did as she was told.

CHAPTER
NINETEEN
THOM

HE'D FOUND the perfect place: a depot on the outskirts of Farragut. It'd be sheltered for a time, and workers would have retreated to warm themselves by the geothermal vents ahead of the ice storms. Exterior temperatures would drop to almost a hundred below at the peak of the storm. The Godfather's men would be long gone, ripe for the taking.

Of course, Thom didn't want to steal anything from the warehouse, and whatever he borrowed wouldn't leave the building. Though he doubted the mobster would draw that same distinction.

But with the building abandoned, it would vanish into the cold shroud of the oncoming storm, invisible to thermal vision. That is until Thom activated the building's heaters. That spike would be picked up by satellites like a flare at night.

During a storm like this, not even the Godfather's goons would poke their heads out to inspect that. But a Paladin...if they were lucky, at least one would come out to investigate the supposedly abandoned hovel, where he'd find some carefully laid evidence, such as a parked shuttle. And he'd come storming in for his Imperial prize.

Which is when they'd spring the trap.

But Thom had to be sure the building—and its contents—would

suit their needs. And Osyen had locked down the shuttles to prevent certain noble parties from wandering off like sacrificial lambs. So he went looking for Osyen to clear the lockdown.

Nobody had seen him for the last few hours. Adelaide and Roche had last been with him interrogating Lars, but Roche insisted he had retired to his stateroom hours ago. Rash confirmed this. Zatia was voraciously eating—again—but hadn't seen Oz come or go.

Scouring the ship from end to end, Thom finally heard Osyen's voice murmuring down from the Jump Deck. What possible reason could he have to be up there?

"I know you can hear me."

Thom squinted and cocked his head. He might've been calling down the hall to Thom, but the tone of it was wrong, too soft and plaintive. It was more like an appeal, desperate and on the edge of tears. Was he hurt?

Osyen sat on the ground in one corner of the deck, his head craned back to rest against the bulkhead. His Adam's apple jumped as he swallowed back nascent tears and quiet grief. "Maybe you'll read this when you wake up or maybe...maybe we'll laugh about it in the morning. It's kind of pathetic, I know it. But I gotta get it outta my head."

Osyen took a strong sniff of the air, filling his lungs. And his brows furrowed in disappointment. "I used to *know* you were around. And I took that—I took that for granted. I don't...I don't have something to give you right now. Hope the meringue was up to expectation." He smiled up one cheek, half of his face still petrified with shame. "We're kinda pinned here at the moment. I just wish...I wish I coulda taken you somewhere nice. Somewhere we weren't getting shot at all the time. Wouldn't that be a thing?"

Thom leaned on the doorframe. It felt wrong to eavesdrop on this private moment, but it somehow felt worse to interrupt. So he just listened.

Osyen opened his eyes, staring upward at the crusty steel ceiling pocked with neglect and age. "I said I'd take care of you, and I meant it. I just...I might have to break that promise, Lily."

No answer. And Osyen's voice cracked with barely contained tears. "Wake up. Please."

He couldn't make this ask now. Osyen was in no condition to make any decisions. Thom would have to make them for him.

———

It had been child's play for Adelaide to crack the cipher on the shuttle lock, and she bid Thom and Milardi a safe flight to the surface. As safe as flying through the leading edge of a frostbitten maelstrom could be.

"Would ya look at tha'?" Milardi uttered, slipping into his old Colonial affectation. "How tall ya think?"

Thom studied the holographic projection on the bulkhead pretending to be a window. The image stuttered and skipped, vertical tears every so often as the cameras struggled with the cold. Even inside the shuttle, Thom could see his breath condensing in billowing white clouds.

Weasel hadn't lied. This was the kind of storm that wiped out lesser civilizations, let alone a city. A roiling white wall marched across the tundra like an invasion, its leading edge curling in on itself as the system advanced. Flashes of hot lightning lit the storm from within, offering a momentary glimpse into the toothless maw of the great wyrm that now descended to feed. This was a thing larger than mountains and deserving of a name in an ancient tongue now lost to memory.

Once embroiled inside that chaos, they wouldn't make it to the shuttle alive, let alone fly out.

"Hard to believe this thing comes every year," Thom whispered.

"Sometimes twice," Milardi said. "They call it the Big One."

Thom shook his head. "Some people, no respect."

"What, you got a better name for *that*?" Milardi pointed at the cold hurricane.

Off the cuff. "They named him Ingohla, The Jawless One, he who devours and is never sated; he who would lay us all to slumber, even during break of day."

Milardi shivered. "You put way too much mustard on that."

"Yep." He didn't put any effort in. Thom had never even laid eyes on the storm, but those words came to him like he'd spoken them before. Spoken from the heart—or from memory.

"We've got a few hours," Milardi said. "I'll put her down by the depot, and we can commence with the snoopin'."

A rough bang and lurch, and the shuttle came to rest on the ground. The hatch creaked open, filling the shuttle with a blast of snow and the howl of the wind. Even ahead of the storm, it was bitterly cold, and the air stung Thom's face like the hardened leather of a whip.

No environment suit would've saved them here. All there was to do was layer up in leather and furs and blitz for the cover of the depot. It was an expansive structure, with a domed roof to accommodate larger cargo. Several docking slots for flying vehicles and loading docks for ground-based transports ran the perimeter, allowing for any number of vehicles to deposit and retrieve their wares.

Milardi and Thom jogged up to the nearest door, which chimed as they approached. It wanted access to biometrics, but hardly anything sophisticated. Combination of cheap and low importance.

Milardi hopped from foot to foot as he tried to hold every part of him as close to core as possible. He hiked up his coat sleeve and raised his Entiglas, pulling up an old friend's rodent face. The computer program faked the voice to perfection: "It's Weasel. Would ya open up already?"

Happy chirp and chimes. And the door clicked. Milardi cackled, throwing the door open and darting inside.

Part of Thom expected them to be met with angry guns, but nobody was there to greet them. With the lights off, Thom couldn't see exactly how deep the warehouse went, but the way the darkness seemed to eat the reverb of his voice made it feel abyssal. What he could make out were stacks of mismatched crates and gear in rows stretching for what must have been half a mile. Markings in some unknown dialect were painted on the cement floor, denoting where they were in the depot at any given time.

He tried to memorize the swooshes and swipes of red paint, lest he forget where the shuttle was.

"So," Milardi asked, "what exactly are you hoping to find? Plasma cutter? A big heavy crate?"

"I don't know yet," Thom confessed, "but if I was looking for a ship-caliber weapon to take out a single person...I go looking around an industrial yard."

"I feel like we could drop these goons into a steel foundry and they'd just start swimming laps."

This wasn't a factory site anyhow. There wasn't food or water stored here, but metal tools by the hundred—entire crates full of screws and rivets, steel plates and glass. Spent torn clothing lay in disheveled heaps in one corner, ready to be boxed up or burned.

"You know," Milardi started, "you and me could just take up shelter in town. Plenty of hidey holes far away from the shooting."

The very notion made Thom wretch. Osyen had saved Thom from obscurity in the Pan & Pantry; Rashida was one of the first people alive who had ever made him feel valuable. Roche, Zatia, Adelaide, Lily. They didn't just share an oxygen supply with him.

"You have a remarkable ability to detach from trouble," Thom noted.

Milardi shrugged. "Call it a survival instinct."

Thom lifted a tarp to peek at the metal bits underneath. Nothing but spent gears with broken teeth. "Looking over your shoulder is a survival instinct."

"I've heard it all before, Maestro. Not tryin' to advocate mutiny, jus'...I try not to stand in the way of bullets."

What did he think he was pushing for? Or was he just giving an idea oxygen to see if anybody else sang the same tune, only to claim he wasn't serious when nobody else pitched in? "Got any more good advice?"

"It was good 'staying alive' advice," Milardi corrected. "Not real sure myself that it was good advice."

Thom kicked another crate, taking out some of his frustration. Milardi was thinking of fleeing, and Zatia wasn't liable to hang out if they ever got clear of this. Who knew what Adelaide would do the moment they were out of danger? She might just beat the nobility off of Rashida and Osyen would just watch, stepping in only to prevent a murder.

This little cozy home had gotten so loud lately.

"Hey, kid," Milardi said, raising a hand. "What do we think of that?"

Thom jogged over to where Milardi stood, craning his neck back to take in the full wonderment of it.

Milardi had found a priceless gem in a barrel full of sand. An enormous drill, mounted on a piston, probably three meters across at the bit. The jaw of a once great HML-68 Mining drone, now hanging distended from a collection of chains.

They must get used in the geothermal operations, cutting additional sources of heat for the colony. They likely had to ship new parts in frequently for these, as the motors burned out or the teeth broke. But here sat either a retired drill or a brand new one.

Either way. "Yeah...This'll do nicely."

CHAPTER
TWENTY
ROCHE

RIGHT NOW, all Roche could hear was the creaking of the building, the howl of the wind, and the aggressive patter of ice against the corrugated steel walls. It sounded like a thousand fingernails tapping against glass, searching for the crack. It was enough to blend into a kind of white noise, but when combined with almost any other sounds...it felt like a blanket wrapped about his head, squeezing tighter and tighter.

He could never sleep like this. But to his luck, he was not the only one with this struggle.

Zatia stood on a loading dock, just barely under shelter from the blistering winds. Licks of snow and curls of white dust whirled about on the ground mere feet in front of her. She hugged herself, rubbing warmth into her arms. Underneath the pink and violet waves of her radiant hair, a white felt had grown in.

No wonder she got such vibrant colors if her natural hair was that shade of platinum metal. Roche couldn't imagine what it would be like trying to die his slate black mop, even if they could gather disparate strands into anything worthy of it.

They'd long since lost sight of Farragut proper, all the buildings lost behind that billowing white, but the ambient orange glow silhouetted some of the taller buildings on the horizon. Flickers of distant lighting gave glimpses of the city, the thunder too far and buried under the storm's other exultations.

But Zatia's tiny frame still stood taller than anything else out there, like a young girl standing on the edge of a dock before raging tide waters.

"Any sign of the mechanical horror?" She didn't respond to him, so he pressed on. "You should come back inside."

"I've got a heater going," she said, nodding to a small device at her feet and the futility of its glowing yellow coils.

"You have an abnormal amount of faith in a three-kilowatt secondhand hotbox."

She shrugged. "Don't need people's faith if you can get the job done. I look cold to you?"

Roche walked up to her side, lowering a hand down to warm near the little coils, roasting fiery gold in the midnight air. It must have been at least twenty below out there, but she wasn't even shivering.

"Lars made any noise?"

Roche almost chuckled. The Engineer had dispensed many creative complaints before being walled up in the *Aurum*'s smuggling compartment but he hadn't made so much as a peep after he was told the risks of the Paladin finding him. A call for help would just as easily summon his doom, so he better pipe down.

He risked a quick wireless link to the *Aurum* to check on the poor bastard, and sure enough, the compartment remained closed and locked.

Zatia gave Roche some side eye as he connected back to the ship. "Thought I'd see you nuzzled into Milardi's side for warmth?"

"His delights are many," Roche admitted, closing the connection with a blink. "But they're fleeting. And a man of his build doesn't exactly put off much heat."

Zatia chuckled at that. "Yeah, his chief exports would be sharp elbows and performance anxiety."

Roche looked aside. No, Milardi could probably use a bit more anxiety to go along with all his braggadocio and charm. "It's too loud in there."

She nodded, looking out on the whipping currents of snow. "Not like it's any quieter from where I'm standing."

He'd reveled in quiet. The Jump Deck of an active ship had its bells and whistles, but it largely left him to his own devices. People weren't chattering in his ear and nobody argued and glass wasn't breaking and...and it was quiet.

"We can just stand here," Zatia offered, "if that's good for you."

"That'd be nice."

Storms were lovely balls of chaos. There were sequences of repeated patterns, but each occurrence had a mildly different expression. Winds shifted, snows drifted, lightning reached down from a distant heaven to strike the ground with such beautiful vitriol. Sometimes they'd start fires, or simply detonate their target as a million trillion water molecules all snap boiled in under a second.

"Volume was..." Roche started, "Volume was never the problem."

"Too many versus too much?"

He nodded. "Not this. This is just right."

Zatia tapped her foot on the ground, almost impatient. She stared out at the storm with a sigh. "Everything's loud to me right now."

"Buzzing?" Roche asked.

"All the time."

"Want to trade?"

She laughed off that suggestion, but then her face soured. "I hate storms. Not like a phobia or nothin'. Just..."

"Can't punch a storm if it breaks a window or forces a door?" Roche guessed.

Her voice was so quiet, he almost lost it under all the noise. "No, you can't."

Can't kill a force of nature. If the storm comes, it comes, and it stays as long as it likes, and it takes what it wants.

"Storm hit the farm once," Zatia said. "What it didn't blow over, it buried in six inches of water. Whole year's crop, gone in jus' ninety minutes. Hardest winter of my life. Everybody made it through, but Pops…he was different after, y'know? He just couldn't run the field like he used to. So my sisters and I, we started helping with the daily duties. 'Got to pull your weight, got to.'"

"You were a child," Roche muttered.

And her eyes flashed like the silent lightning on the horizon, locking him into her clutch and pulling him in. "I was hungry and there was only one way to eat. So we worked, and we worked. And my Pops, he got sicker and sicker, so we worked more and more. Worked until my hands were bleedin' on the tools. And that's when Marcie got sick…"

He knew where this was going. "And you had to pick up even more weight."

Zatia exhaled, dismayed and shuddering.

The stims. She had started that young. "When did you leave?" Because she didn't end up on the *Aurum* because of her proficiency in agriculture products.

And Zatia's eyes finally let him go, looking back to her stormy view. "When I found out Pops wasn't sick. He was never sick. He'd worked his children to the bone because he thought that's what he was *owed*."

And she showed him just what he was owed, did she? Roche imagined the many ways he knew Zatia could've delivered that news.

But whatever she did, she didn't articulate. She just sighed. "We had one use to him: labor."

Why was this on her mind right now? It wasn't just the storm that had brought this on. Or the absence of her stim package. Her brain was locked on to this unresolved memory.

"What if they catch us by surprise?" she asked, turning fully to face him. "It happened before, at the pub. What if we can't pin it down and somebody gets hurt?"

"Well," Roche mused, "if this doesn't work, we're all dead, so I have to imagine injury to be at least in the top ten percent of possible results."

"Don't...*fra tow mi zu*, plughead," she cursed. "Not today."

Fighting the Paladins was *her* idea. This insane gambit came from her overly developed sense of adrenaline. What could she possibly be so wound up about?

Whatever it was, she didn't say. She just turned back to face the storm, eyes glittering with water, her face kissed with frost. Was it tears, or had her breath condensed to her face, snap freezing into a gloss?

"Lots of people got hurt at the orphanage," Roche offered.

"What, like sprained ankles?"

"Sure" Roche said, nodding. "There was this one. I don't recall his name. But he gashed his leg open on a tree stump, took a terrible fall. Everything about him was twisted afterward, despite the best medicine. And he thought that...he thought he'd never work right again, now that he couldn't climb."

"'And that kid was 'me'?" Zatia mocked.

"No, my..." Roche's smile was bittersweet, looking down at the ball of plugs and cables that replaced his wrist. "I'm not as poetic."

Zatia shrugged it off. "Roche, you're being very sweet. I hate it. Go away."

How does he go about telling her this? How Osyen and Milardi sat over her in the medical bay? Thom fretted in the halls, blamed himself for something he couldn't have controlled? Rashida took to preparing her brushes and dyes, so that the two girls could have a moment's calm when Zatia woke up? How Adelaide went back to work in the engine room rather than lay awake?

Zatia didn't see any of their worry. The glow of the heater cast a long shadow across her face, and she refused to look at him.

"I've never had people care about me. Never had people I care about either. No one in the orphanage looked after one another." Roche turned, bringing his full countenance to bear on her. "You're worth more to these people than what you can do for them. You understand?"

She didn't look at him, eyes taking a tour of that frosty horizon for some sign of an exit to this conversation.

Roche slumped. "Of course. Can't breach the contract now."

"This is—and always has been—a job, Roche," Zatia grunted at him. "I didn't sign the charter for anything other than my cut."

Roche blinked at that. "Then that's all you should expect."

He waddled his way back inside and didn't look back.

CHAPTER
TWENTY-ONE
ADELAIDE

THEY HAD VERY LITTLE WARNING. Every so often, the perimeter teams would pass messages back to the team inside the depot, and the inside crew would bounce something back. It worked both as early warning and as bait. If they didn't receive their requisite response back, then the Paladin was both nearby and alerted to their presence.

Some folk could sleep through that stress, but Roche, Adelaide, and Thom just stared at the clock, counting down the minutes for each check-in. And when the clock turned over, everyone drew in a breath, expectantly waiting Zatia's brush off.

But nothing came.

Roche muttered something to himself. Thom put a foot into Osyen's side, shaking him awake. The captain gurgled something amounting to — "What is it?"

Thom didn't offer an answer, but instead roosted on his crate. The boy looked like a compressed spring, a scrunched down coil of copper held steady by a pin.

Rashida sat up from her improvised nest of bedding and fabric, looking toward the door with nervous anticipation spiced with dread. She trembled, like a helpless bunny rabbit under the fangs of some greater beast. The girl was bait for a trap and had no way to personally defend herself from a threat like this.

Of course, if this didn't work, maybe she could talk it to death. They'd tried everything else.

Adelaide put two fingers to her lips, planting a kiss on them and swiping it in the air, finding it empty and wanting. Nathaniel used to gripe when she smeared oil on his cheek. What might he say if he saw her now?

He'd say, 'Go get 'em, tiger.'

Which is when Zatia came stomping in, slinging the door shut behind her. "Either y'all are asleep, or we have company. Either way, *wake up!*"

Thom leapt to his feet. "Alright. Two by twos, don't lose your buddy. Help out your friends and pull 'em in to the box."

Roche stood up and grabbed Rashida by the hand, pulling her down an alley full of crates. Thom and Osyen scampered off, with Milardi and Zatia setting off in another direction. Soon enough, everyone had vanished into disparate corners of the depot's mysterious rows of stock.

Each of them could run far better than the aging mechanic. And besides, the linewoman actually knew how to operate this console with some fluency.

Adelaide clambered up to the crew cabin of the magnetic crane. It was a rather exposed glass box, but it was tempered and vacuum packed to shield the user for long hours in cold weather. So at least her heat signature wouldn't give her away.

She just had to keep her head and lie low. If the Paladin really was here, she needed the rest of the gang to draw attention. If she sent a radio broadcast, that could be tracked like any other echoing noise right on up to her haven.

Which would cause a swift and ruinous end to the day.

The crew would have to locate the Paladin and then drag him back under that crane and do it all without being killed by the most advanced cybernetic assassin to have ever lived. It wasn't the most complex plan that Thom had ever come up with, but not everything needed seventeen steps.

The waiting was killing her. Her hands shook and her teeth were grinding, and she picked at the dry patch of skin on her chapped lip, peeling it back before tearing it away. She couldn't even smoke a cigarette up here—the smoke would be a dead giveaway. So she just had to...manage.

Somehow.

How did folk get through a day without causing mischief and pain? She had every compulsion to break the glass in front of her.

The console had once been hard-locked with the driver's thumb print and heart palpitations, but all she had to do was loop the power line out of its housing and wrap the copper leads to one another and she'd bypassed the security system. From here, she could make three quick button presses to pull the trigger on the world's simplest gun.

Adelaide had a pretty good view of the depot, or at least every part not shrouded in darkness. And it was that much easier to see the ball of electric plasma, sending wide spotlights of green and yellow streaking up every lane. The light swept from left to right as the ball punched outward. She saw the explosion of mustard yellow fire that crackled into life before she heard the cacophonous thunder.

That was Osyen and Thom's corner. The Paladin had come from the city center, as expected, pinching them off from their shuttle and pressing their backs against the storm.

Nowhere to run.

Sure enough, Thom and Osyen came whipping around the corner, running like Hell itself dogged their heels. And it might as well have, as another shot came whistling out from the corridor they came down.

The ball of green plasma ate through a large crate and whatever complex crone inside. Licks of electricity grabbed on to anything nearby and set it ablaze. With each impact, the ball shed a layer of itself, leaving bits of ionized material behind and slagging any metal, stone, or wood it touched until the electrical flame had given all of itself, splattering against a steel crate.

Something told Thom to grab on to Osyen, and he reached over, snagging Osyen's waistcoat and pulling him to the ground—just as a plasma ball snapped through the space Osyen had once occupied.

And that's when the Paladin came into view, clambering through one of the blazing holes it had carved, arm cannon extended.

"There you are," Adelaide muttered.

Osyen grabbed Thom, pulling the boy on top of him and tumbling behind another row of boxes. The Paladin didn't even slow down, punching another shot through the boxes right in front of Thom's nose. The lad was a few inches away from getting a replacement face. As it stood, the electric arcs of sea-foam green set their remaining cover ablaze.

The Paladin's voice was tectonic, filling the space like a monument to sound. "Where is the girl?"

Adelaide swore she heard something staticky as someone tried to push a powerful radio over the Paladin's jamming. It didn't turn, but it did pause, that circlet on its scalp picking up something new...

Zatia standing bold and broad, her tonfa blades locked in each hand. "Do I fit the bill?"

The Paladin didn't even look over at her. He simply raised his arm and fired. The plasma ball of green death rocketed towards her, and all Zatia did was smile.

The psychopath raised her blades, sweeping them forward and up—slashing through the dense burning plasma sphere and separating it like it was any other fruit.

With the magnetic binding broken, the plasma quickly dissipated into a harmless green haze, sprinkling around her like a dusting of emerald snow. Zatia's shoulder smoldered with some embers catching the cloth of her tunic and some bits of her hair singed...

But she just cut a plasma ball in half.

That got the Paladin's full attention. It broke contact with Thom and Osyen, building into a sprint toward Zatia. It had found a potent enough threat. The pixie girl flashed her teeth and stuck out her tongue like a hissing cat, matching its energy, and she charged right at it.

They all thought they were so clever. Adelaide saw Milardi swooping in from a side angle, wearing some forklift loader arms ready to slap the Paladin into next week.

The Paladin didn't even look over, sensing the trap. It swung its great big gun arm across its frame, striking Milardi hard with the bulk of the barrel, solid enough that Milardi simply vanished backward into a pile of boxes. Getting within melee range of this human tank was a piss poor decision that it had punished Milardi for.

The Paladin took aim again, firing off more shots at Zatia. If one shot didn't kill this little fey, perhaps she'd suffer under a volume of fire.

Adelaide smirked. He was welcome to try that trick all day long.

She had sat with Roche and Zatia, modifying those blades with powerful electromagnets in the cross-guard. What had once been simple and compact hidden blades for the pixie were now competent defensive tools capable of deflecting plasma, lasers, and chunky enough to even survive bullets of a certain mass. They had to lean on the Replicator to broaden the steel, which accommodated the upgrades—but added weight.

Zatia had insisted that wouldn't be a problem.

And stims or not, Zatia was still a ball of scar tissue and muscle fiber with bright hair. The girl swung her blades with renewed confidence, batting aside and dispersing the Paladin's shots as they came in.

For a hot second, Adelaide thought the little girl was going to try to scrap with the Paladin...

Oh, no. She actually was. Don't do that. Did she not see what had just happened to Milardi?

But the girl thought herself special. Zatia went high, kicking off a crate to get altitude and slashed at the Paladin's face. It's fist caught the telegraphed attack easily, squeezing hard down on the edge. If the edge lacerated its hand, the Paladin didn't react.

Quick as a dancer, Zatia twisted up, planting both feet into the underside of the Paladin's gorilla palm and pushed off. She torqued her hand free of the blade's restraints and came tumbling to safety a few feet away, her one remaining blade dragging a line of sparks off the concrete floor.

And she looked back up at that cyborg, hunger in her eyes.

The Paladin dispatched her simply, hurling her own blade straight back at her. Zatia twisted herself to one side, trying to parry, but it wasn't enough. The throw was considerably faster than the plasma shots.

The blade sunk tip first into her shoulder and staked Zatia to a crate. She cried out, almost more in rage than anything else. The unnatural bend to the blade made for an uneven, ragged entry, tearing flesh and ripping an ugly channel that spouted blood like a fountain. And the fact that Zatia now hung from it wasn't doing her shoulder any favors. The blood that stained her tunic betrayed how bad the injury was, quickly dripping down her front and onto the floor like red snow melt off a mountain.

Osyen and Thom were trapped, one shot away from obliteration. Zatia hung helpless, and who knew what happened to Milardi? This plan had gone pear-shaped extremely fast.

She had to do something! But what? Adelaide examined the controls, scouring for anything she could do. Power-line, hydraulics. Something!

The Paladin took one step.

"Looking for me?"

Everyone looked over to Rashida, standing radiant under the warehouse lights. Her skirt hung over one leg dusted with frost, and the tailored pants underneath masked light armor plates on her shins and thighs. Her blouse billowed in some unseen wind along with chords of her wet hair, hanging thick across her forehead and eyes—a battle-maiden of legend.

She tucked her chin, the gravity of what she just did suddenly hitting her. And whatever momentary flash of courage that had buffeted her evaporated into two simple small words: "Oh shit."

The Paladin raised his cannon arm, forgetting every other threat...at her.

She dove to run—and the Paladin adjusted his aim, tracking her through the obscuring crates, gear, and stacked panels. Each shot rained hot shrapnel and threw piles of screws or melted machinery. Rashida had to bob and weave, faltering in her speed and balance so as not to be taken out by incoming balls of electric death or by splattering metal slag.

But she was headed straight for the kill box. Adelaide felt her breath hitch up. Come on, girl. Drag him in. Drag him! She was almost there.

But she was down low, in amongst rows of metal crates. Adelaide was high and could see the Paladin approaching, like a monster in a cornfield, lumbering and plowing on through.

She couldn't help herself. "Rashida, incoming!"

Rashida heard the call and slid to a stop. But what she clearly thought was going to be a bolt of energy crashing through the wall of cargo on her left turned out to be the Paladin itself. It slammed through the barrier, sending metal chunks up in a splintering rain.

She froze, looking up at the goliath. It could shoot her. Crush her. Strike her so hard her organs turned to jelly. Maybe it would pop her skull open between its thumb and forefinger?

It reached for her...

And so Rashida produced a small cartridge, ripping free a cord and tossing it up to the Paladin's head. And she curled away, shielding her face.

The light it cast out pierced every shadow, lit every corner. A thunder clap in the halls of the depot. And the Paladin stumbled, groaning.

It reached out for her, blinded, but oh so close. She looked up in time to see its hand descend. The flashbang had bought her a few seconds, and she'd squandered them in her shock.

But it had bought Milardi the precious moments he needed. Twin steel claw hands, painted hazard yellow, wrapped about its wrist, holding it back. The bloodied gunslinger snagged hold and pulled with everything he and the exo-arms could muster.

The Paladin raised its other arm—and a bloody Zatia slipped between its legs and slammed her broken tonfa blade down the barrel. The glowing green immediately dissipated, and they could hear an ugly crunch, the magnets within pulling and pushing in so many directions that the blade glowed with heat. Whatever electro-magnetic fields were generated to control the plasma did not appreciate a high-strength magnetic metal being jammed into the system. It almost instantly turned the hardened Silksteel weapon into a molten ball of lava inside the Paladin's arm.

The Paladin actually screamed, slinging both arms in anger and spraying the hot yellow metal across the floor. He flung Milardi into the air for the second time.

But a larger hook wrapped about the Paladin's neck, leveraging it backward. Wheels screeched and motors whined as a storage cart tried to haul the Paladin away.

Roche had cable-hooked up to the motorized cart from his wrist and was walking alongside as it tugged on the Paladin's thick throat. The Paladin dropped a leg backward for leverage and sank into a lunge, keeping its body low and hard. Adelaide could hear the cart's gears slipping all the way up in the crane.

When Osyen did the most insane thing she'd ever seen a man do. He charged out of the dark and actually body checked the Paladin. Either the Paladin was harder than he expected, or the Paladin hit him back, because Osyen crumpled to the ground, favoring his shoulder.

But it was enough. The big guy started to slide backward, pulled away from his quarry. Away from salvation. Away from the Pilgrim.

It panicked, flailing and reaching, which only further compromised its leverage. Roche drove the Paladin straight on backward.

Right into range.

And Adelaide threw the switches. Power, safety, and hitch.

Hoisted up into the dark, high enough to build up some proper momentum. Silksteel cable unspooled with a hiss off of the drum as the crane let thirty tons of geothermal drill fall directly on to the Paladin's head, leading with a bit designed to core out permafrost and compressed iron ferrite.

It saw the threat coming, never turning its head as the Paladin raised its one good hand like it meant to catch the ball passed its way.

But as Lars had promised, physics was immutable law and there was only so much strength that could be manufactured. There was a single flash of rainbow colors as the deflector shield tried—and gave up.

The Paladin's giant hand was summarily crushed against its side, pancaking flat all the way down to the shoulder. And the Paladin's feet sank almost a foot deep straight down into the concrete floor from the weight of the impact, sending spiraling cracks out from its position.

The big cybernetic assassin twitched, spasmed...and settled still, buried in the cold floor.

Thom emerged from the shadows, joining the rest as they inspected the kill. He settled down next to a panel, draping himself over it, exhausted.

Milarci looked over at Zatia and slipped out a giggle of relief, exhaling pressure and pain and fear. Then that giggle grew to a laugh. And she joined in, cradling her bloody shoulder as the both of them—

The Paladin turned its head and loosed a baleful roar, shaking the drill hanging on top of it. Everyone leapt back in shock as the Paladin reared.

Everyone except Thom, who almost casually reached down for a switch on a nearby panel and flipped the drill on.

The bit turned and took the Paladin's head off in the first pass, grinding and sinking onto its prey like a feasting animal, chewing the Paladin down into nothingness.

The crew all settled, frozen in their shocked poses as they listened to the abusive end. Thom didn't stop the drill for another five minutes until it had cut right through the floor and into the glacier underneath. When it was finally over...neither blood nor machine remained.

"One down," Thom whispered. "One to go."

PART THREE
UNMARKED GRAVES

"Evidence of things not seen is the phrase commonly associated with faith. But what do we have when historical evidence is overwhelming, when our very human senses provide us with tactile practical evidence of the supernatural, of the wonderful? Do we use it to verify, to enshrine?

Why, we bury it, of course: for the mysticism carries more power than any tangible totem."

PROF. ORDEE, C.H. (2226). *THE ROOTS OF OUR FAITH: THE HISTORICAL REVISIONISM OF THE PILGRIM*

CHAPTER
TWENTY-TWO
TYCHO

THE NOTIFICATION REVERBERATED around the deck as everyone internalized what that message implied. The crew of the *Intrepid* was minimal, really just a handful of deck officers and a complement of marines. They were there to support the Paladins in logistical matters, not conduct operations of their own. And they'd all heard the alarm, each in a quiet denial of its meaning.

The Jump Deck was spacious with some living quarters in the halls behind. But the most focus was on the two sleep pods built specially to accommodate the enormous Paladin chassis. Tycho looked over at the empty pod to his left, door open and charge cables hanging loose.

"'How was He to live in their absence'," one officer quoted the words from the Gnostic Librum. "...*Viator Dul.* Go now to the Road."

A Paladin slain. They go to the Pilgrim now, Tycho thought, to join the Sojourn as promised. Their last act one of perfect service. They had made contact with the enemy and laid down their burdens in that pursuit. He could only hope his end was as glorious. He'd serve with every step, every kill, every breath. And finally, he'd bear witness to those violet eyes—

// Data corruption detected in partition NT-618. Quarantining. Warning: Formatting additional wetware for storage.

Not that. No, the Pilgrim. The Pilgrim's eyes. He'd stand in the glory of the Sojourn, not...

The boy. There had been a young man at the compound, and at the tavern before that. So strange and curious and wonderful and familiar. Tycho consulted every databank, every record: Thomas Hugh, child of Admiral Ulysses Hugh, known confederate of criminals and outlaws.

Nothing special. Nothing worth noting.

And yet, when he laid eyes on the boy, something radiated from him. A power, a presence Tycho hadn't felt since his confirmation.

// Data corruption detected in partition AN-714 & 629 & 211. Quarantining sections. Warning: Additional corruptions detected in core system sectors.

Tycho blinked and swiped his hand over, pulling free all the cable connections to his pod. Who that boy had been or would be was of little consequence. If he found the boy, he'd find the target. And he no longer had assistance in this task.

He stood up, and the thud of his boots drew the attention of half a dozen crew members.

He required deployment instructions. Tycho glanced around the room, and the crew avoided his gaze.

But the little foul man, Magnus, did not hesitate. He moved over to a crewmember's console, leaning over them to study the holographic display of glittering colors. "Where did we lose them?"

"Outside of Farragut...leading edge of the storm. There was a heat signature and a shuttle sighting at a storage depot. He went to investigate."

Magnus sighed, hiding his instinct to curse. "Is it possible that he entered hibernation to survive the cold?"

The officer jabbered a set of guttural noises before getting his mouth to obey. "I mean, the units have...programming to handle adverse weather conditions, but the storm is still two hours out."

Meaning only one thing. This target, this Rashida Izan de Tylmirande and her cohort, had actually slain a Paladin.

Now...this was a target worthy of him.

// Data corruption detected in partition TH-Q11. Quarantining. Warning: Formatting additional wetware to accommodate storage requirements.

His head ached and sweat cut a path through the grime on his cheek, and the fingers on his left hand had gone numb.

They had killed a Paladin.

"What could possibly be in..." Magnus mused out loud, like he was consulting an internal library. And a smile crept up his cheek, revealing those sharpened teeth. "Clever girl."

"Sir?"

Magnus called out to the room, looking over at Tycho. "Find me every other storage depot in Farragut, specifically ones storing industrial-grade equipment. It's the closest thing to heavy ordinance they'll have."

Tycho took a single step. "She'll be there?"

"Not yet," Magnus assured him. "But she'll come."

Wait for her? No. Tycho was told to hunt her, to walk the Path. Not to sit idle.

Magnus sensed the apprehension. "A hunter doesn't always chase his prey. Sometimes he lies in wait where he knows the prey must go. Stalking the waterfront—"

Tycho shook his head. Program principles were very clear on this issue. He was to pursue and destroy.

"They're emboldened," Magnus promised. "They think themselves immortal. They won't take such care a second time. They'll make mistakes. They set a trap for your brother, and we will set one in kind."

"No," Tycho said, a single booming rebuttal. And it set everyone on the deck on edge. He felt the temperature rising, the thud of their hearts suddenly spike in power and pace. And the single trooper that thumbed his safety.

How curious, how swiftly they set to violence. They only trusted what they could control. And that control gave them a sense of security and self.

A Paladin draws his purpose from his life's pursuits.

"You want to avenge your brother?" Magnus asked, daring to step in close to Tycho. Not a sign of trust or companionship, but dominance. He wanted to show he did not fear the goliath, but the metallic sting in the air said otherwise. "You want to kill this girl?"

"Vengeance is not the will of the Pilgrim," Tycho cautioned the little man.

Magnus tilted his head in deference, conceding the point. "The Pilgrim wants this girl dead. And she seeks weapons to resist him. She will find them in these depots."

"Will she be there?"

Magnus hesitated. "We'll be there first. And she will come to us."

That was not a hunt. That was not his directive. He had been told to hunt this girl.

Magnus's lips tightened, uneasy with the absence of answer. "She seeks ways to kill Paladins, and we will remove that from the field—and snare her in the same movement."

This effete, ineffectual dilettante. He thought himself so clever.

Tycho simply blinked, unimpressed. "You are certainly free to do so."

Magnus summoned every ounce of bluster he had in his thin frame. "And I order you to hold with us."

// Mission Parameters consult

// Call engagement procedure: pursuit

// Call engagement trigger: immediate

// Call engagement collateral: total

// Determination—kill on sight, pursue without delay, eliminate all obstacles

//This is the Pilgrim's Will

Tycho closed the command line in the blink of an eye. He looked back down at Magnus. Would this little Consort to a noblewoman, the very same man who ordered Tycho's creation, prove to be an obstacle to the Pilgrim's will?

"I serve the Pilgrim in all ways," Tycho said. "You serve...ambition and station. Your service is conditional."

Magnus drew himself up to his full height. "My *whole life* has been a service."

// Corruption detected. Warning: Corruption detected. Warning—

// Cascade Variance. Cascade Variance.

And Tycho's spear unlatched from his back. And the Regulars all drew their weapons on him. They had never been loyal to the Pilgrim, and they stood in Tycho's way. "To yourself."

Magnus's eyes went wide. And he reached out with both hands, to either side of him, bellowing the order: "Stand down, all of you! Stand down!"

Far too late.

Tycho reached for his spear—and the movement betrayed their intent.

The same Regular who thumbed his safety, so eager to be a hero, so skittish and twitchy. He heard Magnus yell and saw a flash of movement. Before he internalized what the words meant, he took the first shot. The bullet connected squarely with Tycho's deflector shield at the side of his head, briefly flickering the protective bubble, as it skipped the round off to the side.

Tycho was sure to kill him first.

CHAPTER
TWENTY-THREE
ZATIA

THERE WERE a few sounds in her life that she associated with genuine joy. Fists banging on tables and hollering loud enough to lift a roof, the clinking of glass.

The sound wasn't usually the beeps and whistles of the AutoDoc tooling away on patients while the line for attendance strung out the door. There were smiles and laughter, arms cupped around waists and folks leaning on doorframes. It was like the waiting room for severe medical attention was actually on the street outside a popular bar, even as Milardi held a rag to the side of his head and Osyen's arm hung from a sling.

All things considered...everyone walked away. No wonder they were flying high.

Zatia stepped out of the medical bay, genuflecting to Milardi. He held his hand out, mocking a reverence back to her, as he strolled on in for his turn at the machine. Adelaide manned the controls, inputting the reported symptoms—even the old crone had a smile pasted on her face.

Zatia rolled out her shoulder, testing out the skin patch and artificial tissues binding the muscles back together. Thom caught her eye, giving her an inquiring thumbs up. She cocked her wounded arm backward, chambering a punch, but the boy just squinted at her, daring her to follow through.

It stung like she'd been burned by a cauterizing iron, but she wasn't about to tell him that. So she just lowered her arm and gave him a nod. Yeah, she was fine. Don't worry.

But her stomach gave a grumble, answering for her.

"What's for dinner?" she asked.

Thom smirked. "What do you want it to be? We live in the future."

"Roast pig. Open fire. Moonlight and whiskey."

"I can do the pig, the whiskey, and a dark room."

It was her turn to give the skeptical face, narrowing her eyes. "You don't drink whiskey. You're like, what, twelve?"

"You're like a biscuit older than him," Osyen said, breaking from his conversation with Roche to hurl that comment. "You shouldn't be drinking either."

"You're welcome to try and stop me."

"No. This I cannot do. But him?" Osyen jerked a thumb towards the scrawny little brains. "I can stop him with a suitably high shelf."

"Challenge accepted," Zatia said, drawing a whiplash turn of the head from Thom, who had no idea what he just got volunteered for. She squared up on Osyen. "You stash the whiskey, and if Thom can secure it before morning, he gets to drink whatever he wants."

"Or," Osyen countered, "I'm the captain, he's a kid, and he doesn't get to drink until he's eighteen."

"The brain doesn't stop developing until twenty-five," Roche offered with a pointed stare at Osyen, who was plenty young himself.

"You're not as funny as you think you are."

"That's not true," Roche said, flat. "I don't think I'm funny at all."

"Oy!" Adelaide groaned, waving her hand in the air. "Short and easy with all that heavy breathin' out there. We're at six percent on our oxygen stores."

Zatia folded her arms across her chest, putting on a more serious face for Osyen. "Kid killed a Paladin jus' like you and me. There's seven folk in the universe who've done what we've done, and those people should be able to have a drink together."

Osyen tapped a foot in thought, scrunching up his face like he was trying to compress it as small as he could. He had to bind up everything so that he didn't betray the thinking going on—or to convince folk that thinking was actually going on. All the traumatic head injuries he'd received, he'd probably developed a thicker skull and a small brain to compensate.

Thom raised his hand. "I feel compelled at this natural lull in the conversation to say I don't really like whiskey."

"I don't like it either," Zatia said without turning around. "I jus' don't much like myself either."

Osyen smirked, raising a pointed finger. "One drink. And it'll be all...ceremony-like."

Roche immediately broke from the line, ambling off to his room as fast as his physique would allow. "I've got just the thing!"

Osyen threw his hands up in the air, snagging onto the grating overhead to hang. "I swear, I'm not really in charge of anything anymore."

"If he finds it before morning...?" Zatia asked again, waggling an eyebrow in daring.

Osyen ground his jaw and rolled his head on his shoulders, the heavy thought clearly overwhelming what little muscle control he had. "No, we're not—but go set a table, and we'll do this proper-like."

"Done." Zatia turned toward the galley, but not before giving Thom a good sock to his shoulder. The kid fell back and bounced off the bulkhead, back up to a standing position. Didn't even complain. More evidence that the little man wasn't really flesh and bone, but some other mysterious material.

She jogged up the short set of stairs and turned into the galley. She was going to need to pull out the table and get some chairs and glasses.

But Rashida sat alone, drawing a spoon across an empty plate. Powdery crumbs like sugary concrete were all that remained on her dish. She looked up at Zatia's high-energy entry, and the two froze. The noble lady's sour note instantly poisoned Zatia's mood.

"Was it good, at least?" Zatia asked.

Rashida shrugged and made a very Milardi-like grimace, her big mouth curled into an elastic frown. "Scratched an itch, but I wouldn't call it satisfying."

Zatia popped up onto the galley counter to fetch the glassware down from the good cupboard. "We're going to be inducting Thom into the Liver Abuse Society. Want a single or a double?"

Rashida's eyes fluttered as she looked at her empty plate. "I'll pass. Thanks."

That thousand-yard stare, the tension in her wrists and shoulders, the head hung low. Zatia knew the look well enough. But the lady of a million fashions and a hundred faces wasn't her friend. Was she?

If not, then why did her chest sour and her gut hurt seeing Rashida wrapped so tight?

Zatia set the glasses down on the counter and hopped down. "You're halfway to a lifetime of freedom, debauchery, and as much villainy as you can stomach. Why so gray?"

Rashida pushed a crumb around the edge of her plate. "Because they'll keep coming."

Zatia shrugged and her shoulder griped a bit, reminding her that patched was not the same thing as healed. "And we'll keep killing 'em until they figure it out."

"You really think so?"

"Come on, have a drink with us. You can braid my hair and talk about pretty boys in seedy little bars. I'll talk about knives. It'll be fun."

Rashida finally looked up. "You don't understand. Magnus will not stop."

"Magnus," Zatia said with a scoff. "I'mma drop that little skeleton onto a cold dark moon without a helmet."

"We kill the Paladins, they'll simply send more," Rashida said. "Possibly more dangerous fiends we haven't even conceived of."

"And we'll kill those. Magnus too."

Rashida shook her head. "We kill Magnus, and they'll simply appoint a new jailor to hold the chain. This isn't something we can just burn down."

Zatia nodded, leaning against the table. "Not my first archenemy. I know the drill. Leaving home the way we did usually makes a few."

"When did you leave your home?" Rashida asked.

Zatia smiled, remembering her father's delicious cocktail of pity-seeking and rage-spewing exclamations. He'd start a sentence in one tone and finish it in another, never quite sure which manipulative tool would work anymore.

She felt her bicep twitch, and she flexed the arm tight, clamping it to her side. "Couple years. Why?"

Rashida's eyes focused up, tracking across Zatia's hair and down her shoulder, studying the patched-up clothes and the belted weapons and the visible scars. "Because you're still there, more than a little bit of you."

The words came out of her mouth like a reflex, with a pleasant melody. "Screw you, Rashida. You don't get any whiskey."

Rashida raised her perfect brow, and that brilliant light sparked up in her eyes. "Never asked for any."

Her biceps twitched again, this time rolling up her shoulder.

No. No.

She knew what was coming, and what it would do, and she refused. She reached over with her other hand and pinned her arm to her side. "We're going to kill this last Paladin," Zatia promised through clenched teeth, "and the Engineer is going to get your shot of whiskey when we do."

Rashida turned back to her plate. "He deserves it."

"And you don't?"

The lady didn't answer that one, swiping a lock of hair out of her face, but still staring down.

Zatia pressed her. "You deserve whatever you can take, not what they give you."

Rashida huffed at that. "Sometimes we deserve what we are given, even if we did not ask for it or want it, Zee. We have not halved our troubles today. We've doubled them."

"You know what I think?" Zatia said, almost slurring. "I think..."

She thought Rashida was scared to turn and face her captor. She thought Rashida was scared to really, truly walk away from Imperial pageantry and power. She thought Rashida laid awake at night terrified that without her bloodline, nobody would actually want her for anything else. And this was the end of that road, when even her vaunted family didn't want her anymore. If her own blood had no use for her anymore, why would anybody else?

None of those words got out, but the intention must have, because Rashida nodded. "You're not telling me anything I don't already know, Zee. Drinks before or after dinner?"

Zatia felt her lip twitch and her arm seize. "Why do you care?" she asked.

And Rashida sighed. "So I know when to be scarce."

"You want to go, go," Zatia snapped. "You've been nothing but doom and gloom since that sentient bone guy showed up. Used to own every room you walked into. Now you don't even own the air around you. You want to be free? Take it back from him."

Her left knee wobbled, shaking. And thankfully, Rashida was staring at her plate, deep in internalized conflict, so she didn't see Zatia dash for the door. Perhaps she thought Zatia had simply stormed out, missing the fact that Zatia mostly fell down the stairs, clanging to the floor.

No call outs, no alarm. She half expected Lily to poke their head out of the wall with a bellowing voice of concern. But the AI was locked in their own sleep. Nobody was there to notice or care.

It was getting worse. So much worse. Milardi had said withdrawal, he'd said seizures. But those were supposed to get better with time, not this. She could feel her heart skipping and her vision blurring in and out, like a bad signal on a video feed.

If they knew she was getting worse...

She hauled herself up and down the hall to her dormitory. A kick to the door open was the last thing she could muster before she fell inside. She remembered seeing the floor hit her in the face. But she didn't feel it. And she stared at that floor until feeling returned.

RECORDED DREAM DATA, DATE: 2241.19.04

PATIENT: THOMAS HUGH

// Warning: Electrical event detected. Beginning Diagnostic Scan.

It's so cold.

Can you see where you are?

It's...I can feel the wind. There's...something billowing, like curtains...my hands are shaking.

Take your time with it. This process can be disorienting, even for folk who know what they're doing.

People like you?

Well, if I'm perfectly honest, there are no 'people like me'. Everyone thinks they're unique until they meet someone like them.

True enough. But...I am unique.

// Warning: Tachycardia response detected. All other biological signatures stable and normal.

I can...the wind? Where did it go?

You're not outside anymore. The moment is changing.

Why is it changing? That—how could that be?

It's...difficult to explain.

You seem to know what's happening.

You're being made aware of something that hasn't yet happened. Because of that knowledge, you then chose a different path.

And that changed something?

// Warning: Secondary heart rate matched and confirmed. Isolating signature.

The further you are from an event, the more likely observing it actually changes it. Basic Quantum state observance: To observe something is to affect it. But in this case...

I'm seeing the future?

// Warning: Pulse ox falling.

Remember to breathe, Thomas. You had quite a bit to drink.

Sorry, it's just...how do you know I was drinking?

You snore when you drink.

How do you know I'm snoring? Are you in the room with me?!

I'm not sure this will be comforting, but no, I'm not.

...you're right, that wasn't really better. How do I know all this is true and not some nightmare?

None of it is true. And all of it is. It won't be true until it happens. Do you feel that wind now?

Yes, it's back. I'm outside again. There's...snow. A storm.

See how it all shifted? How the image bends and warps as you discover new things? Your foreknowledge changes what you'll do when you're awake...which changes what you see now, which then changes your foreknowledge. And so on and so on. The image will keep shifting until you settle on a choice.

How do I lock it down?

You keep looking at it. And if it doesn't drive you mad, you'll eventually find what you're looking for.

...The further out it is, the more variables to account for.

There you go. You understand.

Hardly any of it. Why is this happening to me?

Because, Thomas...it already happened.

// WARNING: ATRIAL FLUTTER DETECTED. PULSE OX FALLING INTO CRITICAL LEVELS.

What do you mean?

Wake up. They need you.

But—

Wake. Up.

———

Thom sat bolt upright in bed, the alarms blaring from his bedside. And he could hear Milardi pounding on the doorframe. "Oy! Maestro! You good in there?"

"Yeah," Thom called back. "Yeah, I'm okay."

At this point, Thom didn't really want to go back to sleep ever again. Because what he saw there...was the wreckage of the *Aurum*.

CHAPTER
TWENTY-FOUR
ROCHE

"ALRICHT," Osyen started the meeting on a cheery note, "with the human artillery taken off the board, that just leaves us with the gauss-powered Olympian."

Lars sat up in his interrogation chair, sipping from a paper cup of tea. The taste was nothing to be inspired by. When Roche was left in charge of stocking the galley and the Replicator, he tabulated the cost per carbon-unit against nutritional value and selected the most efficient distribution of resources.

Which meant unsweetened, no cream, and highly caffeinated. At least, that's what was most useful to him. The rest of the crew groused and moaned, but nobody wanted to take over the role from him. So they continued to grouse and moan while Roche stocked whatever he liked.

Lars sipped the tea like it was delicate and pleasant, and not slowly dissolving the cup in his hand, the potent mixture already dripping on to the floor. "Olympian?"

Osyen struggled to explain. "He throws stuff real good."

Lars grunted at that. "Perhaps he excelled at hand-to-hand combat and improvised weaponry. The philosophy of the program was to lean into the patient's existing skill set, not try to remedy any gaps."

"Gaussian grip controls," Roche explained. "Anything magnetic within a decent range, he can grab and then propel at high velocity. All he carries with him is a kind of spear, or javelin."

Osyen nodded in confirmation. "And when he loses that spear, boy has a habit of making new ones out of just about anything close at hand."

"He's likely to bring down a mid-size freighter with a flick of his wrist." Lars smiled, paternal and wicked. "This is a mid-size freighter, isn't it?"

"We operate at under five hundred kilos, so we're technically small," Roche said. Osyen glared at him, wide judgmental eyes. "It's the industry standard. You don't want to misrepresent storage capacity."

Osyen sighed, trying to reset the moment. He draped himself over a chair back, bringing himself down to Lars's level. "They're wireless transmitting Gods, so we have to assume they know how we did the first one."

A crooked, insidious smile from the old Engineer. "So you require a new method of regicide?"

"Paladins aren't kings," Osyen sniped. "And neither are you, ol' man."

"Yes," Lars said, rubbing his hair with one hand. "This Paladin will likely know to look up."

"Are there any other strategic weaknesses to the Paladins?" Osyen asked, point blank. "Anything you've forgotten to mention?"

"Unless you think we can wait them out," Roche offered, "let the Cascade run its course."

Lars considered the math on that one. "Implausible."

"Oh?" Osyen huffed with a raised eyebrow.

"He won't have long to find you," Lars explained, "so he won't take long. And he will suffer no delays. You can fight him on chosen ground—or in these very halls. But he will find you. He's motivated."

Roche sighed. The Paladin thinks he's going to the Sojourn, to Heaven—but only if he pursues Rashida with every dying breath. Zealotry brought out the most irrational behavior. Tactically, Roche would want to extend his life, not waste its remaining seconds ending others.

"What if he needs more time?" Osyen asked.

"I don't follow."

"Maybe." Osyen paused, tongue jammed in his cheek. "Maybe he has a run of bad luck? He doesn't root us out. Now he's going to be the first Paladin in history to fail, and he needs to do something."

"Paladins don't require luck."

Osyen wind-milled his hand in the air. "Yeah, yeah, yeah. But *what if* he does? Can he maybe hook up to another set of hardware? More hard drive space that's not corrupted? Would that buy him more time? To find us?" That swift addition on the end of the sentence was doing some heavy lifting.

Roche blinked. "Osyen, are you asking because we can't sit and hide—"

"I'm just asking!" The bite in his retort was more than the moment called for.

Lars's eyes narrowed, the wrinkles around the corners deepening into crevasses dug out with hard years and moral flexibility. The only person missing this shift was Osyen himself. "Technologically possible," Lars began, "but pragmatically unsound."

Osyen cocked his head. "Walk me through it."

"Maintaining a long-distance wireless connection would increase rates of corruption. So he'd need the space to be close at hand to minimize that effect."

"He'd have to plug into a ship," Osyen filled in the blank. "No more walking around without a hard-line connection? He'd become a Paladin bolted to a freighter or a corvette."

"Precisely."

And then came the real question. "And if the ship plugged into him?"

Roche winced. "Osyen—"

"Answer my question, Lars, and do remember that I have a gun."

Lars puffed out his chest, taking another sip of his tea, drinking in the irony of the moment. "Your hypothesis is muddled. Why would a Cascading ship's navigator merge with a Cascading Paladin?"

Osyen didn't blink. "I didn't say anything about a ship navigator."

"You didn't have to, boy."

Roche took a steeling breath. This had gone off the rails fast. Osyen wasn't talking about the Paladin's capabilities.

"The only thing," Lars said, nice and slowly, "that a Cascading AI requires is additional uncorrupted space in which to occupy."

"See?" Osyen said, trying very hard not to glare at Roche. "Was that so hard?"

"It was miserable," Lars mocked, "but I'll manage."

"Good," Osyen said. "What would you need?"

"To do what?"

"To patch Lily into me."

Roche's jaw dropped. He couldn't be suggesting that. He couldn't be.

But no matter how horrified or distressed, Roche couldn't make a sound. It was like someone had sealed away his voice in a little box and the key lost in some other box in a long-forgotten corner of his mind, beset with dust and cobwebs.

"Would you need specific tools?" Osyen asked.

Lars sighed. "It's not a matter of technology. If commands can be sent to the ship's mainframe via wireless or direct link, then the ship simply needs permissions to write into a formatted partition. But that's about where you'll lose control."

Osyen squinted. "How do you mean, lose control?"

The Engineer glared at him. "I don't think I need to explain how the human brain is not a magnetized hard drive. You cannot choose what parts of the brain the computer will overtake. There's a reason this procedure kills almost every subject. It might over-write the automatic functions governing regulation of the heart and lungs. It might compromise the nervous system. In a best case, you forget your favorite food. In a worst case, the process outright kills you."

Osyen threw his hands in the air, almost like a celebration. "Well, day of days: you have yourself a willing patient."

"A willing patient with no history of augmentation," Lars pointed out. "And you *don't* have a willing doctor."

Osyen's eyes narrowed. "How could I convince you?"

"And at what point in this discussion will you dispense with the charm," Lars asked with narrowed eyes, "and switch to threats and hate to get what you want? It won't work."

"One out of a hundred odds," Osyen reminded him, "is hardly guaranteed failure."

"Do it as many times as I have, and yes, it is."

Osyen's lip twitched, almost a snarl. "You know, I've met a lot of people in twenty-five years. Never met somebody with the ability to save a life who just refuses to."

"Ah," Lars clucked, "we'll start with guilt, shall we? Guilt and shame?" He glanced at Roche. "Wake me when he grabs the pliers, would you?"

If Osyen had something to stab the Engineer with, he'd have buried it to the hilt right there. Lacking that, he did so with words. "You deserve the guilt. Refusing to save someone, you may as well have pulled the trigger yourself."

Lars was unimpressed. "I've pulled many triggers, boy. I'm just through with pulling triggers, expecting anything to change. It never does."

———

Osyen had almost fled around the corner and out of sight by the time Roche got out of the door. "What was *that* all about?"

The words stopped Osyen. And the captain spun about, marching back to Roche at full speed. "If I stay in that room with that gray-haired lunatic, I was liable to airlock him. So instead, I took a walk."

"I've seen you lose your temper, Oz," Roche said. "It's not an infrequent sight. I meant, why did you ask him that question?"

"You want to have this conversation now?" Osyen asked. "Out here? In the hallway?"

"We all love Lily—"

"No!" Osyen's voice filled the entire ship, from end-to-end. And the second was far smaller. "...No."

There were no tears in his eyes. Tears, after all, came from sadness. An explosion of emotion. This was hollower, like a piece of him had been scooped out and scrambled and put back in as rage.

His voice shook like it was working its screws out. "If we can find a way to save Lily, then we can Jump to safety—"

"Look at my socket," Roche instructed.

Osyen's brow scrunched up, and his eyes bounced around his head. Where was he going with this?

Roche raised up his wrist, a crunchy and dry stump of cables interfacing with flesh. Socket ports inflamed and grimy patches of skin, itching boils, and cracking calluses. "Do you know what this is? To me?"

"It's how you connect to the ship."

"No," Roche said. "It gives me a hand. This bundle of copper wire and steel plating? It's *freedom* to someone who never had it. This isn't a handicap, this *is* my hand. This isn't something you sacrifice to get; it's what you get because *life* had other plans. Sickness, accident, or birth."

Osyen took a breath and tried to exhale out his anger. "You're saying I don't understand what it's like for you?"

Roche felt like melting into the floor. He felt like changing his name and diving into a trash chute. He felt like running away and crawling into bed or closing a door and never opening it again. But his friend needed him right now. "I'm saying you don't understand what you're asking *him* to do. This isn't a process done *electively*. Eye implants, skin grafts, limb replacements—they're done as restorative, not curative. If you survive the surgical implantation—which is a big enough 'if' as it is...then you face the download. You might save Lily, you might! But we're talking about direct line access to your brain, and not as a Jockey line to interpret telemetry. But actual read/write privileges to your gray matter! Even if you succeed, how long would Lily be stable again? A month? Two?"

Osyen grunted. "I know I'm willing to try."

"And *what if* it works?" Roche supposed. "You'll have doomed Lily in an entirely new way. Because every single day they're alive...they'd be consuming you, bit by bit, forced to occupy more and more space in your head. Until you are gone. Put yourself in their shoes: could you live like that, Oz? Where Lily woke you up from a dreadful slumber with such special news: you're cured! But every morning, that cure cost a piece of someone? And that the choice...was made *for* you. Because I know what Lily would say to that. They'd *never* put you in that position."

Osyen hung his head, grinding his jaw and clenching his fists and finally stamping his foot. A silent tantrum in private.

Finally, Osyen lifted his head, tears in his eyes. "I thought...I thought I found a way out."

No more words. Roche opened his arms, and Osyen rushed in, sweeping himself into a hug. Roche was a big guy, and he gave very good hugs.

There was nothing to be done for Lily. The only hope now was the Godfather's grace. And Roche quietly knew that a gift like that would exact a horrible price.

That worried Roche deeply. Because Osyen just proved what he was willing to pay.

FOR SUCH A SMALL ship full of such joyful folk, it had gotten surprisingly hard to find anybody on the *Aurum*. It was as though everyone had retreated to disparate corners, retracting far beyond the public spaces and back into their tortoise shells after just one day of glory.

Rashida's door was closed, locked, and no sound of activity. Not altogether unusual, but she wasn't even emerging to take meals anymore. Thom wasn't in his room, and if he wasn't in some obvious place, the boy was most likely tucked into a ventilation shaft where nobody would ever reach him. Osyen seemed to have evaporated into thin air and taken Roche with him.

He expected to find Adelaide in Engineering. All there was to find was Zatia.

The little pixie was nuzzled up against the reactor core, the internal bronze piston still tumbling in a lazy rotation. Frost clung to unused conduits on the edge of the room, building up impressive crystals reaching far enough to snag clothing. But within a few feet of that reactor, an inviting hearth of warmth and pleasance. And Zatia has cuddled right up to that heat source.

"I'll bring you a cup of hot cocoa, shall I?" Milardi said.

"*Fra tow, skel.*"

Milardi raised an eyebrow at that greeting. "Nice to see you too."

"Do I look like I want company?"

She was shivering, huddled against the heat source. She gripped her right arm tightly, holding it close across her stomach. "You look like you had another seizure and you don't want to tell anybody."

A tremor ran through her, end to end, but she never took her eyes off of the wall.

"Hey," Milardi said, crouching down. "This is me. We could do this in Medical if it'll make you more comfortable, but I think we both know it won't."

She didn't dare move. Perhaps she was hoping the reactor would thaw her out. "I...laid on the floor. Don't know how long I was there."

"Did you hit your head?"

"No. At least I...I don't think so."

He'd known Zatia for a few years and not once could he recall seeing the boisterous and abrasive young girl this small before. She was crumpled up like something discarded, trying to occupy the least amount of physical space possible. It was like she was hoping she'd cave in on herself and cease to be.

"How bad was it this time?" he asked.

And that made her lash out. She snarled at him, but still refused to even look at him. "I don't know! I wasn't exactly looking at a clock."

He let the air cool for a moment. Riling her up would not help anybody. And if the last few days had been evidence, it might end in blows.

"That's two seizures in three days," Milardi cautioned. "Increased aggression, lowered inhibitions—"

"What 'increased aggression?' I'm always like this."

"You killed a man in cold blood on the train job—and then killed the dock guards at Farragut. You're leaving quite a few more bodies than usual, Zee. Is your memory also *fukacta* or are you just being stubborn?"

She cocked her head. "Just stubborn. As always."

227

He forced a smile and settled himself down beside the reactor core. It was surprisingly pleasant, with a baking heat glowing off the metal. "You gotta tell Osyen."

"What's he going to do about it?" she asked. "Sit me in a corner?"

"Zee, I've put enough holes in heads to know that brains are complex and fickle things that don't much like being meddled with. They're unique special little sunflowers and yours is not behaving."

"Well, I've never been the obedient type," she said with a shrug.

"I'm not being funny. We don't know what's going on in your head and until you let me in there, I can't help sort it out."

"It's not exactly slowing us down." She stared into the rough palms of her hands. "I'm handicapped and we're still rolling right over the very best the Imps got."

"You think we 'rolled right over him?'" Milardi asked, jaw hanging loose.

"Yeah." A simple answer as she reset her shoulders against the warm metal, flexing out her fingers and shook out her foot.

Milardi blinked. "Well, then...if there's nothing to worry about, do you mind if I just sit here a bit? It's nice and toasty, and my room is only kinda warmer than the surface of Titan."

She didn't respond. Just closed her eyes and leaned her head back against the reactor with a gong.

Milardi looked up at the catwalk encircling the room, frost-kissed railings and the blue hue to everything. It was like the ice was taking over, claiming the ship as its own.

"You remember your first day on the *Aurum?*" he asked her.

She shrugged. "First few months was kind of a blur."

"I don't remember my first day."

She finally looked at him, her head falling to one side, cheek against her shoulder. "Well, you were pretty drunk for most of it."

"I'd been running with Fiona for a few years," Milardi said, "had a natural break point. When she found out who I'd signed on with—'cause she always found out everything—she offered me a tidy salary. Just to make reports. I didn't know you all, and I knew her so..."

Zatia's eyes sharpened. "Are you apologizing for something we found out about three months ago?"

"Couldn't just let me get through it?" She slugged him in the shoulder so hard, a sharp pain rolled all the way up into his neck. "Ow!"

Zatia rolled onto her knees and brought herself square up to face him. "If you're going to be so slow on the uptake, just don't even do it."

"I disagree."

"Oh, you disagree?"

Milardi's face was as still as the frozen iron around them. "I do. Better late than never. Doesn't make it any easier."

"See, now I'm just mad at you all over again!"

Squaring up on her was like challenging a wild animal, but he made himself do it. "You were still mad. You'd never stopped. And I never...like, I said sorry to *everybody*, but not to you."

She couldn't match his stare, choosing instead to scan him from head to toe, looking perhaps for what piece she might remove first. Or unable to meet his challenge.

"I could've left the crew right then and there. Fiona would've taken me back without a second thought. But I *chose* to be here."

"I'd say, dodged a bullet," Zatia quipped, "but then, look at *us*. We're not doing better."

Flippant, dismissive, avoidant. Everything at arm's length. Give her a reason to believe. "I'm sorry, Zee. You're supposed to trust me out there, and I was...I was lying to your face the whole time. How do you trust someone after that?"

"Generally speaking? I don't," Zatia said with a grimace.

Milardi sighed. "We want you here, Zee. I want you here. Thom does, Oz does. You know how much Adelaide likes you and Rashida...You're a crass, rough, and remarkable young woman. And I'd have you watch my back before anybody else I've ever worked with."

"You've worked with some mean people," she said, impressed.

"Yes, I have. But I didn't trust any of 'em."

229

Her lip quivered, but her brow tightened, forcing a frown. And her voice came out so very weak, like a warning that hurt to say. "You can't trust me."

It wasn't because of her worth, or skill or character. Her own body had betrayed her. How could anyone trust her right now?

"Sure I can," Milardi said without missing a beat. "You'd lay down your life for this crew out of sheer spite."

That got her to laugh, pulling it out of her like it had been stuck to her ribs with barbs. But once it was free, she relaxed into it and leaned back against the reactor. "Nobody kills me without my consent."

"Yeah, there better be a party," he said. "Get together all my worst enemies. Put everybody in one room and we just have a big hurrah full of booze and good music."

A diabolical giggle. "And they all work together, make the ultimate master plan that finally brings me to my knees."

"They work and work, through the night and past the dawn." Milardi fished a flask out of his jacket and took a pull. The cold had gotten through to the metal tin, helping to bring out the notes of vanilla and smoke. "And somewhere between the hair of the dog and the champagne hour, something clicks."

Without even asking, she reached over and plucked the flask from his hand. She threw her head back and poured right down her throat for a full two count, before handing it back to him, wiping her lip on her sleeve. "They finally have it figured. But we'll need to work together."

He laughed, letting that scenario peter out like a flame out of fuel. "Your seizures are going to get worse, you know," Milardi stammered out, afraid to soil the friendly exchange with foul notions.

She grunted an agreement. "I know it. But are we going to break?"

"Many, many times," Milardi said with his smile creeping up his face. "But if you make your living punching holes in folk, you better know how to patch 'em."

"Break it, bought it?"

He nodded. "I've got your back, Zee. Always will. Cut 'em up?"

She smiled back. "Cut 'em up."

CHAPTER
TWENTY-SIX
OSYEN

THEY HAD WANTED a repeat of their first plan, swoop in to an industrial depot and use what they found to mulch, squish, or flatten the final Paladin.

They saw the fires before they even got close.

Osyen would have thought the fierce cold and the biting wind would've long since extinguished anything out there, but whatever had caught refused to bend to something as trivial as nature. This alone was plenty alarming.

But he had no real sense for how alarming until they could make out the wreckage.

"*Fra tow mi*," Milardi cursed under his breath. "It must be two hundred meters long."

An image came into view through the snow. The wreckage bore the insignia of the Imperial Orchid, the blue and white almost camouflaging it with the weather.

"When it was in one piece," Osyen said, looking toward Rashida. "Hazard a guess. Is that Magnus's ship?"

"I don't have to guess," she said. "That's his, alright."

"Looks like this spot's taken," Zatia cautioned. "They've even got a fire to keep warm."

"That'll be their fusion reactor," Adelaide pointed out. "Reaction is self-sustaining, so that fire will burn for a couple months more, at least. But it's not stable with all these contaminants."

"Meaning what?" Osyen asked.

The old lady lit a cigarette right there on the Jump Deck. "Meaning it'll go bang-bang whenever it feels like it."

"It's settled," Zatia said with a clap of her hands. "We get the Hell out of here."

"No," Osyen said, causing the young bruiser to throw up her hands in frustration. "Not yet, at least. Roche, put us down outside the perimeter and then get clear."

Zatia froze, her eyes bugged out. "Did you not hear the prognosis of thermonuclear explosion?"

Even Adelaide shook her head. "I said whenever it feels like. Not in the next five minutes. The Godfather will get a containment team out here long before that happens. Settle down."

"What are you hoping to find in a derelict Imperial frigate?" Rashida asked.

"I know what I'm hoping we don't find!" Milardi quipped.

He knew that this was the ship that brought two man-machine hybrids into his orbital vector, the same ship with the most available intel on his enemy. If he wanted answers to any of his problems, they were on that ship. And whatever happened here, it was now an opportunity too good to pass up.

Maybe the Godfather's goons were on the way right now. Maybe Imperial salvage teams. And even if they weren't, this was still insanely dangerous. Because the Paladin might very well be lying in wait.

But maybe there was a kill switch. A control mechanism, or method to issue orders. Maybe there was data on critical weaknesses.

"It's entirely likely this is a trap," Thom noted.

"Even if it didn't start as one, it is now." Osyen leaned over Roche's chair. "If you don't hear from us in ten minutes...then, I don't know, come get us."

Roche coughed. "Due respect, Captain, if I do not hear from you in ten minutes' time, you're already dead."

"Fine," Zatia said, "then just come get me."

"Adelaide, Zee, Milardi, and Thom? Suit up. Rashida?" Osyen paused. She was transfixed by the horrors below. "Stay with Roche on the ship."

She whispered back, her voice raspy and grumpy. "If that's what you want."

Zatia raised her hand. "Can I stay too? They might need security."

Osyen grabbed her by the wrist and lowered it. "Enviro-suits and cold weather gear. Let's go. We're on the clock, scavengers."

"Ah," Milardi said, "so today we're scavengers. I was wondering."

Roche touched the *Aurum* down a good kilometer away from the fire. Osyen checked everyone's cold weather gear personally before pushing them toward the airlock. Temperatures outside were frigid before the storm rolled in. Now? Triple digits below zero with winds over sixty miles an hour. Exposed skin would freeze like crystals and shatter like glass.

But they had to keep the ship safe. So they walked through the snow and the blizzard, rope lines around each other's waists like they were children. If the Paladin struck now, they'd be completely defenseless.

The alternative was to wander in the cold and potentially lose each other to the storm. There were no safe options anymore.

They approached the crash site with weapons out. Paladin or no, Imperial survivors were liable to be unhappy to see them.

The storage depot loomed high over the crash site, a divot in its land. The ship itself wasn't much larger than the *Aurum*, with the back third as primarily gear and machines, and living quarters and crew deck just forward of that. This boat didn't want to draw attention, and it didn't need to support many.

The first batch of wreckage was mostly industrial, torn up thrusters and the like. It was also where the scar in the snowbank began, implying the ship had flopped onto the tundra at speed. Perhaps the Godfather had finally decided to give some payback. If true, then anything he could want was likely in a lockbox and on its way to a bunker, out of reach.

Maybe they missed something...

Being inside the crash shielded them from the weather somewhat, the maelstrom of ice hanging mostly overhead. But much of the manmade bucket was already being reclaimed by Farragut's Big One.

They made their way through fire control on up. The crew bunks were maybe twenty. Milardi paused at the armory lockers, but they had sealed up when power was lost. Without power, what could he hope to recover?

Maybe he could take them back to the *Aurum*, slice and hack from relative safety...

The Jump Deck of the frigate was a sight. Twin paired rows ran forward of a command station, with the rows flanking a central computer bay. Except for the twinkling of the fires quietly chewing on their fuel, everything was dark. Everything was quiet.

And no bodies.

"Damn," Osyen said, holstering his pistol. "No Magnus."

"It's his ship alright," Thom said, muffled by his face covering.

Osyen was about to ask how he knew. But when he turned around, he saw why. Two ten-foot glass tubes were inset in the wall. Cables and conduits dangled from above, and one of them had a foot and a half of frozen liquid in the bottom of the chamber. The glass was cracked on the other, likely from the impact.

Made sense. If the Paladins were unstable, they'd need a stable way to transport them to theater before turning them loose.

But where was everybody?

"Think they survived the crash? Made for the depot to get out of the cold?" Zatia asked.

Maybe. But until he saw a body, Osyen would not assume Magnus or the remaining Paladin had shuffled off the mortal coil.

"Well, no crew," Osyen noted. "They took battle damage?"

"No way to know if there were escape pods," Adelaide noted. "Not when half the ship is buried in the ice pack."

"Uh, boys?" Zatia said. "Would someone taller come check this?"

She was standing to one side of the deck, on top of a snowdrift. But even with that natural stool, she couldn't get close enough to examine what hung over her head. A twisted bit of metal.

More than likely, it got that in the crash? The whole place was curled and warped.

Maybe...too many maybes...

Milardi and Osyen stomped over, but both paused at a respectful distance. The chunk of metal wasn't structural or some natural piece of the ship bent out of shape. It was lanced into the bulkhead at a clean ninety-degree angle—and stained red.

If there had been a body here, it had been...removed.

"Thom," Osyen whispered, "call in Roche. We need to get back to the ship."

"What is it?"

Milardi drew his pistols like they'd do him any good. "Our Paladin friend just went AWOL, that's what."

Osyen! Rashida's voice blared over the back channel. *Osyen, do you hear me?!*

Her voice was so loud it felt like it was going to split the back of his head open. Everyone winced, and Osyen grabbed the collar of his shirt, like he could muffle it. *Rash, you just flagged your position for a very angry cyborg. This better be good.*

It's Weasel! Weasel is—

And the audio cut out.

No.

Osyen took off, running back down the frigate's open hallway— meeting a baton to his face, clotheslining him to the ground.

Zatia growled and roared, matching the storm's ferocity, but she did nothing. And Milardi dropped his pistols with a polymer clatter. When Osyen could focus his eyes again, he understood why.

A gun barrel pressed to his cheek. And Weasel's little face looming over him, split from end to end with a fatuous smile. "It is so good to see Family again, isn't it? I forgot to ask before: how was that drink?"

CHAPTER
TWENTY-SEVEN
RASHIDA

OSYEN? Rashida bounced the message again, getting nothing back. *Osyen, answer me!*

The *Aurum* rattled and groaned. The high clouds of the storm were full of ice, effectively hiding their exhaust and their heat signatures, not to mention from the casual eye. But it wasn't doing any kind things to their ship systems. They couldn't wait here for long.

"Come on, come on, Oz," Roche muttered.

Despite their excellent hiding spot, they had been lucky enough to see three of the Godfather's picket ships come by over the top of the storm clouds to descend on a clear trajectory for the depot.

The Godfather, it seemed, had finally had enough of the fireworks in his backyard.

"We can't just sit here," Rashida thought out loud.

Roche nodded with a sigh. "If you have any bright ideas, I'm all ears."

"I'm not really one for clever thinking."

"Don't sell yourself short," Roche said. "Just because you've never had to think outside the box doesn't mean you can't."

She almost chuckled. Her schooling had been for how to break bread, speak to strangers, and recite complex philosophical quandaries from memory in three different languages. Rescuing her shipmates from gangsters in the middle of a blizzard was a little out of her depth.

Finally, they heard something back. *We're fine, Rashida. We'll come to you. Stay put.*

Something in his tone, his delivery, sent a chill up her spine. And she knew for a fact that Osyen was not fine—the Weasel and his goons were probably introducing themselves at that very moment.

Rashida looked down at Roche, sharing her displeasure with expression alone. And his was similarly blanched.

That 'all clear' had absolutely not come from Osyen. But from someone else with a radio and the ability to mimic voices.

The ship groaned as the primary aerial thrusters fired up, heaving the *Aurum* higher into the atmosphere and out of the storm head.

"But the others—!" Rashida objected.

"Are in a lot less trouble than you and me!" Roche stressed. And she felt the floor shake as the ship pushed up and away—

Clang.

Roche's eyes drew upwards to the rivets and steel plates overhead. "Oh no..."

Rashida jogged to the Jump Deck hatch comb and keyed a random code into the panel, as long as the system let her. And then the door slammed shut, locking them in.

"That's your brilliant plan?" Roche asked. "Do you even know to open that door again?"

"You think I did anything but slow him down?" Rashida pointed out, stomping back across the deck. "Are there any other ways in?"

Roche blinked, his eyes glazing over with that thousand-yard stare, as he consulted some record or other. "Piping for air and heat in the sub-floor, runs the length of the keel."

Rashida dropped to her knees. "Might be a way out of here. A-hah!" Under the co-pilot's seats, there was a square door that opened up, a dark crimson glow of safety lights beaming up from the guts of the ship. It was going to be a tight squeeze, but...

"Escape for you," Roche said.

Her stomach dropped, and she looked back at him. Roche was a large man; he'd never fit through that hatch.

She couldn't leave him behind! The Paladin would...

But his mind was still deep inside the ship. "Temperature drop in the ship's galley. We have a hull breach. Fifty meters back, you should find a similar hatch letting you out in Engineering. If you can get to a shuttle, you might escape him."

"I'm not leaving you, Roche!"

And he smiled. "Well, I can't come with you. That doesn't mean you should stay."

He was so calm about that notion, a serene look on his face, like he was looking out over a beautiful sunset or snow-capped mountains far away. A soft, forgiving smile flashed across his face for a moment, before he sniffed hard, and the lingering water in his eyes became obvious. "Get outta here."

Her panic froze her for half a second. There had to be another way, another choice. Something she'd missed.

But with no more time to think about it, she dropped into the hole and closed the hatch behind her.

The space was barely wide enough for her to lie down in, and with the hatch closed, it was nearly pitch black. The courtesy red lighting only helped her make out indistinct shapes and conduits running around her. It was akin to a nightmare, where every shadow was solid and every shape was closer than she thought.

She had to shimmy herself along the floor, brushing against metal pipes and panels so cold they felt like they burned her skin. She tried to crawl slowly at first, modulating her breathing and movements to make as little noise as possible. But the longer she lingered on some patches, the more that the cold metal felt like it clung to her skin.

Rashida never thought herself as a dexterous woman and that thought was proven true in this instant. She thought she'd caught herself on something, pinched and unable to move. Truth be told, she'd simply lost purchase and was flailing in the dark. How Thom did this kind of ductwork for almost a year was unfathomable to her, let alone why he would *choose* to hide here.

A boot slammed into the panel next to her head, and she held her breath, wary that even exhaling would echo through and up to the person standing ten inches above her. But the owner didn't even slow down, as it—and several others marched back up towards the Jump Deck.

If the Paladin had come, he had not come alone. Or were they blessed, and these invaders were more of the Godfather's men?

Curious, that she'd consider that a blessing. They'd likely extend her the same sanguine hospitality.

In almost ten minutes, she'd gotten a mere halfway up the length of the ship, and she had to pause. The hatch on the opposite end of the tunnel seemed to taunt her, just as far away as it was when she started. Gasping for breath, she muttered. "If these people don't kill me, this ship will."

"On the contrary!" Rashida jumped, twisting and lurching as much as the cramped space would allow. Peeking out of the floor in front of her...was the mustachioed face of Lily. Their right cheek and eyebrow drooped like a melting chocolate, the physics simulation losing whatever held it together. "I would personally see to your demise, before I let any pirate scum have that honor."

Rashida gasped. "Lily?"

"Increasingly one of many fragments," Lily said, "but yes."

Rashida could've cried. "You've got to warn Oz."

Lily's face spasmed, their jaw unhinging and wrapping around their head before snapping back to normal. "It's...too late for that."

Rashida sighed, lowering her head to rest on her wrists.

"I cannot keep secrets from them, so I must be brief. I am speaking in rooms throughout the ship to mask your presence on the Jump Deck/Galley/Landing Gear Assembly."

Rashida scrunched up her eyebrows. But she wasn't on the...ah.

For now, at least, the Cascade was working to her advantage. A deteriorating AI would likely scatter whoever was trying to find whatever it protected. And if that AI was also lying, it would make for a clever little maze for intruders.

"I can open the way for you," Lily said, "but I cannot hide you from their eyes. If I open only what you need, they will know where you are."

"Okay..." Rashida whispered, "so open everything."

"Are you quite sure?"

Rashida nodded. "Everything but the Jump Deck. Do it."

The breeze tugged on her hair and it took what little warmth there was along with it, cutting so hard that it stole her breath. She tried to hold it back, but her chest ached with the effort, like she'd taken a gulp of the void itself.

Lily's face twitched, out of sync with her voice. "Go. Now."

Rashida crawled to the exit, the steel plating sticking to her knees and wrists with each overhand reach. She heard boots pounding overhead, scattering in a hundred different directions.

The engineering hatch had crusted over with a frost, but with little moisture in this section, it couldn't seal. Rashida spun around to plant her foot against the panel and gave it a good shove. The hatch cracked with a hiss, releasing the fine white mist and a glow of yellow onto her face.

The hatch had opened underneath the grating of the main catwalk, but there was a nice six-foot drop to the work area below, where Adelaide used to spend late nights tinkering. Rashida pulled her head and shoulders out to look around.

Right above her, two men—pirates by their ragged layered clothes —were bent over the railing, one of their melting boots right by her face.

"I heard it, I just don't see anything!" one of them barked at the other.

"Eh, it's these old Perseus ships. They're all bangs and whistles, all the time. And you hear that AI?"

"Spooky *s'ivan zu trit*," the pirate said with a shiver.

She couldn't get out of the hatch with those two right there. They'd almost certainly spot her. One held his rifle low, the barrel uncomfortably close to her head. The gun itself was missing a handful of pieces, including a dust cover, revealing the spring and magnetic assembly underneath. It'd be a shame if he got a pile of snow or rocks into that. The whole thing might shear apart in his hands.

The muzzle drifted absently over to her, like it heard her mental insult. And for a split second, she was looking down the barrel of a poorly maintained battle rifle held by a slouching glory-seeking minion.

She was no fighter.

But an illusionist...

Lily, give me intercom power, she bounced.

Lily's stuttering voice cut in a few moments later. It was taking them an awfully long time to process. *A word of caution: the Paladin has surely detected this back channel communication.*

The Paladin's not here yet, Rashida countered, *and I need the intercom. Quickly.*

There was no more resistance. She felt the twitch as the intercom line connected to the radio implant in her neck. Old and creaky Perseus ships, huh? Let's see how superstitious these young gentlemen were.

Her voice echoed through every weld in the ship. And all she did was give them a girlish giggle.

The pirates looked at each other. "What...and I mean this with all due respect...*the fuck* was that?"

"Skitter, patter, pecking away," Rashida said over the intercom, her voice ethereal and panning from room to room, like it was carried on the wind. "Skitter, patter..."

"The AI, ya think?" one pirate whispered, shrugging.

So Rashida doubled down. "Get out of my house."

They shouldered their rifles, one thumbing his safety. "Come on out, little girl! We just want to talk."

"They all want to talk," Rashida whispered. "They always want to talk. I want to play."

One of them inched forward, sweating from just about every available surface on his body. "Maybe we uh..."

And his friend promptly slapped him on the back of the head, almost earning him a gunshot response from the twitchy pirate. The sensible one just cocked his head. "Do not talk to it."

"What were you going to do to it?" the sweaty one asked. "You going to shoot it? It's a *ghost.*"

"That ain't no ghost. You know how I know? Because ghosts ain't a real thing."

As if on cue, Lily's giant blue face filled the room, a growing azure howl. They loomed over the pirates, unhinging their pixilated maw.

The pirates screamed and raised their rifles—peppering Lily's holographic head. The bullets ricocheted around the room, skipping and punching holes.

Lily descended on them, melting right through them, the floor, and disappeared into the wall. Both pirates took a moment to catch their breath and put their pounding hearts in order.

Rashida eyeballed the smoking divot in the steel next to her hide-out. Maybe the bluff had been too good.

Finally, sensible pirate chuckled, slapping his sweating buddy on the back. "You shoulda seen your face!"

"Oh, really? And look at you, Sir Guns-a-lot! You know that's a reactor core you just peppered?"

"Oh, sure, act like you weren't shooting too. I see how it is."

Fine. Let's step it up a notch. *Lily...close all the doors.*

You're a sadistic person. I enjoy this discovery.

Rashida nodded. *And get the lights.*

With a bang loud enough to compete with the gunfire, every door on the ship slammed shut. All of the light had been scooped out, some black bag over her head. Lily had a moment of genuine inspiration, powering down the reactor core too, leaving the pirates and Rashida in absolute darkness.

The only light Rashida had was the surprised flash from a pirate's gun barrel, strobing the room with three distinct glimpses of the tableau.

Something wet and gurgling, like a mountain spring. The metallic bang as a heavy weight settled onto the steel. And then the smallest voice, whimpering in the shadows. "V-Verner? Verner?!"

Red emergency lights kicked on—and Rashida found herself face to face with the pirate. His mouth hung open, blood leaking from it like a busted filter. He swung back and forth, dangling over the catwalk's railing, his eyes unfocused. A hole had been etched clean through his throat, dribbling a small stream up his chin and to the deck below. His movements came in tiny swells as he tried to pull a breath, his muscles spasming but the air whistling out of his throat.

The pirate above gibbered and gasped, shaking in terror at what he'd done. He dropped his rifle, letting it hang from his sling. He only had eyes for the damage he'd done. "Oh-oh, god. Oh no, no..."

Reduced to a frightened little boy in just five seconds flat, the pirate scrambled for the door and began clawing at the steel, trying to peel it open. "Somebody! Anybody!" Like the ship heard him, the door hushed open, and he tumbled through it, disappearing into the *Aurum's* interior.

Rashida stared at the dying man, as his jaw worked over and over, his eyes blinking and unfocused. If he recognized her, or even saw her at all, his face never showed it. A kind of calm fell over him as he came to stillness. The only sound in the bay was his blood dripping to the floor.

She pulled herself out of the hatch and settled herself gently, dropping herself unfortunately right into the pirate's blood pool.

"May I say, well done," Lily said. "An inspired approach."

She'd killed him. He was alive. Then she came into the room, and now he was dead. She had just said a few words, and now...

Lily's face melted out of the space in front of her, extending a hazy hand to her. "Rashida, you must listen to me now. They will return to—this space—soon, and you must seize this chance to flee."

"Yeah," Rashida whispered, staring down at her shoes and the growing red puddle. "Where are the others, Lily?"

A quiet murmur as Lily considered the question. "I have found them. But you will not like it."

TWENTY-EIGHT
ADELAIDE

IT WAS A STUPID GAMBLE, going down to that ship. But she had to admit, she didn't expect the Godfather's fangs to be what ultimately closed on them. Now they sat in a pirate hold, stripped of their weapons and jammed in a closet.

The ship was a retrofitted medium cargo hauler, older than the *Aurum,* and with quite a few more cubbies and hidey holes. The gangsters had no need to hide or smuggle, so they had stripped away all the excess components and crammed in armory lockers, living quarters, and even a wet bar. What good was kidnapping if you couldn't get drunk while doing it? That always fueled the best decisions.

Every surface was rusted, pitted and pocked. They had shown this ship no love. Adelaide found herself scoffing as she examined the degrading state of the metal grating overhead, locking the prisoners away from the half dozen flickering lights.

In the ship's heart, far from an easy chance of rescue, the *Aurum's* crew languished. What had been guest quarters had been consolidated with a knocked-out wall, the steel beams that used to support a wall still dividing the room like old fence posts. They'd even dug to remove the furniture and the bolts that held them steady.

All they had to greet them was the bare floor, sanded to make it further uncomfortable against bare skin.

Two guards stood just outside at the door, cradling their stun batons. She could hear the idle hum of electric charge, a white noise in their small space.

Zatia paced back and forth like a caged beast. Thom hung off the side of the dividing beams like they were his playpen, swinging from one to the next to pass the time. Milardi did the same in an opposed path, swinging high over the lad whenever they crossed paths, only to scrunch up comically small whenever it was his turn to 'go low.'

Not Osyen. He sat down against the wall, back pressed flat, and stared at the door, eyes narrow. Plotting something horrible, she was certain. His plots were never more than emotionally valid wishes. He'd figure out what he wanted to do, and Thom would sort out how it was actually done.

She took some comfort in that Thom didn't seem the least bit distressed.

They all perked up when the lock on their door clanked, and they had to shield their eyes from the glaring outside lights. They pressed a very smug and bloody Roche through the door, slapping the door shut behind him.

Milardi rushed to the big jockey's side, slinging an arm under him. "My baby boy, look what they've done to you!"

"I'm thirty-one, Jackson."

"'Least they had the kindness not to pick at your implants too much."

"They pick up Lars?" Thom asked.

Roche winced. "He's having brandy and regaling them with his time in captivity."

"Prick," Adelaide snorted.

Osyen nodded to Roche. "That's everyone, huh?" he asked, with a marked point.

Roche had a black eye, but that didn't stop him from discreetly winking. "We are pan fried, sir. Our goose is proper cooked."

Adelaide tried to hide her sigh of relief. There was still one crew member unaccounted for. It wasn't her favorite pick, but they were not out of this game just yet.

Osyen glanced at Thom, forcing a pleasant little smile. "Any big ideas we should be made aware of?"

"Sometimes," Thom said, as he swung around the support beam, "it's more about not doing something."

"You know how I like to do nothing," Adelaide said, "but this really strikes me as a time to get on with it."

He shrugged. "It's just not our turn yet."

A sing-song self-satisfied voice echoed through the steel, like along the surface of an empty tank. "Thomas Hugh!" The crew turned toward the door of their cell. Even through the small slit, Adelaide could recognize Weasel's chin and sneer. "Someone has been naughty."

"I tried to get him to be," Milardi matched the gangster's tone like they were belly up at a bar. "But it didn't take. I mean, look at his haircut! Could clean the floor with that."

Thom's ashy-brown hair did look like the fuzzy end of a mop. She mentally ran through a handful of the chromatic dyes she'd given to Zatia, give the kid a radiant green or something more interesting. He always was quite taken with her colors.

Thom just shook his head, waving him off the issue. Milardi was full of hot air on a good day, but on a bad day, it was like he found reserve gas. He was just blowing smoke.

"There's a fairly hefty finder's fee for the lad. For you all, in fact. I imagine there'll be a bonus for returning you..." Weasel lingered, relishing the implication, "...intact."

"You don't mind me asking," Osyen chirped from the back of the cell, "what's the take on us? Like, collectively?"

"As a set, no particular bonus," Weasel said. "But—all tolled—you come in at a cool two million."

Milardi coughed, offended. "Who in their right mind thinks I'm worth a million? I mean, you all are fine, I guess. Two hundred here or there? But I'm *at least* a mill and a half."

Weasel was fed up. "You speak another word that isn't book-ended with 'sir', and I'll be delivering you in a casket."

"Sir, you're very kind...sir," Milardi said, teasing the time limit on that rule.

"Who's doing the buying?" Osyen asked.

Roche said it at the same time Weasel did. "Admiral Ulysses Hugh, Imperial Navy." And Weasel groaned in frustration. "The fat one ruined my big reveal!"

Roche went from jovial to rage mode, peeling off of Milardi and slamming into the door hard enough that Adelaide had to jump back. "This one is ready for round two whenever you get your breath back."

Roche seized, and Adelaide could hear the crackling of the stun batons being jammed into the ready-made ports. Osyen and Thom lurched forward to grab him, but Milardi held them back with wide a sweeping arm. "Don't touch him!"

Roche gripped the doorframe with his hand, locked up and shivering and cursing in barely audible grunts. But a man loaded down with as many augments as he was, he was no stranger to electric shock. And he brought his other arm across his body, swiping his wrist with a thud and breaking his grip. He staggered away from the door, gasping, fresh blood trickling from his lip.

Milardi swept in, leading Roche to rest against the ground and checking him over. Roche gave him a brief nod. It would take more than a steady electric shock to disrupt a man who was more or less half metal himself.

Milardi smiled, planting a sweet kiss on to Roche's forehead and rubbing the tufts of hair on the crown of Roche's head like he was looking for good luck. Roche patted Milardi's hands to comfort him before spitting more blood into a corner.

Weasel slithered on the other side of the door, flitting in and out of view like a cobra in its basket. "Whatchu think boys? Should we gas 'em, box 'em, and ship 'em? Or bring 'em to the meet, juicy and spittin'?"

"You arranged a meeting?" Adelaide asked.

"Oh-ho-ho! The iron lady does have a voice!" Weasel taunted. "Yes, that's usually how this business operates in polite company."

"Then you're already dead."

He flashed a smile. "Lotsa folk prettier and meaner than you have made the same threat through this very door."

"I ain't threatening you," Adelaide said. "I've got plenty of reason to want you and everybody you know dead and buried. When I threaten you, I promise you'll know it. Right now, I'm warning you."

Weasel squinted, thinking himself so very clever. "Admiral Hugh is a man of law, a businessman. And he honors his debts."

"He will. But something a helluva lot meaner is going to beat him here. It's going to rip through your ship and crew like you're made of tinder."

"Oh, the Paladin?" Weasel asked, looking down his nose at her. "Lars has been very forthcoming."

"Then you know plenty about what's coming," she urged him. "And if you're a smart man—which you seem to carry yourself as— you'll let us out. Right now."

Weasel swept his arms out wide, like he was about to welcome a hug from some invisible sky God. "Children of the Master have no fear of metal men or towering starships."

Adelaide snorted. "Pride goeth before the fall."

Weasel chewed on the notion, almost considering it. But then he waggled a finger at the door. "Now I know why you tucked your chin and held your tongue before. You're tactical with your words."

Adelaide knew better than to hit the door, but lord did she want to. She wanted to wrap her fingers around his squirrelly little neck and wring it out like a wet towel. She wanted to grab a good torque wrench and sink it into the side of his skull to do some adjustments to the inside. But she just squeezed her fingers, the broken and cruddy nails biting into her palms.

"Blessed be your steps," Weasel sassed, as he turned away.

"I ain't joining some Pilgrim's Path!" Adelaide shouted after him. "I'll be seeing you in Hell, you son of a bitch!"

Osyen groaned. "Eh, it was worth a shot."

"He wants to know what it sounds like when I threaten him?" Adelaide seethed. "I'll feed him to my turbines, that's what I'll do."

"I don't care what anybody says, I'm not cleaning that up," Thom said.

Zatia chuckled. "You'd never get it all out, anyway. You'd probably have to buy a new engine block."

"Could always sail it as is. Just call it a ghost ship," Milardi quipped. He stood up tall, hooking a thumb in his jacket, adopting a classic High Imperial accent. "'My, my, what is all this blood doing in my cabin? The ventilation system seems to be oozing again.'" He took a step to the left, slouching back into his natural posture, hip cocked out and arms folded across his chest. "Oh, that? We have a wraith. Just watch your step. It's sticky when drying."

"Anybody have any last confessions?" Osyen asked, head tilted back against the wall. "Window's closing."

Roche shrugged. "I like to think we worked out all of our family secrets, but if somebody is holding out on us, now *would* be a good time."

"Gentlefolk?"

Osyen ground his teeth. Weasel's rodent face was back at the door. "*What*, Weasel?"

Weasel nodded to the guards. "Open the door."

There was a bit of a fuss behind her, but all Adelaide could feel was her blood boiling up in her chest and forearms. He was actually going to run all that talk on her and then remove the one barrier keeping him safe? What a cocky bastard.

But the guards didn't leap to action, instead eying one another with confusion. "Boss?"

"I'm not in the habit of repeating myself."

More confusion. "Boss?"

Weasel rolled his eyes. "Is that all you can say? Did someone extract the rest of the vocabulary from your head with a pair of pliers?"

"No, Boss."

"Oh, good!" Weasel snapped. "We have a whole second word. But I don't need more words. I need more action. Open it up."

Thom stood, dusting himself off with a knowing smile on his face. Adelaide studied the kid, trying to parse out what he was expecting to happen next. But he had the confidence of a gambler who'd already played out the hand.

"You gave us strict instructions not to open this door," one guard said, "even if it was you that asked us."

"I gave you that order, did I?" Weasel asked, snarling at the guard. "Now watch me give you the order that overrules that one. Open the cell."

They looked at each other again...and the door seal cracked.

There he was, silhouetted in the doorframe. The little gangster stood tall and confident, almost regal. She was going to beat that out of him.

"Now get to the escape pods," Weasel said. "We're abandoning ship."

"Boss?"

Weasel snapped back hard again. "Boss, Boss, Boss—We're abandoning ship and I'm not leaving our payday in the wreckage, now am I? Get going, lads!"

"But why don't we take the..."

Osyen didn't wait another second, surging through the door and kicking one guard at the wrist. The stun baton clattered to the ground. His friend lunged for Osyen's exposed back—but Zatia leapt onto the exposed arm, dragging the hand to the ground and wrenching the baton from his grasp.

Milardi strolled through the open door, head held high, drawing a deep breath of freedom. He looked down at the crumpled guards around him, as Osyen and Zatia finished up in a parade of sparks, like a man trying to not get his boots wet in a swamp.

Weasel folded his dainty arms across his chest, smirking at the gang. "Took you long enough."

Adelaide stormed over the threshold, gripping Weasel about the throat and planting the gangster against the opposite wall. She leaned in close, looking deep into his little dark eyes. "I promised you...you'd know when I was threatening you."

Osyen stepped up to her side. "Adelaide, break his neck or let him go, but we're kind of on a schedule."

Weasel's throat let out a squeak under her fingers, the muscles in his throat straining. Yet strangely, his arms were pinned at his sides, stiff and orderly.

He wasn't fighting her. Not like he could stop her. But still...it wasn't as satisfying to see him welcome his end.

Fine.

Adelaide let him go. Weasel slumped to the ground, coughing and hacking. She pointed down at him. "When you're ready to face up to what you've done, you come find me. Until then, stay outta my way."

Weasel coughed. "Awfully nice to see you too." And he reached for his throat, pulling his jacket collar down to reveal—

A holographic collar.

Weasel's face fell away, brick by brick, lowering the electronic veil. And it was Rashida Izan de Tylmirande, in all her Imperial glory. Dressed to the nines in gangster uniform, slender suit and ragged tie. She'd scuffed up her face and hands on something, and oil painted one cheek.

Milardi's jaw dropped. "What the Hell have you been up to?"

Rashida laid crumpled against the wall, eyes bugged out and rubbing at her throat. "Minor heroics. Deception. Subterfuge. The usual."

Zatia just started applauding from the side with a soupçon of belly laugh.

Adelaide blinked and extended a hand to the noblewoman crumpled on the ground. Rashida shrugged off the brutal greeting and took her hand, pulling herself to standing.

"Suits you," Adelaide said, nodding at the uniform.

Rashida chuckled. "I get that. That's funny."

"I suppose I should—"

But Rashida waved her off. "No apologies. I might've guessed that would have been the welcome. Let's just move on to the next problem, shall we?"

Yes, Adelaide thought. Do what you can, make mistakes, learn from them...move on. But that had very nearly been an egregious error. How would she have moved on from a mistake like that?

"Where's the *Aurum*?" Osyen asked.

"They're towing it between the three ships," Rashida explained. "We fight any one tether, and we'll just pull everyone out of the sky."

Roche nodded. "We can cut the anchor on this ship, but how do you propose we cut the other two?"

And that's what made Rashida grind her teeth. "I didn't do this whole adventure alone."

It was strange to hear that familiar bass voice in such a meek and tender tone. *Hello, Osyen. You have gotten—*ksssh*—into quite the pickle. Perhaps I could be-be-be of service?*

Osyen immediately fell into the nearest wall, pressing his back against the bulkhead. His breath fell shallow and ragged. "Hi..."

Hello, Osyen. I understand your feelings. But know that I was never far.

"They're getting worse by the second, so we have to work fast. If we can get access to this ship's Jump Deck," Rashida explained, "Lily can cut the lines by remote. Then Roche flies us all out of here."

Thom nodded. "Okay, everyone, game faces. Zee, Milardi, and Osyen: think you can escort Adelaide up to the Jump Deck for some fun 'n games?"

"We gotta get everyone else back to the *Aurum*," Milardi cautioned.

"I can handle that," Rashida said with conviction. "We'll get ready to fly, you cut us free."

Adelaide smiled, liking that energy. "Time for a grand escape?"

Zatia rested both stun batons on her shoulders, while Milardi cracked his knuckles. Roche wiped the blood from his chin, and Rashida gave a firm nod. Adelaide looked over at Osyen, the young captain staring into the middle distance.

Adelaide snapped her fingers in front of Osyen's face. "Oy. You copacetic?"

"Yeah," he said. He looked up at his crew, a playful spark coming into his eye and a warm smile across his face. "Let's get dangerous."

CHAPTER
TWENTY-NINE
THOM

HE'D SEEN the royal lady do a great many things—Rashida had transformed garments for form and function; she'd stood in the face of lords and thugs; she'd slammed a shuttle craft into the side of an Imperial carrier.

But Thom had never seen her throw an elbow into a pirate's head. As soon as she came through the doorway, she cut loose. She accompanied the blow with a sharp and shrill cry, like she might shout her strike through his head. He turned just in time to catch the attack square to the bridge of his nose.

It was the ship's galley—larger than the *Aurum's*, and definitely more populated. At least ten men looked up, slack-jawed. They were wearing the Godfather's best. Armor, helmets with holographic displays, and shiny new guns.

"Greetings and complications, my dear folk," Milardi spouted like a showman. "We are tonight's entertainment."

And Lars Hedlop was halfway through a bottle of fine whiskey, looking positively crestfallen. "Shoot them! Shoot them, you fools!"

Zatia wasted no time pouncing on Rashida's victim, tumbling through the door to drop a heel onto his head as she launched herself at a poorly prepared second man—she'd managed to bounce from one man straight on to the next, like the floor was lava. She landed on him like she'd sunk claws into his chest, pulling him down to the ground as a shield.

Every shooter in the room turned to follow the little goblin, aiming anything they had at her. But all they hit was countertops and their friend, peppering him with holes and blowing red spatter across the backsplash.

Two goons grabbed Lars, putting his head down and running him toward the door. They assumed the escaping bandits were after Lars for the second time. The two wannabe bodyguards broke from their colleagues and instead laid gunfire on the *Aurum*'s crew, trying to suppress them at the door and keep them from entering further.

But Milardi weaved in behind Rashida and between gunshots. He ripped a pistol from the fallen man's holster. And he was an artist with it, tucking it into his hip and tapping rounds into the room. He placed the shots with precision, snapping the men down before they realized what was happening. One man tumbled down behind cover, using one of his own friends as a shield from Milardi on his way to the ground.

Osyen used this moment, rushing in with head low. He snagged a chair, dragging it along the floor right up to the closest goon. As the grunt raised his pistol to shoot, Osyen swung the light piece of furniture, connecting with the poor bastard's hand. Osyen kept the spin going, swinging the chair over his head like a flail and coming back around to clock the goon across the jaw.

Zatia stood up, glaring at Osyen. "All the tools available, and you grab a chair?"

"He's down! What, you want me to do it with style points too?"

"What about Lars?" Milardi asked.

"Leave him," Osyen grunted. "We got what we need from him."

Milardi shrugged. "I dunno. A cybernetics guy seems like a nice pickup."

Adelaide sneered, looking down the hallway to see if the old bastard was lingering. "He's made his choice."

Zatia hopped from behind the counter, pointing an aggressive finger at Rashida, but her smile said pleased. "Nice elbow. Drive it from your hip next time. All the power comes from your legs."

"How do you punch from your *legs*?" Rashida asked.

The lights suddenly cut out, replaced by flashing yellow emergency lights. A klaxon of hateful whining filled the air. If the gunshots hadn't alerted the entire ship, that alarm sure did. They'd soon have half of Hell falling down on top of them.

Zatia nodded at Rashida. "I'll show you later."

Osyen pointed to one door. "Rash, get Thom and Roche back to the *Aurum* and get it fired up."

Thom tapped the back of his head. "I'll be checking in. If you don't hear from me—"

Osyen nodded with wide eyes. "I'm sorry, how many close encounters with him do you think I want in my life?"

Milardi pressed a pistol into Osyen's hands and tossed another to Zatia. "Let's go, children. Let us away."

Osyen's eyes lingered on Thom, Rashida, and Roche, panning over them like he was committing their faces to memory. And then he broke into a jog, following Zatia, Milardi, and Adelaide down the passage to the Jump Deck.

Roche tugged on Thom's shoulder. "Not to put too fine a point on it, but we shouldn't linger over dead pirates when living ones are on the way."

Thom nodded and followed them out towards the waiting *Aurum*.

The passageways were quite irregular, with dangling cables and exposed piping running the length of the concave tunnel. Thom recognized patch jobs and repairs when done by folk with only a cursory understanding. Any of these exposed hazards could trip someone in a hurry or snag on an arm, yanking out coolant or gray water. Nobody wanted that.

How's it looking? Thom asked over the back channel.

He was pleased to get a fairly irritated response from Osyen.

Thom, I've been gone twenty seconds. I appreciate the concern—but I am being shot at. So, if you don't mind?

At least he answered. So the Paladin wasn't close at hand. If he was...

The storm below them had not been kind to Magnus's ship, and it wouldn't be any more kind to the *Aurum* should they fall out of the sky. The extreme cold and the gnashing teeth of the winter wind would sap the crew of life in seconds. If they survived a crash, the weather would kill them before the Paladin could.

"Get down!" Rashida urged, pressing Roche into the wall, tucking his frame behind the silhouette of the exposed piping. The big jockey stuck a hand back, pressing Thom to safety. Thom reached back, but with nobody to shield, he was just waving his hand in empty air.

Pounding feet as a full squad of pirates stomped through an intersection ahead. They carried long arms, some kind of gaussian carbine, and wore thick ceramic plates on their chests and shoulders. It was hardly inspired, but Thom could think of little that would be more effective armor while on a budget.

And Weasel was leading them, thin suit, and gun in hand.

Crash party, Roche bounced, *you have a platoon of heavy infantry on approach from the starboard side. Carbines and armor.*

Thank you, beautiful, Milardi said. *I'll handle it.*

Weasel is with them, Thom cautioned.

I'll handle it, Milardi repeated with a bit more joy in his voice.

Coast clear, Rashida led them on to the airlock.

A single guard stood watch, feet pointed out like a duck and his armor ill-fitting. The flashing lights made it hard to make out his features, but he looked quite young. Probably no older than Thom himself.

"I doubt he's alone," Rashida whispered.

Roche looked left, up, and down—before finding what he wanted. A serial bus outlet on the wall, a dangling exposed plug with no cover, lay exposed from some hack job, and was then abandoned that way. He rolled up his sleeve and pulled out a cable. "Get ready to run."

"What are you going to do?"

"I'm going to hijack his head's up display. Once I'm sure he's alone, I'll surround him with very angry bees," Roche said with maddening specificity.

"I'm sorry?" Thom blinked at the image. "Bees?"

"Not real ones. When he runs, we run. Sound good?"

Rashida worked her jaw, computing that idea. She glanced at Thom, as if to ponder how her life and its many wonders had brought her to this rusting hull, in this besotted suit, with these beautiful people.

It was the happiest Thom had ever seen her.

Roche plugged his cable into the outlet—

And instantaneously, the pirate recruit swatted the air. First, just a buzzing sound. Nothing too intense. But less than a second after swatting at an invisible bee, the kid had a moment's pause. He's in space, where did the bug come from? And his eye slid left, examining the environment.

Another buzz, and another involuntary swipe. This time he pawed at the side of his helmet, trying to remove whatever he *thought* had landed on him.

That's when it really started. And the kid yelped in confusion, and he lowered his rifle, waving his other hand in the air.

Rashida took her moment, rushing the pirate. Before the kid could parse out the sounds of incoming feet, she lunged, shoving him with both hands into the wall. The gear was not light, but he wasn't a big lad either. Her inertia was plenty to lift him off his feet and bang him into the opposite wall.

She stripped his helmet off and pressed the gun's barrel across his throat, pinning him. "Go, go!" Rashida called out.

Roche and Thom ran past the guard and through the airlock hatch.

The kid tried to talk tough, aiming his snide remarks at the escaping prisoners. "The M-Master will see to you!"

"And I will put bees in your brain forever," Roche promised. "The doctors will never get them all out, no matter how much you pay them."

The kid's eyes flicked between Roche and Rashida, finally whispering to her. "He-he can't do that, can he?"

"My dear boy," Rashida said with a smile, "you wouldn't be his first."

And that sent chills up Thom's spine. She had heard an objectively bizarre and unachievable threat, and she just leaned into it, lending her gravitas and credentials to it. Thom couldn't help but picture the wax-filled apiary that would grow in a human skull. And he filed that one away into the nightmares folder in his head.

Oz, we're on. What's your status?

No response for a second. Then: *On my way to you,* Osyen bounced. *Don't worry.*

Thom's face went pale. "He's here."

Rashida let the boy down, ripping his rifle from his hands. "Get to an escape pod. No more kidding around. You have to get out. Get out!"

Something about her urgency, the extreme shift in tone, sent the boy fleeing with his tail between his legs.

"What do we—" Roche started.

But Rashida shouted him down. "You get this ship ready to fly *the moment* we're loose! Go!"

He nodded and jogged off to the Jump Deck. Whether they stayed was immaterial. If they hung around, they simply risked their deaths. If the Paladin could cut off the escape, he could pick off the crew at his leisure. They'd have to find another way to get Osyen and the others to safety.

If they didn't get free...they'd crash in the tundra, in the heart of the blizzard, assailed by the elements—

Thom's brain froze over. It was going to happen. What he'd seen in his dreams. The crash, the fields of ice, the storm. The Paladin was going to crash the *Aurum*, kill everyone. This was the future he saw...

But the image was not set, constantly in flux. He could stop it. If he only chose differently...

"Thomas?" Rashida read the decision on his face. "They'll be alright. Thomas!"

He didn't wait for her permission. Thom jumped back onto the pirate ship and slapped the door shut in her face. He could hear her calling out to him, pounding on the glass. Pleading with him.

He could save the crew, save the *Aurum*. He knew he could. He had what no one else did: he knew what hadn't worked before.

He had touched the Icon, the Pilgrim's hand. He had glimpsed the future before him. And he knew that future could change.

Thom looked at the concave passageway behind him, listening to the klaxon of alarm bells and the flashing of warning lights. A slight breeze pulled at his skin, and he could almost hear a crackle, like the oncoming of frost adding its crisp to the air.

It felt like standing in a graveyard, in the presence of the Paladin, like the scent of death. Not his first confrontation with that elemental force...

CHAPTER
THIRTY
MILARDI

GUNSHOTS ALWAYS HAD a strange smell to them. Not like a chemical burn, but something akin to ozone. It charged the air and always made the hair on his arms stand on end.

Milardi picked up two more pistols, jamming them in his jacket. Every dead pirate or gangster just meant more guns for his many, many pockets.

The Jump Deck of the ship was rather large and obnoxiously had a glass view port. They could see straight out into the maelstrom. Osyen had entered the room and put three rounds into the ceiling, sending the crew scattering. They weren't gangsters by trade—just pilots trying to make a living. The one hero that went for a gun, Milardi shot in the hand.

Adelaide worked to disconnect the AI core from the console. It was laborious work, on her back under a desk. The AI was liable to counteract anything Lily tried to do, so it had to be removed.

By contrast, Zatia had entered the room with two stun batons, ambidextrously working over the big beefcake of a guard that had been stationed on the deck. He was more muscle than anything else. Milardi couldn't be sure if he flexed every time he breathed, or if his muscles rippled through his shirt by nature.

The meathead growled at Zatia with each hit, swiping with ham-hock fists to break the snapping electric batons' link to him. But fifty thousand volts always found a way to pull back out of reach, to slip back in and crackle against his skin. She left him peppered with tiny red stab marks wherever the prongs struck home.

He got one good backhand onto Zatia's face—and she used the rotational energy to roll into a hands-free cartwheel, kicking him right back.

The heavy slumped to one knee, low enough for Zatia. She pressed off of the back wall, flying past him and cracking her knee across his temple as she went.

"Zatia! I need you to stop playing with your food," Osyen shouted, "because we've got *company!*"

Milardi looked over. Osyen was hunkered down behind a bulk-head, streaks of yellow and white tracers zipping past his shoulder and bouncing off the steel. A formation of armored grunts had taken up residence down the hall, peeking from cover to lay down some impressive fire.

Zatia tumbled over her handiwork, falling behind the same steel desk Adelaide had chosen.

"I can get the door closed!" Adelaide shouted.

"Don't wait for my permission! Get over here!" Osyen yelled back, blindly firing around the corner, but all he was going to accomplish was getting his hand shot off. The Godfather's response squad was good and well bunkered in.

But none approached. Milardi wasn't entirely sure how they would down such a narrow space with their own team firing at their backs. Unless...they didn't intend to.

Diversion.

Twin grenades sailed down the hall. Osyen managed to get his foot out, kicking one right back at its owner. The second bounced right on over beside Milardi, sliding to a stop a foot or so away.

He had just enough time to whimper. "Oh, crap."

The shell cracked, emitting a thrumming high-pitched whine—it was what Milardi thought Hell's waiting room sounded like. Osyen crumpled to the ground, and Adelaide thrashed, clutching at her ears. Milardi flailed at the grenade, trying to silence it, but to no avail.

Zatia stood up, completely nonplussed and eyes sharp. He glimpsed her, even as his eyes fluttered against the noise. Her rainbow hair dancing in the air, a cut on her lip dripping blood like she'd just torn out someone's throat with her bare teeth. She glanced over at Osyen and craned her neck to look down the hall as the attackers held their ground.

The stims, all of the chemistry swirling in her. Trying to overload her nervous system now must've been adorable.

And she flourished her batons, ready for work.

Just as a side door opened. A full platoon of armored heavy soldiers pressed on the door, ready to breach with hate and aggression.

And she met their charge, swinging a baton low to chip the live stun grenade up and out the door.

They were well trained, immediately diving away from what they had to believe was an explosive device. Zatia went to work, slamming from one attacker to the next, striking for knees and throats. She left one stun baton behind, its twin pronged lead jammed directly through one guard's helmet and stuck in his face.

Milardi shook his head, pressing himself up from the ground. He could still hear the screeching, but it had run off down the hallway accompanying the grenade itself. And while Zatia was skilled and aggressive, she was only one person—and they were many. The rest of the platoon filed in, carbines tucked into their shoulders.

They opened fire, one shot lancing through Zatia. She tumbled aside, but Milardi could make out the spray of blood she left over a console.

They were good troops, taking the room with precision. With Zatia suppressed, they turned on the rest.

Milardi pulled the first of his stolen brace of pistols and thumbed the battery charge open. No matter how fast they thought they were, these regular ol' human boys couldn't beat the speed of a bullet. He blasted the first goon to round the corner once, twice, three times. That ceramic ballistic plate was built to take a heated laser blast and would crack with a kinetic strike. The curvature of the mold did what it could to throw spalling lead away from vital neck and arms.

But it did no good at all on the fourth shot. Five, six, and seven shredded the poor lad, leaving him a filet on the ground, armor broken and blood seeping.

Milardi chucked the useless pistol, drawing another. It was far faster to draw a fresh gun than worry about fishing out a magazine, especially when he didn't really know how this particular weapon operated.

Osyen woke up and joined the party. Rifle braced between the wall and his side, he blasted the room, mowing down anyone that tried to get close.

With the breaching force suitably occupied, Zatia popped out from behind her cover, throwing her remaining baton at the goons in the doorway. It bounced off of their helmets, hanging in the air—and she caught it on her way to them, slamming the crackling electric prod into one man's neck.

Zatia didn't even look up, feeling a commando's gun barrel press against her—and Milardi put a round through his eyeball. She wiped at the blood dribbling down her lip, and finally let her wounded arm hang limp.

Milardi dropped the third empty gun. "Wind's whistling right through you, Zee."

Zatia reached over to the console, closing the offending door that had just disgorged almost a dozen armed—corpses—into the room. She almost tripped over one body while picking at her ear. "I gotta tell you: never thought I'd be happy to have tinnitus."

That wasn't why. Milardi knew that whatever neurological damage the stims had done to her made her far less susceptible to neurological overload.

The gunfire might've abated, but that didn't mean that Weasel or his brigade of meat and metal had gone anywhere. The gangster called up the hallway. "Give it up, Osyen! There's nowhere left for you to run to."

"Weasel!" Osyen shouted back. "Do those badasses you run with know your name is Leonard?"

Muttering, muttering down the hall. And Milardi had to chuckle.

Osyen beckoned Adelaide over. "Get this door shut," he said.

"Too happy to," she said, grasping a panel on the wall with her aging claws and popping it open.

Milardi was almost impressed until he saw it dangling off its one rusty hinge. She hadn't won; the metal had just lost.

The ship lurched underneath them, tilting hard to one side, metal groaning and scraping. Osyen clutched the doorframe, eyes wide. "Addy?!" he shouted in confusion.

The old woman shifted her feet, but otherwise hadn't reacted to the rocking floor underneath her. "Don't call me that." She pinched together two wires, twitching away from a slight shock. It must not have bothered her too much, as she just wiped her hand on her pants.

And the blast door slipped shut. Weasel and his goons were pounding on it in a matter of seconds, bellowing threats and orders.

"Why are we listing?" Zatia asked, clutching her shoulder. "Did we do that?"

Osyen stepped off the doorframe, taking command. "Adelaide, get Lily some contact and cut that anchor line! It's time to get motivated. Milardi, would you mind? She is leaking everywhere."

"I've taken over your job," Zatia coughed at him. "I'm getting bullet wounds on top of my stab wounds."

"Yeah, we're proper siblings now." Osyen snapped his fingers at Milardi, pointing to the smear of blood Zatia was leaving on the furniture. "Milardi? Any day now?"

But Milardi couldn't answer. He had no idea how anybody could pay attention to anything else.

He stared out of the windshield...to see one of the gangster frigates spiraling forward, thick black smoke trailing from a deep gash in its hull. A slain monster flopping onto its side, tugged through the air by a thick umbilical anchor tied to its brothers. Shrapnel and debris peeled off its carcass in waves, vanishing into the white storm clouds.

The only thing that could cut that much damage would be an anti-aircraft battery. Or worse.

"My God..." Milardi murmured.

A single shred of metal tumbled towards them, slamming hard into the Jump Deck's window, sending cracks along the five-inch glass down along the entire frame.

"I'm almost there!" Adelaide said, frantically typing on the console.

Something came hurtling right at the window—and the Paladin's heavy boots stuck hard to the glass, sinking into the thick material. His bald head looked up, encrusted with frost along his jaw and under his nose. And his eyes glittering yellow...

"Out!" Milardi shouted. "Everybody out! Now, now, now!"

As the Paladin brought his fist down into the glass, shattering the window.

Everyone fell to the Deck floor, a vicious and unforgiving cold spitting into the air. The wind tugged at Milardi's jacket and he could feel his hair tightening up with crisp ice.

He rolled over to see the Paladin standing over him.

He pulled two pistols, burying shot after shot into the Paladin's chest. And to no surprise, the refracting bubble of energy showed itself with every blast, deflecting the chunks of metal off and away. Perhaps if he got closer, he could get inside that shield—not that being closer to this thing was necessarily a good thing. He'd seen first-hand what had happened to certain barkeeps.

Milardi fired until his guns ran dry. The Paladin courteously waited for him to finish. A mech would've just killed him, pushed right through that last stand to snap his puny human neck. But a man? The Paladin wanted him to plainly see without distraction how useless resistance was.

Adelaide swung a cracked sheet of metal panel—and the Paladin just reached out with one hand, magnetically pulling the sheet to itself. Adelaide couldn't let loose her grip in time, and found herself pulled along with it, letting go in time to be thrown across the room.

The serrated panel hovered over the Paladin's palm, quivering in anticipation, as the Paladin looked down at Milardi. No words, no taunt, no questions. But he was taking a moment to consider his kill.

How polite. Milardi closed his eyes...

And felt hot steel spackle across his face, coupled with gunshots. Bullets struck the deflector shield, shattering against the superior force, throwing subsonic shards at Milardi's face and neck. They dug fiery trails up and down his front.

In between the deafening thuds from his rifle, Osyen bellowed at the Paladin: "Hey! Big guy! I'm right here! You want your *princess*?! I've got—"

He never got the last sentence out. The Paladin hurled the steel plate at Osyen with a blind flick of the wrist. The shot was dead on, so fast that Osyen probably never saw it.

For the first moment of contact, it sliced right through Osyen's rifle, shredding it into a hundred bits of steel and polymer. But at the unfriendly end of the rifle was a hand, and a wrist, and an arm. The metal javelin shredded flesh just as easily—the edge was broad enough that it sliced Osyen's arm off right at the shoulder.

The captain howled, flopping to the ground like a flank of meat in a butcher shop.

Never breaking eye contact with Milardi, the Paladin stomped directly over to Osyen.

The Paladin gripped Osyen by the jaw, heaving him into the air up to his eye level. "I know she is here, Osyen Belt. Where...is the girl?"

Whimpering and dripping on to the floor, he cursed through clenched teeth. "*Fra tow ni laska*...she's dead!"

The Paladin yanked him closer, still staring straight at Milardi. Osyen's feet dangling in the air. And it sneered. "Deceit is a sin."

Osyen grimaced. "Yeah...you mentioned that before."

They couldn't kill this thing. Not here, not now. All they could do was distract and escape. How would he...

Zatia had made her way to the exit, pulling Adelaide to her feet. They beckoned for Milardi to follow. Osyen had this thing occupied. What were they going to do? Peel Osyen away from its fingers? There was nothing they could do now.

Maybe...maybe there was one thing...

The stun grenade. It wasn't much, but it was a loud, high frequency sound. If it stunned regular folk, it might do something to a Paladin. Right?

What other choice did he have?

Milardi caught Zatia's eye, and pressed his hands over his ears, then pointed down the hall—back where they'd tossed the stun grenade. Her eyes went wide, and she darted back. Adelaide shook her head, urging him to abandon whatever stupid plot and flee.

The whole time, the Paladin just stared at Milardi, as if daring him to try something. But so long as he laid there motionless, the cyborg was happy for Milardi to wait his turn.

But its colossal head cocked when he heard Zatia pick up the grenade down the hall. And when the metal ball scuffed off of her hand, faintly whistling through the air, clanking once, twice off the ground right into Milardi's grasp.

Then, right there, the Paladin dropped Osyen to the ground—and pulled free his floating guillotine blade from the wall.

Milardi twisted the grenade, priming it, and tossed it lamely up into the air. It had to give the room everything it had.

And the little ball of metal screamed. The Paladin didn't flinch. But he did...pause.

Milardi held his hands over his ears and rushed for the front of the Jump Deck. His feet crunched on the loose glass powder, almost slipping out from under him. And he stopped at Adelaide's console, ready to cut the anchors—

And he heard...he heard Thom's voice? "No, Milardi! Don't do it!" He sounded so earnest, terrified.

Too late.

Milardi punched in the command, and he watched as the great tendrils let loose from the limping frigate. It drifted off to the side, falling low and out of sight to grind into a happy new home in the ice below. Two more tendrils whipped into view, with the *Aurum* cut free.

Job done, Milardi whirled around to see Thom standing in the doorway, held back by Zatia and Adelaide—

And the Paladin cut off his view of them as the monster drove his roughened metal shard through his chest.

He'd been shot before. Three times, in fact. Nothing like Zee or Oz. And he'd been stabbed once, on Ostia. But this...he felt the bones of his rib cage crack and give way under the enormous force, the click of the metal against the console. There was a frightening amount of...clarity. And it didn't feel like anything.

He reclined against that metal, draping over it. A curtain of black closed around his vision, pulsing with his heartbeat.

The Paladin leaned in close. "Bless your burdens, for the road is long."

Milardi coughed. He'd never...never been a...very religious man...

CHAPTER
THIRTY-ONE
ZATIA

THE BASTARD. The monster. The *fra tow* cyborg had cut Milardi in half at the waist.

"No..." Thom whispered, crestfallen against the doorframe.

The Paladin turned, its stark features illuminated by the howling storm outside, and Milardi's blood coating its hands.

Osyen. Osyen! He was still moving. He was digging in his waistband, producing a standard clotting kit. But he was fumbling with it, unable to focus.

She could leave him. She should leave him. He was stuck in a room with a killing machine that had just deleted Milardi, and left Osyen in a state that would basically guarantee death. Going back into that room was akin to suicide.

She didn't even give it a second thought. She darted to Osyen's side, and to her shock, actually got there. His eyes were fluttering, his fingers twitching. "Gotta go...into shock now..."

"Shut up," Zatia said, grabbing the kit from his hands.

His socket was a right mess, but it was a clean cut. Apply enough force, and just about anything would cleave through human flesh. His arm itself...wasn't exactly in one piece, much of it still stuck to whatever bits of the gun it had been close to.

Okay, so less of a cut—it more accurately detonated his arm. There were bits of it smeared across his face and chest, as much as on the wall.

"This is going to hurt," Zatia said.

And she didn't wait for his response as she pressed the spongy material into his wound. His eyes opened sharpish, but he didn't focus on anything, immediately slumping into her side. At least he wouldn't bleed out, if he didn't die from what he'd already poured onto the floor.

"You." Zatia tensed at that metal voice. She turned to see the Paladin, pointing an empty hand towards Thom. It was impossible for that voice not to command authority, but it sounded distressed. "I've seen you..."

Thom blinked a few times, stunned, tears tumbling down his face. His lip quivered, almost a hateful snarl. But he took a step forward. "...You killed him."

"Who are you," the Paladin asked, "who have touched the face of God?"

What? The Paladin could *tell* Thom had used the Icon? How?!

Thom glanced at Zatia, his expression hardening. And Zatia slunk low, grasping Osyen's leg. With a forward tumble, she pulled the man up onto her shoulders in a fireman's carry. And she stood up.

Thom looked back at the Paladin with hate and blood in his eyes. "I'm the man who's going to kill you."

The Paladin surged forward, ripping a console out of its mooring and flinging the entire blocky desk out of his way.

But Zatia was faster, already at a full sprint with Osyen draped over her back. She hit the doorframe with one foot, rebounding and shooting down the passage. Adelaide pressed a foot into the wall and ripped out the power cables with both hands.

Thom jumped back just in time as the door slammed shut. The Paladin's impact left a hand-shaped impression in nearly a foot of solid steel.

"Anger keeps you moving," Adelaide urged. "Fear keeps you alive. Now run!"

Zatia and Thom took off, Osyen on her back and Adelaide in tow. They could hear the Paladin tearing through the steel, wrenching his fingers through it and pressing it aside. Ten inches of solid Silksteel was bending at its touch, like it was tin foil.

And all too quickly, Zatia heard the pounding of its feet, increasing in percussive tempo.

A blue face projected out of the steel, waxed mustache and flouncing hair and baritone rage. The face inverted, transforming into the Paladin's stony visage, before flickering out of view.

Lily Well, that was predictable.

Lily! Zatia called out, *Tell me we're good to go!*

Do not distract me, flesh bag, Lily growled through static. *I will dismantle this de-de-demon!*

The skipping audio wasn't a comfort. The Paladin excelled at engaging with AI countermeasures. Lily would not have any more success than any other program.

But they were doing some work. The cabinets in the galley were flying open, spitting everything onto the floor. Lights were flickering and doors shaking. The floor seemed to vibrate as vents blasted cold air. This ship was officially haunted by the ghost of Lily's rage.

"Wait!"

Zatia slid to a stop. Who had called out? They...they had everyone, didn't they? Who had she forgotten?

Weasel. The gangster was running down the passage behind them, desperately trying to escape the monster at his heels.

Adelaide sneered—and closed the door on him.

Weasel slammed against it, pawing at the glass. "What are you doing?! Open this door right now!"

"His name was Nathaniel," Adelaide hissed. "I want that name in your head right now. I want it to be the last thing you ever think of."

Thom cautioned her. "Adelaide—"

Adelaide's arm shot out at him, an open palm halting him mid-word. But her eyes never once drifted. She wanted to see this. She needed to.

Weasel pounded on the doorframe, tugged at the handle, swiped his card at the console. Nothing. Nothing did anything. Weasel ducked in and out of view, obscuring the tin window in the door.

And one time he came up, and he went down—and the Paladin was standing right behind him. Weasel never came back up. The Paladin simply raised his glowing magnetic hand, and a splatter of blood went up over the glass.

"What happened to 'fear makes you run'?!" Zatia demanded.

"I look scared to you?" Adelaide muttered, turning with a hollow, distant stare and stomping off down the hallway.

Thom pointed at Zatia's side. "You're bleeding."

"Everybody's bleeding!" she hollered at him. "Move your ass!"

The Paladin slammed the door, and they could hear the metal squeal under tension. But then the big cyborg suddenly stiffened.

Lily's voice could have been detected by radio telescopes across the system. *You have dealt with machines and with men. You have fractured computers and broken bone. I have yet in my lifetime to meet your like, nor am I like to see your kind again. Which is what makes your destruction...so sweet.*

Whatever Lily was doing made the pounding stop. So Zatia didn't question it. She just ran. But she did hear Lily start to scream a moment later, before their voice cut out. And the pounding resumed.

*You're going to hate this, but uh...*Roche's voice was shaking, even over the radio. *You're going to have to jump the gap.*

What does that *mean?!* Zatia asked.

Don't worry, I'll catch you.

That's not more comforting!

They could feel the wind pressing on them before they ever saw the light. The blanching white of the storm filled the airlock passage —and they all realized that the spaceship that was supposed to be there, was not.

"He's right," Adelaide said, "I do hate this."

276

Thom straightened up. "If you've got a better idea…"

Zatia didn't wait for anybody else to speak. She just started running for the open door, trusting that something was going to be on the other side. Her boots beat against the steel grating, her shoulders ached from Osyen's weight.

Every survival instinct in her brain urged her that open pits were not for jumping. Not for jumping!

But she leaned into that little voice in her head that just wished a bitch would.

And she pressed off with her last step, jumping out of the side of a pirate frigate. The snow storm raged properly below them, but the snow and ice whirled around them all the same. The damaged frigate had long since slipped away, and they could barely see the second one peeling off into the clouds. The torch that stood against it all, Farragut's central geothermal tower, stood tall, a flaming testament in defiance.

And then there was the *Aurum*, hanging close a few hundred feet underneath Zatia, engines screaming at full to keep up, twin candles in the pure white.

But no airlock, no opening, no cushy landing. What kinda plan was this?!

Zatia fell, headed straight for the side of the *Aurum*'s knobbly hull. She was going to pancake across that industrial visage and bounce off to her frozen tomb below.

But right as she reached the apex of her fall, the *Aurum* turned, swinging its fat ass forward—with open cargo bay door ready, like an open glove. The opposite wall swung about hard, cargo netting ready. Roche was swinging an entire spaceship around to catch three people out of the air.

And it worked like he'd practiced it. Zatia, Osyen, Thom, and Adelaide slipped through the opening, rolling into that netting, before slumping to the deck.

Zatia popped up, half expecting the Paladin to be standing there with them. But the gangster frigate was disappearing into the storm, as the *Aurum* blasted off in the opposite direction, up into the sky. Satisfied, she collapsed backward into the net, arms splayed wide and gasping.

Rashida ran over, clapping her hand over the big red button that closed the hangar bay doors. "Everyone alright?" Rashida's eyes went wide as she tracked onto Osyen. "Oh my God…"

Zatia pushed the captain to the ground, unable to lift herself, let alone another person. She barely pointed at him. "Get him to Medical now!"

Rashida dropped to one knee to help, but then she finally counted the heads. "Where's Milardi?"

What could she say? What could anybody say? He was gone. Not even the courtesy of a goodbye drink.

Rashida picked up what the silence meant. And Zatia fell into the netting to pass out for…however much time as she needed.

―――

She woke up in Medical, the AutoDoc bringing her out of anesthesia with soft music and cheerful sounds. She blinked the crunch out of her eyes, working the tension out of her jaw.

She looked down to see the fresh skin patch on her shoulder, a neat little messy burn hole over the top of the mottled scar from the spear strike. Then there was the gut shot from the transport and…she had been collecting an impressive set of wounds in the past few days.

Zatia wondered how quickly this one would heal. And when her next seizure might take hold.

The Medical Bay was empty, so she hopped off the AutoDoc, shrugging on a shirt and pulling on her pants. The skin patch complained, but a hit of painkiller and a belt of whiskey would take care of that. She paced up the hallway and into the galley, looking for something to quiet the more common pang in her gut.

Thom sat alone, draped over the table, finger tracing the lip of his glass of water. He stared at the surface like an attentive friend, taking in anything it had to say.

She spoke, her voice raspy from lack of use. "Get you a man who looks at you like that."

Thom stirred, and his eyes lit up at the sight of her. "You're awake!"

"It has been known to happen," Zatia said with a smirk. But then the uncomfortable possibility hit her. "Is Osyen?"

Thom didn't say anything for a painful moment before he nodded. "He's uh...He's not doing a whole lot of talking."

"I wouldn't either," Zatia conceded. How long had Thom been sitting in the galley, alone like this? Had he been the one to drag her to Medical? If she'd been asleep the entire time since Osyen got his treatment...

Thom swallowed hard. "I'm uh, glad you're okay though."

Zatia dragged herself over to the Replicator, head low and not acknowledging the boy or his kindness. She punched in the code for a sandwich toasted bread with ham, cheese and more cheese. The sandwich began assembly, darts of light stitching together the order before her eyes.

Thom didn't take her indifference for the hint that it was, and he cast another line out. "I thought I had it planned out so well. I thought I could—"

And she just snapped. "What were you doing?" she asked. "There *was* a plan. And you were supposed to be back here on the *Aurum*. Instead, you came barreling back in."

"I thought..." Thom swallowed hard, his eyes flitting about as he concocted some preposterous lie. "I thought I could help."

"Did you? Did you help?"

Thom looked back down into his water, searching for something at the bottom of that glass. "I just...I don't know what to think anymore."

He withered, sinking into his chair and studying his hands.

She knew that look, and she knew how to treat it. Pulling her sandwich out of the Replicator, she punched in a new order for some drinks. This took less time, but when it was finished, Zatia pinched the two glasses and stalked over to the table. She sat down across from him and slid a glass of whiskey over to the boy.

Thom studied it for a second. "What's that for?"

"The thinking," she said. "The next one will help with the sleeping."

She'd seen him shove an entire muffin down his throat in half a second, so it wasn't all that shocking to see him pound the whiskey like he was throwing it over his shoulder. He gingerly set the glass back down on the table, feeling the burn rise in his chest and throat. And after a valiant battle against it, he coughed hard.

Zatia raised an eyebrow but held her tongue. The boy had tasted real hard liquor for the first time not a day before, and now he was already using it to soothe his sorrow.

PART FOUR
THE PROBLEM OF EVIL

"Considerate readings of available texts imply limitations on the Pilgrim's omnipotence. For instance, that the Pilgrim did not appear to humanity during our captivity on Earth. I must confess that the continuing existence of suffering certainly implies a shortcoming. Why else would a child starve and the rain in our skies burn the flesh, while feudalism continues to spread?

Where has the Pilgrim gone to, in this, our hour of need?"

PRIVATE DIARY OF PROFESSOR
CHARLES H. ORDEE, PH.D. RELIGIOUS
STUDIES AT THE ROYAL ACADEMY,
DATED 2227.

CONFISCATED DURING HIS ARREST
SUBJECT TO SUMMARY DELETION

RECORDED DREAM DATA, DATE: 2241.22.04

PATIENT: THOMAS HUGH

You said it was the future!

// WARNING: NOCTURNAL EVENT DETECTED.
   // SECONDARY HEART RATE ISOLATED AND LOCKED.
   // BEGINNING STABILIZATION TREATMENTS.

I understand that you're angry.

Don't patronize me! You showed me the future. I saw their bodies! The storm, the crash. You said I could stop it.

You saw the future. You saw it warp and change under your hand.

Milardi is dead! I couldn't stop it!

Yes, he is. But your presence stalled the Paladin's actions, bought the lives of your friends. Had you not intervened, every soul would have been lost.

How can you know that?

The future is not a stable thing any more than the past is.

...Okay, well, that's a concept you're going to have to take some time to explain.

Fair. I didn't intend to crack that nut just yet. My apologies.

He's dead...

I know.

Tell me this. Is there a future...was there a way to save him?

...No.

Warning: Heart Rate elevated.
Notifying Ship Physician.
Warning: No Ship Physician On Board.
Registering Cardiac Emergency.

So wh-what, that was supposed *to happen?!*

Everything that happens was supposed to—

Don't give me that crap! For one gulaw minute, you're going to give me a straight answer! No more riddling, no more sideways, no more half-truths.

Those are all I have. Whatever guidance I have to offer may no longer be true the moment I give it to you.

Because foreknowledge of the future changes the future?

Yes.

I don't want this. I don't want to know! Leave me alone!

// Warning: Hypoxia state detected
// pulse ox ninety-three and falling.

Neither did I. But having the ability to affect something does not make you responsible for the chaos of an entire universe. You can make choices that better your world—but the world is going to react to those choices itself, make choices of its own in response. You saved the crew of the Aurum with your actions. The death of Jackson Milardi...is not your fault.

I know.

You did not kill him.

I know.

You saw the future and took an action that saved five people. The world is brighter today because of what you did.

I should've saved six.

CHAPTER
THIRTY-TWO
OSYEN

RECORDS SAID three days went by. To him, they all blended together into an unforgiving slurry. He spent most of the time in bed, staring at the ceiling of his stateroom. Every time he shifted, he reminded himself of the...absence.

"Lily?" he croaked. "Lily, are you...are you there?"

There was no response. Strange. He distinctly remembered the AI on Weasel's ship—balking and rocking like any normal day, ready to confront the universe. But no matter how much he called their name, they never answered him.

Perhaps the Cascade had worsened, or the Paladin had...if the Paladin took them too...

Osyen couldn't bring himself to cry. He just felt drawn downward into his bed, the scratchy plastic sheets binding him. Pulled him down, down into an abyss. His legs felt heavy and his mind cloudy.

He wanted to hear Milardi's voice, ragging on him for something or other. He wanted to hear that Colonial accent ringing up and down the halls. He always shouted when he got excited, and his excitement was infectious. He always...everything with Milardi was an 'always', and never a 'never.' He said yes to so much.

He wanted to see Thom's stupid grin and Adelaide's scowl, see Rashida's latest project and Zatia's latest scars.

He wanted to see Roche's quiet, contemplative power stance on the Jump Deck. It was like seeing the man wrapped in a blanket before a crackling fire. The jockey took such comfort there, such strength.

He doubted Roche would have that countenance ever again.

More than anything...he wanted to feel Lily's invasive eyes watching, feel their presence, and hear the bite of their observations.

He wanted the before—before Farragut; before the Boolean, before the troubles. It had grown so quiet on the *Aurum*.

On the third day, Osyen tried to get up. He managed to get himself upright easily enough but found pants to be rather complicated. He never thought he'd be happy to have suspenders.

Then he set his foot on the bottom rung of the ladder, looking up at the doorway above him. Sure, he could swing himself up, maybe brace himself against the backside of the narrow space. But it had become a tiresome affair.

They built plenty of ships with accessibility in mind. He might have to look into getting one.

No. He wanted this ship, this crew, he wanted Lily and Milardi and everyone else. He wanted what he had, what had been taken from him. He wanted to scream and cry and punch a hole through the wall.

He didn't want to fix the wall, and he'd probably break his hand doing it. Which somehow made it worse.

So he just sat in his room for another day. And on day four, Rashida came knocking.

"Oz?" she asked, tentative.

"Yeah?" he grumbled from his bed.

"Can I come in?"

He didn't answer, so she took that as an affirmative. She came down the ladder, balancing a plate in one hand. Some delicate pale-yellow foam with flecks of gold.

"What's that?" Osyen asked.

"It's uh...the lemon meringue tart," Rashida said. "Lily still had the recipe saved."

His last gift to them, and now she brought it to him? "I'm good," Osyen muttered, "but knock yourself out."

Rashida set the plate down on his crowded nightstand, sliding it with two pointed fingers into a safe and stable spot. "You've got to eat something, Oz."

"I figure I can go longer without, seeing as there's less of me." Osyen let his head flop to one side, staring up at her with a blank expression. "What, I don't even get a courtesy laugh? That was funny."

"Bit gallows for me," she said, trying to avert her eyes.

"Yeah well, when it's your neck, you get to make the jokes."

Rashida grabbed the spoon and cut off a chunk of the meringue. For looking like wisps of cloud, they had surprising rigidity to them, and they broke like plaster. Like a sweet crunch.

He nodded at it. "How is it?"

She took a bite, and he watched her put on a good show of expressions. Eyebrows up as she considered the mouthfeel, the texture, the tartness. She bobbed her head from side to side and then set the spoon down. "To be honest, I've never had much of a sweet tooth."

"Yeah, me neither." He looked back up at the ceiling—and even that simple motion made his shoulder nub spike with pain, whining a bit at being jostled. He pulled his lips tight in annoyance. Any movement he made seemed to cause pain.

But Rashida had come in here with more than just dessert. "I was talking with the others about...a plan."

"Oh, we've got a plan now, have we?" Osyen asked. "Hijack a fusion reactor? Hit him with a train? Or maybe we drop this bad guy into a sun like the last one?"

"I'm leaving."

That made him sit bolt-upright, so fast he nearly hit his head.

Grumpy shoulder be damned. "Rash, I swear to you: it makes *nothing* better."

"The Paladin—"

"Doesn't fix the price on our heads. It doesn't help Adelaide get her husband back. It doesn't get Admiral Hugh off of our tail. It doesn't—"

She stamped out his fire with a sharp tone. "I wasn't asking you, Oz. We've come to a decision. I'm going."

"Who's we?" he asked. "Because I need to beat them about the head with a length of sturdy pipe."

Her face was stone. "Everyone, Oz."

Osyen scoffed, looking away at the scratches on his wall where his boots always kicked. "Not everyone."

"Everyone who showed up," she said, her voice laced with acid.

She had been pounding on the walls to get out since the Paladin's appearance. At this point, she wasn't going to be taking any input from him. She wasn't here with an apology or a condolence. She wasn't trying to threaten him or coerce him into giving something up: do this, or she'll leave.

No. This was an announcement.

"Go then," Osyen grumbled. "Walk on outta here. And when you do, I want you to keep walking until you find the east side of Hell. Send me a note when you find it. I've always been curious to visit."

"Osyen—"

He'd spent four days barely able to move. And suddenly, when she came into his room with that sweet dessert, that look in her eye, and this crazy plan...he could leap to his feet. "You *can't*...let them win."

She shook her head, big brown eyes full of pity and despair. "Oz, they won.'

No. Because if they won...then there was never getting anything back.

"Says you."

"That's a child's answer."

He felt more like a child every damn day, a scared little boy. All he saw was yet another Imperial official knocking on the door and demanding, demanding, taking and taking...

"Milardi's gone," she said. "Lily might just be beyond repair. How much more are you going to let them take before you—"

"Let them?!" Osyen snarled, sitting bolt upright. "You think I haven't tried to stop this?"

Hands on hips and tilted head, curl to her lip. "I see you curled up in bed feeling sorry for yourself."

He narrowed his eyes. That was...uncharacteristically hostile of her. "I guess a man is not allowed to recuperate."

"You're not in here healing, Oz! You're hiding."

"And what am I hiding from, oh mysterious soothsayer? Responsibility? Or maybe I'm in a not-insignificant amount of agony."

"You're hurting. Yes," Rashida conceded that point. "But that's not why you're down here. If you were in pain, you'd hop over to Medical. Instead, you lie down here in the dark, so you don't have to face your failure."

He laughed. "My failure?"

She didn't come with a dagger for his ribs or a poison for his ear. She hit him with a hammer. "Failure to protect them."

"*Fra tow zu*," he cursed at her.

She threw her hands up and turned away. "Happy trails, Osyen. I hope you have a long life of keeping your head down."

What a fascinatingly quick disengage for the accomplished duelist. Osyen blinked. "What's your game?"

She paused at the ladder, like he'd thrown a steel hook into her back, anchoring her. "I'm sorry?"

"Can't con a conman, Rash." He stood up, and he almost retched from the vertigo. But he held himself together, masking it with a wrinkled nose. "The meringue was a nice touch."

Rashida hadn't come into his room to convince him to get up, inspire him to wake up and join the fight.

She came down here...to find an excuse to leave.

But she doubled down. "You'd get them all killed? Just to satisfy—"

And he closed the distance with one big step. "You're trying to piss me off." And her guilt exposed itself in a flash as she looked away. He laughed. "You tried to leave once already, didn't you? You got into the shuttle, got all nice and comfy in the seat. You grabbed the controls. But you couldn't do it. Because you've never felt more home, more safe, than right here. What, you go to your death? Best-case scenario, you're back in a glass case on Aspen IV—or maybe all the sunny way back to Earth. Now, you want this ship to keep on being? Keep on flying? For that to happen, you have to go. And you fought with it, you chewed on it, but you just couldn't stomach it." He lowered his head, forcing himself into her line of sight. "Not unless you get me to kick you out. Now then...then it's a helluva lot easier, isn't it?"

His barb struck true. She was an exceptional poker player, a trained Gnostic priest and a noblewoman with Dunsweir upbringing. Plastic expression was a survival trait. But he saw the involuntary contraction of her pupils as adrenaline surged.

"You. ." He shook his head. And he laid down his cards. "I didn't stand up to Magnus because you work for me. I didn't fight all this time because of a contract or a charter. I did it...because you are my family, a sister, and a friend. And I've lost too many of those already."

"They will keep—"

"Of course they'll keep coming, Rash! In the history of your glorious Empire, they haven't achieved a single damn thing that wasn't down the barrel of a gun. And they will keep doing it so long as it works."

Rashida hung her head. "This is my family too, Oz. I love them."

"Then don't...leave them," he begged. He couldn't bear another absence, another loss.

But they always left, he thought. In the end, they all left. His mother, Fiona. And now he was losing these people, too.

Rashida turned away, grabbing the ladder firmly.

"Don't go." His voice barely escaped his throat, like a sickness had seized hold of him.

Rashida hung off the ladder, waiting patiently for a rebuttal that would keep her here. She was such a radiant beauty, a talented craftswoman. And a good friend.

She would be...a hard person to lose. But he was going to lose her. One way or another.

He nodded, turning back to his bed. He couldn't look at her another moment. If he did, he might have to stop her. "Thanks for the dessert. But I'm not really hungry."

She sighed. "Yeah. Me neither."

He listened to the chimes of boot on metal as she climbed up, until the clang of the door closed her off for good. The meringue sat on his nightstand, fractured dulcet clouds.

Meringue: A Terran European desert, traditionally from whipped egg whites and sugar, with a lemon tart base. Wisps of brown where the sugar had been caramelized.

Lily would've loved it. Lily had loved it. It just made him angry.

CHAPTER
THIRTY-THREE
ROCHE

OSYEN CLAMBERED up the ladder and out of his cabin with the combined forces of stubbornness and ingenuity. He'd managed to dress himself: the buttons of his overshirt hung open, exposing his undershirt and a hint of bare chest. Despite that, he was leveraging himself up the ladder with slow but consistent progress.

Roche looked down with no small amount of alarm. "Cap'n!"

"Don't look so surprised," Osyen grumbled. "I was hurt, not buried."

Roche extended his hand, snagging Osyen and heaving him up onto the deck. "Don't take it the wrong way, Oz. Just impressed."

Osyen nodded, trying not to glance at Roche's augments. The jockey had some personal experience with what Osyen was going through.

"How ya feelin'?" Roche asked him. It was a simple enough question, open-ended. And Osyen could answer as much or little as he was comfortable. Osyen just gave him an affirmative grunt. All Roche could expect, he supposed. "Should I gather everybody? Get us some space to think?"

"No," Osyen said, head low. "We just hang out for a bit longer and our troubles...it'll all pass us by. I could kill for a muffin." He started to stomp off toward the galley.

Roche's brow furrowed. "Pass us by?"

Osyen paused, the fingers of his hand rubbing across the grating on the wall. His open sleeve hung at his side, an empty drape of fabric, like its contents had been drained away. "Rashida is...uh..."

No. She couldn't be meaning to actually go through with that. Osyen had to stop her. Somebody had to stop her.

"You're just letting her go?" Roche asked.

"Ain't got any right to interfere," Osyen muttered.

"Of course you do. She signed the charter like the rest of us, went to the Boolean 'n back. She's family."

"Thought you were all in agreement?"

They were, out loud. Nobody had the strength to say no to her. They needed him to do that.

"Stop her," Roche said.

"Ain't that simple."

Roche coughed. "Of course it is. It's your ship."

"Yeah, it is." Osyen turned, eyes unfocused and balance drifting. "Make sure a shuttle is tanked off and ready for her departure, would you?"

This was it. This was the end. Rashida would leave and take the Imperial dogs with her. But then how long would Zatia stay, or Thom? Adelaide was only here to get her husband back, and they had demonstrably failed at that task.

He'd be alone again.

But all Roche said was: "Yes sir."

Roche dragged himself up to the Jump Deck. Each step felt like a march closer and closer to his death. To a cold and empty black. He'd have cherished that silence, but only when it was adjacent to such jovial, comforting noise. Silence beside silence was not a comfort, but an abyss.

He wanted to hear laughter in the next room, the clink of glasses and the bustle of feet. And he wanted to be welcome at that table, to come and go as he needed. That folks would leave him be but always be within reach. If they were gone...

He couldn't let them go. But how could he fix this? He needed the others, some space to think. Space to think...they needed space.

That's it. He could fix Lily. He knew how to do it. The Engineer had been very specific. Lily just needed more uncorrupted space to expand into and it would stall the Cascade.

They needed space. Roche had space to spare. It wouldn't cure Lily, but it would buy them time...

And start the clock on Roche himself. But at least he wouldn't be alone.

The Jockey reached over and cranked the hatch to the Jump Deck closed. Rashida had locked it with a pin code before, so Roche just did that again with about sixty two alphanumerics. That would take the crew a good while to beat.

Roche plugged a cable into an open socket and promptly scrambled a code that would take days to crack.

And he heard Osyen's voice call out: "Roche?!"

Roche ambled over to his console, settling himself down into the chair. He had all the necessary connections, with a direct interface to operate the *Aurum's* suite of systems. It was simply a matter of partitioning a section for Lily to expand into.

What would he lose: his childhood at that greasy orphanage? Perhaps the first ship he'd ever flown, feeling weightless and powerful? Or would Lily take his life...

"Roche, what are you doing?" Osyen demanded, his voice muted by six inches of steel.

"What's going on?" He heard Zatia call out.

"I don't know. Roche just locked himself on the Deck."

They'll know soon enough. They'd understand.

Roche reached under the console, pulling free a binding of cables. He needed to pull free a data cable of sufficient bandwidth to allow acceptable read/write speed. Would he ever be able to go wireless again? Or would he be forever tethered to the *Aurum* and its processors?

It would be as good an adventure as any, to plunge into the unbound.

Osyen must've seen what Roche was up to through the glass, because the entire timbre of his voice changed, accented with pitch and desperation. "Roche! No! Roche, stop! It'll kill you!"

It most surely would. The Paladins were eventually eaten alive by their companions. And Roche had warned Osyen against this exact path, that Lily would be cursed to know that they were killing their donor.

But if Lily was to consume someone, Roche would happily volunteer, that his family might have a long and loving life. Osyen would have Lily again, and he would know that this was his gift to them. He would know all that...wouldn't he?

He pulled the cable up and clicked it into place on his wrist.

"*Roche!*" Osyen bellowed, pounding on the door.

The crew badgered, talking all over each other. "It won't open!"

"He's encrypted it. Skip the code, and just cut the power!"

"What does it look like I'm doing, jackass?!"

"Roche, just hang on!"

"What is he doing?"

Osyen was breathless. "He's fusing with Lily."

Roche felt the barest hint of connection, the spark of life somewhere in the drive-space.

// OS 15.3.571—Detected. Beginning Integrity Analysis.

// Warning—Extensive Data Corruption Detected. Boot in Safe mode from External Source?

// Negative

// Warning—Unable to Achieve Consistent Q-Calc. Execute ScanDisc for Repair Mode?

// Negative

// User Input Required

// Additional Storage Allocation, Partition BIO-1A.

While the crew was working on the door, Osyen had snapped. The captain was simply beating on the glass with his fist, bloodying his knuckles and leaving streaks of red without even cracking the seal. He was trying to break in through the one structural weakness he could find. Pity that glass was built to contain multiple atmospheres of pressure.

// Partition Identified: BIO-1A. Warning: This Partition is Wetware Storage.

I know, Roche said. *You can yell at me about it when you wake up.*

// User Confirmed. Access of Wetware Authorized.

It pinched, quite a bit more aggressively than he thought it would. It was like a persistent static shock at the base of his skull as electricity flowed freely. The neuron pathways were wired for this kind of transfer—but what fresh paths would be carved, new links made?

In a flash, he saw the three-story block of the orphanage, all the children jostling in the yard, and a lonely boy off to the side. The mud still sliding off of his cheek as voices called and jeered at him.

He saw—

He saw...a handsome man of unnatural height, a long coat billowing in the unseen wind. He flashed a winsome smile. Roche could feel the man leaning against his shoulder, a laugh rippling up through their connection and back into him, transferring the joy back and forth. His eyes—

No. Not that, not Milardi. Please. Leave that. Don't touch that one thing ..

A single pinch.

And that man...he looked so familiar, but he couldn't place from where. Had he been at Ostia or from the Core, perhaps? A merchant?

The electric pinch stopped—and Roche slipped out of his chair, the cold steel greeting his shoulder with a hard clap. Nausea seized him, and breakfast started bubbling up inside him. But...what had he eaten? Tasted like fried fish? Had he eaten fried fish for his first meal of the day?

He did not know how long he was on the ground when he felt a hand turn him over. Osyen locked eyes with him—and the captain sighed, collapsing over Roche's body in relief. "You scared me, you stupid, *stupid* man!"

"He's alright?" Rashida asked, hanging in the doorway.

"I'm fine," Roche struggled, wiping at his front. "I'm embarrassingly covered in sick, but I'm fine."

"You son of a bitch," Osyen cursed into his side. "You crazy son of a bitch. We thought we lost you."

Thom nodded his head. Roche could swear the boy was nothing more than flustered by the commotion, now set at ease by the result.

The entire crew had poured onto the Deck. Little Maestro Thom sank into Roche's open chair; Adelaide already occupied herself, examining the damage Roche had done to his console, bussing up the cables and panels; Zatia gasped for breath after some great exertion; and Rashida lingered in the doorway.

Everyone was here. The family was whole.

No, they were missing one face. A happy blue face.

"Lily?" Roche asked. "Care to give the captain a full diagnostic?"

Osyen's face paled, his heart stopped. And he didn't dare move, lest he jeopardize the result.

Pixels slipped up from the Deck floor, forming into a head: mustachioed, long voluminous hair, and a voice that could shake mountains. "Hello, Osyen." Rashida gasped from the door, which Lily snapped on to. "Do not act so surprised, your highness. Death has no hold on those that do not live."

Osyen reached a tender hand out to cup that holographic face. His fingers passed right through the image, but that didn't stop Lily from leaning into the touch. "I know, Osyen. I missed you too."

"We did it, Milardi," Thom muttered.

"Milardi?" Roche asked. "Did we take on a new crew member?"

Adelaide jerked at that sentence and bumped her head on the

underside of the console. Zatia's brow twisted in a kind of anger, clenching her fist like she was preparing to deck him. And the tears that had built on Osyen's hopeful face suddenly tumbled down his crestfallen cheeks.

Thom...Thom withered like a plant denied water.

Everyone had such abject looks of horror.

Roche knew he must've made some kind of faux pas. At the orphanage, people stared like that whenever he'd made some inexcusable statement or gesture. "I'm sorry. I've done something rude. If you introduce me to him, I'll make up some story or other. No need for a fuss."

Lily slid in front of Roche, their disembodied head gliding to a stop on the floor next to him. "I'm sorry, Roche. So very sorry."

Why was everyone so dour about this? Roche was no good with names and faces. It wasn't the end of the—

Of course. Memories. The process of restoring Lily, fusing them with his cerebellum: he knew Lily would take up some residential space in his brain. Which, it stood to reason the process might rob him of learned skills, automatic functions, or memories. The hard drive space was now dedicated to primary functions of another entity entirely.

This Milardi figure was clearly someone he was supposed to know—but no longer.

"Tell me everything."

CHAPTER
THIRTY-FOUR
THOM

WITH LILY STABLE, they finally had a good option: get the Hell out of Farragut. They took turns on the Jump Deck with Roche, trying to explain what Roche had lost. There were multiple gaps in his memory. He'd forget common words but remember the most bizarre details. He remembered the pub in Farragut, but Milardi was...curiously absent from his own recollection.

Whatever specific details he remembered, Roche was quite cagey about.

Thom found his own shift up front to be...disquieting. They sat in silence for what felt like hours. A snap in the air, just waiting for the proper connection to set off the bolt of lightning.

Finally, Roche broke the tension. "What was he like?"

Thom took a deep breath, searching for strength. "He was...always happy. He walked everywhere like the party had just started. Or, y'know, that he brought the party with him."

"Was he close with anyone?" Roche asked. "Should we...once we're free and clear, should we be informing anyone? Any family?"

Thom shook his head. Any family Milardi had, if there were any...

Zatia was his partner-in-crime, a pair of chaotic devils. Osyen was his brother, two like minds in pursuit of freedom. Thom was his trainee, someone he guided through the nuances of the wider world like a shepherd to a lamb. Rashida was a kind of rival, both skilled in the arts of manipulation and charm. Milardi always appreciated her proficiency in political arts. So much more subtle and full of craft. And Adelaide, the brutal and crass mother he'd always wished for, honest to a fault and an uncompromising moral pillar.

But Roche was more than family. Roche was his other piece, everything he wasn't, that complemented and completed, modified and supported, broadened and captured.

And now...Roche didn't even remember him.

"I'm sorry I don't have a lot to say," Thom stammered.

"It has been an eventful day," Roche over-enunciated. "If it's any consolation, I do enjoy the company. Even quiet company."

"Good to know that hasn't changed," Thom quipped.

Roche didn't take his eyes off of whatever invisible displays he was tracking. "I should hope that I haven't changed at all. But then again, I wouldn't be able to compare back to who I was before, could I?"

Thom pursed his lips at that haunting idea. Roche existed only in the ways he tied with Lily now. Where did the AI end and he begin? And would he ever recognize the difference again? And how would the slow slide of Lily's condition begin to overtake Roche? Would it take days, weeks?

"I was making a joke," Roche said.

"Yeah, but it turned into a quiet bit of lingering horror."

"That's what makes it a good joke. It sticks with you."

Thom disagreed. "Comedy makes you laugh, reflect, introspect."

"Must be my sense of humor," Roche said with a shrug.

He stared wide-eyed at Roche, who still stubbornly refused to make contact. But a smile did crack across his face, and Thom breathed a little easier. That might not be the old Roche precisely, but he recognized that little of Lily leeching their way in.

A single light lit up on Thom's display, painting his face in strobing red. That finally drew Roche's attention, his blue implanted iris tracking independently over to Thom's side of the Deck. "Were we expecting a call?"

Thom didn't recognize the pin code. It could be Magnus, the Paladin, or any other new Imperial bounty hunter. "Get Osyen up here," he said, as he accepted the connection.

And the holographic display folded up into view—revealing the peculiar weathered face of a familiar Imperial Rear Admiral. 2nd Grade, 3rd Naval Bombardment Wing. He signed off every letter with that designation.

Thom's heart couldn't decide if it wanted to skip a beat or stop entirely. "Admiral Ulysses Hugh."

Hearing Thom's voice pumped fresh anger in the admiral's veins, the very sight of his son causing the tendon in his neck to flex. He spoke with rigid authority, despite the raging undercurrent. "Rogue KC-28 Perseus, designation *Aurum*...you are wanted for crimes against the Empire and her People."

Thom nodded. "Yeah, that's roughly what I expected."

"We have blockaded the only Jump Point out of your system, Thomas. You cannot run."

"What's the matter, Admiral?" Thom teased. "Not like you to wait outside for me to come to you. Can't tread on a lowly mobster's turf? Afraid to own a *second* civil war?"

"From what I understand...you cannot remain in that space either."

"We've been remaining pretty successfully for the better part of a week," Thom offered.

"How much longer do you think that luck will last?"

Thom twitched, remembering the Paladin's voice chewing on his ear with its deep and baleful voice. "Long as it needs to."

"Attempts to resist me..." the Admiral lingered on that possibility. "...will be met with the full might of the Empire's justice."

Fun. Dad was threatening him now. What a delightful change of pace. It was like holidays at home.

"Always love these little chats of ours," Thom said.

"Your actions in the Boolean have caused a great many headaches across the length and breadth of the Empire."

"Yeah," Thom acknowledged. "Who sent us there again?"

Osyen burst onto the deck in time to see the Admiral's next threat. "You will surrender to me, Thomas. Or you will burn."

And Thom spoke before Osyen could. "I already know that won't happen, so spare me the theater."

Hugh's nostrils flared like an angry bull. "Do not test me, boy—"

"Don't test *me*," Thom challenged. "We've already killed one of your deniable ops badasses, so don't think a second one is beyond our reach. Now I don't doubt you intend everything you say, but like everything you say, you fail to follow it up with action. When you're ready to talk instead of 'declare,' I'll be waiting."

And Thom pressed the holographic monitor down, silencing the complaints of the aging military officer.

He looked over to the door to see Osyen collecting his jaw off the floor. "I have so many things I could say."

"Hit me," Thom said, reclining in his chair.

"For one, you clearly *did not* need me. I could've finished my breakfast," Osyen said, listing off his fingers. "For second, please do not taunt the man with an Eisenclad Dreadnought! Aren't we in enough trouble?!"

Thom waited for a number three that didn't come. "Two is many. Okay. Sorry, you implied that there was more."

Roche raised a wrinkly eyebrow. "I don't think we needed any *more* than those two, to be honest."

Osyen sat down against the wall, sliding down to the floor. "That's great. That's perfect. We get Lily back, a way to freedom. And now the Admiral pops up, just in time to slam the door in our face."

Thom shook his head. "Took him long enough to come collect on Weasel's call."

Roche took some amusement at that. "He was probably pretty confused when Weasel wasn't answering hails."

"So with an Imperial blockade, we're right back to square one," Osyen moaned. "Can't run. Can't stay."

Can't run. No, can't run *away*.

Thom spun about in his chair. "Sure we can. We can still run. We run right to the one person who can help."

Osyen tilted his head, daring Thom to put that thought into the air.

Thom chewed on his cheek as he flew through the flurry of details. "Oh, yeah. We're going to turn ourselves in...to the Godfather."

Osyen sat forward, as though Thom needed this explained to him very slowly. "We go to the Godfather, and he's going to fork us over to Hugh for a hefty payday. If he doesn't skin us and put us right on the mantle next to Adelaide's husband. And *that's* assuming the Paladin doesn't get us first."

"That's exactly it though," Thom said. "The Paladin will come, while we're being moved."

"Yeah...but then everybody dies," Osyen drawled, assuming he was missing a piece, but it was just not apparent to him which one.

No. Thom was certain of it. He knew how this would play out. He had seen this. The wreckage he had seen before was not the *Aurum*. It was the Godfather's.

"The Paladin will come..." Thom promised, "...and we'll kill him with the Jump point."

"No AI is going to harm a passenger with a quantum calculation," Roche said, with a tension in his body. "They'll shut themselves down before they let that happen."

"Yeah, we had some experience with that," Osyen chirped.

"No *functioning* AI," Thom pointed out. "But I'll bet a human can do it. Roche? Part AI, part *human*. You can decide independent of hard-coded safeguards to foul up the calculation. You can do what an AI could never. You can jailbreak Lily in ways they only dream of."

Roche's look sharpened, a kind of horror that dawned into glee and back into horror again. He ran a quick diagnostic calculation.

Someone prompted their appearance, as Lily rose up in front of Thom. "Boy. That is diabolical, indefensible, and immoral. I love it."

"We turn ourselves in to the Godfather," Thom postulated, "steal Adelaide's husband right out of his pretty little hand, let the Paladin wreck up the place, and then kill a super-soldier with a galactic Jump by rearranging his genetic code. While Hugh is left to pick through the Godfather's pieces, we escape neat and tidy, with everything we came for."

Osyen took a steeling breath and leaned forward. "Walk me through it, step by step. First off: how do we know the Godfather won't kill us?"

Thom smiled. "That's my favorite part: The Godfather won't kill family."

"And," Osyen noted, still not picking up the scent, "we were never inducted into the clan. Not to mention that being Family didn't stop him from offing Adelaide's husband in between shrimp cocktails."

"Wrong kind of family," Thom said, enjoying the cryptic delivery. "We happen to know a blood relative."

That got Osyen's attention. But it was Roche who jumped in. "How long have you known this?"

"Since about this morning," Thom said. "I saw it in a dream. It's hard to explain, but trust me."

Osyen considered that insufficient answer and Thom's history of success. "Alright then, my next question: who is the mystery cousin?"

CHAPTER
THIRTY-FIVE
RASHIDA

THE GODFATHER'S ship was something out of a fairytale, a majestic and wonderful piece of art dangling in a sea of stars. The chrome and silver dart, manufactured for comfortable atmospheric and galactic travel uninterrupted, was a feat of engineering. It could not have been simple to build, nor cheap to maintain, and something told Rashida that the statement was more important than the function.

The *Aurum* fit into the Godfather's flagship like it was meant to, easily towed into one of four separate interior docking bays. And a firing squad awaited them.

But what Rashida had not expected was to see a well-dressed, lean figure at the head of the line flashing his sharpened teeth.

"Magnus," Rashida greeted him as she marched down the gangway. "You survived your run-in."

He tipped his hat to her in formal greeting. "By the skin of my teeth."

"You sure it's not somebody else's skin you haven't picked out of your teeth?" Zatia sniped from behind.

Magnus signaled, and the guards circled up around the crew of the *Aurura*, securing weapons and forcing bindings onto their hands. Rashida kept her chin up. "Why not simply put a bullet in my head and be done with it?"

"I told you in Farragut," Magnus chastised Rashida's poor memory, "that your death is a last resort. The Dunsweir want you home. And having experienced the pressure I can invoke…you have made the right choice."

"The Paladin's not going to stop," Thom stated, off-hand and matter-of-fact.

Magnus strolled over, clicking his cane on the floor with each stride. He stopped in front of Thom, squaring up on the Maestro to appraise and grade. Thom gave the same unimpressed assessment of Magnus, shrugging at all the finery and nobility.

"Hmph," Magnus huffed, "I suppose one cannot always curate the company we keep."

"I know you can't choose your family," Thom said, "until you abruptly decide to."

"The Paladin has served its purpose, completed its task," Magnus said, turning back to Rashida. He laid a hand on her shoulder with an affirming squeeze. "He has brought our lady home, and for that, he shall walk the Path of the Pilgrim for all eternity."

"Somebody better tell him that," Osyen said, grimacing as the Godfather's goons patted him down a touch too roughly.

"Osyen Belt. I see your encounters have not yet taken your tongue." A glee flashed across his eyes. "I might have to rectify that oversight."

Not even the least bit intimidated, Osyen stuck his tongue out, daring the dignitary to come take a bite. And Magnus took the bait. He pushed past Rashida and Zatia and Thom, drawing a hissing breath.

And the moment he got in range, Osyen head-butted the nobleman with a wet crunch. Magnus stumbled backward, favoring his delicate nose that now seeped blood between his gloved fingers.

The goons immediately set about beating Osyen, striking him with batons in his gut and across his shoulder stump.

"Stop it!" Rashida demanded, but nobody heeded her words.

But it was Adelaide, who stepped in between the guards and Osyen, staring cool death into their faces. "You lay another hand on him, and you better be ready to kill me."

The threat gave the guards pause, but they gripped their batons, ready. Magnus waved them back with a bloodstained hand, playing off his injury with a smile. The blood had flowed down his lips and stained his teeth. "It seems he is damaged enough. The Godfather will determine his fate."

"You owe subservience to the Master, do you?" Rashida asked.

Magnus didn't answer. He just waved for the guards to do their work.

They affixed the group with collars, large brassy things. And with a flick of Magnus's hand, a shroud of darkness wrapped about her face. A simple cloth would have sufficed, but like everything on this ship, they found importance in the theater and the expression of it. They were not simple thugs, but sophisticated people with technology. As if the mere presence of science implied a society.

The guards pushed the group on, heaving Osyen back to his feet. They marched deep into the ship, only once being set down for some reason or another. She thought she heard scanners being passed over them. A great many alarms kept going off on Roche, and the jockey muffled cries on two occasions.

They were inspecting his implants.

Then they were walking again, and she was hit with the smell of cinnamon incense. She heard the crackle of a wood fire, felt the glow of its heat against her back. They had stopped in the center of some wide room, every guffaw and chuckle having a peculiar echo of it. It had the feeling of being at the pulpit, an empty congregation hall at the chapel.

And when the shroud fell, she soon saw why. The room was domed, to make it feel more open, and a cadre of bodyguards and sycophants lined every available shadow. Other individuals, Magnus included, who believed themselves worthy of esteem and attention sought the light, gathering in little social clumps as close to the center of the room as they dared to go.

They all wanted to be...what had Weasel said? 'Under the Master's sight?' But each faux nobleman knew that drawing the focus of that same sight was more threat than strength. It felt like being back in the Royal Court, and with good reason. The room was more auditorium than anything else, with a recessed center and terraced seating rising up in every direction.

To be at the bottom of the pit was to be...under the sight. Rashida looked down to find a brass eye set into the floor, with three lines up and down. The center of attention.

And seated high at the edge of this arena: Anze Orchikov, the Godfather himself, reclined on a chaise lounge.

He wore a stylish three-piece suit, but no blouse underneath, revealing the barest hint of his chest. And his hair, a shock of pure white, like the snows of his planet, so bright it almost glowed. She had hoped for a decadent slob or a sleazy, unkempt fool. She didn't expect a chin she could split wood with and a charming tilt to his smile—let alone that she would recognize him.

"Surprise," came Anze's lyrical whistle tone, a drip of smokey rasp to it. "Good to see you, cousin."

"Cousin?" Adelaide almost spat the word, a sudden heat coming off of her that threatened to cook Rashida's arm.

Anze smiled, wide and welcoming. He popped off his seat and strode on over in a kind of diagonal walk, teasing and casual. He grabbed Rashida by the shoulders, and he planted two formal pecks on each cheek. His thumbs rubbed back and forth in idle familiarity, and no matter how soft and pampered Anze's skin was, it felt like sandpaper against her bicep.

"I have to admit, I was worried about you. I'm so glad to see you well. Haven't seen you since you were oh..." He lowered a hand to her waist, measuring the height of a small child.

She remembered it well. His hair had been brown then.

"Felix," Rashida murmured in greeting.

And there was a cold emptiness in his eye upon hearing those syllables. "Call me Anze. Everyone else does, when they're not using honorifics." But he mirrored the softness of her smile, the playful bow of her head. Perhaps that look in his eye was reflected in her own.

"Anze Orchikov...is one of the Dunsweir?" Zatia asked.

"Well," Anze said, equivocating, "I wouldn't say that. Am I a blooded member of the elected house that governs Imperial interests across the galaxy? Not if you ask them."

Rashida looked about the room, taking it in. The glowing hearth at her back, the thick stone mantlepiece stocked with sculpture and paintings—

And a simple, unadorned urn, no design or embellishment. That right there...had to be Adelaide's deceased husband, laid up like any other trophy, just one of a collection.

"On a little vacation sabbatical, are we?" Rashida asked, turning her eyes back to Anze.

"Hardly a little one at this point!" Anze laughed at his own joke, drawing a polite chuckle from the crowd. Anze puffed up at that response, swelling with pride at the call and response. "My disappearance from public view was barely noticed, and the Family would like to keep it that way. At least here my talents are appreciated, where they might otherwise be scorned. I think you can relate."

"That's why the Navy won't come to Farragut," Rashida said, "why they won't interfere in your affairs. Because the Godfather's affairs are Imperial affairs."

Anze's eye twitched, a mild flutter really. The others wouldn't have seen it, wouldn't have picked up the subtle way his chin lifted or brow tightened.

But Anze slipped his mask back on again in an instant, recognizing a worthy player of court banter. "That's your problem, cousin," Anze admitted. "You still think of things in terms of nations and kings. Farragut has no need for all that politics."

"Yeah: obey me or freeze to death," Osyen grunted. "Real egalitarian paradise you got here."

Anze's eyes flicked over to Osyen, assessing the man's injuries in a nanosecond. Rashida bowed her head, whispering. "Osyen, shut up right now.'

"Now, now," Anze urged, gesturing at the absent limb. "The man has paid the price of admission. He should have the right to say what he wishes, I think."

Osyen cocked his head, biting his lip. "I think you have something that belongs to my friend."

Anze chuckled, freely and loose, waggling his shoulders as he did. The playfulness in his posture was not matched in his tone, nor by the curl to his lip. "Trust a pirate to think only about who owns what. Did you know that my officers own more of this operation than I do? It's true."

"So why they following you?" Osyen spat the question.

And it was not the first time Anze Orchikov had been metaphorically spat on. His body locked up for an instant, like he'd been frozen to stone, a fixed expression. But then the corners of his mouth tilted into a smile. "Because I built the enormous thermal generator that powers every minute of their lives...Mr. Belt."

The intonation, the inflection, implied that he hadn't financed the construction. He meant that literally. That was the basis for the myth, Rashida thought. He had brought warmth to the tundra.

"You truly believe Admiral Hugh will simply let you walk away with his bounty when you're just as interesting a catch?" Rashida asked.

Anze's smile was carefree, a song in his heart. "Darling girl, money is for people who need it. I am giving you to him because you torment my world. And I want you gone." That smile widened, a touch of mercurial glee. "He couldn't hold me if he tried."

Roche leaned over to Osyen. "What's 'money?'"

And Osyen just rolled his head back to stare into the ceiling, beleaguered by his circumstances. What a moment to ask such a fundamental question.

Adelaide was finally through with Anze's posturing. "Princeling playing warlord," she muttered.

Anze scanned the group. He wanted to know who'd said that, but couldn't locate the source, his eyes moving from Osyen to Zatia...to Roche.

And he sniffed the air, like a wolf smelling the hen house. And he found a beating heart within that drew him to his full height, looming over Roche. "Well, aren't you interesting? Something...else pumps through your head, doesn't it? You're haunted, lad."

"Begging your pardon, Godfather," Thom spoke up, "we have not been under the sight of one so potent in many years."

Anze squinted at Roche, still rapt in his studies of the jockey. "You have not been under the sight of anyone like me, I promise you that." His focus on Roche was otherworldly, a sixth sense about him. He could sense something off about Roche, something out of place.

Thom drew his attention with an aggressive maneuver. "When did you first experience the Pilgrim?"

And Anze blinked. Like there was a computational error in his head.

He pivoted on his heel, spinning to face Thom. "What did you just say?"

"You are Dunsweir," Thom said, "but that hardly makes you special. Many in the royal halls claim to have experienced the Touch. Rashida herself is also of the Family, but she's not like you, is she? You are..." Thom cocked his head, studying Anze with a painter's eye, trying to capture whatever elusive quality that evaded words.

"What am I?" Anze asked, breathless, like he was taking in some incredible beauty.

And well, Thom had developed quite a gift for gabbing. "You're excommunicated. Cast out for your truth, adrift. No place, no family. And yet, you secured an entire planet, free of Imperial control. You've sculpted a life for yourself from the ice and snow. No mere man—prince or pauper—could succeed in such a feat. Not without the Pilgrim's blessing."

That twitch of the lip again, and Rashida thought she saw the glimmer of a tear building in his eye. "And you?"

"Me?" Thom asked, trying to act all humble.

"You know the Touch, don't you?" Anze's voice was low, like the hiss of a snake or like he was afraid to speak a secret too loudly. "No. Not that. You're something else."

"I'm a cabin boy, sir."

"You mock me?"

"Quite the contrary," Thom demurred, throwing a glance at Magnus on the sideline. "I see greatness that not even the Empire's most potent weapons could hope to dim."

Anze smirked, but not out of pleasantry. There was a terrible focus spilling from his eyes, like scalding oil in a hot pan ready to flash over He stalked over towards Thom, head low like a wolf approaching a lamb. "I fear no machine, no weapon of war. And I provide safety, Thomas Hugh. Safety you and your friends may avail yourselves of."

And Thom raised his chin. "We're not safe here. And you know it too. The Paladin will come before you can get to the Jump Point. He'll kill your men, and even endanger yourself—though you *will* escape unharmed. Your ship destroyed, your foundations eroded, and the six of us...will walk out of here all the same."

Anze considered Thom for a long moment, before pirouetting on his heel again to face Magnus. "What have you brought me?"

The skeletal Consort knew how to behave around the daggers and vipers of Court. He took two clean steps out of his little crowd, and bent sharply at the waist, proffering his head. "Sir?"

"Have you brought me a joke?" Anze asked, gesturing at Thom. "If it is a joke, I must admit—biting, incendiary, even a tad distasteful with the open Gnostic heresy. I admire the spunk." And the temperature in his tone flashed to a cold that burned. "But I think we both know that nothing *funny* is happening right now."

Magnus looked over at Thom, vibrating with quiet hatred. Anze gestured for him to stand, as if raising him to his feet with the gesture.

And Magnus was pulled to standing, shaking and grunting, as if in pain.

Rashida got the unsettling impression that this wasn't a threat, but a demonstration.

And Anze turned to them, like a teacher to his students. "You see that? This man understands real power." And Anze's pupils dilated, fearsome focus on Thom. "You have that real power too, don't you?"

"I don't know what you mean."

"Lie to yourself," Anze said. "I did too. It's a perfectly rational response when faced with the impossible. But the longer I refused it, the more it burned."

Rashida glanced back at Thom, trying to gauge the boy's response. He wasn't asking if Thom would kneel. He was asking why Thom didn't make others do so.

And Thom had no answer.

A long pause, accompanied by the longest silence Rashida could stomach. It was like Anze had petrified, roots of stone shooting down through the floor and up through his feet. Thom spoke with a freedom no one else dared. Not even her.

And finally, Anze coughed a laugh. He pointed one finger at Rashida. "The lady stays here to enjoy her last moments of freedom. Consider it a 'get the fuck out of my space' present. Take the others to holding cells. Their bounties are to be distributed, properly and equitably."

Rashida looked over at Osyen. There was a flash of natural panic in his eyes.

As the soldiers led the team out, Anze locked eyes with Thom, a cold void behind those Dunsweir green eyes. "Leave the boy with me."

The four of them vanished behind their black shrouds, pushed and dragged out of the door by a dozen armed guards taking no chances: weapons drawn and keeping a suitable distance, especially from little Zatia.

Before Rashida realized it, two aides had swept in, pressing a glass of warm mead into one hand and draping a warm fur about her shoulders. Anze took her other hand, leading her up to his dais, gesturing for her to sit by his side.

And Anze shivered, leering at Rashida. "The boy...you know what he is, don't you?"

CHAPTER
THIRTY-SIX

OSYEN

HE COULD HEAR the echo of their steps off of the walls like they were pounding on his head. Masked in inky blackness was a helluva way to instill subservience. It blinded him, but it also magnified his hearing, making every sound deafening and intense. It was so easy to be overwhelmed by a cough or a squeaking boot heel.

Everyone else had been cuffed, but they didn't quite know what to do with Osyen. So instead, they lashed his arm to the middle of his back in a permanent wrist lock. And then marched him, pressing on the center of his wrist.

Thom was stuck back there in that Auditorium, perhaps halfway to becoming a trophy for the wall.

No. That boy knew what he was walking into, and Osyen doubted he would've mouthed off so much if he hadn't been painfully aware of what would happen. Thom might not be fine, but he wasn't dead.

Not yet anyway. Not like it was a condition that could scare him anymore.

The others were marching around him, somewhere in the dark. They were waiting for his call. Do the thing, start us off. But he found it difficult to say the words.

Someone in the brigade of troopers was slick with sweat, every step like he was sloshing through a swamp. With each footfall, a new wet and crunchy gasp—and Osyen could hear Milardi's blood sloshing to the floor.

Lily, he bounced back to the ship with a quaking voice. *Lily, can you hear me?*

I can hear you, Osyen. What do you require?

Uh... Osyen stumbled on the question. *I could use a hug and a whiskey right now.*

I'm afraid I'm not in a position to offer either of them at this time, but perhaps if you remembered your survival instincts, you might get one or both at the end of the day.

It's going to get ugly, Lily. How are you not terrified?

The computer didn't answer for a long moment. *I suppose I've never known a time when I wasn't, Osyen. I've always been afraid you won't come back. But I'm always comforted by my memory: that you always have.*

Osyen drew a breath. *I can't promise I will this time. You know what's out there.*

Don't promise it then, Lily said, whispering into his ear. *Just jump.*

The hairs on his neck stood on end, like they felt the brush of lips against his skin. And his heart quickened, and he squeezed his hand tight.

And I'll be there to catch you.

A second passed, maybe two. But then he went to take a step...and found no ground. His stomach pressed against his ribs. He kicked his feet in the air, finding nothing at all as he floated upward.

The grunts and chatter of confusion around them told Osyen it had worked: Lily had flicked off the artificial gravity in that section.

And Zatia took full advantage. He heard the slick of a single long blade releasing from the bangle on her wrist, its spring-loaded concealment. And when the steel hit her cuffs, a single sour note rang out as they snapped.

She was blind, in close quarters with her friends, with a sword. And they had guns, their sight. But guns weren't of much help without the ability to brace against the ground.

Grunting, gunshots, bangs, and the singing of metal—suddenly Osyen was ripped back into daylight, as his shroud deactivated. Roche tugged the collar off his head—in time for him to see Zatia shoot across the hallway, kicking off of the roof to slam down onto a guard with both blades.

Three other men were dead on the ground. Adelaide had pinned one guard by throwing her body at him, but that was going poorly for her. The guard had started to bash her face with a clenched fist.

Osyen flew over, slamming the heel of his boot into the guard's temple with a crunch. But he couldn't stop to check on Adelaide. The other guards had locked themselves to the floor and walls with magnetic boots. And they raised their rifles in unison, finally comfortable.

Give me gravity! Zatia demanded.

Osyen's hair fell in front of his eyes, and a great shrug pulled him downward. And the magnetically locked guards were suddenly pulled off line, sagging hard off their ankles. Some even started to slide down the walls.

Zatia crouched low, leaping forward to cleave through the helpless guards with her blades. She didn't look back, absolutely certain in her work. One strike, one kill, and Osyen was having a hard time disputing that, given the amount of blood making its way onto the floor—

—Milardi's eyes, as the blood pooled.

When Osyen blinked that sight out of his mind, Zatia was standing over the last guard. His rifle was on the ground, and her blades laid across his throat.

"Zee!" Osyen shouted, more emphasis than he needed.

But she heard him, pausing. Enough blood had been spilled. So she drew her blades back, clacking the guard across the face with the flat. "Go on now, git!"

The guard did not dispute this good fortune, taking off.

Osyen shook off the sweat like a wet dog. "Everybody alright?"

"Are you?" Roche asked. Osyen couldn't vocalize his answer, but wide eyes and raised brows were plenty enough for Roche.

Adelaide clucked her tongue at him. "I think I have a tooth loose."

Osyen huffed, helping her to her feet. "First hurdle down: now we take the Jump Deck. How's Lily?"

"Actively engaged with the Orchikov house countermeasures," Roche said, head tilted as he consulted Lily's database hack. "The AI is cordoning off critical systems, but I do have Tier One Access. Blueprints and schematics. Jump Deck is that way," Roche said, pointing directly at a bulkhead of pipes and plates.

Everyone stared at the wall in frustration. "Hey buddy," Zatia sang, "that's a wall."

Roche's head bobbed with disdain. "On the other side of it, Zee."

"Okay, then how do we get on the other side of it, *Roche?*"

"Ah," he said with a wandering eye. "I see your point."

Adelaide shook her head, two fingers in her mouth wiggling the loose tooth. "It's amazing any of you made it to adulthood."

"Don't pick at it," Osyen scolded. "It'll fall out."

Adelaide forced her arms to her sides, sticking her tongue out at him. She then gestured down the hall. "Lead the way, then. Someone will be coming to inspect all the *gunfire*."

"Hop to it!" Osyen said, grabbing a guard's carbine. "Do it like you're getting paid."

Zatia pointed at it, blood still dripping off her blades. "You can fire that thing left-handed?"

He studied it for a second, bracing against the wall. Ambidextrous safety, good size, clean grips. But the mag looked finicky with no specific release. It was a grab and tug situation. Someone thought that was superior, for some reason. "I mean...I'm screwed if I need to reload it."

"So shoot the next guy, pick up what he drops," she said that like she was explaining the rules to a game.

The Godfather's cruiser was not a military ship. In truth, it was a luxury liner. Osyen caught Adelaide dragging her hand along the wall. "What is it?"

"Jus' fine craftsmanship," she mused. "Any chance we can break it?"

"I don't know if *we'll* break it, but I do expect it will get broke."

"Good enough for me."

They came upon the hatch to a large pressure door. Osyen had seen this kind of thing before; it was an emergency measure designed to keep the Jump Deck a habitable little space in the event of a hull breach. In fairness, it was probably a perfectly functioning little life pod.

And it was child's play for Adelaide to pop the panel and safely extract a cable for Roche to patch into. They had the door seal cracked in ten seconds flat.

It was not a large space—it didn't have to be. There was room enough for maybe three people to sit at different consoles. The fresh-faced young men, one of them augmented and plugged in, turned to see the door lifting to reveal the cadre of badasses silhouetted by the hallway lights. Osyen couldn't help but smirk: that sight could've been their wanted poster.

Osyen walked into the room, a one-armed man with a rifle tucked into his hip. "Okay! Everybody up, everybody out! I have had a bad day and I *will* make yours worse."

Zatia flourished her blades, pointing to the door.

The three deck officers exchanged looks and promptly stood up from their stations, shuffling out of the door without so much as a peep.

But Roche said two syllables. "Uh-uh."

Prompting Osyen to plant his gun barrel into the chest of the augmented jockey before he could get out the door. "Deactivate the deck lock you just triggered."

The man was a good liar, feigning fear and confusion. "You-you think there's a deck lock? Why would there be—"

"Is my compatriot a liar, then? The pleasant gentleman literally jacked into the wall?" Osyen asked. "I need this thing to fly, not crash when I try to operate a ship that's all locked up. Y'hear me?"

"There-there isn't a deck lock! I mean, we have all kinds of security features in place. And what with all the shooting, maybe your friend... I mean, he's unfamiliar with the architecture—"

Osyen lowered the rifle to the top of the man's foot. Which changed his tune. "Yes sir," the jockey said as he stumbled back to his station.

Osyen followed him over, gun at his back. The jockey plugged in, eyes sliding towards his friends at the door.

"I know you think you're about to be the hero," Osyen threatened. "But you're not even a character in this story. And let me fill you in on who I am." He said it with his chest, low and full. "I ain't the hero either."

The jockey nodded furiously. But then his pupils dilated, focused on something far away. Osyen knew the look, glancing back at Roche, who had the same faraway look.

Lily? Osyen asked, tentative and testing.

They didn't have time to answer back, because that's when they heard chatter from the escort ships. "Unidentified commercial freighter. This is Farragut fleet vessel *Astrid*. You are on rendezvous course at high speed. State your intent."

A shiver went through the room when they heard Weasel's voice. "Pleased to be catching up to you is what I am. This is Leonard Osland of the *La Conte*. Push me a docking boom, I've got wounded."

Roche waved a hand, throwing up an amber schematic of the approaching ship. There was battle damage across the entire hull, with ugly belly scarring and a shattered view port midship. They all tensed at the sight of it—

That was him. It was the Paladin. They knew he'd come by any means necessary. And here he now came, in Weasel's commandeered brig.

Osyen didn't blink. "Destroy it."

The augmented jockey tensed but was unwilling to flinch with a gun barrel at his back. "Exactly how bad guy are you?!"

"That's not who you think it is," Osyen said. "We saw him die. And that's the thing what killed him. If you don't want to join him, you will fire everything you have at that brig. Right now."

The jockey nodded, pushing his message along through the cord. And soon, they heard the security vessel chime in. "Farragut Fleet Vessel *Astrid* reporting: reduce speed and prepare for remote boarding."

No answer back. And Osyen nodded. "There you have it. Light him up."

And they saw the *La Conte*'s engines fire, shooting gouts of blue out of the back half the length of the cruiser itself.

Some idiot repeated his warning. "*La Conte*, reduce speed or we will fire on you."

Osyen yanked the kid up from his seat, passing him off to Zatia and her blades. She rested one across his clavicle with a raised eyebrow. "Roche! Get us mobile!"

"Happy to, Cap'n!" Roche plopped himself down into the seat, plugging half a dozen cables into requisite sockets across the board. And instantaneously, Osyen felt the ship list underneath him.

With Lily's connection and Jump Deck command, Roche could issue some very high-profile orders. "Confirm, confirm. Farragut Fleet, weapons free. Destroy that ship."

They watched as shots came sailing in on the orange hologram, slamming into the hull. Gases expelled and fire erupted, like a primordial earth. Bits of steel and composites sailed off into the black like a mineral rain.

And suddenly, the ship popped, like the pressure from inside it was simply too much. The great metal beast breathed its last, exploding into glittering starlight.

Osyen pumped his fist in the air, letting his rifle fall slung. *Thom! We got him! Popped him at the perimeter.*

And the voice he heard sent a cold ice flow through his bones. *Prepare yourself for the journey, liar. I will set you on the Path myself.*

Osyen turned back to the team, crestfallen. "Okay...and I thought I was both clever and lucky."

"We know you're neither of those," Adelaide slandered.

"Ha ha," Osyen deadpanned. "Roche, get us to that Jump Point and calculate a—"

"I can't."

Osyen blinked. "What do you mean, you can't? You could like four hours ago."

"The *Aurum* isn't hard-lined into the ship like it's supposed to be. It's just sitting loose on the deck. I don't have Lily."

Zatia pushed her captive towards the door. "Go find yourself a good size escape pod."

"There are no escape pods for crew, just the Court!"

"Then go find a pretty person to kiss on the last night of your life. Or—steal—one—of—the—pods! You call yourself a criminal?" She shoved him out of the door and out of sight, whirling around. "What do you need to get access to Lily?"

Roche stiffened, consulting some specs before answering. "There's a universal fuel and data conduit that should be connected to the bow. Since we're captives, they had no use for fueling our ship. Connect that line, and Lily should be able to enter the system."

Zatia nodded at Osyen. "I'll go. You protect the plughead."

Osyen's response came out of his head before he formulated the thought. "No!" The Paladin was out there. If she left...she wouldn't come back.

People kept leaving...

She wasn't in a mood to debate this. "You have *one arm*, Oz, and didn't do so hot against this thing last time. I can do this. And it needs to be done!"

Adelaide slung her kit and gave the young murder-ball a clap on the shoulder. "I'll watch her back."

Osyen looked them over: grandmother and granddaughter, stern and spattered in blood. The two of them had been some of the most mercenary, some of the most disconnected. And here they were, leaping at danger for each other. For him. For family. No promise of pay, or even survival.

Fiona left to pursue her own ambition. His mother was taken, probably dead.

Milardi.

"You better come back," Osyen said.

"I'm coming back," Zatia said, clenching her blades, "or I'm taking that thing with me."

"How?" Adelaide asked, hard and crusty.

"I don't know! We found a heavy thing for the last one."

Osyen shook his head. "We're on the clock. We're Jumping just as soon as you get this thing plugged in!"

Zatia stowed her blades back into their bangles, and she threw herself around Osyen's shoulders, giving him a big hug. "You're not losing me that easy, y'hear?"

The idle patter of metal shards against the ship's deflector shield drew their eyes up. Somewhere in that steel rain, they knew was a pair of boots...

He nodded and pushed her away. "Go save the day."

"You know how I do!"

THIRTY-SEVEN

THOM

HE HAD EXPECTED TORTURE, idle cruelties from cruel men. But Anze had offered him a seat instead. Even as the staccato hail of shattered starship pecked at the hull, setting everyone's teeth on edge, Anze reclined and sipped at the purple drink in his thin-stemmed glass, a dainty balance.

Rashida sat upright, hands folded on her lap. She eyed the concoctions that had been brought as refreshment for his guests. And Thom hadn't missed that Magnus had taken up a post behind her, out of sight but close enough that she could feel him breathing down her neck.

"Not a shellfish man, eh?" Anze asked Thom, as he picked over his plate of tiny pink creatures. "They're an acquired taste. Most seafood is."

Thom looked up at Magnus, the skeletal Consort standing at Rashida's back, just where Thom had seen him a dozen times in his dreams. Everyone in the room was where they should be.

Anze glanced over at Rashida, nudging her with his foot. "You're allowed to relax. You're not going to the gallows. Take a load off, have a drink, some food."

She didn't budge. "Is home a terribly relaxing notion to you?"

He sat up, setting his drink aside, folding his hands across his lap. "It's not. Home is a place...riddled with distasteful people enamored with their own power and the invocation of it on a population too stupid to resist. They inflict themselves on an unwilling universe and call themselves 'Imperial' without a shred of irony."

"You'd send her back to that?" Thom asked.

Anze stood, sweeping his feet along the floor to rest a boot on either side of Thom. Trapping him.

No. Anze never did this in the visions, in the dreams. This was different. And Thom knew the rules: difference meant change. Unexpected change.

"I hadn't decided," Anze mused, sipping from his drink. "You think I shouldn't?"

Get him seated. Get him back in his chair. Sit him back down! If he didn't take his place, then the future Thom had seen wouldn't come to pass.

Thom shook his head. "You don't care what I think."

"Wouldn't have asked if I didn't," Anze reprimanded. His green eyes panned over Thom, squinting with assessment. "Nervous?"

"Of course," Thom whispered.

Anze leaned forward, pressing him. Far too close. "You seemed so insightful before."

"Lucky guesses," Thom said.

Anze smirked. "Foolish men have luck. Folks like us..." He lingered on that, as if unable to put the concept into words.

"Folks like us?" Thom prompted.

"Oh come now, child. You must sense it. There's an...air about you. You stare down dragons and demons with unearned confidence, daring them to strike you down and knowing that they won't. Because they can't."

He saw a kindred spirit. He saw mutual power, a worthy adversary—or ally.

"We don't have to see your father," Anze offered. "We could go somewhere else entirely. Oh! We could see him destroyed, if you like. Would you like that? He is encroaching on my borders."

Thom didn't want to see Admiral Ulysses Hugh ever again. He wanted to bury the man under solid rock and take all of the memories with him. He wanted to scrub the man from his life.

But did he wish him harm? No.

Anze sighed and flopped backward onto his lounge—where he belonged. "We'll revisit the topic when the problem is more immediate. Get a nice impulse decision out of you."

"Leave him alone," Rashida said, and Magnus promptly restrained her with a hand to her shoulder.

"I'm offering the boy options," Anze said, never taking his eyes off of Thom. "He is free to take or leave as he pleases."

It wasn't a complex offer. Anze was asking Thom, and whatever mysteries he had...to join him.

"I'm more like you than you think, Thomas," Anze promised. "My father never cared much for me, either. Never really had the time, what with his responsibilities. His love was the Sermon and the Pulpit. Admiral Hugh doesn't seem to love much beyond power over others."

For a hot second, Thom forgot the entire plan and just spat an insult into Anze's face. "I have a family, thanks."

Anze sighed, disappointed. "Where are they, Thomas?"

I know you're out there, Thom bounced over the radio . *And I know what you want. Come to me, and you will find her.*

Anze's face immediately soured. "Speak up, lad. I don't think the rest of the room heard you."

Rashida didn't so much as blink, twitch her neck. Nothing at all. Masking was her game, control of every muscle in her face.

Thom was less talented. "I didn't say anything," he said with a twitch in his cheek. Fiona had heard the back channel with an implant of her own.

Would Anze have stooped to such risky tricks? No, no, this was something far more ominous.

Anze never broke his withering stare, unblinking, petrifying. "You exist under my sight. You think there is a thing you can do that I am unaware of?" The Godfather rose to his feet like a sheet of silk pulled by a string, fluid and quiet. For a man of shorter stature, he commanded complete attention, and those green eyes were impossible to ignore.

Thom didn't move a muscle, lest he brush them off course. "It's not really what I do, per se. But I know things you wouldn't believe."

"And I have power you cannot yet fathom. I can feel your heart racing. The synapses in your brain, alight with special fire. And I heard you call for help."

Bluff or not, that was curiously timed. Thom had no reason to believe Anze was lying. Could the Master read minds? Thom drew a refreshing breath. "You want a prediction?"

Anze was happy to play. "Hit me."

"I won't." Thom nodded at Rashida. "But she will, in about thirty seconds."

Long pause and sucking silence from the room. Rashida, wide-eyed, glared at Thom. What the Hell was he playing at?

Anze chuckled at the thought, spinning himself on his lounge, playfully leaning forward to give her easy access to his chin. "I still think of you as little Rash in my head, scuttling between chairs, pony-tail bouncing. Show me how you've grown, Dunsweir."

"Twenty-three seconds," Thom said.

"You're awfully sure of that count," Anze said, taunting Rashida with a stare. "You sure she has the guts?"

"It's not a lack of gumption, Anze. The lady is waiting for the precise moment where it will inflict the most harm. Fifteen seconds."

"And what happens in fifteen seconds, Thomas?" That sentence was a threat. "Does little Lady Rash find her spine?"

And Thom had one of his own. "That happens in ten seconds. But the more interesting thing happens right about now."

He was off count by maybe one second, as the Paladin crunched through the roof of the auditorium, landing squarely at the bottom of the room in a cloud of dust and sparks. It creaked and groaned, straightening up to its full height. It raised its bald head, wisps of frost tinging its lips and eyes.

And it looked at Rashida.

Nobody waited for the order—as every soldier in the room snapped up weapons.

Magnus promptly threw Rashida forward, flopping her before the Paladin like a sacrifice to an altar—and Thom was awfully glad the little rat bastard did.

The guns went off before she even hit the floor. And the Paladin's deflector shield lit up, hurtling ricochets in random directions all around the room, shredding furniture and men alike. Thom dove for behind Anze's dais, trying to put some thick metal between him and the chaos. Magnus flopped to the ground next to him, clutching at his shoulder. Blood flowing between his fingers.

Unlucky. Thom couldn't really muster sympathy for the man.

The Paladin was unconcerned with the chaos, only eyes for Rashida. He stuck out a hand, magnetically peeling a gun from a goon's grasp.

"Stop!" Anze shouted—

And the deflector shield fizzled and vanished. The gun he had magnetically pulled went sailing past, skittering across the ground. The Paladin lurched and twitched, paralyzed. His eyes went dark, and he looked so very heavy.

Anze stalked down the terrace towards the Paladin. "The human body is so full of electricity it makes my teeth ache, but a metal man? Now, there is *so much* power in you. Trillions of little electrons zipping back and forth. Building blocks of the universe. We used to think we had harnessed this elemental power. It drove our entire society for centuries." He tutted and tilted his head in disappointment. "We had no idea it didn't belong to us. It belonged to the Pilgrim."

Thom stood up from his hiding place. Anze Orchikov, the Godfather, had stopped the Paladin in its tracks, slowly shutting down its systems, starving it.

With a glance. With a single word. With nothing but intent.

And the Paladin whimpered. And it made Thom feel...right. He watched as the Paladin strained, teeth gritting, as though some great weight pushed him to the ground.

The crowd cheered as Anze stepped forwarded, pressing the titan down. Crushing him. Systems shut down, stalled out. Equations required to keep him moving, to keep him alive, were collapsing. The servos that gave him strength, the sensors that gave him sight...all of them, failing.

They could end it right here, Thom thought. Anze was perfectly capable of opposing anything that ever threatened them. And isn't this what they wanted? To get into his grace, to beg favors?

He could bargain for his friends' lives, set them up nicely. See that Nathaniel's ashes were returned to Adelaide. Set everyone right.

And the Paladin looked over at him, panic in its eye. It had failed. It would die, alone, in the dark.

Good.

Good? What would Milardi say to that?

"Stop it," Thom muttered, repeating the words with more strength. "Stop it."

"What's the matter, seer?" Anze hissed. "Are you adjusting your predictions?"

The Paladin trembled, gritting its teeth. Swallowing a cry of pain.

And its baritone groveling very nearly covered the crack of a single gunshot.

Magnus braced himself on Anze's lounge, popping a shot out of the end of his cane into Anze's back. The Godfather may be the master of electricity, but there was nothing he could do about an exothermic chemical reaction hurtling a lead slug.

Anze grabbed at his back and tumbled to the ground.

And the Paladin roared to life, a growl growing into a battle cry to shake the walls.

Which is when Rashida stood up and decked Magnus, throwing a right cross that would've made Zatia proud. The Consort flopped to the deck, knocked out cold. Thom kicked his cane aside, disarming the Consort.

Anze cursed and groaned, favoring his side as he forced himself to his feet.

The Paladin rose from the deck, dripping sweat and eyes flashing yellow. Gnashing teeth at Anze. Whatever furious vexation he had for Rashida would wait—this man was an actual threat.

"Run!" Thom said, pushing Rashida toward the door.

No one had the wherewithal to stop them, too focused on peppering the Paladin with gunfire as it advanced on their leader with heavy, creaking steps. Anze bellowed commands, each one freezing the Paladin for a moment. But the pain in his back would always break his focus and the Paladin would resume his pressure.

They didn't wait to see what happened next. The two rounded the corner at a full sprint into the hallway.

"You expected all that?!" Rashida berated him.

Thom looked back at the auditorium, afraid of what he might see. "With some loose variation!"

The Paladin was alive, and Anze too weak to resist it now. The chase was on. As it should be. He'd become so enamored with what he had to gain, he almost lost sight of what he had to keep.

"Now what?!" she asked, in between gasps of breath.

"Now we run!" Thom said.

Run, run, run. Until the Paladin catches us, Thom thought. But he didn't dare say that part out loud, or she wouldn't take another step.

THEY ENCOUNTERED precious little resistance on their way aft from the Jump Deck, which was a small consolation to Adelaide. At least the boys back there wouldn't face a whole lot of trouble from this end. But the gunfire and screaming she heard from where they were going certainly made her question her survival instincts.

They had been led away from the *Aurum* with shrouds, but Roche had given them the briefest of plans to the ship before they sprinted off. Didn't help much—they were very quickly lost.

"Hasn't anybody heard of signage?!" Adelaide cursed as she stopped at yet another t-intersection of corridors.

Zatia slid past her, looking down at each one for a clue like they weren't identical. "Maybe Roche got it wrong?"

"Is he known to do that?" Adelaide asked, facetious.

Zatia just picked a direction and took off running again. If they ran long enough and far enough, they were sure to find it, eventually. The ship was only so big, after all.

Adelaide couldn't help but think that they had built the passages to be vaulting and open, as though the builder had severe claustrophobia, making his decision to build pressurized aluminum cans questionable, at best. And so the passages were plenty big for a nine-foot kill-bot with a zealotry setting.

They passed an open doorway—and Zatia slid to a stop, mouth agape. Adelaide caught up to her, peeking around the corner.

It was the Auditorium. And it had been redecorated with the Paladin's signature touch.

A hole in the roof like an open mouth, pipes and conduits dangling. Scuffs and bullet holes were thrown about into every surface with an almost intentional randomness, like there was some complex pattern to pick out if she stared at it long enough. Blood had already started to dry into a cakey black on the steel. Plenty of dead bodies reclined in uncomfortable looking poses, including one gentleman staked to a curved piece of flooring.

"Check for Thom and Rash," Adelaide said.

"If they were here, they'd be dead," Zatia countered. "But if the Paladin's not here, I doubt they are."

Adelaide slunk into the room, sticking to a wall. Just because the machine wasn't here any longer didn't mean it was safe to linger. There were plenty of dead goons, but Rashida's gown was nowhere among the dead. Nor was Thom's raggedy look—or even Magnus's suit. No such easy luck there.

Come to think of it, Anze was not among the dead either.

But Zatia simply marched across the open floor, bouncing down the terrace steps, on over to the fireplace. They had knocked some embers free onto the hearth, singing the clothes on the nearest bodies. Zatia hopped up onto one corpse's back, reaching up high for—

Nathaniel. His ashes.

Zatia plucked his urn off of the mantle. The pot looked to be half the size of her torso, but with two good grips, she was able to easily bring it over to Adelaide.

"I doubt he'd even notice it's missing."

Adelaide's heart fluttered. She had thought often about this moment, and she thought she might cry. She might rage. She might have done so many things. But her actual reaction was more muted, stunned silence. She reached out to take it from Zatia's hands. It wasn't that heavy, really.

She wasn't sure what she expected, to be fair. Apparently, a lifetime weighs about six pounds plus a ceramic pot.

"How does it feel?" Zatia asked, stooping over some dead nobleman to turn out his pockets.

She remembered how Nathaniel howled when he laughed. How he smiled at her when he caught her staring. Nathaniel covered in oil and grime. Nathaniel holding her hand while watching the eternal sunset on Ilum. Standing at her bedside when she was sick, a bowl of soup in his hands.

She didn't feel any better, any worse. She didn't feel like she felt she was supposed to. She was supposed to feel different. She was supposed to feel...

Supposed to feel? Sure, but what did she actually feel?

She thought she'd feel angry. But she didn't. She didn't know what this was, but it wasn't anger, vengeful, or rage. It was...

Magnus. He appeared like a shadow, melting off the wall—raising up his cane like a rifle. He staggered, grunting through pain. Zatia blocked his path to the exit, and he was going to carve his escape.

Adelaide heaved the urn over her head, throwing Nathaniel at her attacker. The ceramic hit the cane first, shattering into a cloud of dust and ash, erupting in a wave of dead husband onto Magnus's face.

Zatia didn't wait another second, rushing the distracted shooter and slamming him headfirst into the wall. He dropped to the floor.

Satisfied he wasn't getting up, Zatia looked back at Adelaide. "Are you certifiable?!"

"I just saved your life!"

"You threw your..." Zatia couldn't say the words, gesturing at the cloud still settling around her. "We're out here, scrapping with gangsters and being hunted by a manufactured *zoldat*. And the moment you get your hands on your husband again—the *whole reason* we're in this hole—you throw him at somebody?!"

"Not just somebody. Look who it is."

"I don't care if you threw him at the *gulaw* Pilgrim!" Zatia whined. "What are you doing?!"

Adelaide glanced at Magnus, still limp on the floor. "Couldn't let him hurt you."

That stopped Zatia cold, her mind grinding on that question. "But...Nathaniel?"

"Nathaniel's gone," Adelaide said. "You're still here. Come on."

Zatia had to reboot her brain before marching out of the door with pockets full of dead criminal money. Adelaide stooped to collect a handful of ashes before she followed.

CHAPTER
THIRTY-NINE
ZATIA

THE HANGAR DECK WAS DESERTED, everything with wings and engines long since gone—except for the fatted and lovely *Aurum* clinging to the deck like a turkey on an ivory platter. Zatia and Adelaide jogged forward, heads on swivels as they checked the surroundings for more surprises.

"Grab the conduit!" Zatia called out. "I'll watch your back."

"Where is everyone?" Adelaide asked.

It was suspicious, sure, but Zatia was not one to question good luck. With no deck crew or guards in their way, they were going to get this done quite fast.

Adelaide gingerly unhooked the refueling conduit off of the wall. The digital connections inside would give Lily access to the Godfather's ship systems and top off the fusion reactor from stores.

A clang-bang from behind them, and Zatia whirled around. The door they came from was just clicking shut, automatic functions. But it certainly hadn't sounded friendly. Whole place was creaking like a haunted house, and the footsteps echoed off the walls like the ship was trying to talk back to them.

Zatia turned back around—to find the Paladin gripping Adelaide by the jaw, two fingers ready to pinch her head right off of her shoulders. Adelaide grimaced, frozen in place, not wanting to taunt the vise that locked its teeth on her skull.

"Hi," Zatia said, clenching her fists. "Can I help you?"

The Paladin cocked its head, blank expression. "Call her."

Rashida. It wanted her to summon its prey.

"I don't know where she is," Zatia said.

"Liar."

Zatia scoffed. "No, for real. I left her in that auditorium room you clearly redecorated. Why don't you tell *me* where she is?"

Adelaide groaned as the Paladin applied pressure. But she held that conduit tucked under her arm, so close and ready...

Enough voltage to set a human being on fire.

"I am trying to be kind," the Paladin admonished her.

Zatia felt her eyebrow twitch, and she prayed it was just dehydration and stress and not something terribly worse. A ringing filled her ears, and her vision darkened, tapering in on the big chunky boy.

And Adelaide let the conduit drop into her hands, swinging the dinner plate sized connector around to contact the Paladin's chest. It was either going to squeeze or let go, no two ways about it. And she was going to get a bit of a kiss from that same flowing current too.

The Paladin howled—releasing Adelaide to the ground. The old woman thrashed for a second, electricity snapping through her veins, before scrabbling away from the monster. Her left leg and arm lay limp at her side, but she could get clear.

Zatia grabbed her bangles, flicking out the blades inside—the tips just long enough to kiss the ground and strike a line of sparks. A battle-cry, and Zatia charged the Paladin.

She remembered what happened the first time she did this: a firm back hand had sent her hurtling across a room. The second time, she'd been able to get a few good blows in before being stapled to a wall with her own blades.

Broken bones, stab wounds, crushed and battered—she'd healed without even a scar. And she had friends to help with the rest.

The Paladin swiped a hand across its front, slapping the thick conduit out at Zatia. The open end of the conduit, a lamprey's maw of pins and connectors and tubes, gaped at her. Zatia dropped to her knees, sliding underneath the foot-wide tube whipping through the air. Her blades screeched against the Hangar bay floor. When she popped to her feet, she brought the blades up—

It raised a wrist to block, but she pulled the strike, feinting up onto her toes and stabbing in with the tips. They pierced, driving a full two inches through the Paladin's shoulders. She yanked them back out before the Paladin could lock her down, slashing across his wrist, tearing at the steel plates and carving troughs in the armor.

Zatia backpedaled away, circling her opponent. "What happened to that fancy deflector shield, big guy? Feeling a little wear and tear?" She gasped. "Did you have to run away from your last fight?"

That got him to charge, a flat golem's expression, like his face had been hewn from stone. And he came at her like a rock rolled downhill. And he reached out for her, squeezing the air like he could choke her from a distance—

—and her swords yanked on her, pulling her off her feet and towards him. She skidded, bouncing off the hangar floor.

Oh right, magnet hands. If she surrendered the swords, he'd filet her with them. So...

She let the force bring her in. She kicked off the ground and flew straight at him, leading with her knee. Make him regret that choice.

The blade stopped, hovering in his hand, bringing her in knee-first like a missile. He raised his other hand, catching her and stopping her cold. But she twisted in his grip, swinging her other leg around to mule kick with all her might directly up and under his chin.

She was small, maybe half his size. He was armored and built to take hits. But it was enough for him to at least loosen his grip on her.

Don't let go of those blades. If she let go, she'd become barbecue shredded beef in seconds.

She didn't want to let go? Fine. He spun the blades, helicoptering them in his hand, and spinning her along with them. It turned her stomach, the world blurring around her.

—and a perfect moment of clarity, as something in her brain clicked into place. It was the world, slow, soft, making sense. She wasn't fast; everyone else was slow.

Like before. That stim pumping through her veins.

She reached out with a foot, pressing off a wall so hard she heard the rubber sole squeal. Her calf muscle screamed, and her gut pulled as her muscles operated at a level that should be beyond them.

The Paladin saw it coming but was nowhere near fast enough to stop it. She twisted herself through his defenses, weaving past his hands to kick the side of his head with her heel. He staggered back, stunned.

Adelaide came barreling in, the conduit in both hands. Like a battering ram, she slammed the hot electricity into his back. The Paladin howled again, the power line of a starship pumping through metal parts and human body.

And Zatia felt his magnetic grip on the blades loosen. She turned them down, indexing the edge, and slashed—right through his hand. Four fingers and a third of palm flopped to the floor.

He wasn't going to be magnetically throwing anything anymore.

The Paladin roared, swinging back at Adelaide, but she was smart enough to abandon her close proximity and flee for the door. By the time the Paladin had come back around, Zatia impaled both blades into his gut, driving them clean through and into the side of a carbon store crate.

She jumped back—but the blades wouldn't come. Leave them. Don't stay close.

She let go, leaving her swords buried in the Paladin's chest as he reached for her.

Zatia looked around her for something, anything. Could she crush him? Squish him? Burn him with jet exhaust?

No—there was the hangar bay door, though.

"Addy!" Zatia called out. "I think there's a draft!"

The Paladin glanced at his lack of a hand, and reached across his body with his remainder, wrenching one sword out of his chest.

"Maybe open a window?" Zatia asked, pressing herself against a wall.

The Paladin raised the sword up, plenty ready to throw it the old-fashioned way. And Zatia took a breath...

...as the howl of emergency alarms kicked in. Her own sword came lurching at her, thrown off-target. Because the crate she staked him to was now sliding towards the exit. Zatia clung to the wall, watching as the Paladin sailed out into the void, stuck to his anchor, drifting further and further off into nothing...

And the bay doors closed again, hiding him from view.

Zatia plucked her sword from the wall, inspecting the edge. "Cut 'em up, Jackson."

CHAPTER
FORTY
ROCHE

AT THIS RATE, gunfire was going to turn into a white noise that Roche used to lullaby him to peaceful slumber. Osyen laid himself against the doorframe, grimacing against the pain of his shoulder as he tried to pinch his third stolen rifle against his hip.

"It's getting awful crowded back here!" Osyen shouted.

"They'll get it done," Roche assured him with no confidence.

They better.

Osyen racked the rifle off of the wall, bracing it against his hip as he sprayed down an unlucky goon who tried to rush the door. His weapon clattered along the floor to Roche's feet, who kicked it back to Osyen. The rugged captain discarded his weapon and reached down for his fourth, inspecting it for any operational quirks. This one was small enough for him to wield one-handed at least.

Speakers crackled, and the heavens shook. It was as though the entire ship had something to say to their presence, but the charismatic voice that seeped from every crevice wasn't the one he expected. "This has been an entertaining diversion, I must say. It's not often my entire world is turned upside my head."

"Anze," Osyen muttered with a derisive snort.

"I must admit to a certain...frustration with you, Osyen Belt.

Your little protege estimated this day with alarming accuracy. For a brief moment, I thought I had his consideration. But that's all ruined now."

Roche glanced around the deck, searching for whatever camera or sensor he was watching them through. But there wasn't anything obvious to find. Lily's rendition of this trick was far more comforting, even if they were to speak the same words. There was something to Anze's words that seemed unhinged, that despite his eloquent vocabulary, he was barely in control of his nerves.

"I wish you well in your endeavors and hope you enjoy my parting gift."

Roche blinked—and felt the timer start. "Osyen, he's sent the reactor core into meltdown. We've got just under ten minutes, on the outside, before it fills the entire ship in radioactive fire."

Osyen's face faltered. They couldn't warn the others with the Paladin still standing. He could try to reason with the Paladin, but the zealot might not believe them—might not care. He would throw himself into his own grave to ensure Rashida fell into hers.

"That's the face I like to see," Anze mocked. "You owe me a ship, Osyen Belt, and since I can't shoot you in the head, I'll have to settle for fireworks. It shall be a spectacular show. Relax: you have the best seat in the house."

Rapid puffs of sound coupled with the briefest pull of air on Osyen's head. He looked up at Roche, grinding his jaw. "He just fired off every escape pod on this ship, didn't he?"

"He did."

"Dramatic son of a bitch," Osyen muttered.

Roche nodded. "Do we make a run for the *Aurum*?"

Osyen swung his stolen weapon up high over his head, resting his arm and breathing hard. And then, with one powerful breath, he pulled himself to his feet. "Better than sitting here waiting to be crisped."

"Well," Roche said, reclining to undo his cable connections. "Least I've led an interesting life. No one can say otherwise."

"Hell, you've got one unlike anybody I've ever known," Osyen said. "What's our time at?"

"Eight minutes," Roche said, sagging, "before the reactor core swallows half the ship in a torrent of fire, and compresses it down to a ball of cooked metal. And the other half gets sucked out into the ensuing vacuum. If the fire doesn't kill us, the void will. Oh, and there's a psychotic super soldier roaming the decks, don't forget."

Something in that prognosis sucked all the power from Osyen's legs, and he leaned against the wall. "Got a preference?" he asked, staring at the floor.

Roche shrugged. "I always thought that getting crushed was a nice way to die. Especially by something very large, very quickly. It'd be like a blow to the head from the world's largest hammer."

"I've been hit by a lot of things," Osyen said with a shiver. "I'd take cold vacuum over getting hit again."

"Not fire?"

Osyen shook his head. "Never really liked hot weather."

No matter how he died, Roche wanted to be surrounded by his friends. At least he still had Osyen there. Suppose that's all he could ask for.

Roche pondered what it might be like—to die. Would he see anything, nothing? He supposed he experienced something akin to it already. He had forgotten so much, he imagined that death wasn't a matter of seeing a light or no light at all—but forgetting what it was to see, to hear, to breathe, taste, or touch. To be nothing wasn't the absence of something but losing the very notion of life as a measurable thing.

"I really thought they were going to make it," Osyen muttered.

And then he heard their voice. *Hello, Roche. I have reserved this comment for some time, but seeing as we face imminent destruction, I have to say you need to organize your thoughts in a more utilitarian manner. It is exhausting.*

Lily? Roche asked.

Who else would have complex and weighty opinions about the contents of your skull? Excuse me, it's our *skull these days, isn't it? And look where you've taken it!*

It was warm blankets and hot cider and pleasant silence, crackling fire and the smell of lavender and dim lighting. Lily had returned, the hard line connected. They had always been ever-present, a friend when all else was quiet. And it had always hurt when he had to leave the ship, leave that voice behind.

No longer. After today's misadventures, a piece of Lily forever with him...he would never be alone again.

The radio crackled the instant Lily stopped talking. "Stop your grinnin' and drop your linen. We've got ourselves a positive ship-to-ship connection!" Zatia sang over the ship's intercom.

Osyen sat upright, hopeful light in his eyes. "Roche?"

Roche blinked, commanding with a thought, and he heard the physical toggle flick over his head somewhere, opening the line. "I have an affirmative link with Lily and have begun Jump calculations. Nice work, you two!"

"Lily, I've got a reactor core—"

"Working on it now," Lily said. "It has passed critical descent, but I can buy you enough time to return to the *Aurum*. I do advise you do so as soon as possible."

"You owe me something big, plughead!" Zatia's voice crackled over the terrible speakers, in between gasping for breath. "And what's more, I just eighty-sixed our Paladin friend."

Osyen jumped to his feet, darting over to lean on Roche's shoulder. "Zatia, do not lie to me! Did you *really*?"

"I watched her do it," Adelaide said. "Blew the cyborg right off the hangar floor. He's spinning in the void right now, stapled to a heavy crate."

A swell of joy rose in Roche's heart, and he reached over, clapping Osyen on the back. His captain simply draped over the back of the chair, laying his arm limp across Roche's front. He muttered into Roche's shoulder. "That is some *sorely* needed good news, you two. Damn fine work."

"Adelaide, we've got a reactor core going critical in a matter of minutes," Roche said. "Sit with Lily and get the *Aurum* fired up. We're coming to you. Lily, start Jump prep."

Already done, Lily whispered over the back channel, and their baritone voice nearly made Osyen melt. He did a little happy dance, shimmying left and right.

Thom's voice chimed in. He was...far less enthusiastic. *Tell me you didn't do that.*

You're not taking this away from me, Zatia said. *No way. That was epic, and I deserve a crown.*

Osyen stopped dancing and started heading for the door. *Didn't see that one coming, didya, Maestro?*

Thom's voice sent chills up Roche's spine. *No...I didn't.*

You're not able to plan for all eventualities, Osyen said. *Get to the* Aurum, *and we'll Jump ourselves the Hell out of here.*

No! Thom shouted over the line. *No, stick to the plan!*

Osyen brought out his authoritative dad voice. *Thom, the Paladin's gone. And this ship is going to parboil us. So you and Rashida drop whatever you're doing, and get to the* Aurum *right now.*

He's not dead! Thom insisted. *He's never dead!*

Roche's brow furrowed. The Paladin might not have perished in the vacuum of space—he'd survived extreme cold before, and there was enough automation in his system, perhaps low-pressure environments were of no concern. But there was very little their cybernetic adversary could do without the ability to push onto something, and Roche very much doubted the resilient bastard would survive atmospheric reentry. Even if he did, it would take him weeks to drift back to Farragut.

The crew would be long gone by then. So why was Thom so worried?

No more arguing, Osyen said. *Beat feet, back to the ship, double-time.*

You have to believe me! He's—not—dead!

He doesn't have to be dead if this ship does his work for him, Adelaide pointed out.

I've seen how this plays out! Oz, please! He's not— And Thom's voice cut out.

Thom? Osyen asked. *Thom, we didn't get that.*

Roche's stomach dropped, and his breath hitched. "Lily?"

The AI's voice could not be interrupted, not with the new link hard-lined from the hangar. But Lily and Roche could feel the cool and crushing presence—moving aft. "I see it."

Osyen waited for one of them to say something, and then the blood drained from his face. "Well...called that shot a little early."

In order to execute a Jump, a computer needed to incorporate the data from every person onboard, so that they might be reconstituted on the other side. The Jump Drive could read who, what, and where everyone was on the ship down to a molecular level.

Which is how Roche saw: The Paladin was still onboard. Somehow.

He must've skipped along outside on the hull, palming hand over hand. Closer and closer to an entrance, or where he might make a new one.

Closer, closer...to Thom and Rashida...

And there was nothing Roche could do.

CHAPTER
FORTY-ONE
RASHIDA

SHE STOOD IN THE DOORWAY, waving at Thom to follow. "Are you out of your mind?!"

Thom was in hysterics, eyes wide on the verge of tears, face flushed, and voice strained. He flailed his hands in the air, like he was trying to beat back a shapeless nightmare. He stood in the hallway, unmoved, a taut muscle from end to end. "This isn't how it's supposed to happen!"

"How *what's* supposed to happen?" Rashida asked.

"She changed something! Zatia!" Thom shouted, tripping over his own words. "When she-she fought the Paladin on the hangar deck. She's not supposed to *airlock* him! Now everything's...*different!*"

The boy looked ready to pop a blood vessel, heart pounding, palms sweaty. His gut spasmed with short and harsh breaths, full-blown panic.

Rashida held open her palms, trying to draw him out of whatever episode was taking hold of him. "Thomas...you need to follow me to—"

She didn't get to finish that sentence. A crunch and a sucking sound drowned out all other noise. The wind nearly yanked Rashida off her feet, pulling on every fold in her clothing like a storm gale into canvas sails.

Thom stumbled into the doorframe, snagging her hand before she could fall over. And the panic came back to him in a flash. Did she dare look behind her?

Carving his way in, scooping bits of metal out of his path, came the Paladin. A gaping hole in his gut, a hand missing all but his thumb. His cybernetic eyes leaked fluid that trailed off of his face and out of the breach. His long coat was torn and abused, mostly a set of rags now.

And he settled himself onto the deck, setting his eyes on Rashida.

"Go!" Thom shouted, slinging Rashida through the doorway and behind him, pushing her onward and away from the threat.

"Roche!" Thom shouted. "Roche, if you can hear me, you need to Jump, right now!"

A loudspeaker picked up, but the voice was fragmented. "I see him, Maestro. Calculating now, but he's...countering my efforts."

One Jump, a single good Jump. Override the safety measures built into the Jump Drive and they could delete the Paladin from existence. Maybe he'd come back missing his head, or with his heart malformed.

One good Jump.

"Stop!" Thom shouted at the Paladin. "You don't have to do this!"

But the giant was beyond listening. Perhaps his ear drums had ruptured in space, or the AI onboard had simply stopped receiving anything from any other source. It strode forward with conviction, heavy foreboding steps.

They turned to run, rushing towards the door at the end of the hall—but the door slammed shut on them. She looked back at the Paladin—and its flickering yellow eyes.

"Lily!" Rashida begged. "Lily, open this door!"

"I'm...trying," Lily stuttered. "He won't let me."

Every ounce of his power, of his leverage, was dedicated to this one small space. Do not let her escape. He waved his finger, and the door shut behind him. The system automatically tried to re-pressurize the space, flooding the room with cool, crisp air.

But the Paladin didn't care about that. There was nowhere for them to run now. He had locked the doors, and only he had the keys.

Thom looked up, down, left, right—for a vent, a door, a damn hole in the wall. Anywhere to go.

Rashida took a step off the doorframe, facing down her assassin. It answered with a single step forward.

"Roche, how we doin' on that Jump?" Thom asked. "Because we're just about out of time!"

"Working on it!" Roche's voice crackled. "But I do it now, and I might rip the ship in half!"

"So rip it in half!"

Rashida didn't turn. She didn't blink. She didn't recoil. The Paladin advanced on her with slow and deliberate steps, like he was savoring the taste of the moment. But he tilted his head, even as he approached...careful study.

Now why would he study her? What was he hoping to find?

The Paladin was close enough now she could smell the oils and metals. Her skin tingled with the open electric hum in the air. And he extended his hand for her.

It was no use. Faithful men could cause so much pain and turn to their flock to call it healing. She always knew they'd turn that knife to her one day. And they would justify it by saying that she had forced them to.

When this was what they were for.

Rashida turned away from her assassin, throwing one last baleful look at Thom. In six months, he had grown so much.

But he was not ready to let her go yet. Thom's shout seemed to ripple the very world. "ROCHE!"

The Paladin's fingers wrapped tight around the back of Rashida's neck and—

—and the world stretched and boiled, skinned alive and shown her own trappings. It was like steel bubbled and blood hardened, and electricity coagulated into thick cords, splitting the air like cracks in glass.

And then, like she could watch the fabric of the universe flex and bend, it all snapped back into place like a rubber band released.

The metal overhead and under them creaked and groaned, bolts straining throughout the hull, like a magnificent set of hands had taken hold and had pulled it from either end.

And the ship was not the only thing taxed by the experience. The Paladin staggered back, reeling from some heavy blow. She could hear the grinding and crunching of something unsupported snapping.

The Jump had worked, to a degree. The Jump had robbed something...crucial to the Paladin. He was not complete. He was...

Pissed off. But it lifted its head, pure hate and disdain. And it took a step closer. And Rashida couldn't mistake the wet slop of something liquid now contained within his boot. Not that it would matter. This ailing half-man would still crush her throat just as easily as before.

"Roche!" Thom shouted. "Whatever you did was good, but not enough! Hit him again!"

"I can't. That's the only one you get."

The Paladin stomped forward, staggering, before tumbling into a wall. The impact left a harsh handprint in the steel. It knocked something loose too, as a steel beam fell from above, penning Thom and Rashida against the door.

Thom turned to work on it, but the panel had lost power. It was only opening with a crowbar now. He tried to work his fingers into the seam but had no luck.

A familiar authoritative voice echoed throughout the ship: "Anze Orchikov, this better not be some kind of trick."

Admiral Hugh. The Navy had been blockading the Jump Point, awaiting delivery. Who knows what state the cruiser had appeared in?

The Paladin grimaced, gritting teeth and pressing itself off the wall. Black oil slicks ran down his cheeks like machine tears smearing battle paint on its face. It took a step, only to realize its left leg didn't answer its calls anymore, being dragged behind.

"Roche, you have to Jump again!" Thom urged.

"I can't! I have a core breach and the heat sinks need time to ventilate. We won't survive another Jump!"

"Rash and I will die, and you will all be shot on sight. Unless— you Jump—again!"

"Jump where?!"

The Paladin stumbled again, falling against the steel bar—the only thing separating them from the cyborg.

It squeezed hard, bending and twisting the thick metal, pressing it down onto them. He might not be able to stand, but he was still powerful enough to kill them.

"Just do it, Roche!"

The world cracked, a million tiny shards spiderwebbing their way along the fabric of the visible world. The Paladin heard it, just as they did. And he looked back, to see the corridor tumble away into an endless black, swallowed by nothing. The silent unraveling came at them faster and faster, peeling reality apart and hurtling it some-where else.

Until the Paladin itself was melted away. Rashida closed her eyes. And prayed.

CHAPTER
FORTY-TWO

OSYEN

HE HAD SEEN SHIPS EXPLODE. He had yet to have the pleasure of being on one as it did. Most people only got to have that experience once in their lives—at the very end.

The core went critical as soon as they exited the Jump, swallowing the back half of the ship in a vortex of plasma and fire. The perfect sphere of radiant destruction expanded and crashed backward in on itself. Anything caught in the blast was crushed down to a ball of dense metals less than an inch across. Crystal black, polished like glass. The hull at the edge of the wreck glowed like iron fresh from the forge.

Unfortunately, that left the cruiser without power, sucking hull breaches across nearly every deck—and no thrusters to pull them out of their planetary fall down to Farragut. What was left of the ship was held together by spun sugar and whimsy.

They had to get back to the *Aurum* and escape before this expensive brick hit the ground with the force of an asteroid. Osyen thought he had mastered running—but not having an entire arm as a counterweight made the process surprisingly difficult. And the floor did not make it any easier, rolling under his feet as the ship rocked back and forth in free fall.

The sight flickered past him as he ran by the view ports in the hull—Farragut's pristine white surface was rising awful fast, and he could see the tongues of reentry burn darting past the glass.

Come on, come on! Zatia grunted in his ear. *Where the* Hell *are you guys?!*

The ship coughed underneath him, throwing Osyen to the floor—right onto his nub of a shoulder. The sensitive patches and stitches screamed at the rough treatment, and he left a smear of blood across the floor as he slid.

But Roche's big hand palmed across his back, scruffing him by his jacket and shirt, heaving him back to his feet.

The two of them sprinted onto the hangar deck, happy to see the *Aurum* waiting happily. Adelaide stood on the ramp, waving her arms in the air.

Osyen saw the clouds outside the hangar bay doors, a rumbling texture of cold and gray, rise to envelope the falling cruiser. Nothing was going to survive this impact.

Roche and Osyen tumbled up the *Aurum's* gangway, bouncing into the cargo netting to lay there, exhausted. *Lily, we're on! GO!*

"Where's Thom and Rash?" Adelaide shouted.

What? They hadn't made it back yet?

But Lily had a more desperate answer. *If the* Aurum *does not detach within the next twelve seconds, we will not be able to halt our descent.*

Goddamn it. Goddamn it! *Roche—get us out of here.*

The Jockey's eyes glazed over as he took control. The *Aurum* snapped off the floor, maglock landing gear disengaging. Osyen tumbled in the netting, slipping to the floor as the big ship lurched up and around, jetting out of the hangar before the gangway had even closed.

Bang went the vertical thrusters—and they were instantly weightless, thrown up towards the *Aurum's* ceiling. Adelaide held on tight by the door, her feet sucked upward, while Osyen himself tumbled up to land hard against the bulkhead. Roche held firm to his cargo netting, terrible focus in his eyes.

Wisps of cloud, ice, and snow spilled into the *Aurum*. And the cloud cover broke, and Osyen could see the ground out the door. Rising fast. Too fast. But he could also see the Godfather's cruiser below, a fatted whale trailing smoke and steam, a carbon-scored nose tilted toward the icy tundra.

Thom was on that ship. Rashida was on that ship.

And it hit, tearing a gash in the ice and throwing up a cloud of snow and fire. Cracks snapped outward in three directions, miles long.

Just because they had hit, didn't mean the *Aurum* wouldn't. That crash site was getting awfully close. The wind howled, and the vapor cloud from the impact soon rose to swallow his view. If they were going to crash, Osyen wouldn't see it happen.

But the thrust that pressed Osyen to the ceiling slowed, and he suddenly had weight again, gingerly bringing him down to the deck. The *Aurum* shot out of the cloud, hovering over the crash site.

A hatch swung open and Zatia popped out onto the deck, all giddy smiles...until she counted the faces. "Where's the others?"

Adelaide looked down at the crash site below them, the echoing drums of cracking ice calling out to them.

Captain, Lily inquired, *I have an incoming hail from the Godfather*.

"I'm sure you do," Osyen muttered. *Put him through*.

The charisma and force of Anze Orchikov had been drained, replaced with an urgency more akin to a distraught parent. "Is Thomas alive? Did he get off the ship?!"

Osyen blinked, and heat radiated off of his skin, through his feet and up to his scalp. He clenched his fingers and clenched his jaw. And after forcing himself to swallow, only then did he give it words. "Repeat that, Anze. You broke up."

"Tell me that Thomas is safe!" That was genuine human concern in his voice, tinged with anger and a sinking pit of grief and denial.

Everyone looked at Osyen. Wondering how he'd play this. What he'd do now. What they wanted him to do.

"You..." Osyen paused, considering his options. "You're *worried* about Thom after all that?"

"Osyen, tell me where he is. Please."

Osyen's answer was like a chilling poison that robbed the breath from your lungs. "He's somewhere under five hundred tons of steel and ice, Anze. Well done. Your plan worked."

There was an ugly pause, but the sound of breathing told him that Anze Orchikov had gone nowhere. He was considering that news. "I.. acted impulsively," the Godfather of Farragut admitted, the words tumbling out of his mouth. "I was caught up in the moment."

"Caught up in the..." Osyen repeated in breathless awe.

"I know my limits," Anze assured him, "and I must admit, I found one of them today. I have been shot, after all. I'm sure you understand."

"No, I don't think I do," Osyen said, glancing at Adelaide to check her temperature. But she had nothing to say or offer. Just an empty stare at the ceiling.

"You know as well as I do, Osyen, that boy is not just anyone. He requires guidance."

"Do me a favor and bleed out already."

"Mr. Belt, my resources are spread farther than you know. You won't be able to hide him from me."

"Hide him?" Osyen growled. "Anze, he might be dead. I don't know what your whole situation is. I don't care anymore. Because if I go down there and pull out the bodies of my two friends, I will rededicate my life to ending yours. You, Magnus, anybody who was involved. I don't care if I have to march up Capitol Hill and put two slugs into the Consul myself, you hear me? If they are so much as bruised, I will end your *bloodline*."

There was a long pause before the icy response. "Good luck, Osyen Belt." And the line clicked dead.

Osyen dragged his eyes over to Roche. "Tell me you've got life signs on that wreck?"

And Roche nodded, swallowing hard. "Yeah...three of 'em."

CHAPTER
FORTY-THREE
TYCHO

// Sys.Kernel Corrupted. Flash memory cores one through four nonresponsive. Thermo couplings in zone one are damaged. Zone three and six are approaching critical temperatures.

// Sys.Power 2%

// Prerogative: Find the Girl

Where was he? He couldn't see. He felt damp and cold. A thirsting wind licked at his forehead like an icy serpent.

// Motor Function Impaired. Oxygen Function Impaired. Toxic sulfide levels detected in blood.

// Unable to stabilize gyroscopic orientation.

He opened his eyes and a hiss of pain flew into his skull, forcing him to clamp them shut again. He raised one hand, pawing at his face. A slick cold crunched under his fingers on his left cheek.

The eyeball had popped, and the viscous fluid had already frozen in the winter air.

The sensor band came alight, picking up the sounds of fire, the cracking of ice. Heat glowed, illuminating spaces no light could get to. He felt the ground underneath him fracture and fragment, hollows that extended three kilometers down. The glacier might take the wreckage in the next few minutes.

She had been so close. So very close. Where was she now?

He pressed his hand into the snow, pushing and pushing until he managed to heave his twisted, bleeding form onto his knees. He swayed in the wind, nearly blown over by its power.

A mere ten feet away, Thomas stood over the lady Rashida Izan de Tylmirande. He was tending to a rather significant gash on her leg. And by the way she was holding it, she couldn't stand.

Good.

They jumped, startled at his emergence. Thomas immediately stooped, trying to lift Rashida onto her one good leg. Together, they hobbled across the difficult terrain. And Tycho did much the same, stomping over rebar and steel plates.

One foot didn't respond to commands, the flesh and metal melted and fused and melted again. But the hinge and rotor at his knee cap still functioned, allowing him to swing the dead leg forward. He cleared a small glacial chasm with ease.

They would not escape.

"Leave me!" Rashida urged.

"Get up, Rash!"

"It's over, Thom."

The truth of those words settled in, and the boy slowed. Accepting. Defeated.

Rashida pushed herself off him, barely able to keep from collapsing on her one good leg. She drew herself up as tall as she could—the noblewoman on her way to the gallows.

Tycho lowered his hand, gripping the edge of a metal plate. It strained and whined against his force, but he slowly peeled off a suitable shard. Something shifted underneath them, and the unsettling thunder of the glacier calving ripped through the air. The sound made Rashida's skin crawl, but she stood tall, her dress billowing in the gale force winds.

But that insufferable boy, that incredible boy, that impossible boy was far from finished. "She named you...after an astronomer."

Tycho paused, staring at Rashida. Who did he mean? Who named him?

"Tycho Brahe," Thom said, turning. "One of the last great naked eye astronomers. She wanted you to look at the stars the way we used to. And you did, once."

// SysAdmin Access, Quarantine Memory — DENIED

// SysAdmin Access, Quarantine Memory, subject: Hellamine, Jeannette K. — DENIED

Why did that name mean something to him? Why did this boy know the name? He squeezed the shard, his fingers pinching out creases in the half-inch steel.

Was that his name? Tycho Hellamine?

"How do I know that?" the boy asked, like Tycho knew that answer. "How do I know that much about you? You can tell me if I'm wrong, if you feel any different. But I'm not, am I?"

Distraction. Deception. Delay and denial. Targets always had a tactic to evade justice. To rationalize their crimes.

Kill. Her.

But his hand didn't move. What could be the harm in listening? They were beyond escape.

That digital intention pressed again. Kill. Her. There was no other way to the Path.

Thom took a step towards the Paladin. "She wrote you letters at Holkstad, tried to stay in touch. You never wrote back...but you read them. You read all the letters." The thought distressed the boy, quivers in his vocal pattern and a spike in the heart rate. "*How* do I know that, Tycho? Tell me. Because—I'm scared. I'm real *gulaw* scared right now!"

Tycho served the Pilgrim. He pursued the Pilgrim's enemies. It was a laborious task, asked only of a few. And he struggled with this burden, buoyed by—

// Memory Corruption Detected. Quarantining Segment KC-112.

Corruptions, quarantines, limits, barriers. Do not trespass on forsaken lands. Cursed, subversive, evil.

They called it corrupted whenever he tried to access it. Not before.

"You want to know how?" Thom pressed. "How I know so much about you? Because I was there, when you were made. I saw it."

Impossible. Tycho had been aware of everyone in the space. He had listened to Magnus speak in the next room. He would've known if the boy had been present.

Then why did he feel so familiar?

"They've told you we're enemies of the Pilgrim," Thom howled over the wind. "But you've known it, you've known it since you first saw me: something didn't add up. So the AI—that program—it put it all out of your mind. It was contrary evidence that drew you off focus, and *that* couldn't be tolerated. You had a mission. And this...you could see everything, and when you see that much, you need something to filter it all out *for you*. To make sense of it *for you*." The boy shook his head, incredulous but smiling. "But you knew...that it didn't make sense. Every time you saw me. And it didn't make sense to me either. But I know now. I know *why*. And I think you do too."

// Those eyes, violet and glittering, like a nebula reflecting a thousand suns...

The memories, like cracks in a dam, came rolling back to him. He remembered letting grains of sand roll off his hands in the sandbox. He remembered his dog, a curious old creature with a squished face and noisy breathing. He remembered those violet eyes.

Whose eyes were those?

"You know what I am," Thom said. "You can see it. Can't you?"

The cathedral. Where he woke up. The Priests. They had something. A relic. And reflected in that dark green ocean, a thousand shards hiding his face...little Thom Hugh, beneath that cosmic shimmering void inside the glass.

"I was there," Thom whispered. "A little piece of me was with you in that room. And that truth, that fact...Your AI detected something that *couldn't* be."

Violet eyes. Such comfort, those violet eyes.

// Unauthorized Memory Access Detected in Quarantined Segment.

// Let me see it.

// Unauthorized Memory Access

// This database is irrelevant to mission parameters

"You don't have to do what they tell you," Thom urged. "If you want to kill us, if you *want* to do that, we're in no position to stop you. Do it. But do it because you choose it. Not because *they* left you no other choice."

// What were the mission parameters?

// All Other Interrogatives Restricted. Engage the Mission.

// User Override.

// All Other Interrogatives Restricted. Priority Action.

// System Query: Why did he know this boy's face?

// Irrelevant to mission parameters. Denied.

// Memory Search: Any precursor instance of Thomas Angelo Hugh.

// Irrelevant to mission parameters. Pursue the objective.

Tycho opened his mouth. "No..."

Rashida and Thom exchanged a look, unwilling to tear their eyes off of the monster for too long. Tycho reached up, his hand twitching. It felt like the air had gone thick, syrupy, like the atmosphere itself was fighting him.

Until he managed to snag his fingers around that golden circlet on his forehead. And he tugged.

Darkness. He couldn't see anything. The world itself switched off. And that companion...that digital voice with an earnest command...was silent.

Tycho reached back, back, back towards what he remembered to those violet eyes. Back before the faith, before the missions, before the commitments.

Silence. Just a beautiful quiet. He hadn't realized how domineering that hum had become, how omnipresent it had been, reminding him of itself.

And he heard her voice call to him...

Tycho kneeled down in the snow, his fingers feeling out the shapes of the metal underneath him. "I promised her..."

Instead of a welcome void or a glittering path lined by starlight, he saw her violet eyes...as he collapsed backward, slipping, falling down the chasm, down into the heart of the glacier. Until the planet's icy embrace was all he could feel.

FORTY-FOUR
ZATIA

THERE WAS a lot of resupply and repair needed to be done to the *Aurum*. Weasel's crew had torn an ugly hole in the galley ceiling that needed to be patched up. And they had shot up the engine room pretty well. Not to mention all the expense.

Thankfully, not much of the Godfather's operation was well-watched at the moment. They were still mopping up the crash site, allowing the *Aurum* to pick out what supplies it needed from cold storage depots without trouble.

Zatia hauled the last crate up the gangway. "That's it!" she shouted. "Close her up."

Roche didn't even move from his spot, blinking once, and the gangway started to seal up. The jockey was squatting in front of one of their stolen crates, shuffling out floating holographic cards before dealing them to Lily's disembodied head on the opposite side. Lily studied them with care before staring back into his soul. "Death does not frighten you?"

"Why should it?" he asked.

"Death is the ultimate unknown, total obliteration of your sense of self. The Far Land from which no data can be collected."

"Not many men have the privilege of choosing their own death."

"Yet my life slowly will eclipse your own," Lily explained.

Roche smiled. "Everybody goes, someday. And when they do, most people go alone."

"But not you?" Zatia asked, dropping the crate atop their game.

But Roche was unmoved—the digital cards weren't exactly disrupted by a physical interruption, after all. "Not me, no ma'am."

"Right," Zatia said with a smirk. "There's a little extra in these, maybe we can cut out a nice little profit out of this nightmare."

Roche blinked. "Profit?" he said, sounding out the word.

"Oh...God..." She rubbed the back of her neck, turning towards Lily. "You want to explain the finer points of capitalism since you're the one that deleted it from his brain. Or do we just take his cut for ourselves?"

Lily's image flickered and Roche's eyes fluttered, computing an entire database's records in half a second. His brow furrowed. "Capitalism: well, that seems unnecessarily cruel."

"How do you figure?" Zatia asked.

"Why build homes only to keep them from people who need them?"

And Zatia heel-turned away from that conversation. She had opened a Pandora's box and had no intention of wading any deeper than she already had. He was already badgering Lily about exchange rates and lines of credit, like he was using curse words.

"Osyen!" Zatia called out up the corridor. "Oz, I might've broke Roche."

"Don't shout," Adelaide grunted as she came out of the Galley, picking at her ear. "It's a great big tin can."

"Ship all warmed up?" Zatia asked.

Adelaide didn't even slow down, marching past her and turning down the steps into Engineering. "She'll hold all the way to Akagi Station. Beyond that, I make no promises."

Zatia leaned on the doorframe, watching as Adelaide bent over the railing to reach for something. "So eager to put Farragut behind you?"

"We staying?" Adelaide asked.

"No."

"'Cause that would've been news to me."

"Anze's still out there," Zatia said, with a hint of bloodlust. "Maybe we track him down and..."

Adelaide pulled a plastic bag from her breast pocket, dangling the small fistful of ash. "Anze may be kicking, but Nathaniel's home."

Zatia's eyes flicked to that little bag, trying not to bust up laughing at the sheer absurdity. "Not angry anymore?"

Adelaide glowered at her, an evil queen's withering stare, leveling kingdoms with a look. How dare she imply anything but?

Zatia nodded. "Right, of course. Stupid me."

She heard the old woman grumbling about some such thing as she walked away. At least she hadn't changed too much, even with her half-victory.

Osyen?! Zatia bellowed through the radio channel as she stomped forward through the ship. She muttered her frustration, "Where the hell are you?"

"Don't shout."

Zatia paused, backing up to poke her head in Medical. Rashida laid upright on her gurney, reading some folksy novelette on her Entiglas. They elevated her leg on a strap, the bone pinned in place by a dozen thin rods jabbed into her skin. But she looked warm and happy, with the blanket draped over her and snug up to her chin.

"I used the radio," Zatia said, pointing at the back of her head. "I physically could not have shouted."

Rashida smiled, soft and full of matronly murder. "You shouted."

Zatia bit her cheek, busted and mad about it. "How's the leg, *principessa?*"

"Torment and woe," Rashida said, "or so they tell me. This fluid line is something else."

Yeah, Zatia thought. That happy juice didn't do her much good anymore, her system long since developing resistance to the antiseptic line. There had been a time when any old painkiller would help her. Now...now, her entire nervous system would up and betray her at random. She was always hungry, and never sure of herself.

But she was sure of these people. Paydays or dry days...they'd still be around. "How are you doing?"

"Good." Rashida almost swallowed the word, her jaw tensing up. "I'm...I'm good."

"Well, you got your life on the other side, like you always wanted. Burned the last bridge back to liveries and elegance," Zatia said. "Any regrets?"

Rashida drew a breath, holding it like she was measuring it, waiting for any quiver or reticence. And she exhaled it, pleasant and satisfied. "Teach me to throw a punch, and how to fall properly?"

"Yeah," Zatia drawled, "I don't think 'tuck and roll' is going to keep your leg from snapping the next time we drop you from actual outer space. That one is pretty much always up to the dice. Whatcha reading?"

Rashida pushed the image, flipping it around for Zatia's benefit. "Proper fantasy. Lizard men, beautiful women, and the people who hunt them."

Zatia's eyes bugged out. "What goes on in your head?"

"Nobody really knows."

"Was just looking for Osyen," Zatia said. "We're all sewn up in cargo. So we might want to make ourselves scarce. You seen him?"

"Not recently." Her eyes unfocused for a moment, staring into the middle distance before she shook her head and came back down to earth. "And...I wouldn't be able to tell you how long it's been."

"Careful with that stuff," Zatia cautioned.

Rashida chambered a response before catching the entire implication. Zatia would know. So Rashida put down her pitchfork and just nodded. "Okay, Zee."

"When you're up and about, can you braid my hair?" Zatia asked.

"Sure," Rashida said with a nod, pulling her book back around. "May be awhile."

"Finish your book first. That'll take you about a week, right?"

Rashida didn't look up, but stuck her tongue out in protest, like a child.

Zatia laughed as she stomped up the hallway. "Osyen?"

"Don't shout," Rashida called after her, matching pitch and tempo with Roche from the other room.

"I—am—*not*—shouting!"

"*That* was shouting," Thom teased from a little cubby over her head. He was curled up into a little ball on the inside of a vent, shoulder propped against the steel grating. But even those bars couldn't dim his smirk.

Zatia propped her hands on her hips, staring up at the Maestro. "When did I become the Osyen in the room? I'm supposed to be cool, calm, detached. Now I'm in charge of a madhouse."

Thom side-eyed her. "When you started giving a damn."

"See, that was my first mistake."

Thom flipped over, fingers gripping through the grating like a prisoner in a medieval dungeon. "Did you try to talk to Roche about housing policy?"

She threw up her arms. "I mentioned getting *paid* for what we *do*. We're pirates. And now he's off on a thing."

"Yeah, I think he's about ready to start burning money in protest."

Her heart sank at the very thought. "Don't let him do that. If he doesn't want it, give it to me. What are you doing hiding up there?"

"I'm not hiding."

"You're in an airway tucked into the ceiling like some kind of alien critter," Zatia deadpanned.

Thom looked aside, busted. What was he supposed to say to that?

"So, explain yourself," she demanded.

He shrugged. "Not doin' nothing."

"Nothing?" she said, skeptical.

He smirked through the bars down to her, resting his forehead against the metal. "You don't understand what a rare pleasure 'nothing' really is."

"You're up there in a vent, staring into the vastness of the cosmos," Zatia scoffed, pointing back behind her. "Adelaide's relaxed, which is beyond strange. Rashida is high on painkillers and wants murder lessons. Roche cut out half of his brain to give to the ship's navigator. And Osyen has vanished into thin air. How did I become the adult?!"

"Just lucky, I guess."

Zatia sighed. "Have you seen the lord commander?"

Thom nodded. "He left the ship about an hour ago. Took a shuttle back into Farragut proper."

He did *what*? Zatia dropped all pretense. Anze was still out there, as was Admiral Hugh, and who knew what else. She emphasized the one word: "Where?"

"He didn't say," Thom said.

"You don't seem alarmed."

"'Cause I know where he's going. May not know the address, but..."

She waited, but the little bastard didn't say another word. "You know a lot these days with very little explanation."

He pretended he didn't hear that, focusing instead on the blank wall in front of him. He had the same expression Rashida had, with tiny darts of the eyes and twitches of his cheeks and hands. Like he was reading the bare steel, like it had something to share.

"What is he doing?" Zatia asked.

Thom's smile softened and slipped away to a kind of regret. "Making a mistake."

FORTY-FIVE
MAGNUS

IT WAS a small matter to pack everything he had into the two large cases. Meticulous folding and compression were easy to do with practiced hands and enough motivation. He clipped their tow tags to his belt and made his way to the door. The cases slid along the floor, following the tag like dutiful and happy animals without so much as a squeak from their wheels.

He could book a transport, get himself to somewhere safe to rest and rearm for the pursuit. Akagi Station would have what he needed, surely.

It was a narrow hallway, cold steel at one shoulder and open doors at the other. He heard families arguing, passionate lovers, and children screaming. The cold air couldn't stamp out the smell of tar, smoke, and sweat that filled every breath. He stalked down the hallway with pace, his cane clicking against the heavy steel floor with an unpleasant echo.

Magnus paused at the lift, adjusting the collar of his shirt against the cold that gripped his neck.

The door opened—and he was about to step onboard. But he froze at the sight.

A floor-length coat, tinged with the snows outside. Heavy workman's boots with broad toes and stout heels. Tousled brown hair, unkempt and ignored by its owner, with a single lock drooping down in front of the cold dark darts of his eyes, speckled notes of black against auburn brown. He looked casual until Magnus noted that the second sleeve of the jacket had been pinned up against his chest—no arm to fill it.

Osyen Belt.

Magnus flailed his cane up at him. But Osyen reached across his body, snagging the cane and yanking Magnus into the elevator with him. Before he knew it, Osyen had wrenched the cane from his grasp, slamming it down on his face.

He said nothing. No taunt, no lectures on morality or feeling. He just began the painstaking task of beating Magnus to death.

"Please!" Magnus coughed in between blows. "I had no choice!"

Osyen wasn't hearing it. He slammed Magnus in the gut and about the face, slinging him into the lift's heavy walls.

The lift doors closed with a happy chime, leaving his suitcases alone at the landing. And he could feel the jerk as the elevator began its descent. Out of the small view port, the snow-capped city of Farragut could only watch as Osyen went about his bloody work.

Magnus fell to the floor and tried to crawl into the nearest corner. Nowhere else to go. "I swore an oath! To the Family! I had to!"

Was the man deaf?! Could he not see Magnus was helpless and pleading for mercy?

Magnus turned about, trying to kick at Osyen's standing leg. But Osyen raised his foot up out of the way and brought it crashing down on Magnus's knee. And still, he said nothing, even as Magnus cried out in agony.

Through gritted teeth and tears, Magnus wailed. "Why don't you speak?! Say *something*!"

Osyen swung the tip of his boot up, cracking Magnus under the chin. Magnus felt something squeal, and his jaw lit up with fire.

"You have a family, Osyen Belt!" Magnus begged. "I know you do!"

No response. He was a man obsessed, consumed with a single emotion. He could not be dissuaded.

Think, Magnus! What does he want? What can you give him? Think!

Osyen picked up Magnus's cane from the floor and inspected the hidden firearm mechanism in the handle. He racked a fresh round into the hidden chamber with a pleasant snap. And he laid the barrel across Magnus's forehead.

"It's your *mother!*"

Magnus winced, waiting for the blow to fall. But it never came. He cracked an eye open to inspect the barrel of his cane held precariously at his temple, ready to scramble his gray matter. But Osyen just stared down the barrel at him, nostrils flared and eyes wide.

Keep talking.

Magnus sat up, pressing his back against the lift wall. "Your mother...is alive, Osyen." Osyen didn't call him a liar, but he pressed the gun barrel to his cheek, and Magnus could feel it click against his teeth. "It's the truth. I swear. I saw it in your file—before I came to Farragut. I was well briefed on Rashida's companions. I swear on the Dunsweir and the Pilgrim's Path. She is *alive*...and I know how you can find her."

If Osyen Belt wanted anything in this universe, it would be her. And Magnus might not be able to provide her, but he could provide enough intelligence to buy his escape. If Osyen was in a bargaining mood.

Osyen didn't lower the cane. But he finally opened his mouth: "Talk fast."

THE END

Follow Osyen's New Quest
And the epic final chapter of the trilogy
in
POWERS OF THE GOLD SERVICE

AFTERWORD

Book Two seems to be the place in my trilogies I put my characters through the absolute ringer. I hope you enjoyed this as much as I enjoyed writing it, as I took the loose collection of like-minded coworkers and really pressed them together into a family of misfits and malcontents.

If you're enjoying the Capital Adventures, please leave a review. It really helps small authors like myself.

Signing up for the Newsletter keeps you on top of the latest news around the Capital-verse.

I also have a cat. I will likely be dropping pictures of her there regularly, as she is a consistent part of my office day. She is bad at being a cat, but she is fat and good and adorable. Sign up and see!

https://www.authorivers.com/

ABOUT THE AUTHOR

Allen Ivers started writing original stories at the ripe age of eleven, largely trying to figure out why the Disney villains on the television box were the way they were. Villains, monsters, and politicians have always fascinated him with their behavior. Twenty one years later, he's still fascinated by bad people and the bad things they do.

Looking to deepen the lore and settings of his universe, Allen set about on a story that would bring the Gnostic religion into sharp relief with his characters and the growing world behind it. And the best way to do that was with a fierce zealous devotee—the Paladin.

Allen now lives in beautiful Juneau, AK where he is somewhere at the bottom of the food chain. You can find his thoughts about writing, politics, and the odd cute cat on his Twitter.

facebook.com/AllenIversSFF
x.com/AllenIvers

ALSO BY ALLEN IVERS